Allie Kincheloe has been writing stories for as long as she can remember, and somehow they always become romances. Always a Kentucky girl at heart, she now lives in Tennessee with her husband, children, and a growing menagerie of pets. Visit her on Twitter: @AllieKAuthor.

Scarlet Wilson wrote her first story aged eight and has never stopped. She's worked in the health service for twenty years, having trained as a nurse and a health visitor. Scarlet now works in public health and lives on the West Coast of Scotland with her fiancé and their two sons. Writing medical romances and contemporary romances is a dream come true for her.

WINTER NIGHTS WITH THE SINGLE DAD

ALLIE KINCHELOE

A FESTIVE FLING IN STOCKHOLM

SCARLET WILSON

MILLS & BOON

First Published in Great Britain 2021
by Mills & Boon, an imprint of HarperCollins*Publishers* Ltd,
1 London Bridge Street, London, SE1 9GF

www.harpercollins.co.uk

HarperCollins*Publishers*
1st Floor, Watermarque Building,
Ringsend Road, Dublin 4, Ireland

Winter Nights with the Single Dad © 2021 by Harlequin Books S.A.

Special thanks and acknowledgement are given to Allie Kincheloe
for her contribution to The Christmas Project miniseries.

A Festive Fling in Stockholm © 2021 by Harlequin Books S.A.

Special thanks and acknowledgement are given to Scarlet Wilson
for her contribution to The Christmas Project miniseries.

ISBN: 978-0-263-29781-2

11/21

MIX
Paper from
responsible sources
FSC® C007454

WINTER NIGHTS WITH THE SINGLE DAD

ALLIE KINCHELOE

MILLS & BOON

For my amazing editors.

Some books come easily.

Others exist because of editors
who push flighty authors like me to be better.

CHAPTER ONE

NERVES FLUTTERED IN Stella's stomach. Getting called to the boss's office was never easy, even when she was quite certain she'd done nothing wrong. She'd run through a litany of possibilities, but still she had no clue what else she could have been called in to discuss other than a potential promotion.

"Dr. Allen, you must've caught wind of some changes happening." The chair squeaked as Chris Taylor leaned back. The chief executive steepled his fingers and gazed at her with a serious expression lining his face. "And I'm sure you've questioned how these changes might affect your own role here at the hospital."

Whispers in the hallowed halls of the Royal Kensington Hospital said that the head of orthopedics could be replaced soon. Rumors floated rampant through the antiseptic-scented corridors since a nurse had caught sight of an employment ad for an orthopedic surgeon. No one had mentioned retirement and none seemed on the verge of a big move, but Stella had sought out the advertisement and read it with her own eyes only an hour before she'd been pulled into Dr. Taylor's office. Her confidence flagged a bit and she barely resisted the urge to cross her fingers or pray that she wasn't about to be fired.

Stella nodded, waiting for Dr. Taylor to get on with it. The man was known for his long-winded explanations of any and every topic of conversation. Stella herself preferred to get to the point quickly and her foot shook as her impatience got the best of her.

"I realize this is your first year with us, so you may not be aware of the particulars. You have heard of The Kensington Project?"

Thinking carefully, Stella nodded slowly. "I have, but only in the broadest of terms. Last year's participants had already returned from their assignments before I came on board here."

"Then you must know it's a medical exchange program of sorts. Four of our own, from various departments, will be traveling to other hospitals across the world to share our groundbreaking advancements. And you've been chosen to share your orthopedic techniques."

"Me?" Stella savored the moment of recognition. Out of all the doctors and surgeons in the elite programs at the Royal Kensington Hospital, she'd been chosen. What an honor! The validation of her surgical skills filled her with pride.

"Yes." Dr. Taylor passed her a file. "If you are agreeable, you would travel to Toronto. While you are there, you will work with the team at St. Matthew's Hospital until Christmas."

"Canada?" Stella gasped. "I've never been to Canada." Stella opened the folder in her lap. Scanning quickly, she tried to absorb as many of the details as possible. The particular that stood out most was that her departure date was within the week and the return date not until Christmas. "I'd be leaving almost immediately?"

"Afraid so. It's rather short notice, but I believe you

to be up for the task." His face took on a more solemn demeanor. "There's one more thing."

Her breath caught as she waited for the bad news that was sure to come with the concern lining his face. Good news always comes with bad, after all.

"In addition to sharing your surgical procedures, we've also secured permission for you to film that television special you've been angling for since your arrival here."

Stella's eyes widened at the news. "I'll be able to film there at St. Matthew's?"

Dr. Taylor nodded. "The producer will have a camera crew film here beginning next week and another to join you in Toronto. I don't seem to have an exact timeline on that. There are a few caveats as noted in the file, mostly legal minutiae that will apply. I'm sure you're familiar with most everything, but do review it for any differences applicable specifically to Toronto. Your contact there is going to be Dr. Aiden Cook. His information is also in the file."

Having grown up on camera, Stella knew the power film had on the general public and its opinion. She'd been trying to secure permission to document just how hard the people in a hospital worked and to bring attention to the sacrifices made to provide healthcare for the masses. Those sacrifices were amplified at the holidays, so she'd pitched the upcoming Christmas holiday as the perfect time for filming. She'd managed to get the support of a network, but getting permission from the hospital had been far more difficult as she'd been refused at every turn.

So, why now?

"Dr. Allen?"

"Hmm…" Stella fought back a blush at being caught woolgathering. "I'm afraid my mind was wandering."

"Are you agreeing to participate then?"

Momentarily, Stella wondered if she ought to decline. Had she only been chosen for the program due to her television background? No, she was quite confident in her surgical skills and the Royal Kensington Hospital would never send her out to represent their good name if they didn't believe in her. Plus, the topic of the show was one near and dear to her heart.

After the briefest of hesitations, Stella said yes.

She walked away from Dr. Taylor's office deep in thought. Excitement filled her at all the prospects The Kensington Project offered. Her motivations for agreeing were threefold.

First of all, it was a wonderful career opportunity. She'd get to share her new techniques in another country and meet a whole new team of colleagues. Expanding her network could potentially open a lot of doors going forward.

Second, and most excitingly, it would put an ocean between Stella and her mother for two entire months. That alone would be reason enough for Stella to say yes. For years, Debra Allen had pushed and pushed to get Stella into television and keep her there. Stella had heard a million times how much her mum had wanted to be an actress, but she simply hadn't had the talent. She'd shoved all those dreams on to her daughter. Being in the spotlight, holding that hint of celebrity status, had often been all that mattered. Occasionally, Stella had wondered if it was her or what she could do for her mum that Debra loved more. She loved her mum, but a vast expanse of water separating them could only improve their relationship.

The third and final reason was that this television program meant everything to her. She'd been keen on getting this program produced for ages. The idea of filming had never been more exciting.

The feeling that her whole life was about to change filled Stella with energy. Mentally, she began listing all the tasks she needed to complete before she left London. There were a lot, so she really should make a written to-do list. She had packing to do before her first ever trip to Canada. Thankfully, she'd kept her passport up to date. She needed to sort her current patient load and arrange for someone to care for her houseplants.

Stella wasn't the sentimental type, but this felt right. It was going to be the best Christmas yet.

She couldn't wait.

Aiden groaned as he opened yet another email from Dr. Stella Allen, the surgeon from the Royal Kensington Hospital that he'd agreed to babysit—*liaise with*—while she was in Toronto. The things he'd do for his kid…

Emergency medicine at one of the busiest hospitals in Toronto wasn't meshing well with single fatherhood. He kept running late, having to rely on his parents to pick up the slack when his job kept him past the scheduled pickup time. The trade-off of coordinating with Dr. Allen on filming her television special and planning the staff Christmas party had seemed worth it in exchange for only working day shifts and no weekends through all of November and December. Now he was second-guessing that thought because she was already grating on his last nerve and they weren't even in the same country.

Dr. Allen had sent him no fewer than a dozen emails over the last twenty-four hours. And the questions? She asked more questions than anyone he'd ever met. And he hadn't even met her yet!

Something in this particular email caught his attention though. Dr. Allen wrote that she'd need to scout the hospital for places to film that would have enough lighting, yet not be too distracting on film. That wasn't the intriguing bit though. Helping her coordinate filming had been part of the deal he'd made with Dr. Stone, after all. It was the next line that sent him off on a research tangent.

She wrote that with several shows behind her, she could evaluate the locations with a glance.

Several shows?

Wasn't this a special one-time deal designed to highlight the struggles of those who worked in hospitals during the holidays? But her words implied she'd done more than this documentary.

He typed her name into the search bar and was not disappointed. Pages of results showed up for her. He settled back and began to work his way through a few of the links. It didn't take long for him to learn everything he needed to know about St. Matthew's newest star.

Dr. Allen had grown up in the spotlight. After an appearance on a show called *Britain's Brightest* at age ten, she had been given her own show—*Stay Smart with Stella*. After that, she had another show while she was in college and medical school.

She had taken time away from her studies to futz about with a television program during medical school and he was supposed to believe that she was one of the brightest pioneers the Royal Kensington Hospital had to offer? Was there a time when she had ever focused all her attention on medicine? Could she really perform orthopedic surgery?

Aiden snorted. More likely, she was the one with the most star power to draw attention to their program.

And the most photogenic.

"Oh, she's pretty. Is she the one you're going to be showing around?"

"It's a bit more than showing her around, Mom," Aiden said as his mother leaned over his shoulder to look at the screen in his hand.

"Well, she's quite lovely. Is she single?"

"I don't know, but it doesn't matter. She's a colleague only."

His mom made a noise of disbelief. "You cannot be alone forever, Aiden. You know, if you found someone new, maybe she could help you shoulder some of the responsibilities."

"Jamie needs stability more than I need a love life, Mom." He resisted the urge to roll his eyes. He didn't have the time or the interest for romance. Where would he find the time? He'd had to bargain for extra duties to get regular hours for the next two months.

"Don't reject the idea before you've even met her." His mom smiled softly as she walked away. "And don't stay up too late."

He sighed. Soon, he and Jamie would need to find a place of their own, but for now, living with his parents was the most stability that Aiden could provide. His son had been through so much upheaval in the short duration of his life and the last thing Aiden wanted to do was add to that.

The low-battery message popped up and it dawned on him that he'd just lost over an hour educating himself about an actress masquerading as a doctor. Dr. Stella Allen was very beautiful and she had an on-air presence that made her seem as if she were talking directly to the viewer. The spark of intelligence in her green eyes lit so brightly that it was visible even on camera. The camera might add ten pounds, but if it did, they'd landed in just the right places on the curvy, dark-haired beauty. Something about her had drawn him in, even in a video. He ran a hand through his hair.

What was he doing?

Surely, he had learned his lesson about getting tangled up with actresses. The last thing he needed was another woman in his life more concerned about the camera than the people around her. Been there, done that, got the two-year-old to prove it.

Stepping across the hall, he watched from the doorway as Jamie slept. Even after months in Aiden's care, Jamie slept with his back to the wall curled up into a tight ball. Aiden still wasn't sure what his son had been through in the two years before Aiden had learned of his existence. Some days, just the thought of what it might have been was too much.

But that was in the past and Aiden was determined to give his son a better future. Jamie's appearance may have turned Aiden's life upside down, but being a dad was the best thing that had ever happened to him. These last nine months had meant a lot of changes for Aiden, including moving back in with his parents and trying to juggle Jamie's therapies and work and a massive custody battle. He had no regrets about stepping up when his son came into his life though. In fact, that little boy was the sole reason Aiden had gotten himself saddled with being a personal concierge for the next two months.

And he was also the reason that Aiden needed to keep Dr. Stella Allen at arm's length.

CHAPTER TWO

STELLA GLANCED AT her watch yet again. Her contact from St. Matthew's Hospital should have been there to pick her up an hour ago. She let out a deep sigh and took her nearly dead cell phone from her purse.

With a few taps she brought up the email she'd received from Dr. Cook confirming that they'd meet here at the airport. Her itinerary had been attached. She fired off a quick missive that her plane had landed and she was eagerly awaiting their arrival.

She hadn't thought to get his phone number and it was a bit too late for that now. Normally, she was far more organized than this, but since she'd only found out three days prior that she'd been selected to come to Toronto for the prestigious Kensington Project, she needed to give herself a bit of slack. She was still quite giddy about being chosen.

Of course, she'd have signed on for Antarctica if it allowed her to put an ocean between her and her parents for two solid months. Her mother had been less enthused at the idea of Stella spending the holidays in Canada, but she could hardly argue about the benefit this could have on Stella's career.

The dilemma of her apparent abandonment here at the airport shook her confidence though. If her mom ever found out, she'd never let Stella hear the end of it. Stella could hear the screeches her mother would have made, reminding Stella that if she'd stayed in the lime-light a bit more, no one would ever forget her at an air-port again.

Pushing an unruly lock of hair away from her face, Stella considered the options and struggled to regain some control. She could snag a taxi and cart all of her luggage along for the ride while she went to St. Mat-thew's and tried to find the elusive Dr. Cook, or she could wait and hope he hadn't forgotten her entirely.

Was there a currency exchange in this airport? There should be, right? She wouldn't be able to pay for the taxi without the proper currency. That should have been on her list of things to take care of before her flight. *Bit late for that now.*

No notifications on her phone meant no reply to the sent email. Oh, she didn't like this. Her teeth worried her lower lip while she mulled over her alternatives.

"Dr. Allen?" a man called from her left.

She turned that direction but the only person looking her way was a father with a small child in his arms. If she weren't looking for someone else, he wouldn't be a bad one to rest her eyes on for a bit. With a wistful sigh, her gaze flicked away from the small family to search for the source of her name.

A tall, athletic frame blocked her view as the man carrying the little boy stopped directly in front of her. His short brown hair looked like he'd been running his hands through it, but somehow the disheveled aspect of his appearance didn't detract from his appeal at all. Stella's heart raced as they made eye contact.

"Are you Dr. Stella Allen?" Apparently, he *had* been the one calling her name and she'd been too quick to dismiss him. Admittedly, she'd been expecting a doctor, not someone on daddy duty.

"Yes, I'm Stella Allen." She flashed him a smile. Had Dr. Cook had an emergent case show up and needed to find someone to pick her up last-minute? Maybe options were slim this evening. "And you are?"

"Dr. Aiden Cook. We've been exchanging emails." His curt tone turned her genuine smile into the practiced fake she'd perfected over years for the cameras.

Straightening her spine, she narrowed her eyes at him. "I assumed that, given the late time, and the presence of a child, Dr. Cook must have had an emergency and sent you in his stead."

Her barb struck home and a small muscle in his jaw twitched.

"I had…" He trailed off, readjusting his hold on the child. "I was nearly here when the day care called in a panic. Jamie was upset and needed me immediately. I apologize for my lateness and any inconvenience it might have caused you."

The apology didn't ring quite true. His words professed apology, but there was a hardness in his brown eyes that didn't agree with the soft words. Somehow, she instinctively knew that he'd leave her standing alone again if little Jamie needed something in the future and she found it hard to fault him for that. Would her own parents have put her first had they been in Dr. Cook's situation? Would they have inconvenienced a professional contact to soothe their upset child? The answer she arrived at was disheartening.

"You could have let me know," she murmured.

"I might have, if I had remembered to get your number." His deep voice still held only the slightest hint of apology. "Are you ready to go then?"

"I am. I've already collected from baggage claim."

He glanced at the pile of luggage at her feet. "Did you bring everything you own? It is a two-month stay, not a permanent move after all."

Who did this guy think he was?

A huff of disbelief escaped her as she followed his gaze to her belongings. She'd brought with her two large suitcases, a carry-on and her admittedly large purse. It was hardly a ridiculous amount given that she was scheduled to spend nearly two months in Toronto.

"I assure you that I've carried nothing unnecessary across the Atlantic Ocean simply for the back pain. Not that it is truly your business, but in addition to clothing for both work and home, I have my computer equipment and materials for my presentation. Believe me when I say that I brought nothing that wasn't an absolute requirement. I hardly overpacked."

The hint of an eye roll he gave when she mentioned her show irritated her even more. The theme of this particular film project had been one she'd been hoping to do since her residency. It had taken her years to convince her contacts to take it on, and even longer to convince a hospital to be open to the project. Now that she'd been given the go-ahead, she was not going to let some grumpy ER doctor ruin the excitement for her.

"Do you have a problem with the fact that I will be filming a television special about the hardworking men and women in and around the emergency department of St. Matthew's? Because I assure you, it was cleared by people well above your pay grade."

His eyes hardened. "Keep your cameras off me and we will have no problem. I have no desire to be on screen at any time."

"Noted." The sooner she could get away from this

man, the better. So much for the warm Canadian welcome she'd been expecting! Although, of all people, Stella should know that what was shown on television and in the media was not always accurate.

"Where is your camera crew?" He growled the question out so low it sounded like a threat.

"Following a bit behind, I'm afraid. It's just me today." She wasn't sure how long the film crew would be delayed, but with her participation in The Kensington Project she'd have plenty to keep her busy. Too much, perhaps, given that she'd be practically performing two full-time jobs through Christmas.

"Well, they'll need to make their own arrangements to get from the airport to their lodging and the hospital. I'm not a rideshare driver."

"Good thing as the poor reviews would keep you from getting fares." She glared at him in frustration. She wanted to get to her rental, take a nice hot shower and hopefully get some sleep, not continue to stand in the airport and banter with a man who clearly wanted to rid himself of her presence. Slipping the strap to her carry-on over her shoulder, she tilted her chin toward the exit. "Could you please show me to where I'll be staying? It's been a rather long day for me."

As she reached for her luggage, his hand settled over hers on one of the handles. Enough sparks flew between them to light up the city of Toronto for the rest of the evening. She recoiled like she'd been burned.

Well, sparks or not, nothing would be happening there. Aiden had a family, and her last relationship had stalled when she'd admitted that she wasn't ready to be a mum. Oliver had wanted to marry quickly and have their first child immediately. Things had ended rather abruptly when she'd confessed that she wasn't sure she ever wanted children.

Toronto held a job for her, not the promise of romance. Although, Aiden was rather easy on the eyes and the mere touch of his hand on hers made her feel things she hadn't felt in quite some time. She rubbed her hand against the fabric of her jacket and wished she could erase the warmth of his touch.

He's off-limits, Stella. Pull yourself together.

Even if she were looking for a bit of fun while she was there—which she was not—it would not be with someone at St. Matthew's Hospital. She was a professional and she couldn't risk the reputation of The Kensington Project, or the Royal Kensington Hospital where she'd be returning to her position in the orthopedic department at the start of the New Year.

"Would you like me to get your bag?" he asked gruffly.

Nodding, she waved at the bag closest to him. "Thank you."

Had the touch affected him the way it had her? She spared a glance in his direction. He was staring at her, his expression unreadable, but there was a twinkle in his brown eyes that made her think he'd experienced something similar.

Aiden balanced Jamie on his hip with his left arm and led Dr. Allen out of the airport while pulling her rather heavy suitcase with his right. Other than a few directional cues, they walked silently into the parking garage. They'd clearly gotten off on the wrong foot, but he didn't have the time or the inclination to make nice with a high-maintenance TV star who enjoyed the limelight.

Aiden didn't even like having his picture taken.

She'd grown up in front of the camera, so he doubted she had any shyness about having a lens aimed at her. He'd watched a good number of clips of her online. It had been simply research, he'd told himself. Just a way of learning what the person was like who he'd be working with day in and day out for the next two months.

Except, he'd found himself watching everything he could find about her, from the childhood show to the solo college endeavor. But it was the more recent clips as resident doctor on a British morning show that held him captive, lulled by the sound of her voice. Her accented speech soothed edges he hadn't known needed soothing. It didn't hurt that she was easy on the eyes.

Not his normal type though.

He glanced down at Jamie and his jaw tightened. Jamie's mother had been exactly his type. Tall and blond, with legs for days. For the one night, he'd been what she was looking for, as well. He'd gone into their evening together with the expectation that he'd never see her again. He hadn't expected a son as a result of that one-night stand either.

Maybe curvy brunettes were more his type now, because he couldn't take his eyes off Stella. The chemistry between them had nearly blown him away. If he hadn't had Jamie to serve as a buffer between them, that bit of argument they'd had in the airport might have gone nuclear. And he didn't just mean in anger. There was definitely a strong undercurrent of interest floating between them.

He needed to ignore it, but he certainly hadn't missed it.

"The information I was given said that a flat had been secured for me near St. Matthew's?"

"Yes." The small one-bedroom had been a temporary

home to a variety of specialists and clinicians. Aiden himself had helped at least two other doctors get settled there for short-term assignments at St. Matthew's.

"The hospital keeps an apartment on lease at a mid-rise building just a block and a half south of St. Matthew's for visiting surgeons and lecturers. There's a shopping center a few blocks the other direction. It's well-placed if you prefer not to have a vehicle while you're here."

He was grateful for the distraction from the turn his thoughts had taken. Replaying those memories wouldn't change the reality and he didn't need to go down that road again. Britney had made her choice, and it wasn't being a mother to Jamie. He had sole physical custody, but until he could be one-hundred-percent certain that Britney wasn't going to reappear and mess things up, he couldn't take any chances. If Britney resurfaced, it could impact the progress Jamie had made. Jamie's needs had to be his number-one priority. Aiden just couldn't let himself forget the pain an actress could cause when she moved on to the next project.

He stopped next to his SUV and fished his keys out of his pocket. Turning off the alarm, he unlocked the doors. He moved to the side of the vehicle, explaining his actions as he went. "I'm just going to get Jamie buckled in and then I'll help you load the suitcases in the back."

Carefully, he buckled his son into the car seat already strapped into the backseat. "There you go, little guy," he said, making some funny faces at his son while he adjusted the straps.

When he closed the back door and turned back to Dr. Allen, she was giving him a softly indulgent smile. When their eyes met though, her expression hardened.

Good. She didn't need to be giving him sweet little smiles. They were barely colleagues. He certainly didn't need her to get the impression that he wanted to be more. He barely had time to himself, and he wouldn't be wasting any of his precious moments away from the hospital on another woman with an eye for showbiz. Stella Allen was only in Toronto temporarily, and he'd do well to remember that, even if she did evoke desires in him that he hadn't experienced in a while.

He popped the hatch and put her two suitcases inside. "Do you want to put your carry-on back here or hold on to it?"

She put the bag next to her suitcases without another word. She stalked around to the driver's door carrying only her purse.

He stood by the end of the SUV and waited for her to realize her mistake.

She opened the door and the color drained from her face. "You lot drive on the right," she mumbled, coming back his direction.

"Yes, we do." He bit back a smile. Working with the woman was going to be entertaining, if nothing else.

"Do not laugh at me," she practically growled.

He chuckled. "Don't make it so easy."

She crossed her arms and rose up to her full height, all of maybe five foot six. Her green eyes flashed her displeasure. The look in her eyes said that she'd kill him and have him six feet under before his next laugh.

It only served to make her more intriguing. In fact, if his son hadn't been with them, he'd have been tempted to soothe her fraying temper with a little wine. Maybe after that, he could take her to her new apartment and see exactly how her curves fit in his arms.

No, he needed to keep it professional. He needed to

keep his distance. Even if her lips begged to be kissed and his hands ached to feel the softness of her skin.

"You are quite rude," she said. He almost expected her to stomp her foot.

"I apologize," he said, with little sincerity. She'd amused him. He wouldn't really apologize for that. His words were meant to soothe her scuffed ego, because if her temper got any hotter, steam might come out her ears. It was tempting to push her until she blew up, just to see if he could goad her into kissing him.

Opening her mouth as if to speak, she second-guessed herself and simply shook her head. She walked around him and got into the passenger seat.

Climbing behind the wheel, he glanced over at her. "Since it's getting late, I thought I would let you settle in at the apartment and then take you over to the hospital for the grand tour in the morning?"

"That's probably best. I doubt you want to cart your son through the hospital. Too many ickies he could acquire."

He lifted an eyebrow slowly. Her unexpected word choice required a comment. *"Ickies?"*

Rolling her eyes, she waved a hand in frustration. "Would you prefer I get technical? We are speaking of a toddler. Forgive me for being a bit casual."

With a shrug, he said, "Point taken."

Carefully, he backed out of the parking space and turned the vehicle toward the exit. The silence of the car quickly became a nuisance. Soon, he found himself making small talk. And he loathed small talk.

"Have you ever been to Toronto?" he asked.

"First time." She scanned the darkened streets as they drove.

"Summer would have been a better time to visit."

A deep sigh escaped her. "I know. One of my colleagues is arriving in Jamaica as we speak. Lucky thing. Although, if I'd been assigned there, it would have been hard to convince my mum that she and my dad shouldn't follow for a family holiday. So, Toronto is better."

"I'm sensing there's a story there." He'd seen her parents in some of her childhood shows when he'd researched her. They'd seemed caring, but her mother had come across as a little overbearing.

"We don't know each other nearly well enough for me to spill secrets that classified."

He snorted. "We don't know each other at all."

"Half my life has been on camera." Her deep sigh filled the car. "The few secrets I have I like to keep close."

"Yeah, I…uh…saw that you'd been part of a few television shows."

That fact alone was enough for him to avoid an entanglement with Stella. After Britney, he'd never get involved with another actress. He was still smoking from the burns she'd set ablaze in his life. Anyone who made their living in front of the camera was no one he wanted to get entangled with. Some lessons took the first time and didn't have to be learned again.

"So, you Googled me?" she asked, and he could hear the mirth in her voice. He imagined her eyes would be twinkling as well if he looked her direction.

He opened his mouth to make a sarcastic reply, but stopped himself. Some topics just weren't worth commenting on. Instead, Aiden kept his eyes firmly on the pavement in front of him. The temperatures had dropped below freezing and he didn't want to risk an accident just to see if he was right about her eyes sparkling in amusement.

CHAPTER THREE

AIDEN MADE THE VEHICLE feel microscopic. His broad shoulders took up more than his share of space in the front, and more than that, he had a larger-than-life presence without even trying.

Stella really tried not to look at him. She kept her eyes firmly on the scenery outside the window—at least what scenery was illuminated by streetlamps. They drove by building after building, but very little could be seen in the darkness of the evening.

"If you'd been on time, perhaps I could have actually seen some of the sights," she jabbed at him, not so subtly. Something about him had turned off her politeness and made her want to provoke him, and she couldn't quite pinpoint the why. Maybe that he was late? Maybe that he'd laughed at her for going round the wrong side of the car? Maybe that he made her want things she couldn't have? "Couldn't your wife have picked up the child?"

"His name is Jamie." The force behind his words drew her gaze. Hands gripping the wheel tightly, he spoke through clenched teeth, "And I'm not married."

"His mother, then."

"Not. An. Option." His tone grew darker, his words

laced with an unvoiced finality, marking the conversation over and unavailable for further discussion.

Curiosity filled her. There was a story hidden in Aiden's reaction. Stealing glances in his direction, she noted the stiffness in his limbs, the way his hand gripping the steering wheel with unnecessary pressure and most of all, the "done with it all" look on his face. For a second, she thought she heard his teeth grinding together.

Not grief, then. Hmm.

Anger?

Definitely anger. The realization only made her more interested in finding out what had happened to wee Jamie's mum. But she'd pushed her luck with the man next to her too much already that night so she'd have to fish for answers later. She worried her lower lip with her teeth as she considered him.

Running a quick recap in her head, she recalled what she knew about Dr. Aiden Cook. It was so very little. He worked in the emergency department at St. Matthew's where she was about to spend the next two months. And he was apparently a single dad to an adorable little tot.

A devoted dad, came the thought, unbidden. A sexy, devoted dad.

No, no, no.

She gave herself a bit of a mental shake. She didn't date dads at home, so she certainly wouldn't start in Canada. She'd decided years ago that children weren't in the cards for her. Why was the idea of dating Aiden Cook even a thought? She closed her eyes tight in frustration. This man was getting far too much of her thoughts and attention.

Her presence in Toronto was for two reasons, and two reasons alone—to present her highly innovative orthopedic surgery technique and film her holiday special. Her career was finally on the trajectory that she herself wanted and she wasn't going to let the shadows lurking in a pair of velvety brown eyes distract her from that path. She inhaled deeply, hoping to cement her resolve, and came away with a lungful of very masculine-scented air.

Of course he had to smell delicious.

The off-limits fellows always did, didn't they?

Aiden broke the silence with a surprise question. "What did your boyfriend think of you leaving him behind to come to Canada?"

The query caught her off guard. It wasn't something she'd expected him to ask. It piqued her curiosity. He must've noticed the sparks between them too then.

"I don't have a boyfriend," she answered softly.

"Imagine that." Aiden snorted. "Did you run him off too with your inability to keep your nose out of private details?"

"I beg your pardon!" Her mouth gaped while she tried to wrap her head around the rudeness of the man. How dare he make such assumptions about her! Blood boiling at the conjectures, the beginning of a tension headache tightened her frame. This man might drive her right over the edge into full-blown insanity. Lord knows her mother had come close more than a few times.

"We're here. I'll help you get your bags upstairs and then pick you up in the morning to go over to the hospital." He turned the SUV into an underground garage. "I'd say you could find your own way tomorrow, but sadly I've been tasked with assisting you while you are here."

"Believe me when I say that I have as little interest in spending time with you as you have in spending time with me." Muscles tensed, Stella waited for him to say something else.

Parking the SUV in a space near the elevator, Aiden said nothing though. She looked his way but he never so much as flicked his eyes toward her a single time. He turned the engine off and hit a button to open the back hatch. The warmth of the cabin disappeared in the span of a blink, replaced with wintry cold.

Stella suppressed a shiver before stepping out of the vehicle. At least the cold was calming the white-hot temper that Aiden ignited. She moved to the back and reached in for her bags only to once again find her hand covered by one of Aiden's.

"It seems our hands like each other even if we can't stand one another," she muttered.

"Hmph." He grunted as he lifted her heaviest bit of luggage out of the SUV. "Maybe you just need to pay more attention to what you're doing."

It wasn't a question. No, Aiden's words could only be described as a demand. It wasn't a statement, but an *order*.

Stella bristled. Who did he think he was? She would not be bossed around by some puffed-up egotistical emergency doctor. Eyes narrowing, she put her hands on her hips. "And perhaps you might listen to yourself there as both times now *your* hand has gotten to the bag *after* mine. Seems you are the one not as aware as he should be of his surroundings."

A noise reminiscent of a growl came from Aiden. "Now, listen here—"

Stella shook her head. "No. You listen. This whole caveman vibe you have might work for some women, but I assure you, it does not work on me. You have a problem with me, then come to me with a calm discussion. Otherwise, keep your anger out of my way. I have a job to do and I won't allow your Neanderthal behavior to derail me."

He moved closer and her breath caught. Heart thudding behind her ribs at a painful pace, she swallowed hard but held her ground. She'd dealt with bullies before and she wouldn't be starting off a new position in fear of one.

Slowly, his hand came up toward her face. Her eyes locked on his, trying to read him, to gauge if she was in real danger. She stood her ground as he merely brushed his fingers along her jawline.

The soft touch of his fingertips against her sensitive skin made her heart pound in her chest. She reached out and grabbed the side of the car to ground herself. The simple graze packed a powerful punch. The gentleness behind his touch and the look in his eyes told her she was safe physically, but Aiden Cook was a dangerous man—to her heart and soul.

"Got it." His words were soft, nearly inaudible, but she had no trouble comprehending his meaning.

Figuring out the puzzle that Aiden Cook presented though?

That was going to be the challenge.

Aiden grabbed Stella's bags from the back of his vehicle and set them roughly at his feet. What was he thinking touching her like that? The woman infuriated him. He shouldn't be thinking about kissing her!

He slammed the lid to the hatch and stomped around her and her pile of luggage to get Jamie out of his car seat.

Keeping his voice even and calm, he spoke to his son.

"Hey, kiddo, we need to go inside for just a minute to help Dr. Allen find her apartment, okay?"

Jamie nodded solemnly as Aiden unbuckled him. Everything the little guy did was solemn. He was quiet unless spoken to. Even in play he made far less noise than most of the two-year-olds Aiden had seen in his life. Nothing broke through the protective wall that Jamie had erected around his heart. At only two, he had already faced losses that most people couldn't understand.

Hopefully, one day soon, Jamie would see that Aiden would never abandon him though. Hopefully, Jamie would know just how much he was loved. Maybe then he would grace them with a smile or a laugh. Until then, Aiden would continue to spend every moment he could with his son, and pray that it was enough.

"Jamie walk?" his soft voice made Aiden's heart swell. The first month Jamie had lived with him, the child hadn't uttered a word. Trauma from his mother's abandonment was what the doctors had said. Even now, Jamie only spoke occasionally. Aiden had sadly related all too well to the feeling of abandonment. Hopefully, his son was young enough that it wouldn't carry over through adulthood for him like it had for Aiden who'd spent several years in foster care after his own birth mother had left him behind.

"If you hold my hand," Aiden said in reply.

Jamie nodded and held a mittened hand up for Aiden to clasp.

"Is he always so well-behaved?" Stella asked.

"Yes." His curt reply would hopefully stave off further questions. Jamie didn't like when anyone talked about him and even a simple conversation would have the boy withdrawing even more.

"Hmm…" She looked like she wanted to say something else but thankfully got the message when Aiden shook his head quickly.

"The apartment is on the fourth floor." He gestured toward the bigger piece of luggage that they both seemed to go for first each time. "May I?"

She waved a hand at him. "Of course, thank you."

He walked slowly toward the elevator so that Jamie didn't have to run. Not that the little guy would complain, but Aiden did his best to make sure his son was comfortable when he could. It was hard when the kid just wouldn't say when something bothered him.

Stella crouched down when they reached the elevator and asked, "Do you want to push the button? I always loved the lift buttons when I was small."

Jamie moved back behind Aiden's leg, peering around at Stella cautiously.

"Is that a no?" she tried again, smiling softly at him. "Last chance," she said, holding her hand over the still dark button.

Jamie tentatively reached a hand, but halted, looking up to Aiden for permission.

"You can push it—go ahead."

Cautiously, Jamie took a step out from behind Aiden and reached out. He couldn't quite reach. He took one more step, and again tried to reach.

Stella eased back.

Still firmly gripping Aiden's hand with his much smaller one, Jamie finally reached over and pushed the button. When the light lit up he made the tiniest of squeals.

Aiden had to fight back a few tears of joy. That was the closest thing he'd heard to a laugh from his son since the day Jamie had come into his life nine months ago. He wanted to thank Stella for it, but at the same time there was a tiny sliver of hurt that she'd managed to pull a response from Jamie that he hadn't yet.

"Good job!" Stella encouraged.

Her enthusiastic words sent Jamie back into hiding mode though, and he ducked back behind Aiden. And clearly the moment was over. Jamie tugged at his hand. When he looked down, Jamie held up his arms, asking to be picked up.

Lifting his son into his arms, he let the boy snuggle in how he liked and then kissed the top of his head. Who knew he'd like being a father so much? Honestly, he'd never planned to have kids. Now he couldn't imagine a life without his son in it. He just wished Jamie were happier.

The elevator doors opened and they moved inside without another word. Stella hit the button for the fourth floor silently. She must have realized Jamie wasn't interested in pushing another button.

"Four-o-two," he directed when they reached the correct floor.

When they reached the door, he fished through his pockets for the keys. He handed them over to Stella to let her handle the lock. Juggling keys and a toddler was something he was still learning to do.

Stella walked in and he could see the approval on her face as she took in the apartment. It was small, but well-appointed. His last apartment had been similar. It was a good fit for a single person.

Aiden rolled the suitcase to a spot where it would be out of the way. He looked at Stella and said, "I wasn't sure what foods you normally eat, but I did stock the kitchen with a small variety of things. Soups, pastas, mostly shelf-stable things. Hopefully, you'll find something to tide you over until you can do your own shopping."

"I'm not a fussy eater, so I'm sure whatever you've provided will be acceptable." Stella shrugged out of her coat and hung it on a hook on the wall. "I do appreciate it."

"Of course." He turned to go.

"Dr. Cook?"

"Aiden, please," he said.

"I want to apologize. It seems we've gotten off on a bit of the wrong foot. We're meant to be working together for the next several weeks, and I would so like that to be on polite terms at the least."

He nodded. "I think we both crossed a line tonight. You must be exhausted from your journey, and my evening got sidetracked. That likely put us both on edge and made us snappier than usual. So, I also apologize for my behavior."

"Well, here's to a fresh start then," Stella said with a smile that didn't quite reach her eyes. She held a hand out to him. "Should we shake on it?"

After the sparks that had flown each time they'd accidentally touched, Aiden was hesitant to put his skin to hers voluntarily. But it would be rude to ignore her outstretched hand.

"To fresh starts," he said, clasping her hand with his.

The early sparks blazed up into an inferno of awareness. He pulled his hand away as quickly as was polite and flexed it a few times, trying to rid himself of the way her touch made him feel. He didn't have room in his life for a woman right now, temporarily or otherwise.

With a curt "Good night," Aiden quickly left, carrying Jamie in his arms.

When the elevator doors closed, shutting away his view of the door to Stella's apartment, he released a deep breath. "Jamie, buddy, don't grow up. Women are bewildering creatures that a man can't decide if he wants to kiss or run from."

Jamie gave him a confused look.

"You'll understand when you're older." His brow furrowed. "Maybe."

CHAPTER FOUR

STELLA DRESSED CAREFULLY for her first day at St. Matthew's Hospital. The brief packet of information she'd received hadn't mentioned the dress code preferred by the administration, but she couldn't be faulted for a crisp business suit with tasteful and comfortable flats. She did slip a scrub uniform and a pair of sneakers into her bag, in case they did prefer her to wear scrubs.

But imagine if she arrived in her pink scrubs to find that surgeons were expected to be in business dress unless they were operating that day? How would anyone take her seriously if she couldn't properly follow a dress code?

No, the charcoal suit was the sensible, safe choice until she learned her way around here. Making a good first impression meant everything. After the rocky beginning with Dr. Cook last night, she needed to start off on the right track at St. Matthew's more than ever.

She applied a minimal amount of makeup—just enough to hide the fact that only two days ago she'd been six time zones away—and styled her dark bob simply. Given that she'd soon be digging deeply into everyone's thoughts and feelings as part of the television special she'd be filming, she wanted to look professional, but approachable. Years spent in front of the camera had taught her to appear unassuming and collected if she wanted genuine responses.

Yet she also wanted to look her best for when she next saw Aiden. Just the idea of seeing him again immediately made her heart beat erratically, like a schoolgirl with a crush. She pursed her lips in frustration. In the mirror, her reflection frowned back at her while her cheeks pinked up.

She took in a deep breath and calmed herself. Dr. Aiden Cook's looks didn't matter to her, even if he was one of the most striking men she'd ever been near. And the chemistry that sparked up between them was no insignificant matter, but he was a grumpy single father and she was not motherhood material.

Her own mother had hardly set a shining example of what it meant to be a proper mum. Oh, Debra Allen had fawned over her, particularly once she'd had Stella's IQ tested and the results came in showing her to be a genius. Stella believed that her mother's actions were based on love—after all, she frequently referred to Stella as her miracle baby—but she was quite selfish and never put Stella first. Was that what parental love was meant to be like? Her mum had never stopped once to consider whether the on-screen life they were forcing her into was what Stella really wanted.

Sure, it had given Stella a tidy little nest egg, but there'd never been any normalcy. Stella's first kiss had been caught on camera. The tabloids knew when she'd been dumped, sometimes before she did. All she'd ever wanted was a normal life.

She was still musing over why she'd stayed in the television business after she'd become an adult when a knock on the door drew her back to her present reality.

As she swung it open, she had to tamp down her excitement to see Aiden.

Pull yourself together, Stella!

"Good morning, Dr. Allen, are you ready to head over to the hospital?" His brown hair shone in the morning light pouring in from the large window in the hallway. It also helped to emphasize just how well-built he was. His broad shoulders filled the open doorway. Even in scrubs, she could tell that Dr. Cook was quite fit.

"Stella, please," she said as she pulled her coat on, hoping it didn't muss her suit too much. The temperatures here were just too low to leave it behind though. Still, if Dr. Cook didn't stop looking at her like that, she might not need any clothes to stay warm.

How could a mere glance from him make her feel so heated? With Oliver, her last boyfriend, she had never had such chemistry. In fact, most of her past experiences had left her cold and uncertain as to why romance was so important to others.

"Stella, then," he said.

She couldn't quite suppress the shudder that the sound of her name on his lips wrought on her senses. His deep voice seemed made to utter her name. She'd always hated her name, thinking it too old-fashioned and stuffy, but hearing those two syllables roll off Aiden's tongue might change her mind.

"I hope you got some rest?" He raised a single eyebrow at her. From the twinkle in his eyes, he'd not missed her unwanted reaction to him. Unintentionally, she'd fluffed his ego.

Great.

Swallowing hard, she chose to ignore the unspoken query and focus solely on what he'd asked verbally. "Indeed, the furnishings are lovely. Once I fully adjust to the time difference, I think I'll be quite comfortable."

"Do you need any of your camera equipment today?" He nodded toward the video equipment she'd laid out on the table.

"Not today. Meetings with the medical director and the head of orthopedics today. And I'm to get my ID badge and stop in at human resources." Stella continued the conversation as she locked the door to the apartment. "Additionally, I thought it best to introduce myself and settle in a touch before pointing a camera at anyone. Hardly the way to make friends, you see. And I won't be doing the bulk of the filming, as that will be left to the film crew once they get here. I'll only be doing some more informal, intimate conversation-type shots."

"If you do bring it, don't point it at me."

His words held a gruffness that she'd started to associate with him, particularly when the subject of her television show came up. She wasn't quite sure if it came as a result of a fear of cameras or a personal vendetta toward show business, but it was hardly something she could ignore. Filming was a priority and it would be hard to get enough material shot without ever catching him on camera when he was her liaison with the hospital.

"At all?"

He glared at her as she stepped into the elevator next to him. "I'd really rather you didn't."

"You have the type of looks that will draw female viewers though." She tried a little flattery, mostly to see if she was correct in her guess at how he would respond.

"Pass." Aiden snorted. His tone made his annoyance clear even within that single syllable.

Interesting. He'd responded quite as she'd expected.

Knowing he was a single parent, she had considered that he might not want the likely aftereffects that his participation on the show might bring. Still, perhaps he might be a little lonely.

"You might enjoy the attention that it brings you." She continued to push him, curious to see if it was a hurdle he'd clear quickly once the initial protests had left his mind. She'd seen more than one shy person put their fears aside in hopes of finding a new love interest. Although, in her experience, men who looked like Aiden would have little trouble drawing attention.

He shook his head. "Doubtful."

"One day, I will get the story from you as to why you are so camera shy."

"How do you know there's a story?" The gruffness returned to his voice. "You don't know me."

Stella shrugged and affected a mysterious air. At least she hoped that's how she looked. "If it was simply that you hated having your portrait taken, you'd have said. My years of experience have taught me that this level of avoidance is more than that. But perhaps we don't know each other well enough for you to share yet."

"Hmph." His frustrated noise confirmed that suspicion, as well.

If she wanted to get to the bottom of his reluctance, she'd have to earn a bit of his trust first. Somehow, she knew Aiden wouldn't trust easily though. What had caused his trust issues? She could see them as easily as she could his problem with being on camera.

Jamie's mother, maybe?

"I have zero interest in being a part of your program." Maybe if he spelled it out specifically, word for word, she'd catch on.

"So, you don't want to find love?" This woman was persistent. Aiden struggled not to snap when she kept pushing him to be on camera. He had already told her he wasn't interested. How many ways did he need to say it? Did she require it in writing?

"No more than I want to be set on fire."

"Everyone deserves love, Aiden."

"So, you've met your soul mate then? The man you intend to live your life with, from now to eternity?"

"We weren't speaking of me." Her cheeks tinted pink when the focus of the conversation shifted to her. The color only served to highlight her beauty.

Aiden had to pull his gaze away from her. It took effort, but he needed to concentrate on the road. "I'm not looking for a soul mate, or a playmate, or any other sort of mate at this point in my life."

Why had he just confessed that? He normally played his cards close to the vest. He didn't share details of his life with virtual strangers.

"But…"

"No buts, Stella. I'm okay as I am."

He couldn't say he was happy. *Content* was even a stretch. But right now, Jamie was the only person he could think of. Maybe once Jamie was more settled and less fragile, maybe then he could consider dating again.

"Your ex did a real number on you, didn't she?"

Aiden's hands clenched around the steering wheel. "Are you willing to tell me all about your exes then?"

"Hardly."

"Then perhaps keep your questioning to yourself." He could feel his blood pressure rising as thoughts of Britney filled his mind. Had his ex done a number on him? Oh, yeah, she had, but indirectly. She hadn't broken his heart by stepping out on him with another man.

She hadn't stolen his money and disappeared. No, what she'd done was much worse. She'd hurt Aiden by neglecting their son, by keeping their son from him. That was not a conversation he was willing to have with a so-called doctor more concerned with filming a television show than with medicine.

Silence filled the car as they continued their short commute.

"There's the main entrance that you'll want to use if you're walking to work," Aiden said gruffly, gesturing as they passed by the front of the hospital. "Employee parking garage is just around the next corner."

Stella murmured a thanks but kept quiet otherwise.

"Where are you supposed to be this morning?" he asked as he pulled into his parking space. They constantly rubbed each other the wrong way, but he couldn't in good conscience leave her with no direction.

"I'm to meet Dr. Stone first thing. Not quite sure beyond that."

He couldn't help but notice that Stella appeared a little nervous. Hmm… So she didn't have nerves of steel after all. Interesting. "First day jitters?"

"I'll be fine," she said, giving him a thousand-watt smile that didn't quite reach her eyes.

"Let me show you to the admin wing before I head down to the ED."

He guided her through the employee entrance without touching her. Touching her had proven to be a bad idea. Every single time he did, it made him think about things and want things that he just couldn't have.

CHAPTER FIVE

No MATTER HOW old you were, the first week at a new job was never easy. The medical director at St Matthew's Hospital had a brusque, no-nonsense demeanor that reminded Stella of the chief executive at her home hospital.

Stella had spent her entire first day with Dr. Stone going over the expectations for Stella's stay in Canada. There were plans for a regular lecture series so that she might share her technique with as many doctors as possible from St. Matthew's and the surrounding hospitals via prerecorded videos. Surgical privileges were extended for Stella if a patient presented who was a candidate for said technique with the understanding that there could be an audience who might view the surgery firsthand.

And, of course, there was discussion on how she might best highlight St. Matthew's for the television program. Dr. Stone had very strong opinions on how she wanted her hospital presented. Stella had given every reassurance that she'd be respectful of St. Matthew's well-earned reputation.

Day two had begun with a quick tour of the facility. So quick that Stella wasn't able to get her bearings at all. Given that it was her specialty, Stella was most in-

terested in the orthopedic floor, but Dr. Stone wanted
to keep moving. With a lingering glance, she followed
the medical director away from orthopedics. She'd have
to explore her temporary workplace more closely later.
They walked briskly through the emergency department where Stella had to bite back her disappointment
when she didn't catch so much as a glimpse of Aiden.
Dr. Stone left her in the human resources department
so that she could fill out some paperwork and get an
ID badge made.

Stella left the HR offices hours later feeling rather
like they'd scraped her bare and stolen part of her soul
with all the forms she'd had to fill out. The picture on
her newly laminated ID badge was her worst *ever* work
picture and she'd begged the clerk to take another. The
man had refused and even had a glimmer of joy in his
eyes when he denied her request. Miserable toad must
have had a bad morning to gain so much pleasure from
causing others pain. At least she only had to carry this
monstrosity of an identification card for two months.

Her week didn't get any better when her third day
at St. Matthew's began with a few wrong turns that led
her into the depths of the hospital. All of the corridors
looked the same and the farther she walked, the less she
recalled having seen before. When she somehow made
a complete circle and ended up taking a second stroll
past the same information desk, she had to admit defeat.

"Pardon me?" she asked the older gentleman at the
desk.

"Guessing you must be lost," he said, with a raised
eyebrow. Amusement lined his weathered face. "You
just went by here a few minutes ago."

"I am." She admitted defeat. "Could you point me

in the direction of orthopedics? I'm afraid I've gotten turned round and can't seem to find my way."

His already furrowed brow wrinkled farther. "Normally don't get asked that one. Most just ask directions to Emergency."

"Well, can you give me directions to the emergency department then? I can make my way from there."

Aiden was working in the ED and he'd surely point the way for her. Her heart rate sped up at the thought of seeing him again, and she tried her best to put that attraction out of her mind.

Why did she have to have a thing for the grumpy guy?

She'd been teased for her taste in men before. For some undeterminable reason, Stella always gravitated toward the guys who verged on being total assholes. In the movies, she loved when the gruff loner fell head over heels for the heroine and was soft only for his woman.

Snarky comments and curt tones were like catnip to Stella. And when they combined with the athletic build and classic good looks in a man like Aiden, well, Stella was going to have to watch herself around him.

It helped a bit that Aiden had made it clear he wasn't interested in her or anything she stood for. He would at least want to keep the distance, even if she strayed across the invisible boundary between them. Despite his apology after their short car ride to the hospital on Monday, he wasn't her biggest fan. He hadn't sought her out at all since. Somehow, inexplicably, that made him more desirable. Her silly hormones had her reacting to a man she didn't even like. Who didn't like her. If she'd gone into psychology, perhaps she'd understand what that might say about her.

One thing she did know was why she was devoutly single. She always went for the wrong guys. Always.

After the way things had ended between her and Oliver, lessons should have been learned. The words coworker and brooding would be numbers one and two on a list of the types of men who should be avoided at all costs. Stella thought she'd learned, but this white-hot attraction to Aiden Cook made it glaringly obvious that her taste in men was still extremely questionable.

Shaking her head, Stella focused on the task at hand—finding the emergency department. When she rounded a corner, she let out a small sigh of relief.

Finally...

Walking up to the reception desk under a large sign that read Emergency, Stella asked, "Where might I find Dr. Cook?"

After looking her up and down, the nurse manning the desk said slowly, "If you'd like to give your name and take a seat, I can page him for you."

Flashing her shiny new identification, Stella replied, "I'd rather you just aim me in his direction. I'm Dr. Stella Allen from The Kensington Project and Dr. Cook is my liaison here. I've only just arrived this week, so I'm still finding my way."

"I'll page him." The nurse smiled the fakest smile.

Stella replied with a fake smile of her own. While she really didn't want to get off on the wrong foot on her first day, she hated having to accept the brushoff. "I'll just wait here then."

"There's seating just there." The nurse waved vaguely to the right where several rows of seating formed a waiting area.

Stella held her position. "I'll sit once you've paged him."

This nurse appeared against the idea of Stella being

anywhere near Aiden. He had implied that he didn't date, but the nurse in front of her didn't seem to have gotten the memo. Stella wasn't going to back down on this matter though. She'd accept him being paged over being sent in his direction, but she wouldn't sit until she saw or heard the nurse actually page him. That way she could be sure it was done now versus an hour from now.

Fake smile falling quickly from her face, the nurse puffed up and sent a glare in Stella's direction that might wither a lesser woman. But Stella had been raised by Debra Allen, the queen of hard looks, and was made of sterner stuff.

Stella's answering look was a genuine smile, because she'd won this round. "I'll wait."

The nurse made a noise that reminded Stella of a growl, but she picked up the phone. "Dr. Cook to the ED desk. Dr. Aiden Cook to the ED desk." Slamming the receiver down, she asked in a waspy tone, "Happy?"

"Very." Stella beamed at her. "Thank you. I do appreciate your assistance in this matter."

She stepped away before the nurse could say another word. Hopefully by ending on such a happy note, she hadn't completely burned the bridge with that particular nurse. She did have to spend the next two months here in Toronto and she couldn't afford to make enemies so early on.

Perched on the uncomfortable chair, Stella waited patiently for Aiden. As she sat there, she people watched. People watching had always been something she'd loved to do, even as a child. She loved to see the little interactions between coworkers and families; the interplay of nonverbal communications and verbal fascinated her. Psychology had been her initial focus, but then she had watched a documentary about orthopedic studies. From that moment on, ortho had become her passion. She'd gone through medical school with the singular ambition to become an orthopedic surgeon. Oh, she'd done the other rotations—emergency, internal medicine, obstetrics—but ortho had been her goal from day one.

Besides being a preferred pastime, people watching also let Stella look for potential subjects for her program. The sour-faced nurse at the desk was certainly not going on camera, unless her attitude drastically improved. A couple doctors strolled past, clearly enthralled with each other. Were they a couple? Adding in a segment on how the stresses of the job affected relationships could be interesting.

Stella dug through her purse for her phone to make a note of that idea before she forgot. The notes app on her phone got a lot of use while she was working on a program. Tapping out her thoughts, she suddenly felt rather than saw Aiden's arrival.

As she looked up, he strode up to the desk. The nurse looked at him with longing written all over her face, but he only barely shot the other woman a glance.

Stella had to squash some longing of her own when she and Aiden made eye contact. Swallowing hard, she rose to her feet as he moved in her direction.

"You paged?" His decidedly annoyed expression caused Stella to bristle defensively.

"She paged. I asked where I might find you." Stella wanted to clear that up. It wasn't her fault that the other woman took it upon herself to be a gatekeeper. "I'm sorry for interrupting your workday. I've had a tour of the hospital and yet wasn't sure I could find my way back to the orthopedic floor. I need to get your number, as well."

The nurse behind Aiden huffed.

Stella's lips turned up in the hint of a smile. She stepped a little closer to Aiden and placed her hand on his bare forearm. "I should have gotten your number when you dropped me off the other night, but I can only blame that slip on jet lag."

"What are you doing?" Aiden asked, his tone dark and low. His long lashes framed expressive brown eyes that were currently glittering with impatience.

"Testing a theory," Stella whispered back as she tilted her upper body slightly in Aiden's direction. Her experiment was wreaking havoc on her own senses, but she continued with her course of action, determined to prove her point.

Something slammed on the desk behind them and Aiden jumped at the sudden noise. His movement only served to bring him even closer to Stella.

"That nurse has a thing for you—did you know?" Stella allowed her fingers to trail softly over Aiden's skin. This might have started as a jab at the nurse, testing a theory that the nurse was attracted to Aiden, but now that her hand was on him, Stella didn't want to stop touching him. "If you are interested in her, now might be a good time for you to go express that interest."

He snorted. "Not in this lifetime."

"No?" She raised a single brow at him.

Shaking his head, Aiden doubled down on his rejection with a glance at the nurse behind him. "I don't date women from the hospital."

"That's just too bad, really," Stella murmured before she could stop herself. She had the same rule for herself, but she could see breaking it for a man like Aiden Cook. Some rules were just made to be broken, after all.

Aiden's eyes darkened in response to her words. He

lowered his head and asked in a dangerously sexy tone, "Are you flirting with me, Dr. Allen?"

Stella's cheeks pinked up in response to his question. Her hand remained on his forearm, her lithe fingers trekking up and down his skin until it was all he could do not to yank her up against his chest and kiss her.

He had always made it a point not to date anyone from the hospital. He'd seen how badly workplace romances could go sideways early in his residency and he'd sworn he would never cross that line. Stella made him want to break that vow in a thousand different ways.

His plan had been to ignore her presence in his hospital and ED as much as possible, given that he'd been assigned to work with her. Knowing he'd be forced to interact with her, he'd accepted that he would have to see her. Yet he hadn't expected *this*.

How could he have expected that The Kensington Project visiting doctor would be the most infuriating woman—who also happened to be the sexiest woman— he'd ever been in contact with?

"You didn't answer my question," he prompted. He reached out and tipped her chin upward until she met his gaze. "Because it certainly seems like you are flirting."

She pulled away and took a step back, her cheeks darkening further. "Apologies. I…" she trailed off. What excuse had she been about to give him? The tidbit about testing to see if Nurse Rita was interested in him might have given her the impulse, but her own attraction was what kept that interaction going.

"If you're curious, I'm not seeing anyone," he said, while mentally kicking himself for volunteering that information. He really should keep his distance from the woman in front of him, but something about her pulled him in like gravity. His own attraction fueled that admission.

"Aww, geez, hold that thought, please. My memory card is full up and I need to switch it out right quick."

Aiden spun around.

A man stood a few feet away with a large camera on his shoulder. "Ah, there's the little bugger," he said as he pulled the small memory card out of the bottom of the messenger-style bag he had slung across his torso.

"I don't want to be on camera," Aiden growled.

"No?" The cameraman looked confused. "The chemistry between you two is priceless. It's the kind of stuff a director's dreams are made of."

"You shouldn't be filming me without my express permission." Aiden narrowed his eyes.

Stella inhaled a sharp breath behind him. He expected she'd wade in and argue once more that he should be flattered to be on camera and extoll the benefits of allowing a lens to invade his privacy.

He turned his glare on Stella. "And I thought you said your film crew wouldn't be here for a while?"

"I managed to finish my previous assignment a bit early," the videographer said, his tone so cheerful and happy that Aiden wanted to punch something.

"Dr. Cook to trauma one. Dr. Cook to trauma one," a nasally female voice called out over the PA system. He had to bite back a curse because the last thing he wanted right now was to run a trauma.

"To be continued?" Stella asked, a hopefulness in her tone that made him want to scream.

What was with these people? Why were they so annoyingly happy all the time? And why was she so gung ho about forcing him to be on camera? "There's nothing further to be said on the matter. I'm not interested."

He let the double entendre in that line stand between them. He wanted to make it crystal clear that he wasn't interested in being on camera or in being with her. Unless it was something physical only, he couldn't get involved.

Stella gave a brief nod, acknowledging silently that she'd caught his meaning. "Do you mind if I tag along on your trauma though? I'd like to see how you run things here. Get the lay of the land, so to speak."

When he shrugged, she fell into step next to him. The cameraman followed a few feet behind, but after Aiden glared at him, he lowered the camera.

Stella ignored the cameraman entirely and spoke as if they were alone. "I'd love to discuss my technique with you when you have a free moment. As an emergency doctor, you'll catch patients first so it would be helpful if you could give me a ring if someone fitting the criteria arrives in your care. I've videos, of course, but it's much more memorable if your surgeons here get a chance to practice it live. Recordings can only teach so much, after all."

"I'd agree with that." He scanned his ID badge to unlock the doors back into the emergency department. "And I'd love to hear more about this revolutionary technique of yours. It must be something for you to be sent halfway across the world to share it with us."

Aiden spared a glance for the cameraman, making sure the camera was still pointed down.

"Revolutionary might be a stretch," Stella continued, her tone modest and free of the boastful arrogance many surgeons assumed when discussing their work. Her eyes lit up with enthusiasm as she spoke though and that told him more than any of the videos he had watched about her medical skill. "I pioneered a technique that saves an average of an hour under anesthesia and it shortens the recovery time which leads to diminished muscle atrophy for patients with a broken pelvis. I have data to support that, if you are interested."

Maybe there was more substance to her than he'd initially given her credit for. He had basic knowledge of orthopedics, like all emergency room physicians, but he had a feeling that seeing Stella Allen operate would be a thing of beauty. While some of the details might go beyond him, he couldn't shake the desire to spend more time with her. The zest in her entire demeanor when she spoke of her technique inspired him to want to learn. She had a certain confidence when speaking of her work that was quite inspiring.

"I'm not a surgeon, but if you think I can help identify patients for you, then I'm interested in finding out more." Not just about her surgical advances, but about her, as well. Something inexplicable drove him to find out more about her, even if it was a bad idea.

They walked together into the trauma bay. He gave the cameraman a pointed look to keep his distance. Aiden pushed all thoughts of finding out more about Stella from his mind, and he turned his focus to the patient before him.

"Fill me in," he said as he gloved up.

"Elderly woman with a possible pelvic break sustained during a fall."

Kismet must have been at work since that very patient turned out to be ideal for Stella's technique. She allowed Aiden to work, not wanting to be a distraction while he stabilized the patient. It would have been great if he'd allowed Henry in, to film, but he'd been so opposed that she didn't want to push any further. She'd have to bring it up when he was in a better mood.

Aiden was really quite thorough and his bedside manner surprised her. The gruff man she'd grown to expect was a real charmer with his patients. He put the older woman at ease within minutes and even got her to smile despite her pain. The gentle confidence he displayed with his patients showed her a different side of Aiden. What had made him so brusque?

"Dr. Allen, do you have anything to add?"

Stella glanced quickly at the list of tests and scans that Aiden had ordered for their patient, Mrs. Upton. He'd ordered nearly everything that she would have done, so she had little to add, although she did ask for a few more specific views to the requested scans.

A short while later, they were looking over the scans together. Aiden gave his interpretation and paused. Stella took that as her opportunity to speak up. "Your assessment that she has a fractured pelvis is spot-on. Might I show you where my skills come in?"

He nodded.

"See that break there," she said, pointing at the screen. "Traditionally, that would be a few pins here, here and there. Each taking time as the surgeon has to be super careful not to farther damage an already fragile bone."

"Right," Aiden said slowly. "I remember that much from my ortho rotation."

"I prefer to do things a bit differently," Stella continued. This was where she was in her element. In the operating room or talking about bones, Stella had full confidence. It was in the rest of her life that she had moments of uncertainty. "My technique came about because I had a patient whose bones were too brittle for the typical plate screw internal fixation. I keep things minimally invasive and, with less damage to the bone and surrounding musculature, that helps both surgical times and shortens recovery."

"So, tell me what you look for when determining which patients are a good fit. What makes Mrs. Upton a good fit, in particular?"

Stella launched into a very technical explanation of patient criteria and a discussion of how the traditional surgical implants were less effective than her procedure. Aiden seemed to be following along, so she continued on through her explanation. Surely, he'd stop her if he wasn't able to keep up.

A short while later, the hospital took Mrs. Upton upstairs to her room. Aiden pulled Stella to the side, his hand lingering on her arm a bit too long to be purely professional. The simple touch sent a wave of interest burning up her arm and into her core.

"Usually my involvement ends when they head upstairs, but I'd like to follow her case and see how it goes moving forward. I'd like to observe when you perform her surgery, if that's okay?"

"Of course. I'll be getting that scheduled as soon as she's cleared for anesthesia with that concussion. I'll let you know."

His lips turned up at the corners. "You did good work today with Mrs. Upton."

"You don't have to sound so surprised, Dr. Cook." His compliment paired with that hint of a smile emboldened her, and she nudged him playfully. "Did you think I got sent here only because of my experience in television?"

Aiden's silence was answer enough. The lack of denial spoke to his beliefs as much as direct words ever could. His skepticism created a gulf between them that had her stepping back as if he'd slapped her.

"You did." Stella stared at him, completely stunned. Taking a step back, she put some physical distance between them. She'd grown to expect that sort of thing from other doctors, but somehow, she'd thought Aiden was different. Or maybe the attraction burning between them had simply made her more sensitive to any cynicism coming from him. "I suppose that explains the cold shoulder at the airport. You were resentful of being saddled with me as you presumed me to be incompetent. Wow."

"Stella, I…uh…" Aiden fumbled for words. "I may have had concerns that you would either pass off the hard cases or need to pull out a textbook to look up how to treat them."

His assumptions left her feeling as though she'd been doused with ice water. Determination filled her, warming her back with a fiery need to show him that she was more than a celebrity doctor. "It's fine. But I will prove to you that I'm here because I deserve to be, not just because a television producer thought I'd be ideal for this documentary."

She'd been proving herself her entire life. Everyone made assumptions about her, depending on how much of her past they knew. If they'd seen her on *Britain's Brightest* or *Stay Smart with Stella*, they liked to toss trivia her way, as if having a high IQ meant her brain was full of bits of useless knowledge. If they'd seen the self-filmed show she'd created and starred in throughout college and medical school, they had seen her minimize her intelligence while trying to date the wrong guys. Even now that she had taken on the guest slot at *Good*

Morning United Kingdom, they stereotyped her into the role of TV doctor who was more polish than grit.

"Stella, I—"

"I said it was fine, Dr. Cook." She narrowed her eyes at him. Aiden Cook was a complication she didn't have time for. She had too many things on her plate over her remaining seven-and-a-half weeks in Toronto, and she certainly didn't want to waste a single second more than she had to on a man who couldn't be bothered to give her half a chance.

"So, I'm back to Dr. Cook then?" Aiden rose to his full height and crossed his arms over his chest. He stared down at her, his eyes hard and his expression grim. "Listen, Dr. Allen—"

"I see you two are getting along swimmingly." Dr. Stone interrupted whatever tirade Aiden was about to launch into as she walked up.

"We are doing just fine," Aiden countered grumpily.

"And yet I have already heard complaints about you not allowing the film crew to work? And that you and Dr. Allen are squaring off in my corridors, although if rumors are to be believed, you can't decide if you want to kiss her or throttle her."

"I'd quit before I kissed her and I don't want to be on camera." Aiden looked so aghast at the idea of kissing her that Stella nearly flinched.

"Good, then you won't mind spending some time next weekend showing Dr. Allen some of what Toronto has to offer."

"I'm sorry, what?" Aiden seemed as thrown off as Stella did.

"You heard me." Dr. Stone smirked at them. "But I'll repeat myself on the off chance that you didn't. I want you to take Dr. Allen out next Saturday and show

her around Toronto. That gives her some time to settle in. I'm sure by then she'll be ready to get out and
about a bit."

"Not sure that's a good idea," Aiden argued.

"We had a deal, did we not?"

Aiden eyed the director before finally nodding. "I'll
do my part, Dr. Stone. You don't have to worry about
that."

Stella's chin dropped. She wasn't sure exactly what
deal Aiden had made with the medical director, but it
must have been a doozy for him to agree to settle down
so quickly.

"By the way, how's the Christmas party planning
coming along?" Dr. Stone raised an eyebrow.

Aiden and Stella both remained quiet.

"I see." Dr. Stone shook her head. "I think it would
do you two some good to find some common ground
on neutral turf. Plan this party. It's going to be on film,
after all. You don't want it to look slapped together at
the last minute. Get to know each other."

"Why would you want him to take me out when
he clearly has so low an opinion of me?" Stella asked.

"I never said anything of the sort." Aiden leaned
her direction, and his voice dropped lower and took
on this sexy, gravelly tone that made her knees weak.
"So, what do you say, Stella? Are you up for spending
the day with me next Saturday? I could pick you up at
nine in the morning."

Stella's heart thudded against her chest both at the
nearness of the man and the enticement in his words.
She was not here for romance; that was a fact. But she
certainly wasn't opposed to spending a day with a handsome man. Even if he was prone to the sulks and mer-
curial as all get-out.

Words escaped her though. She nodded her agreement.

"Perfect. I'll see you then." He sauntered away without a backward glance. His free and easy gait showed no remaining stress on his part from their argument, as if it hadn't affected him as much as it had her.

She stared after him. How had she gone from being angry with him for believing the worst of her to agreeing to a date of sorts within the space of a moment? So much for her determination to stay as far from Aiden as humanly possible. He'd rendered her speechless when he asked her to spend Saturday with him. They both knew she was only in Toronto for two short months. They were both single, and the chemistry flying between them was nuclear. Although they'd had their hands forced by the medical director, they were both fighting the attraction hard.

What could one day hurt? Hopefully those didn't become famous last words.

"He's not so bad once you get to know him." Dr. Stone gave her a knowing smile.

Stella's estimation of the medical director jumped up a notch when she realized just how deftly the woman had manipulated both Stella and Aiden with only a few well-placed comments. She'd have to watch herself around Dr. Stone or she might well find herself in more unpleasant situations than an obligatory outing with a handsome doctor. Her lips turned up in the barest hint of a smile. She loved a good challenge.

"I can't say that I've seen much to like about him just yet," Stella argued.

Except maybe every inch of him...

"You might find that he's like one of those prickly cacti that has the most beautiful blooms if you can put up with the thorns long enough to see it."

CHAPTER SIX

STELLA HAD NO IDEA what sort of day Aiden had in mind for them when he'd been strong-armed by his boss to spend the day with her. She scrounged through the meager wardrobe she'd brought with her across the ocean. She had scrubs, business suits and loungewear mostly. Why hadn't she brought more casual, going-out sort of clothes!

She pulled on the one pair of jeans that she'd brought, shimmying as she tugged them up over her hips. Jeans and a sweater would have to do, since nothing else she'd brought was appropriate. She shifted side to side as she viewed her full-length look in the mirror. The dark shade of the denim helped make her curves look more desirable and less like Stella was a carb junkie. The deep plum cashmere sweater fell nicely and had the bonus of being exquisitely comfortable. Minimal makeup finished off her look.

Before she could second-guess her choice of outfit, there came a knock on her door. Running a shaky hand over her hair, she smoothed it one last time before answering. She hadn't been this nervous about a date in a decade.

It's not a date, Stella.

When she opened the door though, her heart sank.

Confusion filled her thoughts. Aiden had brought Jamie with him?

So it definitely wasn't a date.

Somehow it had never occurred to her that he might bring his son. She'd never spent any time with a single dad before so she wasn't sure of the typical procedures and timelines, but it seemed to her that he'd want to get to know her before involving her in his son's life.

She replayed the conversation in her head, especially after the way they had flirted before that trauma. He hadn't asked her out, no, but they'd been heading that way, hadn't they? His boss had just given them a nudge in the direction they were already moving. Nowhere along the way had he mentioned bringing his son along though.

She gathered herself and smiled at the little boy. "Hello there, Jamie. I didn't expect to see your sweet face today."

Aiden had the decency to grimace. He ran a hand over the boy's hair in a calm and reassuring manner. "I thought we could see the Toronto Christmas Market and try to get some ideas for the Holiday party. It's family friendly. I didn't think it would be an issue to bring him along."

Grump mode reactivated.

With each word he spoke, tension increased in his frame. Aiden's sensitivity when it came to his son was off the charts. How she handled the next few minutes could determine the course of her next few weeks in Toronto. If she messed this up, Aiden would be against her and her life would be infinitely more difficult and far less fun.

She reached out and touched Aiden's hand to reassure him. "It's fine. It was merely unexpected. Forgive me if I made it seem otherwise. If we're still on, I'll grab my coat and be ready to go."

At his nod, she slipped into her coat and grabbed her wallet and keys from her purse. She placed them in the inner pocket of her coat. She didn't want to cart her purse around all day if they were going to be doing a lot of walking.

"Tell me about this Christmas Market."

"It's an annual event. It opened this week. Usually it runs from November through Christmas, and since we have to plan this party, I thought that maybe the market could provide some inspiration." Aiden put his hand on the small of her back and guided her to the elevator.

Though she couldn't feel the heat from his hand through the layers she wore, the gesture warmed her, nonetheless. Stella enjoyed the feel of Aiden close to her. He was near enough to make her feel protected, but left enough space to avoid crowding her. Aiden invaded her personal space just enough to make her hyperaware of his every movement. The nearness filled her mind with the sorts of ideas she'd been unsuccessfully fighting since she'd met him at the airport.

Don't forget his boss quite literally forced him to ask you out.

The market was only a short drive from Stella's apartment, and Aiden's car was still blissfully warm. Jamie sat quietly in the backseat, just like when they'd picked her up at the airport.

Why was the child so quiet all the time? Every kid she'd ever been around had been unbearably loud and bounced from idea to idea. Jamie's somber countenance confused her. She had so many questions, but dare she ask them? Aiden armored up whenever his son became the topic of conversation and she didn't want to push her luck again with him.

The crowd size at the market gave Stella a bit of a surprise. Somehow, she hadn't expected it to be such an event. She'd pictured a small craft market with lots of handmade goodies to peruse. Even before they were fully within the boundaries of the market, she could see it was so much more than a simple craft show. This could only be considered a full-on event.

Jamie pointed at the life-size gingerbread houses with an expression of awe. Stella wasn't entirely sure she didn't have the same look of amazement on her own face. Life-size gingerbread houses were impressive. Were they actually gingerbread or only painted to look so? She made a mental note to find out before the day was through.

"If you like the gingerbread houses, we could maybe do something with them for decorations?"

"Hmm… It is a possibility, of course."

"One that you don't like, even though you like those particular gingerbread houses. Got it." The confusion in his voice said that he didn't understand why she'd seemed noncommittal though.

"I don't want the party to appear childish," she offered as explanation. This event was going to be televised. They wanted it to feel upscale and highlight the best of St. Matthew's, without being formal. Gingerbread houses were a touch too informal, however.

The scent of spices wafted through the air. "Mmm… Mulled wine," Stella murmured, wrapping her gloved hand around Aiden's arm. "Can you smell it?"

He tensed under her touch, but didn't pull away. Should she put a more professional level of distance between them?

"I'm more of a craft beer guy myself, but if you want a mulled wine, then we'll find out where they're selling it. If we have the party on hospital grounds, I'm not sure they'll want us to serve alcohol, or else I'd suggest we add that to the party menu."

"Sadly, I believe you are correct on that. We'll have to do something nonalcoholic. They do want us to have something child-friendly though in case anyone brings their family."

Aiden looked down at Jamie. His love for the child shone in his eyes, as bright and clear as the sky that beautiful November morning. "Maybe some hot chocolate? You like hot chocolate, don't you, buddy?"

Jamie nodded somberly. Not even the idea of hot chocolate drew a smile from him.

Stella worried her lower lip as she considered the boy. She couldn't help but notice that he had few of the typical reactions of a child his age.

"Stop that," Aiden warned, his voice low and firm. "I can see where your thoughts are going and that's not going to be a conversation we will be having today."

"You have no idea what I'm thinking," Stella argued. But she was quite sure that he did. He'd caught her inquisitive looks at his son and was cutting her off before she could ask the questions that sat burning on the tip of her tongue.

"Whatever conclusions you've drawn, I guarantee they are wrong." He looked like he might say more, but he buttoned up tight after a quick glance down to his son. In the way he hesitated, she could see it was private. Maybe he didn't want Jamie to hear whatever it was so didn't feel comfortable talking about it with the child present.

"Oh…" Stella pointed, changing the subject. "Look at that."

Aiden looked in the direction she pointed and she hoped he'd see something interesting. Her goal had been to lighten the swiftly darkening mood and to take Aiden's attention off her interest in his son.

"What?" he asked. "The carolers?"

"Hmm… Yes." She answered without delay even as she scanned the christmas market quickly for the carolers he was looking at. "Christmas carols are one of my favorite parts of the holiday. Do you think perhaps we could incorporate caroling into our party?"

At least she didn't have to try to lie. She wasn't very good at being dishonest. In fact, the slightest lie would have her face lighting up like a neon sign. She may have grown up on camera, but she'd never be a Hollywood star, despite having had a few offers over the years.

"I think that's a great idea. If you love carolers, you will love this then. Follow me." Aiden guided Jamie through the crowd, never releasing the boy's hand. Stella stayed close to him, occasionally letting her fingers clutch loosely at his sleeve. "The carolers here are fantastic."

Thankfully, there'd been something interesting off in the vicinity she'd gestured. It would have been beyond embarrassing had there been nothing but a wall. She hadn't even looked before she raised her hand.

Aiden stopped at a booth just before they reached the carolers. He waved a hand at the confections in front of them. "Do you want some?"

Graham crackers, chocolate and marshmallows covered the table. Stella shook her head. She had never had much of a sweet tooth. "I'm good, thanks. I love the idea of having s'mores at the party, but I don't think admin would be permissive of open flames, do you?"

"Nope. Maybe a cookie-decorating station though? Something to keep people around for a while and keep the kids busy?"

"Hmm, that idea has potential." Cookie decorating was far more practical than gingerbread houses. This was something they could really work with, actually. It wouldn't be expensive either.

"You sure you don't want any?" He gestured again at the s'mores ingredients in front of them.

"I really couldn't."

"Your loss. What about you, little man?" he asked Jamie. "You want some, don't you?"

Jamie nodded, the smallest of smiles turning up his lips.

Aiden purchased supplies to make s'mores and a couple skewers. Where did he plan on making them though?

That question quickly found its answer.

A row of firepits ran the length of the performance area. A few were occupied with families roasting marshmallows and warming their hands against the crisp cold of the day.

Aiden claimed one of the empty firepits and began showing Jamie how to roast marshmallows. Somehow, the man gave his son the space and freedom to learn a new skill while simultaneously ensuring that the child was safe. His interactions with his son showed a softer side to the brooding doctor who she found endlessly attractive.

In that moment, the thought flittered briefly through her mind that family life might not be so bad. There was a certain allure to spending the day almost as a family, although she hesitated to slot herself into the maternal role. With no cameras and no publicity, there was none of the falsehood she'd grown up with.

Her parents loved her—of that she had no doubt. They'd also loved the spotlight. Her mother in particular had thrived under the attention that Stella's television career had brought her. Stella always thought it was like having two mothers, really. The overbearing one bossed Stella around behind closed doors, but the cameras brought out the lovely mum who seemed so perfect and ideal.

The carolers started a new song, enthralling Stella with their harmonizing. Closing her eyes, she relaxed. As she let the music pull her in, the thoughts of her mother drifted out. The harmony washed over her and tension slipped from her as she swayed along with the beat. The music dropped off and Stella opened her eyes reluctantly.

"Thank you for listening to the Candy Cane Carolers! We're going to take a quick break to warm up and we'll be back soon. Enjoy your day at Toronto Christmas Market," the lead caroler announced.

Stella sighed. They'd been so lovely that she hated to see their performance end. Maybe there would be time to catch another carol or two before they went home for the day though.

She looked to see if Aiden and Jamie had enjoyed the caroling, but they'd put their entire focus into building s'mores. Crouched down next to Jamie, Aiden helped the little boy with his snack. He even produced a wet wipe from one of his pockets to clean the excess marshmallow from Jamie's face and hands. What else did he have stashed in those pockets?

A shiver ran through her and she stepped closer to

the firepit. She held her hands over the flames, trying to warm her chilled extremities. "It's so chilly today," she said to Aiden.

He chuckled. "Today's rather warm for November, actually. I take it the weather's not so cold where you're from."

"This is warm?"

"This is warm," he confirmed with a grin that sent her stomach aflutter.

What have I gotten myself into?

Not just the trip to Toronto and all the associated stress, but this connection with Aiden had the potential to be life altering. Her analytical brain was working overtime to analyze all the possible outcomes that these circumstances opened up.

"You two ready to do some shopping?" Aiden picked Jamie up and held out a hand to Stella. "The crowd is rather thick over here. Wouldn't want to get separated, after all."

Stella slid her hand into his. Despite the chill in the air, with Aiden's hand clasped around hers, she no longer shivered from the cold. Warmth spread from her hand and throughout her body. Why did she have to react so strongly to him?

They spent the next couple hours walking slowly from booth to booth. They discussed ideas along the way as inspiration jumped out at them. They'd settled on doing something simple, but traditional. Aiden was vehemently against bringing anything that glittered into the hospital, arguing that they had to give the janitorial staff a break. Stella had to concede when he brought up that point. Glitter was beautiful, but it did make a mess and she didn't want to pile work on any department at Christmas.

When they came upon a small play area, Jamie's eyes lit up. He pointed with as much excitement as she'd ever seen from him.

"You want to play for a little while?"

Jamie nodded shyly.

"Do you mind?" Aiden asked.

"Me?" Stella shook her head. "Of course not! Let him have some fun."

In fact, she rather hoped to see the little boy play. She'd love to see a true smile on his solemn little face. Each of the shy looks he'd given her had already helped him worm his way into her affections.

"Go ahead," Aiden told his son.

Standing by the only opening to the play area, Stella shivered as the little boy ran to a castle anchored in the middle of the playground.

"Dr. Allen, I do believe we will need to get you a warmer winter coat." Aiden took his scarf off and draped it around Stella's neck. His body heat still clung to the knitted garment. "At least until you grow a thicker skin and get used to the weather here in Toronto."

"It's been two weeks here and I've yet to adjust." Snow flurries floated softly in the air and she could see her breath with each exhale. She raised an eyebrow at him. "How exactly does one get used to freezing their toes off?"

He brushed a stray bit of hair back from her face. Lifting one shoulder in a casual shrug, he replied, "I was raised here. I hardly notice it. How are you liking Toronto so far?"

"Busy." Stella turned her attention back to his son who was waving at them from behind the Plexiglas barrier on the second level of the play structure. "Jamie seems to be having an amazing time."

"Is he the only one?" Aiden asked.

"No, today has been quite lovely." Stella glanced over at him, surprised to see that he was watching her. She gave him a wry smile. "The only way today could be better were if it were warmer. I'm freezing even with your kind loan of your scarf."

Aiden stepped closer. His body heat enveloped her and the next shiver that coursed down her spine had nothing to do with the cold air around them. She licked her suddenly dry lips and Aiden's eyes dropped to her mouth.

Kissing Stella was a perfectly acceptable response to the way her tongue teased out over her lower lip, surely. He slid one arm around her waist and pulled her close. Her soulful green eyes had caught his attention in the airport, and even when they glittered dangerously with anger, he'd been intrigued and aching to kiss her.

"Help!" someone screamed.

Aiden pulled away from Stella and moved in the direction of the pleas for assistance. A woman was standing next to a little boy who was lying fairly still on the rubberized flooring of the play area.

"What happened?" he asked, switching into emergency physician mode.

"He fell from the top," she squalled, her words almost unintelligible in her panic.

Aiden glanced up to see that was about six feet. The little one was maybe four. Far too big a height for him to be comfortable.

"Stella, can you take care of Jamie?" he asked over his shoulder, knowing instinctively that she'd be standing there.

"I've got him. You take care of this wee one."

Gently, his fingers kneaded and prodded the child's bones and muscles. No obvious breaks or deformities. That was good. He breathed a sigh of relief when the child began to move on his own and cried out for his mommy.

"Hey, buddy, look here at me." Aiden used the flashlight app on his phone to check the boy's pupils. They were uneven and the left was slow to react.

Crap.

"Has someone called the paramedics?" he asked calmly. He'd learned years ago never to let it show that he had concerns about a patient. That was the quickest way to having a panicked family member go nuts.

When he got an affirmative reply, he returned to examining his young patient. Pediatrics wasn't his specialty, but this kid clearly had a head injury.

"Does your head hurt?"

The kid nodded and then grabbed for his head. "Ow!"

"I know it hurts. Is anything numb or tingly?" No response. "Can you see me okay? Am I blurry or fuzzy?" Again, no reply.

The paramedics came rushing up then, and Aiden turned his little patient over to their capable hands. He took a few minutes to give them the information he had, and his concerns, but let them do their jobs and didn't try to tell them what to do. He hated when people came into his ED and tried to tell him how to do his job, so he wouldn't do it to the paramedics.

They quickly ushered the little boy into the ambulance and sped away with the lights and sirens going. They needed to get the child there quickly so that a neurosurgeon could get a look at him.

Once they were out of sight, Aiden turned to look for Stella and Jamie. He couldn't help the smile when his eyes landed on them. They were sitting together on a nearby bench and Jamie was snuggled into Stella's arms. He had popped his thumb into his mouth. His eyes were closed and it looked like he might nap right there in her arms.

"Hey," he said as he walked up to them. "Thanks for looking out for him."

"Oh, it was no problem at all." Stella sighed. Her face relaxed into a look of utter contentment. "I think he likes me."

Aiden sucked in a breath. His little boy craved the attention of a woman in his life. He hadn't realized how much until he saw how readily Jamie took to Stella and sought her approval. Thoughts of getting Stella back in his arms and kissing her were whisked away on a wave of guilt.

He hadn't expected Jamie to bond with her so quickly. Or even at all... Jamie had been slow to warm up to everyone Aiden had introduced him to. He'd been slow to warm to Aiden, even.

Not that Aiden hadn't been understanding of Jamie's reticence.

After the way Britney had just abandoned him, it was a surprise that the little boy could trust enough to bond with anyone. Aiden swallowed hard at the memory of the first time he'd met his son, pushing the darkness back. If he allowed himself to go down that line of treacherous thoughts, it would ruin an otherwise good day.

"He's tired. We should go so I can get him home for a nap." It was best to get Jamie home and away from Stella before he got any further attached.

Stella gave him a look that said she was aware of his intentions, but she agreed.

They walked slowly to the parking lot. The way Jamie clung to Stella when they went to leave the market made Aiden worry. Jamie hadn't wanted to get in his car seat at all, asking Stella to keep holding him. In an attempt to pacify the child, Stella had climbed into the rear seat with him.

Rather than reassure Aiden, her actions only kicked his concern into high gear. Had he made a real mistake bringing Jamie along today? Stella was only going to be in Toronto temporarily, after all. Stabs of regret spiked through his heart. He should have considered that Jamie might form an attachment.

He stood outside the car and gathered his thoughts. Was it fair to his son for Aiden to be introducing him to women? Aiden certainly had no intentions of beginning anything that might become permanent. Long-term wasn't a relationship status he'd ever wanted applied to himself, but particularly not now that he was a father.

After climbing into the car, he started the engine and backed out of the space. The drive to Stella's apartment was made in silence on his part. Stella and Jamie talked softly in the seat behind him while he brooded on the mistakes he'd made that day.

He hadn't even considered that bringing Jamie along would be potentially problematic. Initially, his thought had been that the christmas market would be a good low-pressure situation where they could spend the day and get some ideas for the employee party. And that Jamie might be a good buffer since their conversations were often volatile. The idea that Jamie might get attached so quickly hadn't even occurred to him. Aiden wanted to kick himself for not thinking of the possibility. It was why he hadn't dated since Jamie had come into his life, after all.

When he pulled into the parking garage at Stella's temporary abode, he stepped out of the car to talk to her briefly. He needed to make her understand how today was not going to happen again. "Today was a mistake," he said bluntly.

Hurt flashed over her features before she shut down all emotion. "Was it?"

Hurting her hadn't been his goal, and he wanted to take her in his arms and soothe the pain he'd just caused with his bald statements. He even took a step closer to her, but he couldn't embrace her like he wanted. How could he both hold her close and push her away?

"You're leaving." He shrugged, as if that were explanation enough.

"And?" Stella raised a brow in question. "This isn't brand-new information that you've only just learned. In fact, you knew the details of my stay in Toronto before I did. I'm uncertain as to why it's suddenly a problem though. You nearly kissed me. You had no problem with that, at least until Jamie fell asleep in my lap. Are you pulling away because you realized that I might be developing a bond with your son?"

He swallowed hard. How could he explain what he was so conflicted about? He wanted her, but he wanted her at arm's length. The only valid defense he could verbalize was to protect his son. "Jamie can't get attached to someone who is leaving."

And neither can I.

The words hung between them, becoming a suddenly impenetrable force separating them. It percolated while they stared at each other, neither blinking, neither seeming to want to look away.

After a moment, Stella caved. "I see," she said softly. "I'll take my unwanted presence to my apartment. Thank you for today. It was wonderful despite the harsh ending."

The stiffness in her back as she walked away from him highlighted how much pain he'd caused her. He sucked in a fast breath. For a moment, he wished that she had known him when he had been fun loving and didn't carry such burdens. But he could wish all night and not change a thing. He wasn't that man anymore. And it wasn't all about him anymore. The walls around his heart had to be strong enough to protect more than himself now. He also had to protect Jamie.

He couldn't let in another woman who was destined to leave.

CHAPTER SEVEN

"DOES POOR MRS. UPTON know that her surgeon isn't really a surgeon, she just plays one on TV?" one of the nurses tittered as Stella came into the operating room.

She released a shaky breath and tried not to react. Bone-weary exhaustion had settled over her an hour ago and she hadn't been able to break free of it. After her unexpected non-date date with Aiden, she'd struggled with insomnia all weekend and had started the week off with a sleep deficit. Between the lack of real rest and the stress of presenting a series of lectures all about the surgical technique she'd developed, she was nearly done in.

She hadn't realized just how much harder it would be to share her technique with surgeons in a different country. There wasn't even a language barrier to contend with, yet each presentation somehow siphoned energy off her like a parasite. Four lectures so far this week had really drained her.

Stella needed this surgery. The boost of energy she always got from performing a complicated surgery would go a long way.

"I'm surprised there's not a camera crew in here." Another nurse snorted.

She paused in front of them and raised an eyebrow.

One of them had the decency to look ashamed of himself, but the other gave her a smirk. "Where are the hair and makeup crews, Dr. Hollywood?"

"Gave them the day off, I'm afraid." She forced a smile. As usual, her defenses were going up because people thought she was all fluff and no substance. In her head, she gave herself a bit of a pep talk.

You can do this, Stella. It's no different than any other day in your life. Show them that you are here on merit and not just because a producer liked your face.

"That's enough," a third nurse said. Her name was Gemma and Stella was growing quite fond of her. They'd worked a couple surgeries together and Stella thought they might become friends. "She's fully qualified and now that she's been here for three weeks, all of you know it. And if it wasn't the television program you were fussing about, it would be something else."

She sent Gemma a soft smile, thanking her for her confidence. At least one person in the room thought she could do her job. If she could bank the number of times she'd heard the bit about only playing a surgeon on television, she'd be richer than the queen.

"Dr. Allen, I'm looking forward to seeing exactly why you are here."

"Thank you, Gemma. Now, if you ladies and gentlemen are done gossiping, let's get to work, shall we?" Stella gave the chattering nurse a hard look. "Mrs. Upton's poor pelvis won't fix itself and I'm the only one in the room qualified to do it. Unless you've gotten a medical degree in the past few minutes? No?"

The other woman paled behind her mask.

Take that, gossipy cow.

The prejudice against her over her television background had long ago grown old. Still, she was determined not to let them see that they had gotten a rise out of her. When they saw that she was affected by them, it let them win. And Stella was far too competitive to let them win.

She checked with the anesthesiologist and received his nod that they were good to go. With a deep centering breath, Stella made the first incision.

"Now, for those of you watching from the gallery, you might be aware that there are two typical options for a surgical repair in this kind of break—external fixation and internal fixation. What I'm going to show you today is a form of internal fixation, although not the traditional way you might have learned during your surgical rotation. Mrs. Upton's had a small procedure a few days after her fall to stabilize, but now I'll be going in to do the permanent fix."

As she continued through the surgery, she described the techniques in detail for the growing crowd watching from above. While she might have felt a little unease at the start, thanks to the rumors one particular nurse was trying to spread, it didn't take her long to get into the zone. There was nowhere on earth Stella had more confidence than in an operating room. If she could lecture from the OR each time, rather than from behind a lectern, it would be so much easier.

Deftly, she handled each incision and the placement of each bit of hardware. Her moves were careful, practiced. She prided herself on the precision of her surgical capabilities. When she was operating, nothing rattled her. With a scalpel in her hand, Stella didn't care at all what rumors might be spread. She was unbothered by what others thought.

If only she could carry that confidence over outside the operating room.

"Like the other forms of pelvic fixation, the goal with this is realignment and stability of the displaced fracture. Getting the fracture well aligned is the first step in a successful surgery and leads to the best possible outcomes."

"Are the surgeries always performed under general anesthesia?" one of the doctors in the gallery asked over the intercom.

"Indeed, they are," Stella confirmed.

"In cases of severe trauma, does having to wait to perform this surgery affect the outcome?"

"Overall stability is of course the first goal. With this particular patient, we needed to wait a bit as she also had quite the concussion from her fall and there was some risk to putting her under anesthesia. Ideally, the surgery is performed as soon as possible after the break."

Aiden slipped into the gallery a few minutes after Stella's surgery was scheduled to begin. The ED had been busy and he'd been unable to get away. He wasn't sure he'd be able to stay for her entire operation, but he'd taken his lunch break with the intent of spending it seeing as much of her work as he could.

He owed her that at least, after the harsh way he'd spoken to her over the weekend, but he hadn't been able to find a way to make the overture. Showing interest in her work seemed like a start, and he hoped to find a way to build on that. Sinking quietly into a seat in the back row, he waited for Stella to resume speaking.

Aiden listened to the joking and the rumbles about Stella being all polished presentation. When one took the joking a bit too far, Aiden felt the need to call him out.

"Hush. Let her work before you try to slam her skills."

The chastised surgeon looked like he wanted to argue, but miraculously kept his mouth shut for the moment.

The gallery quickly quieted as she began to work. Soon, the whispers began again, but this time because they were in awe of her techniques.

Stella Allen was a force to be reckoned with and her skills stood proof. Her economy of motion impressed him. Every move was controlled and precise. It was a thing of beauty. Down in the OR, Stella was speaking, her voice strong and steady as she lectured on the medical techniques she'd pioneered while performing the procedure. Not a speck of weakness or insecurity showed while she was operating. She was flawless.

After the surgery though, she held a little question-and-answer session and he couldn't help but see that she struggled when criticized in any way. Their jabs shot straight to her self-confidence, somehow. Each slight became a barb that she struggled to shake off.

Interesting…

Someone with such a strong connection to the television world should have a thicker skin. Stella should have been practically bulletproof when it came to criticism after growing up in the public eye, but her mannerisms and discomfort today said otherwise.

In fact, there was a fragility about Stella that drew him to her. He wanted to help her. Protect her.

With every snipe that came at her, his muscles tightened more. With every snide comment, every whispered jab, he found himself leaning farther forward, barely restrained from going after the jerks. He scrubbed a hand over his face in frustration. He barely knew this woman. Where was this relentless protectiveness coming from?

"Dr. Stella, when you filmed these clips did you have a full camera crew? Perhaps an advisor whispering instructions via an earpiece?"

Aiden couldn't take it anymore.

"That is enough!" His voice was louder than he meant it to be, but it silenced the scoffing crowd. "Dr. *Allen*—" he emphasized her proper name and gave it the respect she deserved "—is here to show us something groundbreaking and you stoop so low as to tease her and make childish remarks about her? This is the impression you want to leave of our hospital? I, for one, would like to learn all I can from her. We can't do that if we make it impossible for her to teach. Now, either shut up or get out." Aiden glared until the man backed down.

"I apologize for the interruption, Dr. Allen. Please, continue."

Stella beamed at him and he knew in that moment that any fallout he would face for standing up for her would be worth it. It was a given fact that she was leaving in only five weeks. That alone should be enough reason for him to keep his distance. But he found himself drawn to her, despite knowing she was only there temporarily.

There were a few more questions, which she answered deftly when no one was looking down on her for her career choices. Aiden made his way downstairs and waited around outside the OR so that he could try to steal a moment alone with Stella.

He propped a shoulder against the wall and waited for her to come his direction.

"Thank you," she said softly as she drew close. "You might have noticed, but I was a bit uncomfortable there."

Aiden snorted. "I think it was a little more than that."

She sighed. "I've just given you my thanks—please don't make me want to take it back."

He reached out and gently took one of her hands in his. "I wasn't trying to rub your nose in it. It actually surprised me to see how much you were struggling. I'd have thought you'd be so used to it that it wouldn't even faze you anymore."

Stella grimaced. "One would think that, yes, but it's really quite the opposite. I think I'm rather more sensitive about being teased over anything connected with television. I'm always worried that I've only gotten my foot in the door due to my past. I want to succeed because of my medical skill, not because my mum shoved me into a television program when I was just a child."

"My mom shoved me into Scouts Canada when I was younger. Said it was important for a boy to learn the skills they taught."

"And have you used those skills as an adult?" Stella asked, looking slightly amused at his uneven comparison of their childhoods.

"Actually, yes. I make a mean s'more. Jamie loved them, even if you were too uptight to enjoy one." He flashed her a grin. "Seriously, though, I made some good friends and the leadership skills have served me well. Even if I don't go camping on the regular, it's not a bad thing to know how to build a fire or set up a tent."

"I suppose not," Stella said. "My mum wasn't a fan of anything of that sort. Not enough recognition from others, you see."

"Your mom seemed so devoted on screen."

"Of course. She couldn't look bad on camera." Stella gave him a wry smile. "In real life she wasn't always the mother she portrayed on screen."

"I was adopted," Aiden found himself saying. He never offered up that information about himself to anyone.

"But you ended up with a loving family?"

"After a while in foster care, yes." His adoptive family had been the one constant in his life and he was lucky to have found them when he did. The Cooks were attentive, loving, generous and a million other positive descriptors. They'd showered him with love from the moment he walked through their door as a hurting nine-year-old, afraid to let his guard down. Even with all they'd done for him, something had always felt like it was missing. But despite the lingering fear of abandonment he'd been left with by his birth parents, Aiden had been raised by some amazing people. He *knew* he was loved. "Overwhelmingly so at times."

"I fully understand the concept of having an overwhelming mother." The warm tinkle of laughter from Stella made him want to take her in his arms.

He even started to reach for her, but at the last second, Aiden covered the move with a glance at his watch. His lunch break was long over. Honestly, he was surprised he'd made it this long without getting called back to the emergency department. He might be pushing his luck by stretching it out any more, yet he found himself asking for more time with Stella.

"Can I buy you a coffee?"

CHAPTER EIGHT

STELLA'S PHONE RANG before she could say yes to the coffee. She winced at the name on the screen. The producer for the program was calling again. He'd called twice during her lecture, so she really shouldn't put him off again. "I'm sorry, Aiden. Can I take a rain check on the coffee? Afraid I have to take this."

"Sure." Aiden took a step back. He kept the smile on his face, but he couldn't hide the disappointment in his eyes. "You know where to find me."

Frustration filled her as he turned and walked away, but she really had to take the call. Martin was not a patient man, and if he got too put out about the delay in response, he might drop out of the project.

"Hello," she answered, just in time to keep the call from switching over to voice mail.

"Stella, this is Martin O'Connor. I've been trying to reach you for hours. I was worried that perhaps I'd gotten the time difference wrong when I kept getting your voice mail. I received the footage you've sent in so far for the Christmas special and I've had some thoughts."

"Hi, Martin, thank you for getting back to me. I was in surgery all morning and have only just finished." Holding her phone with her shoulder, Stella stepped into a nearby consultation room. People who took private telephone calls in public venues drove Stella mad. "Is something wrong with the material you've received so far?"

"Hmm…" he stalled.

Stella's heart rate kicked up at the pause. Martin was known for delivering negativity with a dramatic flair. Sinking down into a chair, she closed her eyes and waited for the bad news to drop.

"I don't want to say that I dislike it, because some of it is quite good. It needs a bit more punch though. Kicking up the drama would certainly add interest for viewers." Martin's voice held a formal quality she'd come to associate with him. Even with a smile on his face, the older man remained distant. He was a brilliant filmmaker though and having him on board was ultimately a good thing.

"Drama?" Stella asked cautiously. Drama could mean so many things, so she needed to get a bit more clarity. He had a vision for the project, clearly, and she wanted to be sure their ideals aligned. Sometimes his ideas stretched beyond her comfort zone though.

"Yes. We need more of you on screen, as well. And, well, I think the best way to add the interest we need is for you to have a love interest." He spoke of her getting a love interest so matter-of-factly that it could have been like he was ordering her to get lunch.

"A love interest?" she repeated, aware that she was sounding like a parrot as she mimicked his words. None of the various scenarios she'd run through her head had involved herself on screen beyond introductions and voice-overs. And romance? Never even the briefest of thoughts. "Martin, that's not the direction that I want to take this program."

"Darling, it's not about what you want, it's about how to bring in an audience."

She cringed at the implication that her love life might draw more viewers than a proper medical documentary. How had her professional documentary about medical staff who worked over the Christmas holidays devolved into a love story? No, she needed to bring this back on track.

"I'm not interested in turning my life into a soap opera! I'm a surgeon and I don't want to look like I'm only paying lip service to my career in medicine." It wasn't the first time she'd been pushed to have a romance on screen. She'd even cooperated while she was in college, but she'd moved beyond that and her focus now was on medicine. "I'm afraid I need to decline."

"Stella, if the program doesn't have anything of real interest, it won't get the needed ratings. And I don't need to remind you how hard it can be to recover from a flop."

Horror filled her at how hard Martin was pushing this angle. She'd wanted to show the world what working in a hospital was like, not give them a reality TV romance. Would she ever have full control over her life or would someone else always be directing her actions?

No.

She wasn't going to stand for this. Her life, her choice. Stella gritted her teeth. "I am not looking for romance while I'm here. You have to appreciate that I am here to do a job, not find a soul mate."

"It doesn't have to be real. You know how these things go." The director cleared his throat and continued, "Just find a way to bring a touch of spice into it. Something to really draw in the female viewers. They are our biggest demographic for a program of this nature."

"Why me?" Stella asked, despite already knowing the answer.

"You are the star of the show, love." Martin took on the tone of a kindly grandfather explaining something patiently to a child. "We've watched you grow up. We've seen you go off to college and medical school. It's been some time since you've even had a hint of romance on screen. It will be a major draw for the program."

Stella tried not to wince. Being on screen added an extra layer of difficulty to any relationship, as she'd learned the hard way. Now they were asking her to begin a new relationship on camera.

"I appreciate what you're saying, Martin, but I'm afraid it's a no from me. It wouldn't be right for me to start a relationship when I'm only here a few more weeks." Aiden's face flashed into her thoughts as she repeated the refrain she'd been telling herself about dating him to Martin.

"If you want this program to move forward, you will follow directions." His voice brooked no argument. Clearly, he didn't buy her excuses any more than she did. "I'm not saying you have to marry the fellow, but we do need something more than you've given us. Are you an actress or not?"

"Martin—"

"Stella, darling, it's not really optional. Now if you can't deliver the goods, I'm going to be sending a different videographer out soon. Maybe around the beginning of the month? You know, try to get some different perspectives. Amp up the drama a touch. Makes for better viewing."

"I really feel that's unnecessary," Stella argued.

"We shall see." The line went silent as Martin ended the call.

Putting her own heart, and the heart of another at risk for a temporary fling? It wasn't fair to either her or the other person. Think about faking a romance to improve ratings?

There had to be another way.

She took a deep breath and tried to consider the other options. How could she add drama? Would another romance be enough to satisfy that desire? She might pitch the idea and see. Even as she ran through all the eligible people at the hospital who'd agreed to be on camera for her, she knew it wouldn't work. It would have to be her or the director would never be satisfied.

There was a slight hitch in that plan though. The only man at St Matthew's that she could convincingly pull off even a hint of romance with had refused to be filmed.

Aiden wasn't sure if Stella was avoiding him intentionally over the previous few days or if she honestly hadn't even noticed he was there. This was the first time he'd caught sight of her since his ill-fated attempt at asking her out for coffee. The look of concentration on her face seemed far too intense for an empty hallway in the early morning hours. She didn't acknowledge his presence in the slightest.

Now, Aiden wasn't the sort of man who needed all the attention, but something about her expression concerned him.

"Stella," he called after her.

"Hmm…" She came to a stop and turned to face him. Worry lined her face. Something was definitely bothering her.

"Is everything okay?" He could see that it most certainly was not, but he wasn't sure Stella would want to confide in him.

He wasn't the guy people confided in. He was the reliable guy who they called for a ride if their car broke down. He was the one who people called when they needed a night out or a distraction—at least he had been until Jamie appeared in his life. But he wasn't the guy who people spilled their guts to. He didn't know anyone's deep dark secrets. He never had to worry that he'd let something slip he shouldn't because no one shared that information with him.

Did that mean no one trusted him enough? That thought wasn't a pleasant one to ponder. He hadn't done anything untrustworthy, so surely not.

Stella flashed him her fake smile.

Yes, he'd learned to tell the difference, but no he wasn't going to consider what that meant. At least not yet.

"You can talk to me, you know." He gave her what he hoped was a reassuring look. For some reason, he actually wanted Stella to confide in him. He wanted to be the man she came to for advice. The feelings that realization brought up in him would have to be unpacked later. At that moment, he had to focus on what Stella needed, not what she made him feel.

Stella opened her mouth as if to speak and closed it quickly like she'd thought better of what she'd been about to say. Indecisiveness showed on her face. White teeth gnawed on her perfectly pink lower lip.

This woman was going to kill him without even trying.

Was murder by lip biting actually a thing?

He reached out a hand, unable to keep from touching her any longer. "What's bothering you?"

"What's not bothering me at this point?" A harsh exhale combined with a sort of self-deprecating laugh.

"I've had to be on my game one hundred percent here, because my televised past gives people the impression that I'm ignorant, despite the programs quite literally having been born because of my intelligence. I have to prove myself time and again. Unfair, really, because I take it on good faith that each and every surgeon I work with is presumed competent yet I'm not afforded the same courtesy."

She paused, but before Aiden could speak, she began again.

"And the program I'm currently filming? The director wants more drama. Not only drama, he wants romance. And not just any romance. He wants *me* to have a romance. I have to find someone to date on camera or there's a very good chance he's going to pull his support for my program."

"You need to date…" He let the words trail off as jealousy surged up from somewhere deep. The idea of another man romancing Stella didn't sit well. Not at all.

"I'll be on camera with you."

He hadn't meant to blurt out those words, but he couldn't take them back now. And he found he didn't want to. Taking them back meant that he'd have to watch as some other man wined and dined her. He'd have to see her walking the halls of St. Matthew's with her hand on some doctor's arm, that rapt look of attention on another guy's face as she listened carefully to his words.

The stunned look on Stella's face mirrored his own shock at his actions. "You don't want to be on camera though," she said cautiously.

"That's true." Sliding his fingers down her forearm, Aiden gripped her hand and squeezed. "You know what I want less than being on camera?"

She shook her head. With her eyes full of curiosity, Stella waited for him to answer his own question.

"Seeing you with another man," he growled out.

Pink tinted her cheeks. "I see."

"Do you?" He leaned closer, watching as the color in her face deepened. "I have been trying to keep my distance from you, Dr. Allen, but I'm failing at that goal quite miserably."

"Are you saying I make you miserable?" Stella bristled in faux outrage. The sparkle in her eyes contradicted the would-be anger in her words.

"Very," he said with a grin. "But I can't stay away."

Only their hands were touching, but the moment held an intimacy that couldn't be denied. The tension that rose up between them was something to be savored. Aiden couldn't remember a time when only holding hands with someone affected him this much.

"It needs to just be for show though. I don't date colleagues, no exceptions. And I have to put my son's needs before my own. But you and I both know there could be something here." He gestured between them. "Too much for me to stand by while you flirt with someone else."

She raised an eyebrow. "So, let me get this clear. You want to date me, but only on camera."

"Yes." It might be unfair, but he wasn't going to pretend he didn't have concerns about getting involved. By faking a relationship on camera, he got to get close to her, but the relationship would remain surface level. No depth that put him or his son at risk.

"I see…"

"You get what you want. Take the win. Just don't fall in love with me. I'm not looking for anything real."

"Why do you assume I would fall in love with you?" She crossed her arms over her chest.

He whispered in her ear, "I don't want you to, Dr. Allen. I'm just warning you that there's no future here."

The barest glimpse of desire flickered in her eyes before it was replaced by what could only be called stubbornness. "What if your heart's the one in danger?"

"My heart is locked up tight in a vault surrounded by razor wire."

"Is that so?" Stella snorted. "Well, I can assure you that your heart and your body are both safe from any unwelcome advances from me."

He chuckled. While he had no interest in emotional entanglements, he wouldn't say a physical relationship was unwelcome.

"I find nothing about this situation amusing." Anger flashed in her eyes.

"You think you can resist me for another four and a half weeks, Stella? Even if we have to spend time together on camera, appearing to grow closer and closer." He moved in until millimeters separated them. "We can fake a relationship, but you can't fake your reactions to me. Those are real."

"As are yours to me." She ran her fingers along his jaw and it took all he had to suppress the shudder at her touch.

He wanted to deny it, but it would be a lie.

"Dr. Cook to trauma one, Dr. Cook to trauma one."

The timing of that page was fortuitous. A few more moments, and he might have been goaded into kissing her.

"Saved by the bell?" she joked.

"More like punished." He gave her hand one last squeeze. "Think about what I'm proposing though.

Don't go starting an on-camera romance without me today. I'm serious."

What exactly had he gotten himself into by agreeing to be on camera with Stella? He was toeing a line here, faking a relationship with a woman he was really attracted to. The idea of Stella even fake dating someone else rubbed him up the wrong way though.

He'd made the right choice, so why did he feel a little green around the gills about it?

CHAPTER NINE

AIDEN DIDN'T WANT her to date anyone else? And he wanted to be on camera after vehemently refusing? Stella pinched her arm, hard.

Definitely not dreaming. Hmm...

Well, his sudden change of direction was unexpected. And even more so a relief. Drama sold in the television world. Romance was also an audience pleaser. Both would be best. Aiden was the only man she'd met in Toronto who held any interest for her though, so she'd never have been able to convincingly pull off a romance with anyone else. Not even a fake one.

Even though she'd grown up on camera, Stella was no actress. Past directors had gotten so frustrated when she failed to participate as they wished in false narratives. She'd never really mastered the art of subterfuge and she couldn't tell a lie without lighting up like a neon sign.

Honesty was a virtue, right?

Stella rubbed the bridge of her nose, trying her best to wish away the stress headache building behind her eyes. This trip was not turning out how she'd thought it would. It was far more stressful than she'd imagined. The excitement, too, was more than she could have pictured.

All morning, she'd been frazzled, worrying about how she could pull off a fake relationship with any man other than Aiden. Her stomach had roiled and twisted into a giant knot. She drew in a shaky breath. Anxiety had frayed her poor nerves to the point of breaking, and now that worry had all been for naught.

A small giggle bubbled up inside her. She had nearly worried herself ill over a nonissue. Wasn't that just like her?

The arrogance in his eyes when he'd told her not to fall in love with him though made her defenses rise. Who did he think he was? Just because he was absolutely gorgeous did not mean he was irresistible. The way he'd warned her off tempted her to blur the lines between fake and real, to tease him and possibly take him down a peg or two by making him fall for her. Of course, she'd be putting her own heart squarely at risk in order to take him down.

A series of beeps sounded from the phone in her pocket, startling her out of her thoughts. Pulling it out, she read the words on the screen and sighed.

It was a blunt reminder from Martin as to what he expected from her.

Stella, I need the additional footage from you ASAP. Remember to keep it heavy on the drama and the romance. I'm not fussed if it's real or fake, just be sure it's attention-catching.

A second message followed before she could formulate a reply to the first.

And I do mean ASAP if you don't want me to put the brakes on this little pet project of yours.

Stella huffed. There wasn't a chance that she was going to let him kill this program without fighting for it. Now driven with purpose, Stella put her mind toward finding some of the drama and romance that the director wanted to see. It didn't take her long to find a few in-hospital romances where the couples were willing to be filmed and interviewed.

With no presentations to give or surgeries to perform that day, Stella immersed herself in filming. She did short interviews with the participating couples, happily noting that at least some of their answers were dramatic enough to pacify Martin's penchant for excitement.

One of the couples was more than happy to try their skills at acting. Tyler and Gemma excitedly staged a fight in the hallway about how working opposite shifts was putting a wrench in their relationship. Had Stella not been aware that the young couple was acting, she'd have thought a breakup was imminent. Gemma, in particular, was quite convincing and even managed to shed some very real tears.

When Henry turned the camera off, Tyler pulled Gemma in for a kiss. Stella turned away from the heartfelt display in order to give them a bit of well-earned privacy. They'd given her quite a bit of material to work with. It should appease Martin for now.

She moved toward Henry, ready to call it a day with filming. "Shall we take a look at what we managed to collect today?"

He nodded and they reviewed the footage together. While some of it might need some edits, they'd captured a good bit that was usable and Stella was quite pleased with it.

"Leave that out," Aiden called from behind her.

She startled, knocking the camera from Henry's

hand when she spun in Aiden's direction. Her fingers managed to gain a grip on the expensive piece of equipment only just in time. "Aiden, you gave me a fright."

"Sorry about that. Let me just have this for a second." He took the camera from her. Nodding at Tyler, he asked, "You mind?"

Henry took the camera from Aiden's outstretched hand. "What do you want me to film?"

"Just keep it pointed at Dr. Allen." Aiden stepped back as Henry lifted the camera and aimed it in Stella's direction as instructed.

Hoping that her smile looked more genuine than confused, Stella waited to see what Aiden was up to. She didn't have to wait long.

"Dr. Allen, might I have a word?" Aiden asked as he stepped up and into the path of the lens.

"Of course, Dr. Cook," she replied, still no less confused. Her heart rate picked up at his nearness.

"Do you have plans for Saturday evening?"

Stella gaped at him. Her mind refused to process the fact that Aiden had not only asked her on a date, but had done so on camera. His gruff refusal to be filmed still held dominance in her mind over his blurted decision this morning. The surprise rendered her speechless.

Gently touching her hand, Aiden prompted for an answer by rephrasing his query. "What do you say to dinner on Saturday?"

Swallowing hard, Stella licked her suddenly dry lips before answering. "I'd love to have dinner with you, Dr. Cook."

Aiden lifted her hand with an exquisite slowness. His breath was hot and his lips tempting as they lightly grazed the tender skin of her wrist. "Then I'll pick you up at seven."

With her heart racing in her chest, Stella stared after him as he walked away. Her hand still burned with the fire he'd started with his breath and lips and she let her hand flutter toward her chest. Resisting that man might be harder than she thought.

"Wow." Henry lowered the camera. "That was… wow. Martin has been waiting all month for a scene like that."

"Indeed," she murmured.

Twinges of guilt still stabbed at him over how he'd brought Stella into Jamie's life without so much as a thought. And how he selfishly wanted to spend an evening alone with Stella. Thankfully, his mom had been enthusiastic about the opportunity to spend the evening with her grandson while he went on a date.

Nerves fluttered around in his stomach, frustrating him to no end. He was a grown man. He shouldn't be as nervous as a teenager about to go on his first date.

It was his first *real* date since finding out he was a father though. The christmas market hardly counted as a date, even before he'd gotten weird and ruined things. Jamie's presence had served as a chaperone and they'd barely even touched. And a few brief coffee breaks together at work in front of an entire hospital certainly weren't dates.

Starting a romance with someone on camera and in full view of his coworkers went against nearly every fiber of his being, but from the moment she'd mentioned that her director wanted her to get involved with somebody he'd had no choice. He couldn't stomach the idea of her being with someone else, of her touching someone else. Not even if it was faked for the camera.

"So, you have a hot date tonight?" his mother asked with a knowing smirk.

"Moms of grown-up sons should never say the words *hot date*." He shuddered at the connotation that left in his mind. Was she trying to put a damper on his evening? Ugh.

"Tell me about her." His mom's eyes twinkled with mischief.

He grumbled in exasperation. "I will tell you about her when there's something to tell. It's a first date. I'm hardly proposing to her."

"Let an old woman have hope." She sniffed, before hugging Jamie tight. "I'm hoping for more grandchildren in the future. Preferably soon when I'm still young enough to enjoy them."

"Can we not have this discussion again tonight?" Aiden sighed. His mom had been angling for grandchildren since shortly after Aiden had graduated college. He'd been able to push the topic off through medical school and residency, but for the last several years, it had been frequently and passionately brought up. Jamie's appearance had delighted her and now she was eager for Aiden to give Jamie a sibling.

"Only if you tell me about your date," she said, attempting to bargain her way into more information by wearing him down.

"You mean the date that I'm going to be late for if I don't leave soon." The protest was weak, but it was all he had.

She countered his argument swiftly and surely. "All the more reason to tell me quickly."

"You are so stubborn." He could tell by the set of her jaw that she wasn't going to let him leave until he gave her something though. If he held his ground, he'd be late. So he gave in to her demands, giving her a small amount of information. "Her name is Stella. She's an orthopedic surgeon."

"The one you were looking up?"

"Yes. Can we leave it at that for now?"

His mom pursed her lips unhappily, but she nodded. "For now. Will you be home tonight or should I plan to drop Jamie off at day care in the morning?"

"I'll be home tonight," he said. "Can you save the rest of the inquisition for a later date? You wouldn't want her to think I stood her up now, would you?"

"You really like her," his mom said with a look of surprise.

Honestly, he was as surprised as she was that he liked Stella as much as he did. He'd never, ever thought of long-term before her. There was something special about her though that made him crazy, but it could never be anything real since she was leaving soon.

"What are you waiting for then? Get out of here!" His mom practically shoved him out the door. "I won't wait up."

The heat of the chemistry that burned between him and Stella meant he wanted to go home with her, but it was too soon. As he walked to his car, he wondered at that. Too soon for whom? He'd never had a problem taking a woman to bed on the first date before. In fact, that had been the bulk of his past relationships.

Something about Stella though made him want to take things slower, to savor each interaction. Gut reaction said slow would be worth the wait with her, and Aiden had learned to trust his gut. But fake dates didn't wind up in bed. Fake dates put on a show for the people around them and kept their distance in private. He needed to remember that.

He knocked on Stella's door precisely at seven o'clock. Despite her determination, his mother hadn't succeeded in making him late for his date after all.

The door swung inward and he was at a loss for words. His tongue suddenly too big for his mouth, he tried unsuccessfully to swallow and remember how to talk. She was so beautiful it took his breath away. She'd clearly forgotten that they had plans tonight though, because she stood in front of him wearing flannel pajama bottoms and a tank top.

"Hello," she said, dipping her head shyly and breaking eye contact. The softest pink blush crept up her cheeks.

His confidence spiked when he realized she was as unsure as he was about how to proceed. "I was so much more anxious about tonight than I was about Saturday and the christmas market. Silly, huh, when I show up to find you in pajamas?"

"Oh, thank goodness. I was worried it was just me!" Stella's smile shone brightly enough to light up the Toronto skyline and it took his breath away. "I didn't expect you to actually show!"

The more he flirted with this woman, and the more time he spent with her, the deeper risk he was taking in falling in love with her. He really needed to rein in his emotions, find a way to keep Stella at arm's length, but he couldn't seem to make himself take the necessary steps. He tried to repeat to himself the refrain that this date was a fake, but he was struggling to believe himself.

"I thought we'd go out," he said softly. Rather than stepping back though, Aiden found himself stepping closer. He offered her a smile as he stepped inside the apartment and closed the door behind him. "Unless you'd rather stay in?"

"I didn't think it was a real date," she said as she grabbed a cardigan and covered up her bare shoulders. "Really thought that was all for the camera."

"Don't you think it's best we get to know each other a little? It will help our fake relationship seem a bit more realistic." He shrugged. "How can we bond if we don't spend time together?"

"Bond…"

"Plus, a few of the nurses in the ED are going ice skating tonight. To keep the reactions real, it might be a good idea to be seen out and about together. It would lend some visual weight to the hospital gossip."

"I see." She tilted her head and stared at him for a moment. "Give me a moment to change."

Aiden went to the window and looked down at the street while he waited for Stella to get changed. He almost regretted telling her that they were going to go ice skating where they might bump into some of their co-workers. Those pajamas were going to be missed. The thought of them coming off her in the other room sent him into a vivid daydream. He might avoid emotional attachments like the plague, but he was very pro physical entanglements. Especially with Stella.

"Aiden?" Stella's fingers snapped in front of Aiden's eyes. She stood next to him, her face pensive as she contemplated him. "Where did you go? Clearly, you checked out on me."

"Hmm… Maybe one day I'll tell you."

CHAPTER TEN

THE HEAT IN Aiden's eyes when she caught his attention told her where his thoughts had gone, even if he wouldn't put a name to it. Warmth bubbled up inside her and made her nearly giddy.

While romance hadn't even been a blip on her radar when thinking of this trip to Toronto, she wasn't going to pass up the chance at whatever this was between them. Some things just couldn't be faked, and the chemistry between them was one such thing. Vacation flings were an actual thing, right? Outside her norm, maybe, but normal. Healthy, even, as long as everyone was clear on the boundaries.

But how to bring up the topic of boundaries?

Back home, Stella was known to be rather straightforward and blunt. She liked to know where she stood with people and she preferred to be honest about where people stood with her. Her lack of filter had, on occasion, created problems in her personal life. Still, she liked to be aware of the relationship limits. Crossing an ocean had thrown her off-kilter though, and one spark from Aiden's hand had nearly capsized her.

Stella liked plans. She made daily schedules and her calendar was filled as far in advance as she could do so. Her desk was usually covered in color-coded to-do lists and she liked knowing what to expect personally and professionally. The hours she spent setting goals and visualizing strategies helped make her more confident in her everyday life. She feared her world careening out of control and took every step to minimize the chances of that happening.

Her medical career was the one aspect of her life that had never let her down. She'd worked really hard to have a career that was all hers and not under her mother's influence. Psychologically speaking, her control issues stemmed from her childhood and her relationship with her mother. Being thrust into the spotlight at such a young age, without being asked, had made her value the concept of choice. It had ingrained in her a deep respect of autonomy and she did all she could to avoid infringing on anyone else's freedom of choice. She didn't really know what being a good mum looked like, but her own mother hadn't been the best example. No, it was safest all around if she just focused all her attention on what she could control: her career.

So, what was it about Aiden that made her so willing to relinquish a bit of that hard-earned control? Fake relationship or not, the man intrigued her.

"I know ice skating was chosen because of others going there, but where would you normally take a date?" she prodded, curious to hear how the handsome doctor at her side would usually treat the woman he was taking out for the evening.

Aiden's face tightened. He tugged at his collar. Opening and closing his mouth repeatedly, Aiden ultimately remained silent. The question clearly made him uncomfortable.

He looked so awkward that she took pity on him. "Okay, you don't have to tell me where you take your dates."

"I don't date a lot. The women I do date don't expect much beyond a nice dinner or drinks and then some... uh...adult activity."

"I see," Stella said, trying her best not to let her mind drift toward engaging in some adult activity with Aiden. "Let's talk about ice skating then. Are there actual outdoor rinks here or is that another televised myth?"

Secretly, Stella loved watching all the sweet romance movies that highlighted the fun of the holiday season. Sometimes, she needed the assurance that a movie would end as expected, not wanting the anxiety of an unknown ending. Given the many romance movies she'd watched, it never failed to amaze her that there was always a place to go skating under the wintry sky. She was really hoping that it would be an outdoor rink.

"Can you skate?" Disbelief colored his voice.

She affected what she hoped was a nonchalant shrug before she replied. "I've been a few times, but I'm not going to be representing my country in the next Olympics."

"I played hockey up through college." Sparks of mischief shone brightly in his eyes. "Think you can keep up?"

"Is that a challenge, Dr. Cook?" She narrowed her eyes in playful competition. While she wasn't very athletic overall, Stella did like to indulge in games and competitive activities. Deep down, she knew she couldn't truly compete with a former hockey player, but she would have fun trying. "Think you can beat me then?"

Aiden's deep, booming laugh sent shivers speed walking down her spine. "I see no way I can lose. I'm confident on the ice. If you can't skate, you'll end up in my arms. If you can, then we can have a true competition. I don't give up easily though."

He opened the car door for her, moving closer to assist her into the vehicle. When he leaned in, her quick exhale filled the space between them. Aiden must have read the burst of desire that rose up at his nearness. His eyes darkened and his own breathing picked up in pace.

"Get in the car, Stella," he said with a groan. "I'm trying to take this slow, but if you keep looking at me like that, we won't be going ice skating. We'll be going back up to your apartment and we might not make it out again until morning."

Her cheeks burned as she swung her legs fully inside the vehicle. While he walked around to get into the driver's seat, she fanned her blazing hot face. It took all she had not to just invite him back up to her apartment to see if his actions could back his words.

Aiden white-knuckled the steering wheel. "At least being on the ice ought to cool us down."

Stella chuckled at his little joke. "Is that the Toronto version of a cold shower?"

"It'll do the job." He shifted in his seat.

"How long has it been since you've skated?" She hoped that some innocuous conversation might release some of the tension between them. This fake date was feeling far too real at the moment and she wanted to move it back onto more neutral territory.

"It's been a few years," he admitted.

That knowledge gave her a touch of hope that she might not embarrass herself too badly against the former hockey player.

Don't forget that your graceful self landed smack on your bottom twice.

"Hasn't been quite that long for me." She had gone

skating only a few months back, so her experience was more recent. She had that to her advantage.

"Don't gloat yet. I used to live at the rink before I traded my blades for a stethoscope."

"Will you teach Jamie to play hockey when he's a bit older?" The image of little Jamie decked out in full hockey gear made her smile. She'd only seen them on television, but children in sports uniforms always looked adorable. "I bet he'd love having an activity to share with his dad."

Aiden grunted. "I hope so. I hadn't thought of starting him in hockey yet. He's been so slow to warm up to anyone and has showed so little interest in anything, really, that it hasn't been a high priority. I've been trying to gain his trust and get him speaking."

"Gain his trust?" That particular turn of phrase caught Stella's attention. While she wasn't a parent, it seemed to her that children instinctively trusted their parents until given a reason not to. She'd certainly trusted her parents as a child. "Why wouldn't your son trust you?"

Aiden pulled the car over and put it into Park. He sat in silence, staring at his hands where they still gripped the steering wheel for so long that she thought he might not answer.

"It took time for me to gain Jamie's trust because he didn't meet me until his second birthday. That's when his mom dropped him off at the hospital with a note that said she was done being a mom."

His words did not compute and she gaped at him, trying to make sense of what he'd confessed. He was such a devoted father to that little boy, how on earth could he have only just met him?

"I'm sorry, what?" she asked, hoping to get clarification that would help her reconcile the father-and-son duo with whom she'd recently spent the day with the picture Aiden's words painted.

"Look, I..." Aiden paused, as if considering how much to reveal. "Jamie is the result of a one-night stand. I didn't see her at all between the next morning and the custody hearing. We haven't seen or heard from her since. As best as I know, she's trying to make her way out in California. She wants to be an *actress*."

The way he spit out the word *actress* cleared up a lot for Stella. It didn't take a genius to see why he was so against being on camera and why he'd hated her on sight. His past experience told him that actresses weren't to be trusted. Maybe she was helping him to see that she and his ex were not the same, but she imagined the mistrust might flare up again when she least expected it.

This knowledge added another reason to the growing list of why Stella should keep this relationship squarely in the pretend category. If only for her own self-preservation, she needed to remember that Aiden would never consider her for anything long-term due to his prejudice against actresses. Well, at least she knew where she stood in his esteem and would be going in with her eyes wide open if they did progress to anything more than an on-screen romance.

And if they did, it could only be temporary. A fling, at best.

After the way things had ended with Oliver, though, she was hardly planning to settle down. A temporary fling, augmented by some on-camera flirting, suited her just fine.

"Any woman who could walk away from that sweet boy is a fool."

And doubly so for walking away from his father.

* * *

Aiden hated the damper he'd put on their evening by bringing up Britney. He could never forgive her for what she'd put Jamie through. Such a sweet, innocent child and she'd treated him like a disposable plate—tossed in the trash when his usefulness to her ended.

As a newborn, Jamie had drawn a lot of attention her direction. Everyone wanted to see the new baby and it had fed her desire to be in the spotlight. From what Aiden had been able to gather, Britney had lost all interest in the child about the time he learned to walk. That's when the neglect had begun but it had taken another year before she dropped him off at St. Matthew's with the front desk nurse, a diaper bag and a note basically saying, "Tag, you're it, Daddy."

Jamie had been underweight, and still in clothes a size too small. The boy's innocent but terrified gaze had drawn him in. Even before the reality of Jamie being his son had settled over him, a fierce protectiveness for the child had filled Aiden's soul. After giving the boy a thorough checkup, Aiden had begun the legal nightmare of trying to gain custody of his son.

Only the fact that his own parents were already registered foster parents had allowed Jamie to stay with them. Aiden had been forced to move back into his old bedroom for a while to be under the same roof as his son until the DNA tests could come back proving what Aiden already knew in his heart—Jamie was truly his son.

Even now, months later, the mere mention of Britney soured his mood and he didn't see that changing in the future. Forgiving her might take longer than a lifetime. It certainly wouldn't be anytime soon.

"That must have been very hard on Jamie. And you,

as well." Stella reached out and smoothed her fingers over his. "He seems to be quite healthy now."

Aiden entwined his fingers with Stella's and looked over at her. While her words were meant to be reassuring, they only brought back how far Jamie had come. "He didn't speak at all for the first month that we had him. Wouldn't say if he was hungry or cold. He didn't laugh. Barely smiled. All we could get was him nodding for yes and shaking his head for no."

"It must have been hard to see him that way." Stella bit her lip like she wanted to ask more but wasn't sure the question would be well received.

"Ask what you like," Aiden offered cautiously, "but I reserve the right to limit my response if it's too painful to discuss."

Things like how he'd needed to have his son checked for more than just mental and physical neglect was a topic he refused to discuss. It had taken all he had to say the words to the pediatrician to have the exams done to be sure. Words he hoped he'd never have to utter again. Thankfully, it had proven to be "only" neglect and Jamie's exams had revealed no physical abuse. The neglect had caused mental trauma, for certain, but Aiden and the team of doctors he'd hired were confident that with time, Jamie would fully recover.

"I started to ask if you'd had him to see a psychiatrist, but then I realized I already knew the answer. You're a physician. Of course you've taken him to every specialist who might help."

Aiden nodded. "Psychiatrists, play therapy, speech therapy, developmental pediatricians, you name it. He's still under the care of several different therapists and specialists, actually. He's slowly opening up, but it's been a gradual process."

"I'm sure he will once he's learned that he's safe." Shadows haunted Stella's eyes. The intensity of her next words made him reconsider all that he knew about Stella Allen. "In my experience, safety makes all the difference."

"Now I'm the one with questions."

"It's nothing compared to what you and sweet Jamie have been through," Stella whispered. "Let's leave it, as I've had my fair share of times where I didn't feel safe. I don't want to unpack all that tonight. Weren't we going to ice skate?"

"I overshared on the first fake date." Aiden grimaced. The word fake burned like a lie on his tongue. "Does that mean a second fake date is out of the question?"

"You were the one who said we should get to know one another more." Stella's hand was soft as it trailed along his jawline. "I think the evening is still redeemable. But perhaps we should stick to lighter fare for the rest of the evening."

Her touch reignited the blaze between them. The look on her face made him want to take her in his arms, to kiss her until the bright morning light crept over the multistory buildings surrounding them. He hadn't made out in a car with a girl since he was in college.

Stella deserved more than that. So, instead of reclining the seat and pulling her across the console, he put the car back in Drive.

"The skating rink is a few blocks away."

CHAPTER ELEVEN

HAVING HAD LITTLE real experience with relationships that involved ex drama, Stella wasn't sure how to respond to all that Aiden had just disclosed. Her heart ached for all that little Jamie's mother had put him through, and Aiden, as well. She wanted to pull him close and soothe his hurts away, but that would be inappropriate. Unless they actually were starting something up...

Tonight revealed a few of her inadequacies in the dating world though. This fake relationship was feeling all too real. And a bit beyond her comfort level. She'd dated, of course, but something about Aiden, about the connection they shared, felt different. Comforting his hurts involved more than physical care. She'd have to ease the mental angst his past had wrought on his ability to trust, and that would take time. Getting seriously involved with a single dad meant not only being in a relationship with him, but also with the child. And given that she'd sworn off motherhood, that was another red flag on the still growing list of why she shouldn't get close to Aiden Cook.

"My parents used to bring me here every winter," Aiden told her as they pulled up to the rink.

Large lights surrounded the oval-shaped expanse of

ice and created a sparkle effect. Stella gasped. "Aiden, it's simply magical! How amazing that you were able to come here each winter!"

"It really was." Aiden's face lit up at the happiness of his memories. "We'd skate for hours and drink so much hot chocolate that I'd be up half the night with a sugar rush. My hands and feet would be numb from the cold, but my heart and soul were warm from all the laughter."

"That sounds perfect." Stella couldn't quite keep the longing from her voice. She couldn't imagine her mum on ice skates for even an hour. The only time her parents had taken her skating as a child had been on camera and her mum had spent most of the time sitting on a bench bragging about Stella to the other mums. Her dad had been happy out on the ice, but not enough to take her frequently.

Aiden rented them some skates and while they were lacing them up, he asked, "So, what sort of activities did you and your parents do? Besides the trivia shows and television programs, I mean."

Stella snorted, covering her nose at the very unladylike sound that had just come out of her. "You mean besides what was videoed for *Stay Smart with Stella*? Nearly everything had to have an educational component—my mum was adamant about that. Ice skating wasn't educational. Sports, also a no-go. We played quite a few board games and read a lot."

"Educational and fun don't always align."

"Nor do they need to," Stella agreed. Her mum had been determined to keep education as a top priority for Stella, only coming second to the determination to keep their family in the spotlight, and sometimes Stella thought she had missed out on a lot of typical childhood things as a result.

She stood on the blades, gingerly finding her balance. "I don't want to give the impression that I have bad parents. I'm sure they did what they thought was best for me—they just didn't consider the alternatives. They didn't consider my personality in the decision."

Aiden stood next to her, showing far more confidence on the ice than Stella could muster. "Which parts were not to your liking? The board games or the reading?"

"I quite like board games, actually, and I read at least a book a week. I wasn't a fan of having the camera follow my every move." She'd complied with it in effort to please her parents, trying to win a scrap of praise from her mum in particular.

Aiden raised a brow. "And yet you're currently filming another program. As an adult, you don't have to do television anymore if you don't enjoy it."

Stella sighed. His words seemed so judgmental. How could she best phrase it so that Aiden could properly understand her motivations?

"That is true, yes. But this particular program is quite dear to my heart." Television had long since lost the glitter of excitement for her and had become something of a rather expected obligation. She could never truly explain how being on television had bought her a somewhat peaceful relationship with her mum, how it had helped provide an income for her family to supplement their retirement or that she had no idea how to step away without ruining that fragile equilibrium between herself and her mum. So, she smiled at him before changing the subject rather abruptly. "Race you to the other side."

She pushed off and did her best to cross the ice before Aiden. Wobbling a bit, she gained speed. The unmistakable sound of a blade on ice followed her and Aiden passed her in seconds.

He turned and slowed his pace, skating backward just a few feet ahead of her. The cold put some color in his cheeks that made him even more irresistible. He grinned broadly. "Am I racing a surgeon or a sloth?"

"Remember who won the race between the tortoise and the hare?" she teased right back. "Initial speed isn't everything."

He changed directions again, moving toward her with a slow deliberateness. Skating right up to her, he put his hands at her waist and pulled her close. "I can think of a few other activities where slow can be a good thing."

"So much for the ice being as good as a cold shower," Stella breathed more than said as she found herself pressed tightly against Aiden's broad chest. They were on the verge of melting this ice. Were fake dates allowed to be this hot?

Nothing permanent could come of it, but they were also both consenting adults. Why were they denying themselves what they both so clearly wanted?

She threw caution to the wind, wrapped her arms around his neck and kissed him. His lips were hot on hers, contrasting with the brisk air surrounding them. The contrast only made the kiss seem, oh, so much hotter. Her fingers tangled in his thick hair, and when she sighed in contentment, Aiden deepened the kiss.

The sounds of downtown Toronto faded as Aiden's lips moved over hers. All that mattered in that moment was the feeling of his arms around her and the taste of his tongue as it slid along hers.

"Watch out!" someone shouted.

Aiden lifted his head away from hers, and Stella immediately began scanning for potential danger.

She watched in horror as a teen girl skated straight into a young couple, knocking them both over like pins at a bowling alley. They separated like a seven-ten split.

The couple cautiously got back to their feet, dusting the ice shavings from their clothing. Shaken, but seemingly physically fine, they made their way back to each other.

Unfortunately, the teen girl who had careened into them was not so lucky.

One glance at the kid who'd crashed into the couple galvanized Aiden into action. "Her leg is broken. Someone call 911!"

"Are you…?" Stella called after him as he skated over to the girl's side. "Well, I was going to ask if you were sure, but now I see that you're right."

He crouched down next to the girl. "Your leg is broken. Try not to move too much, okay?"

She cried out, "It really hurts."

"I know it does." He pulled his gloves off and tucked them into one of his pockets. "I'm a doctor over at St. Matthew's Hospital. I work in the emergency department. Is it okay if I take a look?"

She nodded.

Aiden gently put his hands on the teen's leg. She cried out as he palpated her leg. "Feels like you've fractured your tibia. Can't let you put any weight on this leg until you get X-rays, but it looks like you'll be spending the next several weeks with a cast."

Tears welled up in the teen's eyes. "I don't want to be in a cast over Christmas!"

Stella appeared next. "I had my arm casted at Christmas once. Everyone drew little Christmas trees and ornaments across it. It was quite festive."

"I think she's got a tibial fracture," Aiden told her. "This is my friend Stella. She's actually an orthopedic surgeon. Do you mind if she takes a look?"

The teen shook her head.

"I'll be gentle," Stella assured her. Her face was still and emotionless as she carefully examined the girl's leg. "I'd say that's definitely broken. The good news is that it's not an open fracture as it didn't pierce the skin. Definitely displaced though."

"Did you bump your head at all?" Aiden asked, using the flashlight on his phone to check her eyes.

"No." She sniffed. "Only my leg hurts."

"Pupils are equal and reactive to light. Very good." Aiden turned and carefully unlaced the girl's skate. "Stella, could you help immobilize while I get this skate off?"

Stella placed a hand on either side of the break and Aiden gingerly slid the skate off the girl's foot.

"Pulse is strong," he told Stella. That was a good sign. In the distance, he could hear the wail of the ambulance. The girl was still talking, pulse was good and she had no symptoms of concussion. All postive news.

They waited with her for the ambulance to arrive and Aiden gave the paramedics the vitals and his preliminary diagnosis. Stella skated up beside him as the stretcher rolled toward the ambulance.

"It's a good thing I geek out over broken bones," Stella said, leaning her head against his shoulder. "First kisses are meant to bring fireworks, not fractures."

"What can I say—I'm an overachiever." Aiden roared with laughter. "This is really shaping up to be the worst first date in history. Or are we jinxed and accidents follow us around?"

"It's not been all bad. Wasn't there a promise of hot chocolate?" She smiled up at him. "Load it with extra marshmallows and I might let you have a second kiss a bit later."

"Bribing me for chocolate already, are you?"

"Is it working?" Her eyes sparkled in the twilight.

"Maybe," he said as he skated away toward the snack stand.

More than maybe.

He paid for two hot chocolates, one with extra marshmallows as requested. What was he doing? He couldn't see a transatlantic relationship working in the long-term, and he had Jamie to consider. But maybe they could enjoy each other until she left at Christmas.

When he turned to skate back to Stella, he saw she was standing in the midst of a group of people. A few he recognized from the hospital. A radiant smile brightened her face.

He skated over slowly and held out her hot chocolate without saying a word. If he were being honest with himself, he was afraid that whatever words came out of his mouth would be sappy or cheesy. Instead, he stood next to her silently and waited for her to say something. When he was around Stella he felt sixteen again—awkward and full of unfamiliar feelings. This woman brought up scary amounts of emotions within him. Eventually, maybe, he'd learn to get a better control over it.

"Aiden, you remember Tyler and Gemma, right? And do you know Ben? He works in oncology at St. Matthew's and guess what? He managed to catch *everything* on film. I was just telling him that I'd love to use some of the footage he captured. I'll have to clear it with Martin, of course, but I think it would be amazing if I could add some clips showing that even when off duty, medical professionals will still step up and take charge. Don't you?" She held the hot chocolate up and let the heat waft over her face. "Mmm…this smells delicious, thank you."

"You're welcome," he finally muttered.

Tyler and Gemma made their excuses and skated away hand in hand, looking very much in love. Ben also said his goodbyes, and Stella waved him away with a smile and a promise to follow up with him about using his footage. She turned back to Aiden with a question in her eyes that he'd really hoped to avoid.

She pressed the issue. "Wanna tell me what changed you from Flirty Frank to Grumpy Gus in just a few moments?"

He shook his head. "It's nothing."

Stella's brows raised. "I'm not sure I agree."

"So, do you really think the footage Ben got will be usable for the program?" Deliberately, he changed the subject, hoping beyond hope that Stella would go along with it.

She stared at him over the rim of her cup, her eyes searching his. The intelligent way she searched his face said she had calculated and came up with exactly the right answer.

He swallowed hard and resisted the urge to shift and spill his guts like a wayward child. What was this woman's sway over him? How could he tell her that seeing her smile like that made him want to do whatever it took to keep her smiling? It was their first date, and it was supposed to be fake. That was a bit too far and he needed to cool it down some.

"I'm hopeful," she said cautiously. "He caught some really good angles. I'd have to get permission from the girl's family, but it would go a long way toward satisfying Martin's request for me to have an onscreen romance, as Ben caught us kissing and working together to keep her calm."

Tension invaded his muscles. Ben had nabbed their first kiss on camera and now it would be broadcast to an undefined number of viewers. He had expected that part of their relationship would be on film, accepted it even, but he'd thought tonight was private. Life on camera would take some adjustment, knowing that everyone would be able to see everything.

He wasn't sure he wanted that. As a very reserved person, the invasion of privacy tonight rankled. He hadn't considered just how invasive the cameras would be.

Did Stella ever have any true privacy? How did anyone ever come to terms with that?

He couldn't help but wonder how Jamie would react if someone pointed a camera at him. Aiden had just gotten his son into the hospital day care, so there was a slight chance Jamie could be captured on film. Would seeing Jamie on screen bring Britney back out of the woodwork so that she could try to exploit his connection to Stella? The answer to that seemed readily apparent. She'd tossed Jamie aside when he was of no use to her, but Aiden didn't think for a minute that she'd stay away if she saw her son on screen.

She'd want him back.

He could not put his son at risk.

"I think I should take you home now."

"Aiden, what's wrong?" Stella reached toward him

but he shrugged off her touch and skated toward the bench where they'd left their shoes.

Aiden's sudden reluctance to talk bothered Stella a lot more than she wanted to let on. He made the barest minimum of small talk as they drove back to her place. But more than his silence, the emotions playing out across his face concerned her. She could see he was struggling with something. Whatever it was, he wasn't yet willing to share.

When they reached her apartment, Aiden got out of the car. What was he doing? He didn't want to talk, but he thought he should walk her in? Stella couldn't understand him.

"Are you going to talk to me or just keep peeking at me like you're afraid I might bite?"

Stella was startled, embarrassed that he'd caught her tentative glances. Wrapping her arms around herself, she said, "You don't have to walk me in."

"Yes, I do." He jabbed at the button for the elevator.

She stepped into the elevator the minute the doors opened. His hot-and-cold behavior left her a little hesitant. Aiden Cook had something of substance about him that drew her in though, even when he tried to push her away. "I've spent the whole trip here in thought, wondering exactly where things went astray."

Aiden winced. "I deserve that. I've been trying to figure out what I need to say too, but the words aren't coming easily."

"Indeed." Stella raised a brow at him. "I've drawn my own conclusions, of course. If I'm wrong, do feel free to correct me. I think you had a bit of a panic over finding out our first kiss was on camera."

"Kissing on camera was part of it, yes." He let out a

shaky breath. "I'm not sure I want my private moments filmed and plastered across the internet."

"I can remove any parts that contain or mention you." Dread seeped into her bones. Martin was going to implode when she snatched the budding romance from his wrinkly fingertips.

"No." Aiden's vehement denial sparked the tiniest flame of hope.

"No?"

"I keep my word, Stella." He took her hand in his. "I was struggling to come to terms with it all. I don't want to promise that I'm one-hundred-percent sorted, but I'm doing my best. No more disappearing act. No more silent treatment."

"Your best is all I can ask," Stella said with a small smile. Prudence demanded that she guard her heart when with Aiden though. She had only a month left in Toronto and what would happen then?

She was hardly about to give up her career for a man she'd only just met, and she was sure he'd be unwilling to give up his and uproot his son for her. Real emotion couldn't be risked. A holiday fling was all this could ever be.

"Was there more than that?" she asked, sensing that he was holding something back.

"It hit me that a certain someone might try to use the connection to you to further her own career."

"Jamie's mum, you mean." Stella hadn't considered that Jamie's mum might come back into the picture. Aiden's swift retreat made so much sense after that realization. If that's where his mind had gone, she couldn't blame him for needing a bit of space. He'd had to fight so hard for his son, and if he thought being with her could put that in jeopardy, it wasn't a surprise that he withdrew. "Hmm... I hadn't thought of that possibility," she admitted.

Aiden had been adamant that Jamie's mum was gone for good, but if she wanted to be involved in the television world, she might do anything to give herself a leg up. Stella had seen a lot of people do a lot of sketchy things for a few moments of fame.

"I hadn't until just a bit ago either. I owe you an apology for the way I reacted. It wasn't very adult of me, and I can only tell you that I'm sorry and I'll try to do better going forward. Opening up is hard for me." Aiden grimaced.

"What do you think she might do?" Stella chewed her lower lip in thought.

Aiden grunted. "Well, from what I was able to learn, she used to take him on set for the extra attention. She might worm her way back into Jamie's life, trying to get close to you and the people you know."

"I see." Stella looked at him closely. From the worry lines around his eyes to the grim set of his mouth, his concern marred his face.

"I hate that she's still affecting my life like this. I'd hoped that when the custody issue was settled she'd be out of my life for good. The thought that she might find a crack that she could exploit to weasel back in, that she might hurt Jamie again... I like you, Stella. A lot. It's just—"

"You aren't the only one to consider," she interrupted.

"Exactly."

"Well, I'll do my best to keep Jamie and any mention of him off camera." She fumbled with her keys to unlock the door. "And she can hardly use a single fake date against you, so I don't think you should worry."

"Does this really feel fake to you?" Aiden moved closer, pinning her to the door with his frame. She sucked in a sharp breath at his sudden nearness. Her hands came up to clutch at his muscular shoulders just before he settled his mouth over hers. The nervous flutter in the pit of her stomach disappeared as his tongue flicked along the edge of her lower lip, tempting her to open her mouth so that he could deepen the kiss.

And man, could he kiss. Flames of desire started at her lips and radiated out until every inch of her body had sparked alive. She returned his attentions with equal fervor.

He broke away, gasping for air. Pressing his forehead to hers, his voice shook when he said, "That definitely wasn't fake."

Stella's cheeks were pink and her lips had the swollen appeal of having just been thoroughly kissed. One of her hands still clutched at his shirt, keeping him close.

Even though she wasn't the sort of woman he'd normally consider his type, Stella was beautiful. The spattering of freckles across her nose made her more approachable. And her curves? Curves like Stella's were what dreams were made from. She was smart and sassy...and leaving in little more than a month.

A small smile tugged at her lips. "No, I dare say it wasn't fake."

"So, where does that leave us when you aren't staying in Canada? Have fun while it lasts?" He brushed a lock of hair away from her face. He searched for emotion in her expression. While he'd love nothing more than to go inside and take Stella to bed, he found himself allowing her to set the pace. Maybe they could just have some fun together, appreciate each other with no pressure to make it permanent.

"Hmm…" Stella's noncommittal sound gave no indication as to whether she was considering his question or not.

He bit back the urge to repeat himself. Instead, he suggested, "We could take this conversation inside."

She smirked at him. "You'd enjoy that, wouldn't you?"

Leaning in, he whispered in her ear, "I'd make sure you enjoyed it too."

"You know, I've never quite understood the joy in party planning. Decor and menus have never been all that exciting for me."

By changing the subject to the Christmas party, she threw a roadblock into the tension that had been building between them. He recognized the tactic.

Easing back, he gave her a little more space. But he couldn't keep the double entendre from creeping into his words. "Maybe you've been party planning with the wrong people?"

"Oh, is that the problem?" She raised a perfectly sculpted brow at him, clearly picking up the second meaning behind his words. "And I suppose you're the right man for the job?"

"Only one way to find out," he teased. He didn't press forward for another kiss though, as he sensed Stella wasn't ready. They only had weeks until she went back to the UK, but if he pushed too much, she might shut down entirely. He kept his tone light and flirty when he made his next pitch. "Let me take you to the Winter Festival of Lights this weekend."

"Christmas lights?" She looked skeptical.

"Niagara Falls at Christmas is an experience you can't miss while you're here." She clearly needed more persuading, so he brought up the party they were planning. "It'll be perfect research for the party decor. We can spend the evening surrounded by the Christmas spirit. What could be more exciting and inspiring than that?"

"Another fake date?"

Lifting one shoulder, he gave a casual shrug. "Why put a label on it?"

Her lips pursed together briefly before she blurted out a question. "And what of your concerns about your son and your ex?"

Aiden swallowed hard. "If there's no camera to film our every move, then there's no need for Britney to find out."

"So, a secret fake date?" Her lips twitched like she might be fighting back a smile.

"A secret fake date disguised as a research trip," he said with a grin.

"Fine. I suppose I'll go."

"Yes!" He pumped his arm in victory. "I should go, before we have any other clandestine activities to disguise."

Stella surprised him by rising up and brushing her lips across his. "Then I'll just say good night."

He waited until the lock clicked audibly as she locked the door behind her before he walked away. Was he getting in too deep with her? With every touch, every kiss, his feelings for Stella grew stronger. This was not supposed to turn into anything real. The line he was toeing was a fine one. If he didn't maintain his balance, Stella

or Jamie might be hurt. It was a real risk, so he'd have
to proceed with caution.

The best solution would be to stay away from Stella
Allen.

If only she didn't draw him in like a tractor beam,
he might be able to do that.

CHAPTER TWELVE

STELLA FOUND HERSELF strolling at Aiden's side on a crisp winter night. The trip down to Niagara Falls had been quite fun. They'd had a lot of lively conversations in the car on the way. She kept sneaking glances at him as they walked through the Christmas light display. He looked so carefree when he was with his son. The Aiden with her now was certainly not the grumpy man she'd met at the airport, but he wasn't the sharp professional from the hospital either. This Aiden was the version she liked the best. This Aiden smiled a lot. He joked, and he teased.

Stella's eyes flicked down toward Jamie. Once again, Aiden had surprised her by bringing his son along for the evening. She'd managed to hide it a bit better this time, avoiding another reappearance of defensive Aiden. And she honestly didn't mind that he'd brought his son the first time; it had merely been unexpected.

A crisp breeze blew past them, ruffling their clothing. Aiden bent and adjusted Jamie's hat, tugging it down closer around the boy's ears. "It's a little chilly out tonight, but I promised Jamie that we'd come see the Christmas lights—even though he's going to be up way past his bedtime."

Jamie gave a tiny little grin at the playful tone in Aiden's voice.

"Normally he'd be in bed soon, but it's Christmas lights. You can only see those for such a limited time. So, we struck a bargain that he'd be allowed to stay up tonight if he napped today. So, what do you think? Are you finding a bit of Christmas spirit?"

"Of course." She wrapped a gloved hand around his biceps. Maybe if she moved a little closer she could share a bit of his body heat. "I'm so happy to have been invited, even if it is quite cold."

"I'm glad you came too." He tossed a look her way that made her feel like they were standing in Death Valley midsummer rather than the middle of a Canadian winter.

Trying for a distraction from the heat building in her core, Stella pointed at the animatronic reindeer that was moving off to their left. "Look at Rudolph! Jamie, what's your favorite reindeer?"

"Wudolph," Jamie answered, exactly as she expected.

"Mine too," she said conspiratorially. She'd always loved the reindeer with the red nose and the courage to stand out too. "Which one do you think is Daddy's favorite? I think it's Dasher."

Jamie nodded solemnly in agreement. Even surrounded by animatronic animals and thousands of twinkling lights, it was hard to get a smile from the little boy. She wanted to start singing a Christmas carol, maybe in a funny voice, to see if she could pull a laugh from Jamie.

Walking along the marked path was a bit like walking through a winter wonderland. Between the slight crunch of snow beneath their feet and the soft flurries falling around them, the atmosphere was perfect for getting into the Christmas spirit. All it was missing were a cup of peppermint hot chocolate and some Christmas carols.

"Dasher? Really? Very funny, guys," Aiden said with a roll of his eyes. "I've always been fond of Cupid actually."

"Really?"

"Really. Cupid seems like she'd be grumpy that everyone assumed she was a romantic because of her name. I relate to the grumpy."

Stella laughed until tears ran down her face. "At least you can admit that you are a grump. I have to say, I thought you were going to be a nightmare when we first met. You had me regretting that I'd agreed to come to Toronto. Turned my impression that all Canadians were overly polite and friendly straight on its ear."

"I admit that I didn't make the best first impression." He leaned closer and her heart rate ticked up at the closeness. "But even then, we had crazy chemistry. Just a touch of our hands was enough to keep me up most of the night thinking about the what-ifs."

"Oh?" She tried not to sound too eager for his answer, but it wasn't every day that a gorgeous man confessed to thinking about you all night.

In fact, to Stella's recollection, this was the first time a man had ever made such a confession to her. She found herself comparing Aiden to the other guys she'd dated, but there was no real comparison. He was the kind of man every woman hoped to find.

That comparison led her to wondering what else was different between her life in Toronto and her life back in the UK. Her career, obviously, was on a path she was happy with back home. Although, other than a few snotty people, the staff at St. Matthew's Hospital had been extremely welcoming. She'd been asked to drinks more in the month of November than the past six at the Royal Kensington Hospital. Okay, so the bar had been quite low on that and she'd only been asked once, by Gemma, but Stella still had to count that as a pro for Toronto.

Of course, her personal life back home was nothing to brag about. She had been longing for the connection of close friends for a while, but none had materialized. She thought if she had more time in Canada that Gemma might become that close friend she'd always felt was missing from her life. And her abysmal dating life would be watched with abject horror if it were to be filmed.

She paused.

How was it that in a month she had a more satisfying social life in Toronto than she'd managed to build in nearly a year in London? And this Christmas was shaping up to be the best one she'd had in years. She hadn't done multiple Christmas activities in the same holiday season in longer than she could remember.

"You okay?" Aiden questioned. They paused to look at a brightly lit two-story-high fountain. "Considering all the festivity surrounding us, you seem a bit down."

"Just thinking."

"Doesn't seem like good thoughts?"

"Hmm… Neither good nor bad, merely confusing." Stella leaned her head against his shoulder. "Simply thinking of how different my life is here versus my life in London."

Slipping an arm around her waist, Aiden pulled her in close. "Do I dare hope that there's at least one thing you like better here?"

She tiptoed to brush a kiss across his lips, mindful of Jamie being on his opposite hip. "I can think of at least two right now."

Aiden smiled before kissing her again. His kiss was far less chaste than the one she'd just bestowed on him. "We are growing pretty fond of you too, Stella."

"My turn kiss Stella," Jamie insisted. He puckered up his little lips and leaned in to smack a kiss on Stella's cheek.

Her heart melted at the little boy's actions.

"Oh, my heart, you are the most adorable creature in existence," she cooed.

"Shall we continue on? There's a lot left to see here."

They continued on, walking through a tunnel of light loops. The colors of the lights changed as they continued to walk, and Jamie was so fascinated that they had to circle back and go again. The lightwork gave the impression of a passage through a portal.

"I wonder if we could set up something similar at the party, maybe for the kids to go through to get to the cookie station?"

"I think that would be brilliant." Aiden grinned. "I know at least one little one who might be more interested in that than he would be in the cookies."

Pointing ahead, and whispering in Jamie's ear, Aiden convinced his son to go on and see more of the Winter Festival of Lights when he wanted to go through the light passage once more. Before long, they came up on what Aiden must have told Jamie about, because the boy squealed with excitement.

A warmth she'd never felt came over her when she saw the pure joy on Jamie's face. He ran ahead to a giant keyboard with music notes on the wall behind it. His giggles filled the air as he ran from one end to the other and the lights changed colors with his steps. Each step played a musical note.

"He laughed," Aiden breathed more than said. He pulled her into his arms and hugged her tightly. "Did you hear? He actually laughed."

"I heard," she said back in a whisper, as if afraid speaking louder would break the spell.

They stood, looking at Jamie playing a few feet away, still wrapped in each other's arms. Stella relaxed against Aiden and he leaned his cheek against the top of her head. Nothing in Stella's life had ever felt more perfect.

"You have a lovely family," an older woman said. "Have a Merry Christmas!"

"Merry Christmas," they both murmured in return.

"I suppose we do look like a family," she said, extracting herself from Aiden's embrace. She was getting too wrapped up in the romance of the evening. She shouldn't be allowing herself to get so close to them. With every moment she spent with them, she found herself wishing circumstances were different and that she weren't leaving in a month.

Maybe she should just step away before she hurt Jamie like his own mother had done? Or gave him the same sort of long-term issues that her own mother had given her. And she certainly didn't want to provide an "in" for Britney to hurt Jamie again.

Plus, she wasn't sure she was the mothering type.

Wrapping her arms around herself, she tried to will away the ache that sat down deep in her chest.

Stella visibly withdrew after the old woman's comment about them being a family. Had it upset her that someone would think they were a couple?

Worse, was she upset that the woman might have

thought she was Jamie's mom? That one dug deep and latched on. Who would be embarrassed by an ador-able little boy?

He could see her struggling. Emotions were flash-ing across her face with unreadable speed. It had to be connected to the woman's words. They'd shared a few light kisses and she'd been content in his arms up until that moment.

"Talk to me," he said. "She upset you. What I'm not understanding is exactly how? And the reasons I'm coming up with in my head are not good."

"You're a dad."

"Yeah."

News flash, I was a dad when we met.

He searched her gaze for the relevancy to that fact. "And?"

"I'm not sure I'm cut out to be someone's mum."

Those words cut straight to his heart, piercing his soul faster than any insult or criticism ever could. The weight on his chest made it hard to breathe. Stella didn't want to be a mother. Or a stepmother, in this case.

"His mom said something very similar at the cus-tody hearing when she signed over rights." He picked up his son and hugged him tight, wanting to shield him from any further pain.

"Aiden—"

"No, it's better that we're honest about what this is, and what this isn't before any of us get truly attached." He sighed. "I was starting to really like you, Stella, starting to think of how we might make something work long-term despite living on separate continents, but this is one thing that I can't look past."

"I'm trying to be up-front about what I'm thinking."

She reached out a hand toward him, but he stepped back out of her reach.

"What about him isn't enough?" She'd seemed to really like spending time with Jamie. Had it all been an act?

Her jaw dropped. She recovered quickly, and argued, "It's not that, Aiden. He deserves only the best."

"It's already past his bedtime—we should go see the falls and then head home."

"Aiden," she called after him, but he'd already stomped away. He stopped at the viewing platform where they could see the colorfully lit frozen Niagara Falls. Its beauty couldn't be denied, even when frustration ran through his veins unchecked.

Stella stepped up next to him. "I've never seen anything like that." Awe filled her voice. "Jamie, what do you think? You like the pink waterfall?"

"Pretty," Jamie said, not taking his eyes off the falls. "Ooh! Blue!"

The lights at the falls changed to another bright hue, casting a bluish tinge across Stella's face. She stared out at the icy waterfall, and he thought he caught the glimpse of tears in her eyes.

Jamie yawned and reached his arms out to Stella. But Aiden couldn't let Jamie get even more attached to her.

"Not right now, buddy," Aiden said, denying his son's request. He tried not to wince at the gruffness in his voice. Hugging Jamie closer, he tried to soften his refusal.

"Are you ready to go?" Stella asked quietly.

With a quick nod, he walked away. No, he came close to running. Power walking had nothing on him as he strode back to the car, eager to put any distance between himself and Stella. How could he have put Jamie in this position again?

Stella trailed behind a bit, reaching the car after he'd secured his son in the back and closed the door.

"I don't suppose we can talk about this?" she asked as she walked up. She'd wrapped her arms around herself like she needed a hug and he wanted so much to reach out and pull her into his arms.

What was wrong with him? Why did he want to comfort someone who didn't want to be involved with him and his son?

"What's left to say, Stella? I have a kid. You don't want to be a mom."

She shook her head. "Aiden, that's not exactly what I meant."

"Isn't it?" He released a shaky breath. "What did you mean then? Because I don't see any other way I could take that."

"I'm not good at this. I've messed up every relationship I've ever started." She looked down at her feet, no longer meeting his eyes. "I don't know what to say to fix this."

"I promised earlier that I'd try to talk more. To not just shut you out when something bothers me." He swallowed hard. His resolve to keep his distance almost broke. He needed to stay strong, for Jamie. "When I touch you, I can see an amazing future stretched out in front of us."

"I can too," she whispered.

"But when you say things like thinking that you aren't cut out to be a mom, all I see is history repeating itself. All I see is another woman willing to walk away from my son to further her career." He should have known better than to try to get involved with another actress.

"Aiden, I—"

He cut her off, not wanting to hear any excuses. "Get in the car so I can drive you home."

They made the car ride to her apartment in silence. The drive back seemed far longer than the drive there had. But he couldn't think of a single thing to say that wouldn't be the start of a fight he didn't want to have in front of his son. When he turned into the parking garage, she glanced back at Jamie.

"He's asleep, so there's no need for you to get out of the car to walk me up."

After pulling up next to the elevator, he waited for her to get out. He paused until she stepped inside and the elevator doors closed, taking her out of his sight. Even though he was angry with her, he needed to be sure she was safely in her building before he drove away.

How could she dismiss his son so easily? Why did women find his little boy so unlovable? Was that a genetic trait? His own birth mother had abandoned him as a child too. He'd been lucky and had been adopted by the Cooks who were the best people he'd ever known. But the question had always lingered in his mind: *Why did my parents not want me?*

From the moment he'd read the simple note that Britney had left with Jamie, he'd vowed to be the very best father he could be. He'd do all that was within his power to make sure Jamie never felt the sting of paternal rejection. Britney had walked away from their one night together without a backward glance, a fact that had never bothered him until he learned she'd given birth to his son.

By the time he reached home, he'd worked himself into a frenzy about the evening. He'd never wanted a woman to stick around before, but now, ironically, the one he wanted didn't want him. His anger with Stella for rejecting his son had spilled over into anger at himself, as well. The fact that her confession bothered him so much told him a lot: he was falling for her.

He carried Jamie into the house, still half asleep.

His mom was there to pass judgement before he'd closed the door behind them. "You look upset."

"I'm fine." He really didn't want to get into it with her tonight. He loved her, but she was one of the most stubborn people he knew and he wasn't sure he had it in him tonight to handle her interrogation without breaking.

She tilted her head and he could practically see the gears turning in her mind. "Jamie, dear, how were the Christmas lights?"

His son ratted him out. "Daddy mad with Stella."

"Traitor," he muttered under his breath. His own son had thrown him straight under the bus.

"Oh, Daddy's mad at Stella, is he?" She took his son out of his arms. "You want Grandma to get you ready for bed while grumpy ol' Daddy takes a shower and calms down?"

Jamie nodded, and his mom headed for the stairs with Jamie in her arms. He couldn't hear the words she whispered, but Aiden was sure his mother was promising things to Jamie that spoiled him rotten.

"So why does your son think you're mad at a woman?" his dad asked from the doorway behind him.

"Leave it alone, Dad," he said without turning.

"Jamie likes her, you know." His father came fully

out of his office. "He's been talking about her nonstop since you went to the christmas market together."

"Jamie doesn't really know her," Aiden growled.

"And you do?"

"I know enough!" He ran his hands through his hair. "She doesn't want kids. She as good as said."

"Hmm…" His dad looked thoughtful. "Not wanting children isn't a defect."

"I know that." And he did. Truly.

"Then you're not upset with Stella, are you?"

Aiden pinched the bridge of his nose. "No, I'm mad at myself for getting involved with someone who doesn't want kids."

"I didn't want kids at first either. Your mom wore me down. I only gave in because it made her happy, but once you came into my life, I found I'd never wanted anything more. I didn't want to be a dad until about five minutes after I became one."

"She said she's not cut out to be a mom." Aiden tried harder to explain to his dad why Stella wasn't an option. "How much clearer could she be?"

"I've only got one question for you, son." His dad paused for effect. "How long was it after you met Jamie before you decided that you *were* cut out to be a dad? Because I seem to recall a similar sentiment coming from you in those early days."

Chewing on his dad's words, Aiden showered and went to bed. Even as he lay there, wide awake, the words bounced around in his head. He'd never known that his dad had been reluctant to have children.

He'd never not wanted Jamie though. He'd been completely taken with that little boy from day one. Had he questioned his ability to be what the child needed? Well, sure. But what parent hadn't questioned themselves at some point along the way? Never once had he considered walking away though.

Not even for a second.

If he were being brutally honest though, he'd never pictured himself as a family man before he suddenly became a father. Kids hadn't been high on his priority list, but once he had a son, it became his top priority. It hadn't taken long for him to realize that being someone's dad was a role he was meant to play.

In certain situations, emotions and instinct showed a man who he was meant to be. Having his son placed in his arms told him he was meant to be a father. The pain he felt at Stella's rejection told him he was meant to spend his life with her.

Sleep eluded him as he let his mind drift to what could have been with Stella. When he rolled over to check the time it was two in the morning. and the notification light on his phone flashed. He had two messages from Stella.

The first read:

I didn't mean to imply that your son wasn't perfect in any way. I think he's the most perfect child I've ever met. Me, though, I'm so far from perfect that I blew an otherwise perfect evening. He is enough. It's me that's lacking.

The second simply said:

I've an IQ of one hundred and sixty. You'd think I'd know a few synonyms for perfect.

He couldn't stop the snort of amusement at the last message.

If Jamie was perfect though, why couldn't she envision herself in his life? Unlike himself, Stella didn't have an obligation to be in Jamie's life. It would be a choice for her.

Did his dad have a point about giving her time? Or would giving her time just prolong the inevitable heartache when she boarded the plane back to her life without them?

CHAPTER THIRTEEN

"St. Matthew's Day care," a frazzled voice on the other end of the call answered.

"This is Dr. Stella Allen. I received a page for this number, but I'm not quite sure why."

"Oh, thank goodness." The woman's sigh of relief was audible. "Could you please come down to the day care? We're on the first level, just behind the administration wing."

"Could I ask why?"

"It's best explained in person." The line went dead.

Curiosity piqued, Stella made her way downstairs. Why would an orthopedic surgeon be called to the hospital's crèche? Surely if any of the children were injured, they'd send them over to Emergency. Or call a trauma doctor.

She buzzed the intercom at the entrance and when she gave her name, the lock clicked open. Hesitantly, she made her way inside. Children played in various parts of the room, some quietly, some not so quietly.

"Are you Stella?" One of the day care workers asked as she walked up to Stella.

"I am." Stella couldn't see anyone hurt, no reason for her to have been called. Her confusion rose.

"Follow me," the young woman said, turning and

heading toward the back. When she opened a door, the faint sounds of crying met Stella's ears.

"Is one of the children injured?" Stella picked up her pace. She had no supplies down here. How was she to handle an emergency? She took a deep breath and calmed that anxiety. She'd have to make do.

When she stepped through the door though, she saw only one child—Jamie. He sat slapping at the hands of the poor childcare provider who was trying to soothe his tears.

"Jamie, what's wrong?" She hurried to his side and sat next to him. While her instinct was to pull him into her arms and cradle him until the crying subsided, she didn't want to upset him further if he didn't want to be touched.

"Stella!" He shouted her name and jumped into her lap. He buried his face against her throat and mumbled something she didn't understand. His breathing came in great hitching breaths as he tried to stop sobbing.

"What happened here?" she asked, trying to keep the anger and accusation out of her voice, although in that moment she wanted to shout at them all for upsetting Jamie.

The young woman who'd shown her in shrugged. "He was playing out there with the others and everything seemed fine. He was rolling a ball with another child, and it was like a switch flipped. He went from content to crying in a matter of seconds."

"How long was he crying?" Stella rubbed Jamie's back as he snuggled closer to her, still occasionally sobbing. Thankfully, the overall intensity of his cries began to reduce.

"A while. We tried to call Dr. Cook first, of course, but the ED is swamped. There was a multicar pileup on the freeway, it seems. Then we tried his grandmother, but she's at a doctor's appointment across town."

"And I was the next logical choice?" Stella couldn't keep the surprise out of her voice.

"When we told him that Daddy and Grandma couldn't come, he asked for you." She gave Stella a soft, telling look. "I'll leave you some privacy to calm him."

Why had she been given that look? The one that said she ought to know how to comfort Jamie. She hadn't spent nearly enough time with Jamie to understand what he liked or didn't. She rubbed his back gently and murmured the kind of soothing nonsense that she'd seen others use, and when Jamie responded favorably, she continued.

Slowly, Jamie's breathing settled into a steady pace and the occasional sobs faded. He fell asleep, his face pressed into Stella's throat and his breath tickling her skin. Rather than making her uncomfortable though, it filled Stella with a longing she'd never expected.

For years now, she'd told herself that she had no interest in being a mum. Stella had been loved, yes, but she'd never truly felt understood by her mum. There'd been a distance between them that Stella saw widening as the years passed. She wanted the distance—more than her mother did—but she needed more autonomy than her mum was willing to give. What if she couldn't give a child what they really needed?

Jamie snuffled a bit, cuddling closer, his tiny little hand clutching at hers. Tears welled up in her eyes. He trusted her implicitly, enough to let his guard down and sleep in her arms. After everything he'd been through, he'd wanted her to comfort him. That had to mean something, didn't it?

One thing she knew—she'd been deceiving herself for years about not wanting kids in her life.

"I'm sorry it took me so long to get here," Aiden told the day care worker. "Where is he?"

"Asleep."

Aiden's heart dropped. Had Jamie cried himself to sleep again? Nausea bubbled up in his stomach at the thought of his sweet baby crying until he couldn't cry anymore. It wouldn't be the first time, but Aiden had hoped it wasn't going to happen anymore.

"They both are," she said with a smile.

"Both?"

She opened the door to the room at the back used for naps and quiet time. Over her shoulder, Aiden saw a sight he never would have expected.

Stella sat in the rocker, eyes closed, with Jamie cuddled against her chest asleep. Her cheek rested on the top of Jamie's head. Matching looks of contentment graced their faces. By all appearances, they were a natural pair.

He sighed.

"I hope you don't mind that we called Dr. Allen down. We tried your mom after we got word from the ED that you might be a while. She couldn't make it either and he was so upset. He started asking for Stella and we knew you two have been seeing each other."

We were seeing each other.

"She wasn't on the list to take him though, but we can update that if you wish," the day care worker kept talking. "He threw himself into her arms the moment she arrived and hasn't let her go since."

And she'd stayed with him.

Aiden swallowed hard at the lump of emotion clogging his throat. In the moment, he could see a future with Stella at his side. He could see her filling the maternal role in Jamie's life.

But, somehow, *she* couldn't.

Was something in her past blocking her from seeing what an amazing mom she could be? Or had he missed a key piece in her background that changed everything?

He didn't know.

What he did know was that the closer she got to Jamie, the higher the risk became that his son would get hurt.

That thought sobered him. The chinks in the wall around his heart that had softened upon seeing Jamie sleeping in her arms filled back up.

"Hey," he said softly, nudging her shoulder. He made sure to avoid touching her anywhere they might have skin to skin contact. "Stella, wake up."

"Hmm…" she murmured, voice thick with sleep. Her eyes opened and she blinked rapidly. "I must have drifted off."

"You did." He nodded down at Jamie. "I need to get him home."

"Oh, of course." She brushed a kiss on Jamie's hair before lifting him up so that Aiden could take him.

He tucked his son into his chest and turned to go. But before he left, he couldn't help himself. He had to say something. "While I should thank you for coming down here to take care of Jamie, I can't help but worry that you've made it harder on him."

Without giving her time to respond, Aiden left the day care. He'd have to talk to them about calling for Stella. It was already going to be hard enough on Jamie when he realized that he'd never see Stella again.

CHAPTER FOURTEEN

"SOMEONE PAGED ME," Stella said as she walked into the emergency department. It had been a generic page, so she had no idea who. She had been trying unsuccessfully to squash the hope that it was Aiden and that his reason for paging her was personal for her entire walk down from ortho. She looked around hopefully, but didn't see him.

"Exam two. Mrs. Upton is back. Dr. Cook asked me to call you down here." The nurse gestured over her shoulder from where she stood on a stepladder behind the desk hanging garland along the top of the bulletin board.

Christmas decorations had started to pop up everywhere at St. Matthew's. A huge tree already took up a large portion of the waiting room, although it had yet to be decorated. Up in orthopedics, the patients had responded favorably to the festive touches and the staff were often found humming Christmas carols as they worked. Stella was loving the vibrancy of the holiday in Toronto so far.

"Mrs. Upton?" Stella's mind went into overtime, running through the details of Mrs. Upton's surgery. Everything had gone well. She'd been healing okay at her follow-up. Had there been a complication that Stella had missed during surgery or one of the exams?

She smoothed her hair and straightened her white coat before hurrying into exam two where Aiden was standing at the patient's bedside. Stella's eyes drank him in like an oasis in the desert. She hadn't seen him since the incident with Jamie in the hospital day care.

He'd ignored her calls. Read, but didn't respond to her texts. And she hadn't even caught a glimpse of him here at the hospital. He must have been determined to avoid her.

Their eyes met when he looked up at her arrival. Tension sparked between them like a live wire. Desire pooled in her abdomen. She shouldn't still want him so much after the silence, but her body reacted to a single look from him.

"Dr. Allen, how good of you to join us." The words rolled off his tongue like a rebuke. As if she had dawdled on her way down rather than arriving only minutes after she'd been paged.

"I arrived as quickly as I could, Dr. Cook," she replied with an edge to her voice. Why did his cold tone make her so hot? Two could play that icy treatment game. She'd show him that she could give as good as she received on that front.

She softened her tone when speaking to the patient though, of course. The sweet, elderly woman had done nothing to deserve the sharpness of her tongue. "Hello, Mrs. Upton, what brings you in today?"

Mrs. Upton grimaced. "I fell again."

"Oh, dear." Stella scanned her patient for visual clues of injuries. Mrs. Upton's skin looked a little washed out of color, but she seemed free of bruising or obvious damages. A glance at the monitors showed that the patient's vital signs were strong. "Can you tell me a bit about what happened?"

With a sigh, Mrs. Upton began her story. "Well, there I was at physical therapy—still at that rehab facility they sent me to, mind you—they had me up and walking along with this wheeled walker. I stumbled a bit, lost my footing and that walker just went on without me. I landed on my left hip. There was a lot of pain so the physical therapist and the doctor there thought it best I come in and let you have a look."

"It does sound prudent." Stella moved over to the computer terminal. Why had that physical therapist let her get so far ahead of them that Mrs. Upton became a fall risk? They should have been right within arm's reach so that they could support her, catch her and ease her down if she lost her balance. Incompetent. They'd be catching an earful from her this morning. "Dr. Cook, have you had new imaging done?"

"We have." His voice was tight. "The results have just popped up and I was about to review them."

Stella tapped a few keys so that she could check the patient's chart and make sure Aiden had ordered all the imaging she wanted to see done. He had.

"Okay, well, let's take a look."

Aiden looked over her shoulder, standing so close that the hint of cedar from his cologne tickled at her senses. She swallowed hard, fighting herself to focus on Mrs. Upton's imaging.

"What do you think?" he said softly, his breath warm against the back of her neck.

"Looks like everything held." Stella squeezed past Aiden, being careful not to touch him. She patted the patient's foot gently. "Looks like it's just bruising. The fracture seems to be healing well and the fall doesn't appear to have hindered that."

"I've already ordered some pain medication for you, as well," Aiden reassured the older woman. "The nurse should bring that in shortly."

He motioned for Stella to precede him out of the exam room.

"Could we chat for a moment?" she asked. "In private."

"We have nothing to say to each other."

She sighed. He wasn't going to make this easy on her at all, was he? "We still have some issues to discuss regarding the Christmas party."

With a nod, he stalked down the hall and into one of the small family rooms where the doctors took patients' loved ones to tell them bad news in private. The door clicked shut.

He crossed his arms over his chest and waited for her to speak. The shields in his eyes were fully erect, and she didn't see the charming man she'd spent time with. No, this was back to the snappy grump from the airport.

"Well?" he prompted. "If you aren't going to get on with it, I need to get back to work."

Stella closed her eyes and took a deep breath. Why had she though it was a good idea to get involved with a coworker again? "I emailed you some ideas on the party and wondered if you'd had a chance to take a look."

"No. But I'm sure whatever you've decided will be acceptable."

"Okay, so I'll just put your name down on the order for the jolly Santa strippers and the naughty Mrs. Clauses then?"

"Sure, Stella. You just tell me what you need me to

take care of." He rolled his eyes. "I'm trusting you to keep it professional and work-appropriate for the rest."

"How is Jamie, by the way?" she asked. "Hopefully what happened at day care didn't upset him too badly?" She'd been worried about that for days now, and when Aiden didn't answer her calls or texts, her worries had nearly taken on a life of their own. "I tried to check in on him."

"I know."

"Is he okay?" Stella tried again. She really was concerned about the little boy. He'd been through so much and if she had added to it because of her actions, she wasn't sure how she'd handle it.

"Do you even care?" Aiden huffed. "Or are you just asking to be polite?"

"I don't think I deserve this much animosity for expressing a personal concern." Stella sighed. "I really don't want to upset your son. I hope I didn't, and I apologize if I have done so."

Aiden was more upset than she'd realized. While she'd known there was a problem, it went far deeper than first glance.

She really had some nerve! Asking about his son like she had a right to know how Jamie was. Like she cared! She'd said she wasn't cut out to be a mother, so what benefit did she gain from acting like he mattered to her?

"He told my parents we were fighting."

"You still live with your parents?"

He had to fight back a growl, but he gave her an abbreviated version of the events that had led to him moving back home. "They're licensed foster parents. They had to take Jamie in before I could gain legal custody. I moved back in with them so that I could be in the same household with my son. His psychiatrist recommended that I not uproot him again by moving out just yet."

"I see."

"Do you?" He started pacing back and forth in the small room like a caged tiger. From the door to the back wall took him only eight steps. "He's had so much upheaval already. And by introducing him to you, I brought yet another person into his life who is abandoning him."

"I didn't…"

"Didn't what? Abandon him? You cuddled him and gave him kisses and then walked away. That's exactly what you did."

Her mouth gaped open and she sank down into one of the ugly salmon-pink chairs the hospital had installed during their last reno. "I never thought…"

"Never mind." He couldn't stand to look at her anymore. Did she really not see that her actions had affected Jamie? He turned to go.

"Aiden, please wait. I know you might have watched some of my programs when you were researching me. But despite how it looked, my mother was never going to win any parenting awards in real life. I was actually a very lonely, neglected child. The bulk of my interactions with my parents occurred on camera. If the red light wasn't on, I didn't exist for them."

"Why are you telling me this?"

"I don't know how to be a mum! My decisions were all made for me for so long that I am only just now learning what I want from my own life." She went and stared out the window over the snow-covered parking lot. "I don't even know what a good mother might look like as I've never had one in my life."

"You are a fantastic doctor. You care deeply for your

patients," Aiden scoffed. "And I think if you would open your eyes, you'd see that you could be an amazing mother. You've already shown more caring than Britney ever did."

She didn't turn away from the window. "After all he's been through, little Jamie deserves better than someone playing at motherhood! Children don't come with a tutorial and I have no idea where to begin."

"Parenting comes with a learning curve. A steep one. And no parent is ever perfect. The most important thing to do is to show them that they are loved." He ran a hand through his hair in frustration. "Stella, I know your parents left you with some trauma, but even if you simply do the opposite of what they did for you, you'd be a better parent than either of them ever was."

He left the room quietly, leaving her to digest all that he'd just thrown at her. He strode over to the desk. "I'm taking my break now."

He took the stairs up to the roof and stood in the cold, staring out over the Toronto skyline. Working on patients wasn't a good idea until he'd pulled himself together. What had he been thinking getting involved with another actress?

Clearly, he hadn't been using his brain, but another part of his anatomy, when he'd gotten entangled with a woman from the hospital. Particularly when her second career was in the film industry. He should have stuck with his normal routine of being alone until his physical needs got too much and then finding someone for a night to satisfy those urges. Then he didn't have to worry about finding someone who would love both him and his son.

Maybe his past had marked him as unlovable. He should focus on his son. He'd been lucky that he'd found adoptive parents like the Cooks. And despite the neglect Jamie had suffered while under Britney's care, Aiden had custody now. If he gave Jamie enough love and attention, maybe he could break the cycle.

The feelings of inadequacy that he'd struggled with his entire life resurfaced. The therapist he'd seen for a while said that his lack of self-worth when it came to relationships stemmed from his own abandonment. It had been amplified when his own son went through the same abandonment by his birth mother. Neither of them had been born to women capable of loving them.

In the past, Aiden had never let a woman get this close. He'd never wanted to. But from the undeniable chemistry whenever they touched to the intelligence that made her eyes sparkle when she talked, Stella Allen had gotten under his skin. The part that hurt the most was that he could see that Stella wasn't really as ambivalent about motherhood as she tried to tell herself. He could see what a loving, caring person she really was. Had anything he'd just said resonated with her at all?

The wind kicked up and Aiden shivered. Still, he stayed out and sucked the crisp, cold air into his lungs while trying to quiet the voice in his head that kept telling him to go find Stella, to do whatever it took to make her love him and love Jamie.

But why bother when she was leaving so soon?

CHAPTER FIFTEEN

"Hey, Stella," Gemma blurted out. "A really hot guy is looking for you downstairs with a camera."

Stella stopped walking and lifted her attention from the file in her hands. She blinked at her in confusion. "I beg your pardon?"

"There is a super cute British guy waiting in the lobby for your presence." Gemma rephrased and slowed her words down as if Stella hadn't heard her. It wasn't the hearing she was struggling with but the comprehension. "He has the most adorable dimples I've ever seen on an adult male."

She wasn't expecting anyone from back home to show up in Toronto. But if it was a good-looking man with a camera and dimples, she could only think of one person who fit that description, and he had no business being at St. Matthew's. "Dark hair and quite tall?" she asked.

"Got it in one. I take it you know who I'm talking about?"

"I do." Stella turned toward the stairs. "Thanks for letting me know, Gemma."

"We still need to find time to get drinks," Gemma yelled as Stella walked away.

"Absolutely," Stella called over her shoulder. She'd

need a drink after she dealt with her unexpected visitor downstairs.

When she reached the crowed lobby, she saw exactly who she'd expected to find. "Oliver, to what do I owe the pleasure?"

"Stella, darling, I've missed you." Oliver took her in his arms and moved to kiss her. She turned her head just in time and his lips landed on her cheek.

"Really, Ollie, we no longer have that sort of relationship. Please, be respectful of that fact."

Oliver rolled his eyes, but released her. "Martin thought you could use my services. He said the footage that's been captured is…usable, but not very inspired. He said it needed more of a cinematic touch."

"A more cinematic touch?" With her fists clenched at her sides, Stella stared Oliver down. When the first of December had passed without Henry being replaced, Stella had thought that Martin might have changed his mind about sending someone else. Her heart sank as she realized that he'd not backed down on that at all. And of all the people he could have sent, why did it have to be the one videographer in all the world with whom she had history?

One of his shoulders lifted in a casual shrug that she'd once found attractive. At least until she learned that Oliver had as much personality as stale toast.

"Martin likes my work, and he knows I've worked with you in the past and can capture your best angles. I know how to flatter you on film, darling. I minimize those luscious curves of yours and slim you down to the perfect look." He winked at her. "Plus, I was encouraged to make the trip."

Stella shook her head in frustration. That was another reason why she and Oliver had never worked—he always wanted her to slim down so that he didn't have to film her at specific angles.

"Oliver, go home. I don't want or need your help."

"Take that up with Martin, darling. I've checked into a hotel a few blocks down. Why don't you plan to have dinner with me this evening? We can go over what footage we still need, then you and I can get reacquainted." He reached out and took her hand. "I promise to make it worth your time."

A gasp off to the side reminded Stella that they had an audience. She snatched her hand from him quickly, but she could already see the disapproving looks on the faces of the St. Matthew's employees clustered nearby.

"You never made it worth my time when we were together, so I think I'll pass." She took another step back. "I have work to do."

"So do I," Oliver said. He swung his camera up on his shoulder. "And that's to follow you around and get some good footage for this program."

She hadn't seen Oliver since they'd broken up several months back. Her decision. Besides the utter lack of physical allure, and the dullness of his personality, Oliver wanted to grow his career in the film industry. He wanted them to take over the film world together and she wasn't sure she wanted that life. But it had been when she'd expressed her concerns about having a family that had created an unbridgeable gulf between them. She just hadn't seen a future with him.

Not like she had with Aiden.

She'd blown her chances with Aiden though. He'd been giving her a wide berth and would barely make eye contact with her. She wasn't sure how to go about repairing what she'd broken. Bones she could mend: hurt feelings, not so much.

Stella hurried back to the orthopedics floor with Oliver following right behind her. The head of the department stopped her, placing a hand on her arm, and silently asked about Oliver by flicking her gaze behind Stella to where he stood.

"Assigned to me from the director. Seems the earlier footage wasn't quite hitting the spot," she said through gritted teeth.

"Hmm…" Dr. Devlin looked at Oliver. "Stay out of my operating rooms. Be extremely careful about patient privacy. And do not get in my way."

As she walked away, Oliver snorted. "Well, she's fun."

"I quite like her actually," Stella countered.

"Give me the tour, Stella." Oliver placed his hand on her lower back. "Then we can get some dinner and get out of here."

"Can I get your signature on a few forms, Dr. Allen?" one of the nurses asked. She shoved the tablet against Stella's arm.

"Certainly," Stella said, using the distraction to once again move away from Oliver's touch.

The brief conversation with the nurse seemed snappier than usual but Stella couldn't pinpoint why. She had only had a few interactions with this particular nurse and none of them had been sour, so she wasn't sure where the animosity came from. She signed the forms quickly and handed the tablet back to the nurse.

For the rest of the day, all of her interactions went similarly. The feeling at St. Matthew's Hospital had definitely changed. The warmth and acceptance that Stella had worked so hard to earn had vanished. She'd proven herself, hadn't she? Had all her effort been for naught? Once again, Stella became an outsider and she wasn't sure why.

Based upon the number of glares, it seemed to be connected to Oliver though. Was it how he talked about her, as though she were a celebrity they should feel privileged to know? Or his insistence on filming every move? Both had to be reinforcing the staff's early belief that she was more TV personality than doctor.

And she hated it.

"Did you hear that she's already taken up with— Oh, sorry, Dr. Cook, I didn't realize you were there." The nurse and orderly who had been gossiping both flushed brightly and hurried down the hall away from him.

It was completely unnecessary. He already knew exactly who they were talking about. Rumors had reached Aiden's ears quickly about the British cameraman who was currently attached to Stella's hip. He wanted to tune out the gossips, pretend he hadn't heard the whispers of how she'd moved on already, but he was finding that impossible to do.

He hadn't realized that word had gotten out to the entire hospital that he'd asked her out, but it didn't surprise him. Neither did the fact that everyone seemed to know they were over. Nothing spread through a hospital like reports of a breakup, not even a virus.

What did surprise him though was that all of his coworkers had rallied to his defense at the perceived threat to his heart. They'd put up walls and shut Stella out in the cold. For a man who had never felt like he truly belonged anywhere, it warmed his heart to see that so many people cared.

Getting the warning that she'd already moved on helped. He'd have completely embarrassed himself if he'd looked up from a patient's chart to see her standing so close to another man so soon. If he'd ground his teeth so much he might need dental work; at least he almost managed to get through their first conversation with the guy present without any reaction.

Key word there being almost.

Then things went a little sideways.

"Stella, I'm going to get the shot from back here since the patient doesn't want to be on camera." The cameraman laid a hand on the small of her back. The touch held a familiarity that said they'd been closer than mere coworkers. Far closer.

The growl that came out of Aiden at that moment would have put a caveman to shame. Stella blushed until all he could think about was throwing her over his shoulder, carrying her back to her apartment and claiming every inch of her.

The cameraman puffed up and Aiden gave him a look that said, "Try it."

He and the other man stared each other down for a moment before Stella stepped between them. "I think that's enough from the both of you."

Neither of them moved.

"Ollie, we should go," Stella said quietly. She pushed at the guy's chest until he took a step back. "Wait for me in the hallway, please."

After he stepped out, she turned and shook her head.

"You are just as guilty as he is of creating a scene, Aiden. I'm going to go before this situation escalates any further. Please let me know if the patient's imagining looks promising."

Aiden followed her out of the exam room. As they walked away, side by side, Ollie, as Stella had called him, smirked at Aiden over his shoulder.

Irritation rose up swift and strong. Who did that guy think he was, walking into this emergency department like he belonged here? Acting like he was the king of the castle? No, this was Aiden's domain and he wasn't going to let that slide.

"Hey, Frank," he called to the security guard. "See that guy with the camera there?"

"Yes, sir."

"Don't let him back through those doors again." It might be petty, but Aiden didn't want to see that smug face sneering at him from behind Stella. "Throw him out of here if he sets foot in this emergency department again."

The bitter taste of self-disgust rose hard and swift. He had to swallow it back hard. It wasn't in his nature to be such a petty, jealous Neanderthal. Was he so far gone over Stella that he would act so out of character?

Yes. Yes, he was.

And he hadn't done more than kiss her.

Maybe if he could do more, he'd be able to get her out of his system. He'd just have to get her back in his arms, and hopefully into his bed, so that he could move on.

CHAPTER SIXTEEN

"I BELIEVE I told you already that I didn't care if it was real or fake. Get my footage."

"But Martin—"

"No buts, Stella, I don't care if your hint of a relationship has gone bottoms up. You're running low on time and I'm low on patience. You have to get that footage and quickly."

And that was how she found herself tracking Aiden down to try to talk to him about his continued participation. She dreaded the conversation, even though she slipped away from Oliver to try to have the discussion in private. Aiden and Oliver had taken an instant dislike to one another and she was quite sure she was the root cause.

"Aiden, might I have a word?" she called after him as he came out of one of the trauma rooms.

He stopped walking and gestured in a vaguely positive manner. "I guess."

Since he didn't seem inclined to seek out any privacy, she stood close so that not everyone in the department could hear their chat. "I was wondering if you might find it in you to keep going with your part in the television special."

"No." His curt, swift rejection was on point with his character, if nothing else.

She tried again. "Martin is being quite insistent about it, really. He loved the footage that I'd already sent."

Aiden crossed his arms, leaning slightly closer. Stella's heart rate jumped up at his nearness, and when the movement brought the spicy notes of his cologne over, she had to swallow hard. "If he loved the footage you sent, why'd he send that guy?"

It hit her then that Aiden was completely and totally jealous of Oliver. It wasn't a mere case of rubbing each other the wrong way, but a classic case of envy.

Interesting...

"Cameramen change if the director feels that things aren't moving in the right direction. Admittedly, I never expected Oliver would be one of the cameramen assigned to this project. We haven't worked together at all since before our breakup. I suspect my mother had a hand in his appearance. She has grand hopes of a reunion between us, but that's not what I want."

"What do you want?"

"To fulfill my obligations to St. Matthew's and The Kensington Project and finish this program. The latter would be much easier if you would reconsider your wish to withdraw."

"No," he repeated. "I don't want to fake a romance with you to make some jumped-up director happy. Get your boyfriend to do it."

"Oliver is no longer—"

One of the security guards interrupted their conversation just then. "Hey, Dr. Cook, I thought you'd like to know I escorted that camera-wielding weirdo out of the building for trying to gain access to the emergency department again. Kept him out like you asked."

He walked away whistling.

Stella turned her full attention back to Aiden. She

crossed her arms over her chest and glared at him. "You ordered security to keep Oliver out? How's he to get the footage he needs if you won't allow him access to your department?"

"Not my problem." Aiden lifted one shoulder in a way that made Stella crazy. She might have been able to ignore the casual little shrug if it weren't for the sparkle of self-satisfaction she saw in his gaze.

"You most certainly do have a problem. And I think it's jealousy."

"Excuse me?" Aiden's eyes glistened dangerously.

"I enunciated rather clearly." She pushed a finger into his broad chest, trying hard not to smooth her hand across those deliciously firm pectorals. "You sabotaged Ollie because you think he took your place in my life, didn't you?"

"You think far too highly of yourself, Dr. Allen," Aiden argued.

"I think you think quite highly of me as well or we wouldn't be having this conversation."

Aiden stepped closer and put one hand on the wall behind her. His voice carried a dangerous temptation. "What are we going to do about this mutual admiration society we have going on for each other then?"

Stella darted her tongue out to moisten her lips and the small action caught Aiden's attention. His gaze locked on her mouth.

"You are killing me slowly," he said, groaning just before he bent his head down to hers. Stella rose on her tiptoes to meet him halfway, their lips reaching each other in eager anticipation. With her arms around his neck, she returned his kiss with more passion and desire than was really proper for a workplace.

Aiden's hand tugged at her hair, tilting her head so he

could deepen the kiss. She sighed as his tongue brushed hers. She wobbled as her knees gave way and he held her against his firm chest, never letting up on the kiss.

He didn't relax his hold on her until the door next to him opened. Then he pulled his lips from her and took a step back.

Stella leaned back against the wall, willing her legs to hold her weight. A couple of employees wrestled a large Christmas tree into the room and maneuvered it into the far corner.

Aiden stood near her, silent, his chest heaving. That kiss had affected him as much as it had affected her, she was sure of it. Although she doubted that he'd ever admit it.

Overhead, a page called out for her to return to the ortho department. "I suppose that's my cue to leave," she said with a smile. "One thing before I go… Oliver and me? Past tense. There's no need for jealousy. Who I end up with in the future has yet to be decided. Have a good day, Dr. Cook."

She walked away before he could say anything else, hopefully leaving him with the image of what could be. With a little effort, and maybe a bit of luck, she'd get the footage she needed and a little bit more.

The knowing look on Stella's face when she dropped that bomb and walked away made Aiden want to punch a wall. She'd all but said, *I know you still have a thing for me.*

That wasn't the part that upset him though. It was the fact that she was right. He did still want her every bit as much as he ever did. He'd illustrated that quite clearly by kissing her just then.

But nothing had changed.

She still didn't want kids and he still had one.

"You know, they say the best way to get over some-one is to find someone new."

He looked over at Rita. Her freshly applied lipstick stood out given how far they were into the shift. Stella had been right; Rita did have a thing for him.

"Who said I needed to get over anyone?"

"Your expression did when she walked away." Rita laid a hand on his arm. "How about drinks tonight?"

"I don't think that's a good idea." He searched for the words to let her down easily, because the last thing he wanted to do was to hurt her. But he had zero interest in going out with her. Even though he hated to admit it, as long as Stella was in Toronto, he didn't see himself with another woman.

"It could be fun," Rita said, laying a hand on his arm and leaning her torso his direction. She was a beautiful woman. He should feel…something. Anything. But, he didn't. And that was the problem.

"It wouldn't be fair to you, Rita. I think it's best if I stay single."

"If you change your mind…" She let the invitation trail off. Her meaning was abundantly clear though.

He nodded at her before walking away.

Maybe it really was best for everyone if he stayed single. He hadn't been lying when he said that it wouldn't be fair to Rita. It wouldn't be fair at all to her or to any other woman if he started a relationship right now. Be-sides, he had Jamie and that's all he really needed, right?

Stella's face flashed into his mind.

She was far more attracted to him than she was Oli-ver. Anyone could see that.

All he needed to do was find a way to convince Stella that they could share something physical while she was here and leave it all behind when she left. The big question was, who was going to convince his heart to keep the emotions out of it?

CHAPTER SEVENTEEN

FOR THE NEXT WEEK, each day when Stella showed up to St. Matthew's she found Aiden in her path at every turn. When they were filming interviews and a few staged clips, he ran interference with anyone who might interrupt. When she lectured, Aiden attended more lectures than he'd missed, even though he'd seen the same presentation a dozen times now. How many times could he watch her perform her surgical techniques on video while answering questions along the way? Wasn't he tired of it by now?

When she operated, he watched from the gallery. He made sure there were no repeats of the poor behavior she'd dealt with early on. And somehow, he still found more questions to ask. Intelligent questions that showed he'd done his research too.

The constant presence could have seemed too much, but he managed to make Stella feel protected. He managed to toe a line between icy and flirty that nearly drove her mad with wanting him. Some days she wanted to slap his face for the insolence. Others, she wanted to take him back to her apartment and do naughty things to him.

Today was one of the latter days.

She'd been summoned to the medical director's office. Per the email, it was to discuss her progress on the television special and how well she thought the lecture series had gone thus far. She'd brought notes, including numbers on how many surgeons had attended her lectures and how many surgeries had been performed at St. Matthew's Hospital using her technique so far. And she had a list from Martin of the final few scenes he still wanted her and Oliver to film. She had been overprepared for her meeting, as was her normal. Everything had gone as planned. Dr. Stone had even hinted that a position at St. Matthew's Hospital would be Stella's if she only asked.

Then Aiden had walked in.

With one shoulder propped against the wall, and a devastatingly sexy grin thrown her way, he turned his attention to Dr. Stone. His devil-may-care attitude had distracted Stella so much though that she completely lost her train of thought and had to be prompted to find herself again. She finished explaining her progress with heat in her cheeks and a desire to slide under the desk and give up her existence. She'd gone from confident surgeon to spaced-out fangirl over a guy in front of her boss. Recovery from that level of embarrassment might never be possible.

Dr. Stone began talking to them both about the staff Christmas party, but Stella found herself more focused on the way Aiden's fingers drummed rhythmically against his thigh.

"Dr. Allen."

"Hmm…" She pulled her eyes away from Aiden to see the medical director looking at her in amusement. Would she ever live this down? Having only a few short weeks left in Toronto might be her saving grace.

If she stayed here much longer, she might actually die of embarrassment.

"Part of the agreement for allowing you to film was setting up this party. We agreed that it will double as a filming opportunity for your special and a nice celebration for my staff. You'll be able to get footage of the doctors 'letting their hair down,' get more interviews as you need and show our employees that we value them. You've come in on budget so far, so good job. I'm still waiting on the final invoices, I believe." Dr. Stone tapped on a piece of paper just in front of Stella on the desk. She gave them both a tight look. "There is another matter. I've heard a few rumors about the two of you, but I expect that you both will be professional. Cordial, even."

"Of course," Stella murmured. She'd really been trying to maintain her professionalism, despite how things might have looked in this meeting.

She glanced over at him, wondering how he'd handle being chastised along with her. His face showed no emotion.

"Do you have any concerns about this, Dr. Cook?" Dr. Stone asked him.

"Not at all." He made eye contact with Stella and she thought she might melt into a puddle of goo at his feet from the intensity. "I'm looking forward to it."

"I turned in the invoices for the lights and the caterer." Aiden held out a couple pieces of paper. "Copies for your records."

Stella had insisted on having paper copies of everything they'd planned for the party. She might have duplicates or even triplicates of some of it. Organized must be her middle name. Complete overkill, in his opinion, but it seemed important to her, so he'd made sure to get the requested copies for her.

"Thank you," she said. "Any surprises?"

"Nope."

He fell in beside her as they walked toward the cafeteria. Thankfully, Oliver was nowhere in sight, so he had Stella all to himself for the moment. She was different when Oliver was around, not the Stella he'd gotten to know. When the camera was pointed at her, she closed off. Did Oliver even see the real Stella? And if he did, did he appreciate her?

"That's good news. We haven't the budget for surprises." Her accent made him crazy. He could listen to her speak all day about the dullest of topics and never get tired of her voice. The idea of her whispering sweet nothings in his ear as he made love to her kept him up at nights.

He wanted to keep her talking, so he made another comment about the Christmas party. "I wish they'd let us take this off campus though. We could do so much better if we weren't having this party in the hospital cafeteria."

At least they'd had a budget for catering and a cake. Most years the staff party had consisted of cold pizza slices and flat store-brand soda. Stella's program must have rated the upgrade. The higher-ups wouldn't want St. Matthew's Hospital to look bad on camera, after all.

"Hmm…" Stella murmured. "I do agree, of course, but unfortunately we weren't given options on that. So we have to make the best of what we were given. And that's a free location with a lot of seating."

"That's one way to look at it, I suppose." The fact that it was free with a lot of tables and chairs might be the only positive beyond the location making it more convenient for more people to attend.

"I try to focus on the positive whenever I can." Stella raised a shoulder in a little shrug. "There's not much point in focusing on the negatives. I'm far more productive when I look at the bright side."

"The bright side to having the party in the cafeteria is that we aren't having to eat the food, as well." Aiden snorted. "Some days the food looks three days old, other days, it looks like they forgot to kill it before they served it."

Stella wiped away a tear as she laughed. "Hospital food isn't very good, no matter which side of the ocean you're on."

A lock of her dark hair tumbled down into her eyes. Aiden brushed it back for her, tucked it behind her ear. His fingers trailed down along the side of her jaw, savoring the feel of her soft skin under his fingertips. He'd been aching to do so for days.

"You are so beautiful."

When she leaned into his touch instead of withdrawing, he moved in to kiss her. His lips grazed hers, tempting, teasing, waiting for her to tell him to stop. She didn't. His arms slid around her waist and pulled her in closer so that he could deepen the kiss.

"And when you're an outsider dating a medical professional you run the risk of them finding a romance at the hospital," a voice cut in, interrupting an otherwise perfect moment. "Stella and I have been dating for a year and a half. She's been here several weeks now, and as you can see she has found her way into another man's arms."

Aiden looked up.

Oliver stood a few feet away, his camera on a tripod

pointed in their direction. He spoke in the direction of the lens. "Romances run rampant in hospitals. Though with the hours they work, most find that they don't have time to meet anyone outside the hospital. Stella and I met on set. It was a whirlwind romance, but I suppose I was more invested than she. I suppose I should be happy that she's not wearing my ring while kissing him."

Aiden looked down at Stella, confusion clouding his mind. He'd never seen a ring on Stella's hand. Not wedding nor engagement. If he had, he'd never have asked her out in the first place. At least he'd like to think he wouldn't have. The chemistry they shared had him doing things he'd never believed he would.

When she didn't say anything, he found himself asking, "His ring?" He winced at the crack of emotion in his voice.

"You didn't know we're engaged?" Oliver asked, glee evident in his voice. Other than sneaking glances at them, Oliver continued speaking to the camera. "We're all set to spend the holidays with my mum and dad too. Wedding planning, you know."

Aiden took a step back.

Stella was shaking her head, tears in her eyes, but she didn't actually deny any of what Oliver had said.

What else could he do but take the man at his word? And though his heart was breaking, he walked away from Stella.

CHAPTER EIGHTEEN

"REALLY, OLLIE?" STELLA finally found her voice. As usual, she froze at the moment of conflict and now it might have cost her everything. From the pain in Aiden's eyes, now wouldn't be the time to chase him down and try to force the conversation. Instead of tracking him down, she spun and stomped over to turn the camera off.

Striding up to her ex-boyfriend, she stopped in front of him and snapped, "Why can't you let me be happy? Is it simply because I'm not with you?"

"It's always been you and me, love." Oliver shrugged. "You simply needed the reminder."

Stella tilted her head and scrutinized him. This wasn't Oliver's idea. He'd never been so calculating. "Who put you up to this?"

"No one," he said, but she heard the lie in his words.

She could see her mother's handiwork behind his actions. "My mum," she said.

"Our mothers thought we should give it another go. My mum's mad about you. And you know yours has always been gone for me, as well." He spoke like their mothers should have supreme say over their lives forever.

Her mother had made far too many decisions over

the years without Stella's input. Stella had gone along with a lot for the sake of peacekeeping, but this was too far. No more.

"I don't care if the queen herself thinks we're a perfect match—there is no us. We are over and we will not be giving it another go."

"No?" Oliver asked, looking confused. "But—"

"There are no buts to this situation. I am not interested in giving it another go. I don't want to be with you. Ollie, you aren't a bad guy, you just have no spine. Find someone who loves you enough to stand up for you when your mom tries to push her about. That woman is not me though. Go home. Please."

She walked away, so angry at herself. Interference from her mum was something she should have expected. Debra Allen had been sticking her nose into Stella's business from the time she was born. Even the ocean couldn't provide enough of a barrier to keep the woman from meddling.

Stella's heart ached knowing she'd probably lost Aiden for good now. The look in his eyes when he'd walked away had been so hurt. He'd believed every lie that Oliver had spewed. It had certainly helped that she'd stood there next to him, gaping like a fish and unable to deny the accusations thrown at her. What else could he do but believe Oliver when she'd been incapable of even defending herself?

No, this one was on her. She may not be able to fix things between her and Aiden, but she had to stand up for herself once and for all.

When she got somewhere that afforded her some privacy, she pulled out her phone and called her mother. It was nearly bedtime there, but she didn't care if she woke her. What she had to say could no longer wait. She really should have done this years ago.

The call connected and Stella didn't wait for a greeting. "Really, Mother?"

"Stella, darling, how are you? Is something wrong? Bit late to be ringing for a chat, not that I'm not happy to hear from you."

Stella strode from one end of the room to another. "It wasn't enough for you to force me into a lifestyle I never wanted, but now you've taken away the future that I do want."

Her mother faked innocence. "How could I—"

"You know exactly what I'm talking about. Having Ollie announce that we're engaged and planning our wedding over the holidays on camera!" Stella paced, her ire rising with every step. "This is your signature move—wait until I'm happy and then ruin everything."

"Stella, this is no way to talk to your mother," her mum huffed, breath loud as it blew over the phone's microphone. "Your accusations are—"

"True. My accusations are completely valid and true." Stella squeezed the bridge of her nose and fought back tears. She really hated confrontation, particularly with her mum, but she'd reached her breaking point. It was time that she stood up for what she wanted in life. "Listen carefully, as I'm only going to say this once. My love life is not under your purview. My career is no longer under your control. And if you cannot respect those boundaries, then I can and will remove you from my life entirely. I'm done."

So done.

"Goodbye, Mum," she said, hanging up without giving her mother time to say anything else.

Having the entire Atlantic between them was the

best thing about their relationship at the moment. If she were on the same continent as her mother, she'd be tempted to move away.

That was it!

Inspiration hit and she knew exactly what she had to do. Things might be over and done with Aiden, but she had one last shot at happiness. And she wasn't going to give up without taking it.

Now she needed to get Dr. Stone on board with her plan.

When Aiden got home with Jamie, his mom looked up from her sewing.

"Is Jamie okay?" she asked, frantically packing her supplies away. "The day care could have called me. I only worked a half day today. I should have just gone by there and picked him up."

"He's fine, Mom."

She stood and moved closer. Testing the temperature of Jamie's forehead against the back of her hand, she nodded when she confirmed he had no fever.

"Are you sick then?" She treated him to the same temperature check.

"Mom!" He stepped back and out of reach before she decided to do more than check his temperature. "I'm fine."

"You're not." She tilted her head and scrutinized him. "But I'm thinking this isn't a physical ailment."

He sighed and sank down onto the couch with Jamie still in his arms. Hugging his son close, he tried to convince himself that Jamie was all he needed to be happy. Millions of people were happily single. He had been happily single up until a certain British doctor squared off with him at the airport. Now nothing about being single made Aiden happy.

"Jamie, buddy, whatever else happens in this life, I promise you that Daddy will never leave you." He kissed the top of his son's head. "No matter what."

"Is this about Stella?" his mom asked as she sat beside him. Worry lined her face.

"It doesn't matter." Reclining his head back, Aiden closed his eyes. Always so perceptive, his mother. He'd never been able to get much past her. He hated that he was adding stress to her life again.

"I think it does. I've never seen you like this over a woman." She brushed his hair back gently like she used to do when he was a child. "Britney made you feel a lot of things, but I don't think it touched this level, did it?"

Britney had evoked a lot of emotional responses in him. With her, the dominant emotion had been anger, leading to an ever-deepening rage that time had yet to fade. Following the anger had been bouts of disappointment and sadness. Yet he'd never felt as lost as he did knowing that Stella's heart belonged to someone else. With Britney, most of the emotions had been tied to how her actions had affected their son. It had never hurt his heart.

"She's engaged, Mom. And she doesn't…" He glanced down at Jamie. "She doesn't have maternal feelings and I have paternal responsibilities."

Aiden tried to use words he didn't think Jamie would understand. Jamie had been asking to see Stella again as it was and finding out she didn't want to see him might crush the little guy. Jamie had been subjected to more than his fair share of disappointments throughout the years and Aiden wanted to minimize any letdowns that he possibly could.

"But you fell for her anyway."

He closed his eyes tight. "I didn't mean to."

"Most of us don't go out with the intention of falling in love, sweetie. Even when we begin a relationship, we take our time and keep our distance until we can't anymore. It's only when we let our guard down that love has a chance." She took his hand in hers. "I found your father when I had just broken up with my high school love. He asked me out and I couldn't think of anything I wanted to do less. But he was persistent, because he could see a future, even if I was blind."

"You didn't have so many obstacles."

"Maybe not, but no one said love was easy." She put her hand on his chest over his heart. "You've kept that heart of yours behind a ten-foot wall topped with razor wire. Consider what it was about her that convinced you to let her into your heart."

"I thought she was the one," he said quietly.

His mother stood up. "Jamie, I was thinking that this might be a perfect afternoon to have some ice cream. Can you think of anyone who might want to eat ice cream with me?"

Jamie nodded with a little smile and jumped down to follow her.

"Love finds us when we least expect it, Aiden." She looked down at him and smiled. "If you want her that much, fight for her. Love doesn't come around every day."

Love might not come around every day, but that didn't mean it was meant to be. She was engaged to her cameraman and going back to the UK in less than a week.

Her future wasn't in Toronto or at St. Matthew's Hospital. And it wasn't with him.

CHAPTER NINETEEN

STELLA STOOD NEAR the doorway watching the doctors and nurses of St. Matthew's Hospital mingle. It was December twenty-third and the Christmas party had arrived. She'd been anxiously awaiting the event to begin and now her nerves were about to get the best of her. If only she were more confident about what she was about to do.

This was her one and only shot to get everything she wanted. There was a chance that it might work, but it was also the biggest risk she'd ever taken in her entire life.

Stella made her way around the room admiring the decor. It was barely recognizable as the utilitarian cafeteria it had been just eight hours before. The tables had been clustered to one side and were covered with red-and-green tablecloths. In the center of each red table sat a small Christmas tree, while the green tables were graced with miniature Santas. Above the tables, tiny fairy lights flashed merrily.

Despite the festiveness of the room, and the general joviality of the crowd, Stella was struggling to be merry. She snagged a plastic wineglass filled with sparkling grape juice just to have something to do with her hands. The mulled wine would have really helped take the edge off her nerves, but they'd strict instructions to make it a no-alcohol party, sadly.

In one corner, there was a cookie-decorating station. Giggling kids of all ages crowded around, jostling each other playfully as they reached for bright icings and colorful sprinkles. Scanning their happy faces quickly, Stella had to bite back her disappointment when Jamie's face wasn't part of the crowd.

The carolers they'd hired gathered along the far wall. Their lovely harmonies added both cheer and ambiance. Stella moved closer to listen. As the melody washed over her, she breathed deeply, trying to steel her nerves for the change that was to come. And it would be coming, no doubt about it. One way or the other, by the end of this party, Stella would know if the changes would fall how she wanted.

To her surprise, people started dancing along to the Christmas carols. The darker middle of the room became an impromptu dance floor as couples swayed and laughed to the music. If only she could let go and dance like that...

Aiden still hadn't appeared. Stella tried to keep an eye out for him, allowing her gaze to drift back to the main entrance every time she caught the slightest movement. If he didn't show up, her plan wouldn't work. She needed him here.

Maybe she could page him?

"Stella! This is amazing!" Gemma wrapped her tightly in a hug. "I didn't think it was possible to transform this toast-bland cafeteria into a practical winter wonderland. The twinkling lights—oh, my heart, are they ever gorgeous!"

It had taken so many strings of lights to create this effect that Stella didn't even want to admit the number.

She'd spent half the night stringing up fairy lights so that they could leave off the overhead ones, but the atmospheric effect of the twinkling made it all worth it.

"Have you seen the cake yet?" Stella asked.

"It's too pretty to eat!" Gemma launched into exuberant praise over the cake and the rest of the decorations. Stella tried to pay enough attention to know when she should nod and when a more verbal acknowledgment was required, but she wasn't giving the conversation her all. The bulk of her focus was looking for one specific person.

Just as she was about to give up hope that he'd show on his own, Aiden walked through the cafeteria doors with some of the emergency department staff. Their eyes met. She gave him a slight smile that faded quickly when he looked away without acknowledging her in the slightest.

He wasn't going to make this easy on her.

She swallowed the last of the sparkling grape juice and wished it had been real champagne. A dose of liquid courage would have really helped in that moment. Sucking in a deep breath, she made her way to the microphone that had been set up at the front.

It was now or never.

"Happy Christmas, everyone. Most of you know me by now. I'm Dr. Stella Allen. I've been on loan here from London as part of The Kensington Project. You might also have seen me with a camera in hand or trailing behind me as I film a television special designed to showcase just how hardworking medical workers are, particularly through the holidays."

There was a slight murmur of agreement, but the crowd largely stayed quiet. They'd clearly all sided with the hometown guy. She had her work cut out for her.

"You're probably wondering why I keep blathering on and wishing I'd put a cork in it and let you enjoy your party."

A few yesses chorused back to her.

"I do plan on that—I promise. First, I have an announcement though. Oliver, do make sure you are filming this."

Oliver flashed her a wide smile and a big thumbs-up. The idiot likely thought she was going to announce their engagement just like he'd planned with her mum. He'd remained stubbornly hopeful even as she'd shut him down with every conversation.

Stella gathered her courage. Her next words would change her life.

"The close of this special program marks the realization of a goal for me—to tie my television past with my medical future. Now that I've accomplished that, I'm saying goodbye to television. This will be my last on-air appearance."

The noise in the crowd kicked up.

"Please, quiet, I've a bit more to say and then I'll leave you to enjoy the celebration." When the silence returned, Stella continued speaking. "Television has been good to me in many ways, but it's time for me to move on from that life."

Her heart pounded and there was a rumble of nausea low in her stomach, but she didn't let her nerves stop her. She had one more big revelation, the biggest of all. Seeking out Aiden in the crowd, she made eye contact with him before she publicly declared, "I've also decided to move to Toronto long-term. I hope you'll be welcoming as I join the orthopedic team here full-time in the New Year."

Stepping away from the microphone, she walked

across the cafeteria to Aiden. He stood next to the elaborate cake that she'd personally commissioned for this party. His expression was unreadable.

She'd never been more nervous. She'd just told the entire hospital and the world that she was moving to a new country, giving up a large portion of her career, and by walking straight up to him afterward, she'd effectively told everyone that her decisions were all for him. Everything was on the line.

She had no idea where things stood with him, but she was finally following her heart. He might reject her outright, but she'd forever regret it if she didn't try.

Holding out an embarrassingly shaky hand, she asked, "Would you like to dance?"

The cafeteria got so quiet that Aiden could hear Stella's heart racing. Or maybe that was his own. Cheeks blushing a deep rose, she maintained eye contact under his scrutiny and that of the entire Christmas party. Everyone they worked with stood watching, waiting to see if he'd accept her outstretched hand or slap it away in rejection.

It took a lot of courage for her to make a gesture that grand.

There'd been a dozen reasons Aiden hadn't wanted to attend this party. Stella making an extreme gesture to him in front of all of their coworkers hadn't even been on his radar. It was almost too much to process.

He grabbed her hand, but not to dance. He led her away from the cake that had a tiny ice rink on top of it with a miniature couple who had an even smaller little boy with them. Stella had taken care of ordering the cake alone, and now he thought he knew why. The scene on top was meant to remind him of their first kiss.

"I can't do this here." He walked out of the cafeteria, leading her along with him. He was not going to have this conversation in front of all of St. Matthew's and a camera. Far too many nosy coworkers had already been given far too much ammunition to gossip about without them hashing this out in the open.

Stella had just upended everything he'd thought she was going to say. He'd expected a speech, but a *Thanks for a good time—I'll always remember it fondly* sort of goodbye since she was scheduled to leave the next day. He'd expected to hear something about how hard the employees worked and how her program would finally give them a shred of the recognition they deserved.

The last thing he'd expected was for her to say she was staying in Canada. Or that she planned to quit television entirely.

He pulled her into an empty on-call room and slammed the door behind them. The wreath on the door jingled merrily as it fell to the floor from the force of the closure. He spun around and faced her. "Explain to me what just happened?"

"I'm staying," she said simply, as if that were enough of a response that it didn't require further explanation.

"I gathered that." He stared at her, trying to get answers from the expression on her face. The look in her eyes told him that he was missing something, something that should have been obvious, but for the life of him, he was struggling to pinpoint what. Nothing made sense. "What I don't get is why?"

"I rather thought that was apparent."

He stared at her, thoughts bouncing through his head faster than he could fully process. If he was coming to the right conclusion, then he could only think of one reason she might do something so drastic as to uproot her entire career by moving to Toronto and quitting television.

"You gotta give me something here, Stella, because my mind is racing and coming to all sorts of conclusions. I don't know if I'm way off base or if I'm reading the situation right." He swallowed hard when she simply stared at him with one raised brow. "Come on, Stella, give me some answers here."

She shrugged delicately, but the tiniest glimmer of worry cracked through her facade. "I'm moving across the ocean for you. Do you think maybe you could at least meet me part way here?"

Moving closer, he pressed his forehead against hers. He wanted so badly to kiss her and it took every bit of his self-control to keep from doing so. She'd made this big gesture, and it was an amazing thing, but it didn't alter the biggest obstacle keeping them apart.

"I was hoping that's what you meant. But, Stella, you gotta know that nothing's different for me. I'm still a single father. That's not changing."

"I'm aware. When Oliver gave his little speech about us being engaged, and I saw the look on your face, I knew I'd lost you. That's when it dawned on me that I might never see Jamie again either. That realization nearly broke my heart. I never thought I wanted to be a mum, but I do want to be Jamie's mum, or at least stepmum." Her voice choked up with emotion. "I don't think I can walk away from that little boy, or his dad. I've fallen in love with you both, you see."

He wanted to focus on the positives in her speech, he really did, but the mention of her cameraman set his nerves on edge. He didn't want to think of the two of them together, but he had to know. He couldn't move forward with Stella if she remained involved with another guy.

"What about your engagement to Oliver?"

"Nonexistent. Dreamt up as a ploy by my mother to keep me under her control. But that's done, as well. Moving to Canada is my chance to get everything I want."

"And what exactly is it that you want?"

"To be an orthopedic surgeon and live a quiet life with the man I love and his adorable son, assuming you will give me another chance." Her fingers trailed along his jaw before gently tracing his lower lip. "I'm here for the long term. If I have to rebuild your trust, I will do so, even if it takes time."

Aiden couldn't wait any longer. He dipped down and pressed his lips to hers. He poured all the love he had for Stella into that kiss. Within her embrace, he found hope for the future.

When they broke apart for air, Stella laughed. "Now I really do have to cart everything I own across the ocean."

"And I won't even complain about it this time."

EPILOGUE

Six months later...

"I GOT YOU a pwesent, Stella," Jamie said as he tossed a small, brightly wrapped box into her lap. "It's fwom me and Daddy. Happy birfday!"

"Oh, it's from you both?" She picked up the color-ful little package and shook it gently. No rattle. *Hmm.* "Shall I open it now?"

"Yes!"

She carefully peeled the paper off. Her heart rate kicked up when she pulled back the wrapping to re-veal a small jewelry box. She popped open the lid and a beautiful diamond ring sat nestled into the velvet lin-ing. She stared at it for a moment, not quite believing what she was seeing.

When she finally looked up, she met Aiden's steady gaze. He got down on one knee in front of her. Jamie wobbled a bit but got down next to Aiden and copied his pose. How cute were they?

Tears welled up in Stella's eyes at the sight.

"Dr. Stella Allen, will you marry me?"

"And me?"

"Yes, of course!"

Aiden took the ring from the box and slid it on to her finger. It was perfect. "I love you, Stella."

"I love you." She leaned forward and kissed him gently. How had she gotten so lucky? "I never expected when I agreed to participate in The Kensington Project that I'd get so much out of it. I thought I'd find a bit of a career boost, make some new professional connections and finally make that TV program. Falling in love wasn't even a consideration, but then I met you."

"Your career didn't quite benefit though," Aiden said, a bit of a wince on his face.

"My medical career will be fine," she reassured him. She'd already settled into a permanent position in orthopedics at St. Matthew's and it had been strongly implied that she'd be in line for the head-of-department position when Dr. Devlin retired. She'd made a quick trip back to the UK to settle her affairs, but she hadn't been able to get back to Canada fast enough. Toronto had quickly become home for her, and it was entirely due to the people. "Getting out of the film industry was a choice I made that I will never regret."

"I can't believe your documentary has already been nominated for an award," Aiden said as he slipped his hand over hers.

"It has been very well received. Of course, it certainly helped that Martin was amenable to cutting out Oliver's ridiculous voice-over and replacing it with the scene where I announced that I was moving to Toronto."

"The farewell to Dr. Stella Allen, former child prodigy, caught a lot of attention."

Giving up her television career hadn't really been a loss, but it had certainly lent a perspective to all that she'd gained. The man sitting at her side was even better than she could have dreamt of. An adorable child sat happily at their feet playing with a toy truck. And across the room were Aiden's parents. The Cooks had brought her into their home with an openness that astounded her. Their visible love for their son and grandson made Stella even more aware of the distance between herself and her parents.

"The personal gains were worth any potential stall my career might face due to the move. I finally feel like I'm part of a family. A real family. Obviously, I had a family, but, oh, I'm not explaining myself very well."

"I get it." Aiden gave her hand a reassuring squeeze. "I spent years wondering why my birth mother abandoned me. Why I wasn't enough. Those insecurities kicked back up when my son was also abandoned."

"You are more than I ever hoped for," his mom said. Love for her family lit up her face. "I hope you know that."

"I do." Aiden flashed his mom a smile. "And you were the best mom that a nine-year-old foster kid could ever hope for. It took me a while to get out of my own way, but I finally realized that family doesn't have to be biological. It shouldn't be something you force out of obligation. Family should be something you choose."

"You are so very right." Stella leaned her head against his shoulder and sighed happily, knowing she'd made the right choices. "Family is not about blood—it's about love."

* * * * *

A FESTIVE FLING
IN STOCKHOLM

SCARLET WILSON

MILLS & BOON

This Christmas story is dedicated to
my two weddings of 2021,
Dillon and Megan Glencross, and Stuart and Carly Walker.
Two beautiful brides and two gorgeous grooms.
Wishing you all the love in the world.

CHAPTER ONE

CORA CAMPBELL WALKED briskly down the long corridor of the Royal Kensington Hospital, wondering if biting her nails might be an option. Her pager had already sounded twice.

As a neonatologist she'd spent the last twelve years of her life listening to the sound of a pager—at some stages it had almost dictated her life. Usually she welcomed it. It meant she was needed. She would be busy. She would be serving the tiny patients to whom she'd dedicated her life. But this time was different. This time it was Chris Taylor, the chief executive of her hospital, paging her, and her stomach was doing uncomfortable flip-flops.

She had to be in trouble.

The long walk wasn't helping. It was giving her lots of time to contemplate all the trouble she could be in. She'd signed for new state-of-the-art incubators last week. She'd authorised two extra staff to work over Christmas, because the same old faces went 'off sick' every year at that time. She promised one remote teaching session a week with a prestigious US hospital. She'd just had her fifth professional paper published on a new pioneering technique she'd introduced last year for neonates between thirty-one and thirty-three weeks. The before and after was quite astonishing, and right now she was wondering if the before had unintentionally shown the hospital in a bad light.

She glanced down as she neared the office. Maybe she should have gone back to her locker and put some heels on for a more professional look? Cora always tried to be dressed in a presentable manner at work, comfortable black trousers, a short-sleeved unfussy red top and her trademark shoes. A fellow doctor had introduced her to them at the conference in the US: flat, and completely machine washable, they were as comfortable as slippers and came in a rainbow of colours—all of which Cora had promptly purchased. They were also a dream when running the miles of corridors to an emergency page.

'Hey, Cora.'

Lucy, the chief executive's PA, was sitting behind her desk beaming like the Cheshire Cat. This didn't look like the sign of trouble.

'How's Louie?' Cora asked automatically. 'Can I see a photo of my favourite boy?'

Lucy grabbed her phone from her bag and immediately turned it to face Cora. Her son Louie had been born at twenty-six weeks, two years previously. Cora had looked after him, and always liked to check on his progress.

A sticky face and wide smile beamed up at her. Louie had a shock of blond hair, and a twinkle in his eye. He was also holding a crayon and had clearly just drawn on a white wall.

'Oh, no! The cheeky wee devil. When was that?'

'Sunday,' Lucy said with a smile as she stuffed the phone back in her bag. 'The decorator had just finished the hallway, and Louie decided he wanted to decorate too.' She shook her head. 'I swear, I just turned my back for second. He'd been sitting right next to me eating a yoghurt.'

Cora laughed and nodded. 'What can I say? He's just trying to keep you on your toes.' She winked at her. 'We teach them lots of tricks in NICU.'

She knew Lucy had worried endlessly about her early arrival. But although Louie was still a little small, he was meeting all his milestones with bells on. Cora shifted on her feet and glanced at the closed door. 'So, spill, am I in trouble?'

Lucy widened her eyes, in the way that only a person who knew everyone's secrets could. 'Dr Campbell, what on earth could you be in trouble for?' There was an edge of humour to her mocking tone.

Cora shrugged. 'I thought of nearly half a dozen reasons on the way down the corridor. You really should persuade him to move office. It would be much better for my fear factor if he were situated right next to the stairs.'

Lucy laughed and shook her head as the intercom on her desk sounded. 'That's for you.' She gave her a wink. 'And I don't think you've got anything to worry about.'

Cora sucked in a deep breath and walked over to the door, giving it two knocks before she pushed it open and stepped inside.

Chris Taylor rose to his feet and extended his hand towards her. Cora was immediately struck by the enormous window and the view of London outside. Even though she'd worked at the Royal Kensington for years she'd only ever been in this office on a few occasions. She smiled nervously and shook his hand. 'I would never get any work done in here. I'd be too busy people watching.'

His normally serious face broke into a smile as he

shook his head. 'I don't believe that for a second. You never stop working, Dr Campbell.' He lifted something from his desk. 'As your newly published peer-reviewed paper demonstrates.'

Darn. He'd read it. That must be why she was here. 'Oh, about that. I don't think you should concentrate too much on the before. The Royal Kensington still demonstrated an excellent level of care.'

One eyebrow arched. 'As I would expect,' he said smoothly.

Cora fought the urge to clear her throat and shift in her seat, conscious it would make her look guilty of something. Chris Taylor placed the medical journal back on his desk and clasped his hands in front of him. This was it. This was the position he frequently assumed in press conferences when he was about to deliver news.

'Dr Campbell, I invited you here today in part—' he nodded his head at the journal '—because of your latest publication, and in part, because of an offer I'd like to make to you.'

An offer? Cora immediately straightened in her chair, every cell of her body on alert. An offer was good—right?

'You've been with us a while, so I take it you've heard of the Kensington Project?'

Cora almost choked. 'Yes, of course.' Everyone who worked at the Royal Kensington knew about the Kensington Project.

It was obviously the correct answer because Chris gave a gracious smile. 'You know that we think of ourselves as being home to the best and brightest in the world. Every year we send four of our pioneering team members out to train staff in other hospitals across the world. This year, we'd like you to be one of those members.'

Something was wrong. Her skin was tingling as if a million centipedes were marching over it. Her mouth had just decided she was stuck in the Sahara Desert, and the thirty-three years of knowledge and experience her brain stored had just vanished in a puff of a magician's wand.

Chris was obviously waiting for some kind of response.

She'd wanted this. She'd wanted this for the last few years, and last year had been sadly disappointed when she'd heard that four others had been selected. She'd gone to a nearby bar with her good friend Chloe and they'd both had a glass of wine to commiserate.

This year though, between her teaching, her research paper, and the maternity leave of a colleague, she hadn't even had a chance to watch the calendar and wonder when the announcements might be made.

Chris was still patiently looking at her, as red London buses and black cabs whizzed by outside.

'Fabulous.' It came out almost as a squeak.

Satisfied, he continued. 'We've had a request from…' he consulted a list on his desk '… Stockholm City Hospital in Sweden. They'd like you to train a wide range of their neonatal staff on the pioneering techniques you developed while working at the Royal Kensington.'

She heard the hidden unspoken message. They might be her techniques, but credit would always have to be given to the hospital that had supported her. Cora didn't mind. The Royal Kensington had frequently put their money and trust in her over the last few years, when she'd outlined plans for improvement, both small and large. Her success rate was good. And even when a few things hadn't quite achieved their goal, there had always been learning for all those involved.

Excitement fizzed down inside her. This was an honour. A privilege to visit another country and teach them first-hand all the techniques she'd learned. Stockholm. Sweden. She'd never been to either before and that added even more to the excitement.

Chris kept talking. 'If you choose to accept, then you'll leave in three days' time—the first of November.'

'Three days?' If he heard the note of alarm in her voice, Chris Taylor showed no sign of acknowledgement.

'The arrangements are in place. You'll be flying into Arlanda Airport and we've arranged for you to be picked up and taken to your accommodation. You'll be there for just over seven weeks, flying home on Christmas Eve. I trust these arrangements will be suitable?'

Cora nodded. Her brain was kicking back into gear and she had a million questions.

'Who will I be working with? Do I get to take any of my equipment?' She frowned. 'How do I transport hospital equipment? Where will I be staying? Who are the others involved in the Kensington Project this year?' She paused to catch her breath. 'You said they requested me? Is that usual? Is that how this normally works?'

She caught the gleam in Chris Taylor's eyes and realised exactly how she must sound.

She gave a short laugh and a shrug. 'What's the weather like in Stockholm?'

There was silence for a few moments and Chris tilted his head to one side. 'Is that a yes, Dr Campbell?'

She jumped to her feet as he stood and held out his hand again. 'Yes!' she said, shaking his hand with an overenthusiastic grip. 'That's definitely a yes.'

He smiled. 'In that case, Lucy has a number of details for you that she prepared earlier. I think it's safe to say you're in very good hands.'

Cora didn't doubt it for a second. Lucy was meticulous with her work.

She let his hand go and moved back to the door. 'Thank you. Thank you. I'll check the rota. I'll need to make sure there's enough cover at short notice. I'll speak to Ron in Medical Physics about the transport and review all my patients.'

As her hand closed on the door handle she realised she was babbling again.

'Dr Campbell?'

Chris's amused voice came from behind her. She looked over her shoulder. 'Yes?'

He glanced at her red flats. 'Buy some winter boots.'

'I have wonderful news!' The door to Jonas Nilsson's office burst open with a bang and Elias Johansson came into the room, his eyes sparkling and his smile wide.

Jonas looked at the mark on the wall and shook his head. Elias's enthusiasm for work had never changed in the ten years that he'd known him.

He was seventy and should have retired years ago, but Stockholm City Hospital's Head of Neonatal Intensive Care was showing no signs of slowing down.

Jonas nodded to the chair across from him. 'What have you been up to now, Elias?' he asked.

Elias gave a hearty laugh as he flopped onto the chair. 'What makes you think I've been up to something?'

Elias glanced at the calendar. 'Because it's… Wednesday? And on any weekday, and on some weekends, you're usually up to something within this hospital.'

'Don't ask permission, proceed until apprehended.'
Elias smiled, with a wave of his hand.

Jonas put down his pen and leaned forward. This was
a favourite quote of Elias's and generally meant trouble.

'I'll ask again,' he said with one eyebrow rising,
'what have you been up to?'

'You've heard of the Kensington Project?' Elias continued without waiting for a reply. 'I put in a request for
a doctor from the Royal Kensington Hospital in London
to come to Stockholm City to teach us some of her new
pioneering techniques in NICU, and I found out earlier
today that my request has been successful. I'll be picking Cora Campbell up at the airport in a few days' time.'

Jonas opened his mouth and closed it again, trying
to formulate his words carefully. 'What? Who? And
no, I've never heard of the Kensington Project—what
on earth is it?'

Elias's eyes twinkled. 'An opportunity. That's what it
is. An opportunity for us to borrow one of their best—
and most published—neonatal experts to come and
share her expertise and knowledge with us. What's
better, she'll be here right up until Christmas. Can you
imagine how much we can learn from her?'

Jonas frowned. 'I have no idea who this woman is.
Do we want to learn from her?' He could feel himself
getting angry. He was very fond of Elias, but the older
he got, the more he meddled.

'Of course, we do!' He winked at Jonas. 'And who
knows? Maybe she'll learn something from us. She
might even want to do some joint research projects.
Now, that *would* be exciting.'

Jonas took a deep breath. As he was Head of Midwifery this new arrival would affect his work schedule
for the next seven weeks. He was in charge of the nurs-

ing and midwifery staff attached to the NICU. A new doctor might want to teach new techniques. Coming from London, she would be unfamiliar with the standards and guidelines, procedure manuals and cross-check of training that Jonas insisted was adhered to within *his* NICU—because that was how he thought of it.

Jonas was a stickler for regulations and paperwork. Having been burned early on in his career, he wanted to protect both his staff and their patients. He knew just how important that was. Every t was crossed, and every i was dotted. He had high expectations of his staff and they all knew it. Woe betide anyone who fell below his standards.

But Jonas had good reason for feeling as he did. A harsh lesson had made him realise how important rules were, as well as listening to instincts. That was what he'd done years ago when treating a patient in the final stages of labour. She'd been insistent in her birth plan that she did not want a Caesarean section unless there was no other option. Surgery as a teenager had left her feeling traumatised and she didn't want to feel that way again. Having a natural birth would mean she would feel in control and Jonas had been with her all the way. Jonas always promised his patients he would do his absolute best to help them stick to their wishes. But when the condition of her baby had deteriorated rapidly, he'd had to move quickly and follow his instincts, advising her that she needed to undergo a Caesarean section. His instincts had been right. All other professionals had agreed.

But when the woman had been diagnosed with postnatal depression following her delivery and made a complaint that he had let her down, Jonas had been overwhelmed with guilt. His actions had saved the lives of both mother and baby. But he still felt responsible for letting his patient down. His emotions got in the way.

The investigation had shown he'd made the right call. And even though he'd acted on instinct, the hospital policies and his rapid note-taking of all events had saved him. From the first time the baby's heart rate had dipped, Jonas had followed every rule to the letter.

That was why he was now the way he was. Rules, policies and standards protected staff against any complaint—if they followed them to the letter. He also tried to ensure staff weren't ruled by their emotions. He knew how deeply he'd been affected by his own, and had always done his best to stay detached from his patients ever since. He could listen to them, treat them well, and be an utter professional, ensuring a high standard of care, but he couldn't ever let his emotions get in the way.

'You should have discussed this with me first.'

'Maybe.' Elias gave a careless shrug. 'But I've put in a request to the Kensington Project for the last ten years.' He wrinkled his nose and looked thoughtful. 'I'm not quite sure what tipped the balance in our favour this time around.' He smiled again. 'But I did write five thousand words about why I specifically wanted Cora Campbell.'

Jonas groaned. This was always going to be a losing battle. He knew exactly what would happen. Elias would happily entertain Dr Campbell every morning, but by mid-afternoon he'd start to flag and arrange for other people to keep Dr Campbell entertained.

Jonas didn't have time to entertain anyone. His job was busy enough, and one of his senior staff was starting early maternity leave in the next few days due to some complications. They hadn't found a suitable replacement.

'Where is she staying?'

He was asking the question, but Jonas had a creeping sensation that he knew the answer.

'With me, of course!' said Elias. I have plenty of space and I'll get the opportunity to show her the festive activities of Stockholm.' He rubbed his hands together. 'I'm quite looking forward to it—the opportunity to see our own city through someone else's eyes. I think it will be good for me.'

Suspicions confirmed. Somehow, he'd known that Elias would offer to host the visiting doctor. He'd rambled around his large home on the outskirts of Stockholm for the last few years, ever since his wife had died. Both of Elias's children were married with children of their own, and lived in other parts of Sweden. Jonas knew that Elias was lonely. He was sure it was part of the reason that Elias refused to retire.

Jonas sighed. 'Tell me again, when does she arrive?'

'November the first. I'm picking her up at Arlanda airport at two p.m.'

'Are you bringing her straight to the hospital to show her around, or taking her home first?'

'Oh, taking her home first. Give her some time to settle in, then probably take her out to dinner in one of the restaurants at night. You'll join us, of course?'

Jonas shook his head, an automatic reaction. He wasn't entirely comfortable with the idea of some new doctor coming into his unit to teach them 'new' things. The last thing he wanted to do was make small talk with the woman.

No. He'd rather meet her on his terms, in his professional setting. That way, he could be clear about boundaries, and the fact that anything that happened in the

NICU involving any of the nursing or midwifery staff, had to be run past him. There. He felt better already.

'I'd prefer to meet her the next day. When she's had a chance to relax and get her bearings. She'll probably be tired after travelling.'

Elias wagged his fingers at him. 'Excuses, excuses. All work and no play makes you a very dull boy, Jonas. When was the last time you went out for dinner? Threw a party?'

Jonas laughed and leaned back in his chair. 'There are enough people in this hospital already throwing parties without me joining in. Did you see the state of some of the medical and nursing students last week? I sent three of them home.'

Elias tutted. 'Finest days of my life. I love a good party,' he said wistfully.

'I'll meet her the day after,' Jonas said, in the vain hope it might lodge somewhere in Elias's brain.

Elias's page sounded and he glanced down. 'I have a patient. Here.' He pushed forward the pile of papers he'd been carrying. 'Read up on our visiting guest. You might find something interesting. We can talk later.'

Jonas smiled and shook his head as Elias left. He knew exactly what the old scoundrel was up to. Every six months or so, he got it in his head to play match-maker between Jonas and whoever he thought might be a suitable companion.

Most of his matchmaking attempts had been in vain. Two or three had lasted more than a few dates, maybe even lasting for a couple of months. But Jonas was too involved at work to invest in a relationship and all of the not-quite-right women had grown frustrated and drifted off.

He pushed the papers to the side, instead pulling up the rota for the NICU on his computer.

He wanted to check who would be on duty at the start of November. He trusted his experienced staff to be able to deal with the new doctor in a polite but efficient way. He might have a quiet word in the ear of some of the other physicians. As he glanced to the side, he caught the title of a research paper: *The Basis of Hypothermic Rescue in Twenty-Six-Week-Old Neonates*. Interesting. He was just about to pull it out when he heard a yell.

'Help! Someone, help!'

Jonas was out of his seat in an instant. As he ran out of the door, he could see a nurse kneeling at the site of a collapsed body in the corridor.

No. No. He recognised the familiar shape instantly.

The nurse was relatively newly qualified. 'Good work,' he said quietly as he bent over the body. The nurse had put him into the recovery position, but it was clear it was Elias. Jonas checked his airway, breathing and circulation. He looked up at the nurse, putting a hand on her shaking arm. 'Maja, put out a treble two call.' There was a phone at the end of the corridor and she blinked and then got to her feet and started running.

Jonas stayed leaning over Elias. 'It's okay, Elias. I've got you. Just take some nice, deep breaths for me.'

He noticed the slight sag of one side of Elias's face immediately and his stomach gave a horrible ache.

Moments later there were thudding footsteps next to him, a portable monitor and trolley, along with a sliding sheet. Eight people moved Elias easily onto the trolley and Jonas walked alongside as they headed to the emergency department.

His head was already spinning. He knew both Elias's son and daughter. He'd make sure he was the one to phone them.

Seven hours later he was still in the hospital sitting by Elias's bedside. Initially, the emergency physician had suspected a stroke, but over the last few hours Elias had gradually regained consciousness and movement in his arm and leg. He was still groggy, his eyes were heavy and his mouth still drooping. His oxygen levels had also dropped slightly.

Elias's son, Axel, burst into the room, much in the way that Elias had burst into Jonas's office earlier. Jonas stood quickly and put his hand on his arm. 'He's okay. It looks as if he's had a transient ischaemic attack. They're going to keep him in and do a few more tests.'

Axel moved straight over to the bed and put his hand on his father's cheek. 'Pappa,' he said softly. 'I'm here.'

Elias's eyes fluttered open and he gave a soft smile, before they closed again.

Axel looked at Jonas. 'He has regained consciousness, but is very sleepy. It's the body's way of letting him heal. They are doing his neuro obs every hour and he's making gradual improvements.'

Axel finally seemed to take a breath. His coat was dotted with snowflakes and was damp in patches. 'Thank you, Jonas. Thank you for staying with him until I got here.'

'Of course. I would never have left him. Now you're here, I'll check and see if his doctor is around to talk to you.'

Axel looked around. He was an engineer by trade but knew his father well. 'What about this place? What about work?'

Jonas shook his head. 'Don't worry about a single thing. I can sort all of that out. If they think he's well enough in a few days, I can help you make arrangements to get him home and see if he needs anything.'

Something flitted across Axel's eyes. 'He was on the phone to me earlier, telling me about some doctor who is coming to stay with him. He was so excited about it. Will you be able to sort some alternative arrangements for that? I don't even know their name.'

'Leave it all to me.' The words came out instantly, even though Jonas was inwardly groaning. Getting cover for their head of NICU would be difficult enough, without the added responsibility of their international guest. Several of the other physicians had extended holidays before they hit the festive period, which was traditionally busy at Christmas. They still had strong staff numbers, but Elias's presence would definitely be missed.

'Thank you so much,' said Axel in obvious relief. He looked at his father with affection. 'I keep telling him he's too old for all this but he won't listen.' His face fell. 'Maybe he will now. I appreciate your help, Jonas.'

Jonas held out his hand. 'Let me know if you need anything.' He pulled a set of keys from his pocket. 'Here are the keys to your dad's house. I wasn't sure if you had a set, so I got them from his office. I'll find that doctor for you.'

The events weighed heavily on Jonas's shoulders as he left. He had complete confidence in the doctors and nurses looking after Elias. He just hoped the situation wouldn't become more serious. Elias was a mentor to him, as well as a verbal sparring partner. He enjoyed his company and respected his work.

As with any hospital, news would spread quickly and

Jonas would need to focus his efforts on making his staff feel supported within their working environment.

He collected his jacket from the locker room, pulled his hood over his head and walked out into the falling snow.

CHAPTER TWO

CORA HADN'T SLEPT a wink for more than twenty-four hours. After her initial news she'd dashed off to phone her friend Chloe, a neurologist who worked at the Kensington too. But Chloe had been in a meeting and phoned her back squealing with the news that she too was part of the Kensington Project and was on her way to Kingston in Jamaica.

Both were delighted and numerous calls of varying length happened over the next few days as they both tried to complete their workloads before leaving.

Cora had left lengthy instructions on the care of some of her babies, including follow-up plans if they were ready for discharge in her absence. She was meticulous about her work, and wanted to make sure nothing was left to chance.

There had barely been time to pack her case, and it had been as she was grabbing some jeans and a jumper to travel in that she'd looked down at one of her pairs of colourful shoes and realised they were totally inappropriate for Stockholm's potential snow and ice.

'Too late,' she sighed as she remembered Chris Taylor's words about winter boots. Running on adrenaline, she caught a cab to the airport. By the time she was checked in, she grabbed the latest crime thriller from the airport shop and a glass of wine from the bar, sipping nervously as she waited for her flight to be called.

Elias Johansson was Head of Neonatal Intensive Care at Stockholm City Hospital and had generously offered to pick her up at the airport and to host her for the next seven weeks.

Initially she'd been taken aback by his offer, but after looking him up online, and reading reports about him, then speaking to him briefly on the phone an hour after Chris had told her about Stockholm, she'd known she'd be in safe hands. He was so enthusiastic about her work. He'd read all her research papers and wanted his staff to learn from her. She couldn't help but be flattered by the experienced doctor's praise. By the time her flight was called, Cora was almost jittery with nerves. The flight was bumpy, with turbulence just outside Arlanda airport. It was a short flight, only two and a half hours from London, and she skidded as she walked from the plane to the terminal.

'I must buy boots,' she muttered to herself, wondering if there might be a clothing shop in the airport. She was shivering too, the temperature drop noticeable from the mediocre winter season that had just started in London. What she really wanted right now was a big fur-lined parka, rather than her loose green raincoat.

As she collected her luggage and walked through passport control and customs, she scanned the waiting faces, trying to pick out Elias from the crowd.

That was odd. She'd thought she would recognise his cheerful face. She pulled her phone from her pocket and checked she was getting a signal. Yip, she'd connected, just as her phone operator had promised, but there were no messages.

She looked around. Maybe she should have a coffee.

There was a good chance that Elias had been delayed at the hospital. The airport was more than thirty kilometres from Stockholm, so there could be a whole range of reasons for him being late.

'Dr Campbell?'

She jumped at the deep voice, then jumped again as she turned around and was met by the broad chest of a Viking.

'Y-yes,' she stuttered, looking up cautiously.

Okay, so she must be dreaming because this was clearly some kind of romance movie. This guy was too good-looking to be real.

'I'm Jonas Nilsson. I'm afraid I have some bad news.'

Well, that stopped the movie dream in its tracks.

'What do you mean?' She was confused, and, even though it was the middle of the afternoon, tiredness was hitting her in waves. What was it about even the shortest of journeys that could do that to a person? 'Where's Elias? He told me he would meet me here.'

A pained expression shot across the man's eyes. He really was a traditional Viking with bright blond hair and blue eyes. 'Unfortunately, Elias had a TIA a couple of days ago. He's just been discharged from hospital and will take some time to recover.'

'Oh, no.' She was a doctor. She knew instantly what a TIA was, and she was thankful that this man's English was impeccable, because the few words of Swedish she'd learned would be entirely inappropriate.

'Is he going to be okay?'

The man nodded solemnly. She could see the concern in his eyes and darned if it didn't make him even more attractive. 'We hope so. His son has come to stay with him. But in the meantime, your visit might not be how you intended. Would you consider rearranging?'

She blinked. She'd just travelled from London to Stockholm and was standing in Arlanda airport. Did he honestly expect her to rearrange?

'Who did you say you were again?'

He put his hand on his chest. 'Jonas Nilsson, Head of Midwifery at Stockholm City Hospital. Elias is a colleague of mine.'

She gave a thoughtful nod and looked Jonas in the eye. Head of Midwifery. It was likely that the Viking hunk would hang around the NICU frequently. Right now, she wasn't quite sure how well she could concentrate on work issues with this guy by her side. 'Well, Jonas, I'm assuming that, even though Elias is currently sick, the unit is still functioning at its usual high standard?'

It was a pointed question and she knew it. His response would be telling.

Sure enough, Jonas Nilsson bristled. 'Our neonatal intensive care unit is one of the finest in the country. We have a broad range of highly skilled staff.' Good. She'd annoyed him. She even liked the little spark of anger she'd seen flash across his eyes.

'Perfect,' she interrupted before he could continue. 'Then I'll do the job that Elias requested. I'll share my skills and train some of your staff in my techniques.'

It seemed that this statement caused an even deeper reaction than the last one.

Which was a pity. Because as he inhaled a deep breath, a waft of his aftershave drifted towards her, like a warm sea breeze. A sea breeze in which any easily distracted female could get lost.

'My staff are already highly trained, extremely conscientious individuals.'

She smiled. 'I'm sure they are. But Elias requested

my presence to share my expertise. I didn't come here for a holiday. I came here to work.'

It was a stand-off. And as she was a feisty Highland girl, this wasn't Cora's first rodeo. She'd dealt with more than one guy like this. A guy who seemed to think he could tell her what to do. Not a chance.

Jonas blinked his extraordinarily long eyelashes and had the good grace to remember she was, indeed, a guest.

He reached his long arm over and grabbed her case. 'Let me get you back into Stockholm. It takes around forty-five minutes. And we'll need to sort somewhere for you to stay.'

'Oh.' The word came out before she even had a chance to think. Of course. Staying with Elias would be out of the question. Jonas gave her a sideways glance as they reached the doors. It was a long walk to the car with very little conversation. Cora had the distinct impression that Jonas already thought of her as a nuisance.

She'd been so excited about coming here, seeing around the unit and training the staff. Getting introduced to a whole new country and city had made the whole project seem even more fabulous. She'd already searched and seen the pictures of Stockholm in the Christmas season. Christmas wasn't her favourite time of year, and she was glad to be away from London and be distracted by a new city. She'd expected the next few weeks to be amazing, but right now her hopes and expectations were sitting like a deflated balloon left behind when the party was over.

Part of the reason she'd dug her heels in so hard when he'd suggested she go back home was that she liked to avoid Christmas at home as much as possible. It brought back too many bad memories. The first, of being the child placed in the foster system two days before Christmas because there was no immediate placement available. No one wanted an extra unknown child at Christmas. It brought back painful memories of sitting in a quiet dormitory with a large decorated Christmas tree. And it was an agonising reminder that she was alone, and essentially unwanted. She had finally been adopted by wonderful parents, but had lost them both years later, so close to Christmas again. This time of year felt almost cursed to her. So the chances of her getting back on a plane and flying home were less than zero.

Jonas had a large four-by-four and he lifted her bright red suitcase into the back easily.

As they moved along the airport roads, she tried her best to fill the silence.

A male midwife. Interesting. And Head of Midwifery at one of the best hospitals in Sweden? No matter how grumpy this guy was, he must be good. Just a pity he was so darn attractive too.

'Can you tell me a bit about the unit?'

His eyes remained fixed on the road. 'We have twenty-five single rooms where families are encouraged to stay with their baby. The layout of all rooms is standardised so staff know exactly where everything is that they will require. Each neonate has their own team to provide consistent care. We have thirty doctors, and one hundred and ninety nurses and midwives. We use a colour-coded system to signify level of acuteness of our babies.' He gave her a sideways glance. 'As you know, Elias is our Head of Neonatal Care. He's responsible for the medical staff in the unit, and I'm in charge of the nurses and midwives.'

Ah...now she understood. When Elias had spoken

to her, he'd very much emphasised how it was a team approach to training in NICU—a principle that Cora had always agreed with. There was no point just training doctors in the techniques. In many units there were advanced neonatal practitioners who were often responsible for caring for the sickest neonates. Some of the experienced nurses she'd worked with over the years had more knowledge and skill in their pinkies than some of the doctors.

'I'm really looking forward to meeting the teams. Do you work much in the unit yourself?'

'Usually I'm in there two days a week. I like to make sure staff keep standards high.'

Cora shifted in her seat. Did he mean he spied on his staff?

He kept talking. 'My predecessor line-managed the staff in the unit with no supervision. It created…problems. I decided to be more hands-on. It also gives my senior staff a chance to fulfil their personal development plans and get study days if I'm there to be the supervisor on that shift.'

Ah. That sounded better. Cora nodded her head. 'I've worked with too many staff who miss out on some of the training opportunities they've wanted because units are short and they can't get time off.'

Did she imagine that, or was it a look of approval?

'Can you take me to a hotel somewhere in Stockholm, close to the hospital?'

He gave a nod. 'If you want, I could try and find you accommodation at the hospital. We have rooms for locum staff.'

She shook her head. 'But then I'm taking up a space you might need. As long as there are transport links to and from the hospital, any hotel will be fine.' She gave him a wary smile. 'You might need to let me take a few notes about the transport links before you leave.'

'What kind of place do you like?' he asked. 'Modern, traditional, boutique, luxury, or hidden away? Obviously, the hospital is picking up the bill, so price won't be a problem.'

There was obviously a correct answer to this question but Cora wasn't sure what it might be. She was here for seven weeks. She didn't want to end up in a youth hostel kind of place, or those very trendy places where you basically slept in a capsule that resembled a coffin with lights.

'Somewhere central,' she said promptly. 'I want to take the chance to see some of Stockholm. See the shops, eat in the restaurants. I've heard it's magical at Christmas and I'd like the chance to see some of that. Oh, and a comfortable bed. I definitely need a comfortable bed.'

For the tiniest second Jonas's eyebrow arched, and heat rushed into her cheeks. 'Oh!' She laughed self-consciously. 'I'm just tired. I've been awake for the last twenty-four hours. I was too excited to sleep last night. I keep leaving notes about some of my patients.'

The expression on his face softened. Finally. She'd said something that met with his approval. Thank goodness. She didn't want to spend the next seven weeks tiptoeing around this uptight guy. He was so hard to read. There had barely been a trace of emotion.

They were starting to move through the city now and Cora stared out of the window at the passing buildings and people. Everywhere was covered in a light dusting of snow. It really was a beautiful place.

Most people were wrapped much more warmly than she was. Before she even had a chance to think about the appropriateness of the question it was out of her mouth. 'Can you tell me somewhere I can buy boots and a new jacket? I didn't really have time to get equipped for the cold.'

'You want me to take you shopping?' His voice practically dripped with disdain and all of a sudden Cora was immensely annoyed. She'd had it with this guy. Cora had always been a girl with a tipping point. She could only grin and bear so much, and then her patience left the room and she let rip. Trouble was, the more annoyed she became, the thicker her Scottish accent got, and it was bad enough in London. Last time she'd lost it there, people had looked at her as if she needed subtitles.

She turned towards him. 'No. I don't want you to take me shopping. Just like I don't want to be treated like a major annoyance. Has anyone ever told you that it's time to work on your people skills? I'm truly sorry that Elias is sick, and you obviously feel you've been lumbered with me, but, funnily enough, I'm a fellow professional and I expect a little courtesy. If this is the way you treat all visitors to your unit, I'm surprised you have any visitors at all.'

The car came to an abrupt halt. She was still fuming. But after a few seconds, Cora wondered if he was about to throw her out of the car. He gave her a hard stare with those blue eyes. Finally, he spoke. 'Your hotel,' he said in a low voice, as if she should have known why they'd stopped.

She turned her head to the pavement and saw a uniformed man walking towards her car door. He opened it and spoke in rapid Swedish that went straight over Cora's head. 'Hi.' She smiled. 'Thanks so much.'

The man dropped into English easily. 'Welcome, madam, checking in?'

She glanced over his shoulder. The boutique-style hotel had glass-fronted doors and a dark carpet running over a light wooden floor. A warm glow came from the reception area, and there were a few large pink chairs scattered around, making it look welcoming. 'Yes, please,' said Cora.

'You have bags?'

Cora nodded and the man opened the boot of the car, pulled out her case and turned towards her. He gave her a wide grin and gestured his other elbow to her.

How charming. She threw a glance back at Jonas. 'Appreciate the lift. Sorry to be such a bother to you. But that—' she nodded towards the doorman '—is what I call a welcome.'

She got out of the car and slid her arm into the doorman's. 'Lead the way,' she said with a smile.

Jonas was stunned. By her rudeness. By her abruptness. By the sharpness of her tongue. By the glint in her green eyes. By the way the second he'd seen her at the airport, his breath had caught in the back of his throat. And by the way he'd treated her since he'd met her.

Cora Campbell was more than a little attractive. She was stunning. He'd never met a woman before who literally took his breath away. What was wrong with him? Elias would be ashamed of him. He knew how excited Elias had been about Cora coming here, and he had been annoyed at only finding out at short notice. But that wasn't Cora's fault. She'd travelled from London to a strange country, to be met by someone other than she had expected, only to find out her accommodation was no longer available.

He'd obviously added to the problem with his brusque manner. What was worse, he'd been completely aware he'd been doing it. He used to be a happy-go-lucky kind of guy, but now he was a by-the-book practitioner. He could count on one hand the number of people at Stockholm City Hospital who'd known him in the early days, so everyone now just accepted him for who he was. He knew he was uptight, but with Cora he'd just gone into overdrive. It was clear she was excited to be here, but he had the distinct impression she could wreak havoc on his orderly unit, with her brimming enthusiasm and plans to teach his staff.

But he was also completely conscious of her immediate impact on him. He was distinctly aware that he'd noticed every single thing about her—the few freckles across the bridge of her nose, the way she kept sweeping one piece of hair behind her left ear. The way her accent got thicker the angrier she got—or the more excited she got. Cora Campbell was *way* too attractive. Jonas had spent years keeping his emotions in check. Spending time around her would be difficult. What if his strong attraction to her distracted him from his job? He'd never dated anyone at work—and it was a rule he meant to stick to.

Truth was, if he'd known about her more in advance, he would have probably looked at the rota and scheduled sessions for her when staff would be free to learn and take part. But someone like Cora, with only a few days' notice, at one of their busier times, could cause disruption in a unit where calm and controlled were the order of the day. It looked as if he hadn't done too well with keeping his emotions in check this time, and his anxieties and annoyance had spilled over towards Cora.

He sighed. It was his duty, as a hospital representative, to make it up to her. He looked at the crowded streets. At four p.m. it was already starting to get dark.

He knew that Elias had booked a nearby restaurant to take her out to dinner on her arrival—he'd found the details amongst the papers Elias had left at his desk.

It was time to put this right.

The hotel was quite literally a dream and Cora couldn't have been happier as she lay in the middle of the deliciously comfortable, huge bed, wrapped in the snuggly dressing gown that had been on the back of her door.

Although the room wasn't oversized, its quirkiness appealed to her. There was a pink chaise longue under the window that looked out onto the busy streets. Thick curtains framed the window. Her bed was made up in rich white cotton sheets, but the duvet was thick, and a giant red comforter adorned the top of it.

Her suitcase was unpacked. The doorman had been great and given her a map of the surrounding area, a list of Christmas experiences to sample in Stockholm, a handwritten note of shops she might like, and restaurants to try. She couldn't have asked for more.

Well. Yes, she could. A warmer welcome might have been a bit better.

She wiggled her toes. Socks. Another thing to add to her list. Thicker socks. The wind had whistled past on the few short steps into the hotel and her feet were instantly cold. As were her arms in her green raincoat.

She rolled off the bed and moved to the chaise longue, staring at the street outside as she nibbled the plate of complimentary chocolates that the receptionist had given her during her unplanned check-in. It was such a nice touch.

There was a large store in the distance, with a variety of mannequins wearing thick jackets in the window. It might be a good place to start.

She was just contemplating what clothes to put on when there was a knock at her door. Cora frowned, and then brightened; this place had been so welcoming so far, maybe it was complimentary wine!

She opened the door and stared into a familiar broad chest.

Jonas took a step back and held up a large bag. 'Peace offering?'

'What?'

He held the bag out to her again and she reluctantly took it, putting a hand consciously to the top of her dressing gown as she bent down to look inside.

Green. Something green. She pulled out the item and her eyes widened in surprise. It was a thick green parka with a grey fur-edged hood. It took only a few seconds to realise this was a good quality item. It was lightweight, even though it was thick.

'You said you needed a jacket. I guessed your size. Sorry, couldn't do the same for boots, but I can take you to a shop if you want so you can get some for tomorrow.'

He was still standing in the doorway, filling most of the space. For some reason, she was reluctant to invite the man who seemed to exude sex appeal from his very pores into her room, worried about how she might actually react. Jet lag could do weird things to a person. In a flash in her head, she saw herself grabbing him by the jacket and throwing him down on her very comfortable bed.

'Elias had booked a restaurant to take you out to dinner tonight. The reservation still stands and it's only a few minutes' walk from here. I take it you haven't eaten yet?'

She was still holding her hand at the top of the hotel dressing gown, conscious of the fact she only had her underwear on. Her head was still in that other place where he was lying across her bed. She finally found her voice again. 'I was just thinking about it.'

He gave a nod of his head. 'Then why don't I wait for you downstairs and, when you're ready, I'll show you where to buy some boots and tell you a bit about the hospital over dinner?'

Cora swallowed, her throat a little scratchy. Now she'd seen her room, she kind of wanted to spend the rest of the night here in complete comfort, watching the world go by—obviously with room service too.

But Mr Antisocial was apparently making an effort. It seemed her earlier outburst had awakened his hospitable side. Thank goodness.

She took a deep breath and nodded her head. 'Give me five minutes.'

Jonas still wasn't sure about this. He actually wondered if she might just leave him sitting in the reception area for the rest of the night. But ten minutes later, Cora Campbell appeared in a pair of black trousers, a jumper and her new green parka.

Green was definitely her colour. It made her eyes sparkle. And he'd been right about the size. She looked perfect in it.

Cora was chatting to an older woman she'd met in the lift. It seemed that Cora was a people person, and they walked towards him talking like old friends.

He got up from his seat and nodded at the older woman as she left the hotel. 'Ready?' he asked Cora.

She gave a small nod and he could sense her hesitation. 'Thanks for the jacket. You shouldn't have done that. You have to let me pay you back. The doorman had given me a list of shops to try later.'

He shook his head. 'Take it as an apology and a welcome to Stockholm.' He gave a half-smile. 'But don't worry, I'll let you buy your own boots. They can cost the same as a small house.'

Cora's face brightened and as they walked outside she lifted the hood of her jacket. For a second, he was almost sorry he couldn't see her face properly now, but he gave himself a shake and guided her towards a crossing to reach the other side of the square.

As they walked around the edges and past a number of shops, he gave her a running commentary. 'Yes, no, maybe, definitely not, only for tourists, and the best bakery around.' He gave a non-committal shrug as they passed another.

Cora stopped and put her hands on her hips. 'Jonas Nilsson, you gave me the distinct impression earlier that you weren't much of a shopper.'

'I'm not. But I've lived here long enough to know where to go and where to avoid.'

He stopped at a shop with a large front window made of tiny panes of glass. It looked like something from the last century. 'This place is pretty unique if you're looking for a gift. Some carvings. Some glasswork. Paintings the size of the palm of your hand. And some unique jewellery. All done by local artists. Come back when you have some time.'

Cora nodded eagerly at the packed shop. 'I'll come back later in the week,' she murmured. 'It's the kind of place I could get lost in.'

They arrived at the boot shop and Jonas held open the door for her. 'This is the place that Nils, the doorman, recommended to me,' she said as they walked inside.

'I'm glad I'm managing to keep to his standards.' Jonas smiled.

Cora walked over to a wide range of boots and immediately started asking the saleswoman some questions. Jonas was happy to wait. At least she wouldn't fall over on her way to work the next day.

And that was what he kept telling himself as he watched her try on a few pairs of boots, before finally selecting a grey pair, fur-lined with suitably sturdy soles for walking in the freezing temperatures.

Cora was animated in all she said and did. The saleswoman was laughing and giving advice as they chatted easily. At one point, she nodded in his direction and Jonas felt a flush of embarrassment, wondering what had been said.

Finally, Cora gave him a bright smile before putting her own very flat and brightly coloured shoes in the large box that was meant for the boots and going to the cash register to pay.

She waved her card, then put her bags over her arm and dug her fingers deep in her pockets as they made their way outside.

'We should have got you a hat and gloves too,' he said.

She shook her head. 'I know how much you love shopping, Jonas. I think you've suffered enough for one day. Shall we go to the restaurant you mentioned?'

He took her to the restaurant, which was near the shipyard and had an interesting view of ships both young and old.

He could see her studying the menu. 'Would you like some recommendations?' he asked, knowing that Elias would have relished this kind of chat. It was something he wasn't generally used to. Jonas was perfectly capable of being a charming date if the desire was there, but he wasn't a man normally assigned the role of trying to charm a foreign visitor. He wasn't even entirely sure he could, when he didn't know exactly what Cora's role would be while she was here, and he still had that underlying feeling that she could disrupt the standards in his unit.

He pointed at two items on the menu. 'Depending on how you're feeling after your journey, I'd recommend this one. It's deep-fried smoked pork belly with turnip, chilli mayonnaise, crushed potatoes and sauerkraut. Or there's this one—herring with brown butter, chopped egg, potato salad, and pickled yellow beetroot and hazelnuts. Or, if you're feeling a bit delicate, I'd go for the grilled Arctic char with pine and butter sauce; you could have a side of smoked pumpkin with that if you wished.'

Cora leaned back in her chair and sighed. 'They all sound wonderful, and to be honest I'd like to try all three.' She took a sip of the white wine that she'd ordered. 'I'm here for seven weeks. I guess I'll get to try a bit of everything.'

The waiter appeared and Jonas waited until she'd ordered the herring, then ordered the pork belly and requested an extra plate. He could let her taste a little. And it was the kind of thing Elias might have done.

It was almost as if she'd read his mind. 'Have you heard any more about how Elias is?'

Jonas gave a nod and sipped his beer. 'I heard from his son this afternoon. Even though he's home, he's still very tired. A TIA for most people is a sign to slow down. He's been running on adrenaline for as long as I've known him. Apparently he was furious that his physician said he couldn't come back to work for at least six weeks—and then promptly fell asleep again.'

Cora drummed her fingers thoughtfully on the table.

He could see her thinking. 'What does that mean for the unit, if Elias couldn't come back?'

Jonas gave a wry laugh as his stomach twisted over. 'I can't imagine the unit without Elias at the helm.' He looked out over the water. 'But I guess I'll need to start. None of us are irreplaceable, no matter how much we think we are. And both Elias's son and daughter are married with families of their own. They don't stay in Stockholm any more, and I have a feeling that both will want him to move somewhere closer to them. Although they live apart, they're a very close family. Elias's wife died of cancer more than twenty years ago, and ever since then, his work and his children have been his obsessions.'

Cora drew in a kind of hitched breath. 'Family is what shapes us all,' she said with a tired smile.

Jonas nodded. 'For the last ten years, he's been like family to me too. But I know I have to step back and let his son and daughter be the ones to persuade him it might be time to rethink. If I said it—' he gave a small laugh '—he'd just be angry with me and give me a list of everything that currently needs sorting at work.'

'Can I help with that?'

Jonas drew back in his chair. It had just been a throwaway comment. 'Oh, no, sorry, I didn't mean anything by that. I wasn't trying to hint. I can assure you, the unit is run to impeccably high standards. You won't find anything lacking.'

He could feel his defences automatically coming down.

Cora gave him a look. The kind of look that told him that this woman could read him better than he thought.

'As you've guessed from the accent, I'm from Scotland,' she said, setting her wine glass firmly on the table. 'So, this isn't my first Highland Fling—so to speak. What I'm saying to you is—' she put her hand on her chest '—I'm a doctor. It doesn't matter what I'm here to teach, or to learn. I'm here for seven weeks. I'm not the kind of person to stand on the sidelines and watch, if I can help. In fact, I've *never* been that person. So, if you need help, rotas, supervision, teaching new medical staff the basic procedures in NICU, then use me.' Her fingers closed around the stem of the glass and the corners of her lips turned upwards. 'In fact, be warned: if you don't use me, I might just step in anyway.'

Talk about putting her cards on the table. 'You like to be frank?'

'It should have been my middle name.'

Jonas took a long drink of his beer. The smell of delicious food started wafting towards them.

'I only found out about you a few days ago. I had no idea Elias had asked for a visiting doctor to come to our hospital.'

He could see her taking stock of those words. If she was as good at reading people as he suspected, she would know there was a little resentment in there.

'I only found out a few days ago myself,' she answered in a slightly teasing tone. 'And I'm not a visiting doctor. I'm a specialist neonatologist, practising pioneering techniques.' The words rolled off her tongue and he wasn't sure if she was putting him in his place or taunting him further. No matter.

'It didn't help,' he added, 'that Elias has apparently requested you before through the Kensington Project. More than once, in fact.'

Now that clearly surprised her. Cora tilted her head to one side. The flickering candlelight in the restaurant made her all the more alluring—in a really annoying kind of way.

'I had no idea,' she said curiously. 'My research papers have only been published in the last few years. I mean, neonatology can be a small world. Everyone generally knows what everyone else is doing. I suppose he could have heard through one of my supervising professors.'

Jonas gave a small smile as the waiter approached with the plates. 'I sometimes wondered if the man ever slept.'

She gave a small smile. 'I spoke to him a few times by video chat. He was fun. So interested. Full of questions. I liked him.'

'And he clearly liked you too.'

Cora's eyes lit up at the plate crammed full of food. He took a few moments to slide some of his food onto a side plate and held it out to her. 'You said you wanted all three. Let's start with two.'

He thought she might refuse. Some women would have. But Cora grinned widely. 'Perfect,' she said as she accepted the small plate. 'Now at least I'll have to behave and not stick my fork into someone else's food.'

Jonas raised his eyebrows. 'Is that how things normally are?'

She'd already taken a small forkful of her herring. 'Delicious,' she sighed, then looked at him with laughter in her eyes. 'What, you were never a medical student, sharing a house with people who ate every item of your food anonymously? Or were the junior in a ward area where you're last to the canteen and only get the old withered leftovers?'

Now it was his turn to smile and nod. 'Actually,' he

admitted as he started on his pork, 'I was probably the food stealer.'

'I might have known that.' She shook her head, then waved her fork at him. 'You have that look about you. At least I'm…' she gestured to the small plate to her left '…upfront about it.'

She was obviously more relaxed now, but as their meal continued he could see she was clearly tired. It was odd. Sometimes he felt completely at ease around her, then she'd say one small thing, one throwaway comment, about teaching, or training, and he could feel every little hair on the back of his neck stand in protest.

'We should get you back to the hotel,' he said. 'Can you be at the hospital for eight tomorrow morning?'

She nodded. 'That's no problem.'

He raised one eyebrow. 'Just a tip, although the hospital food is fine, you might want to eat breakfast at the hotel. Their coffee is definitely better.'

'Noted. And what about tomorrow? Obviously I thought I was meeting Elias. Will I just meet with you, or is there someone else you want me to meet with?'

Jonas frowned. He hadn't really had time to think about it. 'Let's work on the assumption that our chief executive will want to see you at some point. Tomorrow will likely be introductions to the hospital, and its department and staff.'

'And who will help me with the training schedule?' She took the last sip of her wine. 'I'll need to see a list of the staff disciplines to work out who is most appropriate for what session.'

'No.' The word came out of nowhere.

Cora looked up in surprise. 'What do you mean, no? That's exactly why I'm here.'

Jonas was bristling again. 'I think we should discuss

the training elements once you've had your feet on the ground for a few days. Give yourself time to get a feel for Stockholm City Hospital. For the way things run in our NICU. For the staff, patients and parents.'

'You don't want me to upset the apple cart, do you?'

'Excuse me?'

She gave a wave of her hand. 'Sorry, it's a British expression. Probably doesn't translate well.' She folded her arms across her chest. 'Are you averse to change, Jonas? You don't look like a dinosaur. Do you think everything in medicine should stay the same?'

'Of course not,' he said quickly. 'I've been a midwife for fifteen years. There have been changes in practice throughout my career.'

Cora gave a knowing nod. It was maddening. 'Ah, I get it, you're a control freak. It's good to know. At least I know what I'm dealing with.'

She made the words sound so light, so flippant. As the waiter appeared with their coats, she slid her arms into the jacket that he'd bought her earlier.

She tapped the front of it. 'You picked the right colour. Green for go. That's how I am, and that's how I work. If you want to stop me doing the job that I came here to do, you'll have to be quick. And believe me, I can sprint like no other.'

She patted his arm in a way that made him seem like a child. 'Thanks for dinner. I think it's done both of us good. See you at eight.' Then she raised her eyebrows. 'Or maybe I'll get there before you…'

And before he had a chance to respond, Cora Campbell disappeared out through the doors of the restaurant and into the icy night of Stockholm.

CHAPTER THREE

JONAS HAD BEEN in the hospital since five-thirty a.m., but everything had gone against him. While everything was peaceful in the NICU, the labour suite had gone into full meltdown and, as senior manager on call, he had to assist.

Four midwives had come down with some kind of bug, meaning the staffing level was low. Six women had been in full labour, with another ten being observed. He'd had to pull midwives from other parts of the hospital to assist. Six of the staff on duty were newly qualified, and, having been there himself, he was careful to make sure there was enough supervision to keep them confident in their roles.

He'd already delivered two babies this morning, when he'd been called to assist with another; thankfully, all had gone well.

He snapped off a pair of gloves and washed his hands in the treatment room as Linnea, one of the newly qualified staff, came through, eyes sparkling and cheeks flushed. 'Oh, thank you, Jonas. I am so happy that things worked out.'

He gave a nod of his head. He'd stepped in to help when she'd asked for assistance. She'd been right. The baby's heart rate had started to fall slightly as labour progressed, which usually signified problems with the cord. Jonas had allowed Linnea to continue to be in charge of the delivery, while giving her the monitoring support and professional advice she needed to proceed. The cord had been longer than normal and had been wound around the baby's neck. The obstetrician had been alerted and agreed with the decision to continue as the heart rate drop was minimal during contractions. Linnea had been able to deliver the baby's head and gently slip the cord back over, before a healthy baby boy was finally introduced to the world.

'You did well,' praised Jonas. 'It was a difficult situation. You'll come across this again, and you have to judge each one based on the circumstances presenting.'

She gave him a knowing glance. 'I was tempted to ask you to take over when you appeared.'

He shook his head. 'We're all tempted in these situations, and, believe me, if I'd thought it was necessary, I would have stepped in. But there was no need. You're a good midwife. Congratulations on another delivery.'

He could see the clock on the back wall and his heart skipped a beat. It was nearly ten o'clock. Time had slipped away from him.

Things hadn't exactly gone as she'd expected. Cora had arrived at the hospital at eight. She'd taken Jonas's advice and had breakfast at the hotel, bringing them both takeaway coffees. But Jonas had been nowhere in sight.

Instead, she'd found her own way to NICU and introduced herself to the staff, standing awkwardly for a few moments with her coat. Alice, one of the sisters, had taken pity on her and showed her to the cloakroom to get changed and store her gear in a locker. Once she'd changed out of her boots into her more comfortable flat, bright blue shoes and tied her hair up, she'd been ready to start work.

But there was still no sign of Jonas. This time, Alice had directed one of the interns to take Cora on a tour around the hospital to get her bearings. Unfortunately, Hugo, one of the doctors, found himself entirely too charming for words.

Although he asked questions, it was clear he didn't listen, so he didn't realise just how experienced and senior Cora was. It might have been amusing, if she hadn't been stuck with him for more than an hour.

When Jonas finally appeared, clearly looking harassed, he came up on the tail end of a conversation.

'Twenty-four weeks is usually when babies are considered viable, but some babies at twenty-two and twenty-three weeks have survived here at Stockholm City NICU.'

Jonas ran his hand through his blond hair. She recognised the signs of someone who'd just been wearing a theatre cap.

He gave her a sideways glance. 'You haven't told him, have you?'

Hugo had the continued nerve to keep his haughty demeanour. 'Told me what?'

Jonas gave him a stare, and Cora completely understood why. Hugo's manner and tone were clearly lacking.

She bent around him and sighed. 'I have, actually. Twice. But listening is a skill that needs to be developed.'

'What are you both talking about?'

Cora smiled. 'I'm Cora Campbell, visiting specialist neonatologist. I'm here to teach members of Stockholm City Hospital about new techniques and carry out training.'

'I'll take over.' It was clear Jonas was cross.

'But—' began Hugo.

'*But*,' emphasised Jonas, 'Dr Campbell specialises in early neonates. She doesn't need you to define that for her.'

Hugo straightened his white coat. 'Well, I was only—'

'Go back to the unit, Dr Sper. You and I will talk later.'

Cora waited a few moments as they both watched Hugo strut back down the corridor with his head held high and his hands in his pockets.

'You owe me twice now,' said Cora succinctly.

Jonas turned with puzzled eyes. 'Twice?'

'Actually, make that three.'

His frown deepened. She counted off on her fingers. 'One, you were late. Two, I brought you coffee. Three, you left me with Mr Arrogant and Insufferable for more than an hour. So—' she gave a nod of her head '—Jonas Nilsson, you definitely owe me.'

He turned to face her. 'Okay.' He followed her lead and counted off on his fingers. 'One, I was here from five-thirty a.m., but there's some kind of stomach flu going around in the labour ward and I helped deliver three babies this morning, then I had to go in and assist at a potential emergency section. Three, I can only assume it was Alice who told Hugo to give you the tour?' He shook his head. 'She's had enough of him and I appreciate why. I'll deal with him later. He's not a good fit. Elias would have dealt with him, but that's down to me now.' He took another breath but before she could mention his odd counting he spoke again. 'And two, I concede. Did you keep it? I'll heat it up in the micro-wave. I would kill for a coffee right now.'

Cora shook her head and gave a knowing smile. 'Sorry, no. I know who to keep happy. I gave it to Alice.'

A smile spread across his face. He knew exactly what she meant. The sister of the unit was a key partner. Cora was right. And he hated that right now.

He leaned against the wall of the corridor they were still standing in. 'How did your tour go?'

She nodded. 'The only place I've not been yet is the labour suite. But that's the last place you'll want to go back to.' She gave him a careful stare. 'But I need to know how to get there if there's an emergency page for a new delivery—a neonate.'

Jonas shook his head. 'You won't need to answer any emergency pages.'

She folded her arms. 'I warned you last night you'd have to be quick to catch me. I told Alice if she needed shifts covered, I was willing. She gave me a few pro-visional dates until she checked with you.'

His eyes narrowed. Then he shook his head slowly. He looked half impressed and half annoyed. 'This is my unit. My staff.'

She held up both hands in front of her. 'I know, I know.' She gave him her brightest smile, knowing that he wasn't convinced at all.

One hospital tour later and Jonas still wasn't at all sure about Cora Campbell. She was clearly smart and very sassy. But the underlying suspicions of 'disruptive' seemed to glow like a neon banner above her head.

She was looking him clear in the eye and telling him that, absolutely, it was his unit, and she would follow his rules, but the gleam in her eye made him suspect she had plans entirely of her own.

Although on the outside Stockholm City Hospital appeared calm, on the inside it was chaos. And Jonas appeared to be the only person whose job it was to deal with it.

The stomach bug that had affected the labour ward earlier seemed to be travelling at rapid speed throughout many of the staff groups in the hospital. He was beginning to suspect a nasty strain of norovirus, which was notorious for appearing in the winter months.

It also meant he was eight doctors down, three senior managers, around fifteen nurses and midwives, and many other ancillary services. Each time his page sounded, he cringed, knowing he was being notified of another staff shortage. He was lucky that there didn't seem to be any patients affected as yet.

He strode back to the NICU where Cora was standing with Alice, the sister. 'Alice, we've had multiple notifications of staff sickness. Sounds like norovirus. I'm going to contact Infection Prevention and Control. Let's start taking extra safety precautions in the unit. Last thing we need is any of our babies getting sick.'

Alice didn't need to be told twice. Staff were briefed, safety messages reinforced, and even more hand sanitiser sourced, along with additional protective equipment. She also placed a ban on any additional staff entering the NICU.

Sometimes, some of the junior doctors from other areas would come to observe specific procedures. The sonographers frequently had students, as did the physios.

Jonas had half expected Cora to object. This would thwart her plans to teach over the next few days. But instead of creating a fuss, she disappeared off into one of the offices to go through some of the babies' files.

She appeared a few hours later with a clipboard in her hand. She smiled at Jonas. 'I've made a list. You have a number of pregnancies that are being carefully monitored right now. If any of these women deliver early, I think we should look at some of the techniques I've been using back at the Kensington.'

He glanced over the list, recognising several names. 'You won't have time to train our staff—or get consent from parents to try something new.'

She gave a small shrug. 'The staff won't need to be trained in advance. I'll be here. I can start the procedures, speak to the parents, gain consent, and monitor the babies.'

Alice had walked over to listen to the conversation too. 'Sounds good to me. I've read your research. I liked it.'

'You have?' Cora brightened instantly.

'Of course, I have. Elias spoke about you frequently. I thought I'd better keep up to date on what Pioneer Woman was up to.'

Cora blinked, then her cheeks reddened. 'What?'

Alice laughed. 'That's what he used to call you. He was very impressed by your work. I think he secretly hoped to take part in whatever your next research might be.'

Jonas was stunned. 'He never mentioned you to me.'

The comment was unintentional. And entirely thoughtless. Once it was out of his mouth, he realised exactly how it sounded.

Cora instantly looked wounded, pulling back, her eyes darting in another direction. Alice looked at him reproachfully, as if she were an elderly aunt, and rolled her eyes. Her voice stayed calm. 'Well, he wouldn't, would he? Everything here has to go through our ethics committee and you know how long they take. Elias would only have spoken to you once all those agreements were in place.'

She nudged Cora. 'They turned down an application once because they didn't like the colour of the flow-chart.'

Jonas tried to do some damage control. 'Oh, of course, okay. Yes, our ethics committee are strangely unique. They tend to get stuck on some tiny detail instead of looking at the big picture. I'm sure that's why we hadn't discussed you yet.'

Cora gave him a sideways glance as his page sounded again. 'Give me a sec,' he said as he ducked to the phone.

By the time he came back he could see from the electronic notes that Cora had performed one troubleshooting procedure after another. He watched as she put a central line into one twenty-six-week-old baby, and a tricky feeding tube into a twenty-seven-week-old baby who continued to struggle with its sucking reflex. Before he'd had a chance to speak to her she'd moved on, next to one of the doctors from the unit. It was clear he was having some difficulty re-siting a line in a premature baby. She had gloved, masked and gowned up, and was positioning the baby's arm in another way, demonstrating the angle he should use to get the vein.

She was kind and encouraging, giving clear instructions. There was no bossiness to her tone, but he didn't doubt she would take over if required. Her eyes looked over her mask and met his for a few seconds. It was hard to read her. He couldn't see the expression on the rest of her face. He wasn't quite sure what the message was that she was trying to send.

Half an hour later, line inserted and baby settled, she joined him back at the nurses' station as he replaced the phone. 'Go on then, ask.'

'What?'

'The call you got earlier. It was another doctor off sick, wasn't it?'

He gave her a suspicious look. 'Any more of this and I'll suspect you had something to do with all this.'

She shook her head and patted her stomach. 'Not me. I'm fit as a flea. Now, do you need me to cover shifts?'

Jonas couldn't help it. He would have to go against his instincts. It was ridiculous to use a visiting doctor to cover regular shifts. It was even more ridiculous to have a visiting doctor who was a research fellow and actually here to teach his staff, cover those shifts.

'Jonas, don't make me beg.'

As quick as a flash, a thought instantly entered his brain. *Go on, then.* Where on earth had that come from?

He gave a half-laugh, which he did his best to disguise as a cough, and shook his head as he stared at the staff rota. 'We need cover on Wednesday night—and on Friday, during the day.'

'Done.'

Simple as that.

She was looking at him with those green eyes, expecting him to say thank you. And, of course, he should. But Cora had a glint in her eye as if she'd just won something, and saying thank you somehow stuck in his throat.

He leaned one elbow on the counter. 'Earlier, you didn't step in and take over. You just talked him through it. Why?'

She gave him an odd look. 'Because he's a good doctor. He just needs to build his confidence. He could do that procedure.'

'But you didn't know that. You'd never seen him do one.'

Cora pulled back and looked at Jonas in surprise. 'You've worked as a hands-on midwife. Trusting your instincts is everything. You must know that.'

His insides clenched. She couldn't possibly know about how that had affected him in the past. One incident had scarred him for life. He'd trusted his instincts, and hated every second, because he'd had to go against a patient's wishes to save her life, and the life of her child. There had been consequences for those actions. She'd complained about him. And even though the complaint hadn't been upheld, Jonas had never forgotten it. He still felt guilty—as if he had let his patient down. It had impacted on him in so many ways. Instincts were good. But rules were better. Rules were what protected staff.

'But you had no idea about his capabilities.' He could feel himself starting to get defensive.

She gave him the most open look and put her hand up to her chest. 'But I know me. I sense if someone is good at their job. Always have. Always will. I would never have let him carry on with the procedure if I'd had the slightest doubt.' Her forehead creased in a small frown as she looked at him. 'This is a teaching hospital, isn't it? All he needed was a hand on his back, literally, along with a whisper in his ear.' She smiled as she said those words, and it struck Jonas that he wasn't entirely happy at the thought of her whispering in some man's ear.

He didn't want her whispering in anyone's ear except his, and it washed over him as if he were some ancient prehistoric man.

He gritted his teeth and pushed his emotions away. This was exactly what he'd wanted to avoid. Cora Campbell was affecting him in ways he didn't like—not at work anyway.

'I would have taken over in a heartbeat had I any worries,' she said steadily, then she gave him a wide smile. 'I'm good at my job, you know. I'm good at lots of things. You just have to learn to trust me.'

For a few moments, neither of them said anything. Jonas was frozen by her gaze and the way she was looking at him as though she could see parts he didn't want her to see. Who was this woman? And why did it feel as if she were getting under his skin?

One of the paediatric nurses walked past and glanced at them both, slowing and tapping Cora on the shoulder. 'Just to let you know, we start our annual Christmas traditions this weekend. You should come along.'

The spell was broken. For a second he saw a wave of momentary panic in her eyes. Curious. She'd just performed a tricky procedure on a tiny baby with the utmost confidence.

'I think I've just agreed to cover some shifts,' she said swiftly.

'No, you haven't. You're free on Saturday night. You can go ice skating at Kungsträdgården Park.' He knew exactly what tradition his colleague was talking about. Even though it was November, it was sort of an inbuilt tradition for the staff here. They all gathered at Kungsträdgården—the King's Garden—ice rink on the first weekend it opened in November. It was almost like the start of the Christmas season for everyone.

She blinked. 'Where?'

The nurse waved her hand. 'It's right in the city centre. You'll have no problem finding it. And if you do, we'll send Jonas to find you.'

This time it was Cora who waved her hand. 'You know, I'm not that great at ice skating. I'll maybe give it a pass this time.'

Jonas lowered his head. He couldn't help the mischief in his voice. 'Dr Campbell? Something you're not good at? I'll need to see it to believe it.'

She sighed, clearly realising that he had her.

It seemed as though this was a game of tit for tat.

'Fine, I'll go.' But there was something in her eyes. Something he didn't understand.

He put a hand on her shoulder. 'It will be fine, I promise you. We normally meet around six p.m. I'll pick you up at the hotel.'

Then, before she had a chance to find a reason to say no, he left the unit and went to answer another page.

Cora had spent most of the day trying to find a reasonable excuse to back out of ice skating with her new colleagues.

How could she explain to people she'd just met that Christmas was a bit of a black hole for her? She didn't need to do that back home. People knew her. They knew her background and didn't ask questions. When Cora volunteered to work Christmas, most other doctors just accepted the offer gratefully and for that she was thankful. Here, she really didn't want to have those conversations with people she barely knew. Trouble was, from what she'd heard around about her today, this was just the start of Christmas events in Stockholm City Hospital. It seems they celebrated from this weekend, right up until the actual day.

For Cora, it was a bit like being in her own special horror movie.

It hadn't always been like this. Once she'd settled with her adoptive family, Cora used to love Christmas just as much as the next person. She hadn't just loved it. She'd loved it, adored it, revelled in it, and planned a million Christmas activities. But after a clash of terrible luck over a few years, all during the festive season, her Christmas spirit had been well and truly drained dry.

First, her beloved adoptive mum had died unexpectedly on the twenty-third of December after being admitted to hospital with back pain. It didn't matter that Cora was a neonatologist. She still had an overwhelming surge of guilt that she hadn't seen any tiny signs of the aortic aneurysm that had killed her mum in minutes. It was known as the silent killer for a reason. Almost no warning, and, unless detected through a scan, very often deadly.

The following year, her adoptive dad had died after fighting cancer. The light had finally gone out of his eyes on Christmas Eve. Cora knew the true reason that he'd died: he'd lost the will to live after the death of his wife.

So, the time of year that she used to share with the two people she'd loved most—the people who'd completely turned her life around, and given her the reason, will and determination to be a doctor—had been tainted.

Christmas had started to feel like a cruel reminder. Her rational brain told her that was ridiculous. But she was a doctor. She'd seen enough in this lifetime to know that Christmas wasn't a joyful time of year for everyone. Lots of others had painful memories too, and Cora had learned to cope by throwing herself into her work, and by allowing others to enjoy the season the way she'd used to, and giving them the gift of time to spend with their families.

Both of her parents had finally died in the Royal Kensington, so some of her colleagues there knew her circumstances.

Although Cora was usually a positive and encouraging person, this time of year just seemed to cast a shade over her mood. As she pulled her green coat on, and grabbed the snuggly red hat she'd bought in a shop nearby, she tried to push those thoughts from her head. She could put her game face on for a few hours. That was all it would be.

Then she could come back to her hotel room and snuggle up in bed. As she grabbed her gloves, her eyes couldn't help but glance at the square outside. Everyone had been so warm and friendly these last few days at the hospital. Jonas had been there, but not too much. If she hadn't known better, she'd think he was avoiding her, but she'd been too busy at work to pay attention to that little gnawing feeling that he hadn't been around much. Tonight would be different. Tonight, he was picking her up.

Dusk had already fallen and now she could see glistening white lights were everywhere. It really was pretty. The lights were twisted together in a variety of ways, and giant snowflakes were strung between the normal lights. There was a scene in the centre of the square with white reindeer and Santa's sleigh. People were already gathered around it and posing for pictures. All the lights had literally appeared overnight. Last night, there had been none. Then, today?

She pulled the curtains, letting out a wry laugh at herself and her Christmas Grouch behaviour. As much as she'd loved the view from the window of her room, this might be a bit much to see, night after night.

She sighed as she made her way down to the lobby. Again, it was now filled with Christmas trees, and boughs. She fingered the bright pink and purple decorations threaded next to the bright green foliage. Alongside the pink and purple were straw wreaths and small straw goat decorations. How unusual. She'd need to ask someone about those.

Jonas walked through the front door of the reception area, dusting the snow from his uncovered blond hair. Cora saw several of the female staff members take a second look.

She watched them, oddly suspicious as one nudged the other, and they both clearly murmured about Jonas under their breath. Of course other women would look at Jonas. He was tall, handsome, and clearly quite commanding.

But that didn't stop her quickening her steps and giving him a broad smile, along with a loud, 'Hey.' Okay, so he might not have a flashing sign above his head saying *This one's mine*, but she hoped she'd made her point. Taken. Look, but don't touch.

'You ready for this?' His voice had a hint of wariness.

'Of course,' she said without thinking.

'Really?' His brow had the slightest frown. 'I thought you were trying to get out of it earlier.'

She gave a half-shrug. 'Not the greatest lover of the festive season,' she said, not wanting to make up some elaborate lie.

Jonas gave a thoughtful nod. 'Okay.' She wondered if he would ask more, but he didn't, and that actually helped a little. He held his elbow towards her. 'But you can put up with a bit of ice skating, I presume?'

She nodded and smiled as she slid her arm inside his elbow as they walked outside.

'It's only around a ten-minute walk,' he said. 'The park really is in the heart of the city.' As they dodged around a few people on the crowded street, he gave her a sideways look. 'We celebrate the season pretty hard here—just a word of warning that you'll probably get invited to more events.'

She bit her lip and nodded. He still wasn't asking the personal questions.

'And, as another hint, there is a really good word for the hire skates at the park.'

She looked up at him, half smiling. 'What?'

He laughed. 'I heard it in a Sherlock Holmes movie and always wanted to use it.' He leaned down towards her ear, his warm breath tickling her cheek. 'They're dastardly.'

Now it was Cora's turn to burst out laughing.

But Jonas nodded sincerely. 'I'm telling you. They look like skates, but—' he shook his head '—as soon as you hit the ice you'll realise it's all been some kind of sly scheme.'

'You're not selling this,' Cora admitted as they kept walking.

He shrugged. 'Don't say I didn't warn you.'

'So, if they're that bad, why didn't you bring your own?'

'Yeah, I thought about that, but decided that might be a bit mean.'

Cora laughed. 'For who? Me?'

He was still half laughing as he looked at her again. 'It might be a bit much to invite you skating, leave you in the old hire skates, then bring out my professional skates and strand you in the middle of the rink.'

Now Cora was really laughing. 'Why, Jonas, I didn't know you cared.'

'Don't take it that far,' he said quickly. 'I might hire skates with you, but I still expect you to buy the hot chocolate.'

'There's hot chocolate?' She could almost feel her ears prick up.

'Of course, there is.'

They crossed a busy road and Jonas pointed. 'Look, there's the Royal Palace, and Gamla Stan.'

'Does the King actually stay there?' Cora asked, looking at the immense and beautifully lit building.

'It's his official residence.'

'And what's Gamla Stan?'

'Our old town, and one of our most popular tourist destinations. Cobbled streets and colourful buildings, it's all seventeenth and eighteenth century and is one of the best-preserved medieval city centres in Europe.'

Cora stared in wonder. She immediately planned to come back here some time during the day.

They crossed through the park entrance. The lay-out was impressive. The park connected the harbour with the main shopping district. There was an elaborate fountain, a stage, a lawn area, and, of course, a large skating rink.

The rink was already busy. 'What's that in the middle?' asked Cora. She pointed at the enormous statue, with iron lions around it, around which the skaters were circling.

'Oh, that's Karl the XIII. He was King of Sweden.'

They walked closer to the rink. There was a barrier surrounding it that was topped with a wooden fence on which people were leaning as they watched others skating. 'What are the tents?' asked Cora.

'They're warming tepees,' said Jonas. 'A place to huddle when you get too cold. That's where you'll find the hot chocolate, the lingonberry or the *glögg*.'

'Okay, you got me. What's that?'

Jonas smiled. 'It's good. *Glögg* is mulled wine. It's sweet, warm and spicy. Just the perfect thing for a winter's night.' He waved as they spotted other members of staff gathered near the skate-hire booth. 'Come on, then.'

As they approached Cora realised most of the staff had brought their own skates. She waited while Jonas hired them both skates, and strapped them to her feet. He was right, of course. They looked distinctly un-skate-like. And as the other staff stepped on the rink and started spinning off in various directions, she realised just what a big sacrifice he'd made on her behalf.

He held out his hand towards her. 'Don't worry, I'll catch you if you fall.'

'The first time, or all the times?' she asked as she grasped his hand and nearly landed flat on her back with her first step on the ice.

He put his other hand at her back and, since her feet seemed frozen in one spot, gave her a gentle push in the right direction.

Cora wobbled immediately and held out her other hand in a desperate attempt to regain her balance. Jonas just laughed and stayed behind her, putting his hands on either side of her hips and almost pushing her along.

At first, Cora couldn't pretend her legs weren't shaking, but after halfway around the rink, she started to relax a little and leaned back against Jonas.

'Is this okay?' he asked, his voice above her shoulder.

'Is this?' she asked, leaning back a little more. 'You're doing all the work.'

'Just enjoy the view,' he said as they continued around the rink. Other members of staff kept whizzing past them, laughing and shouting and waving.

After a few minutes, several of the girls from the unit came along on either side of Cora and took her hands, pulling her along. She let out a scream, half fear, half laughter as they continued dragging her around the rink. The air was crisp, cold enough to make her want to keep moving, but bearable enough that she wasn't freezing and desperate to get back to the hotel.

She finally collided into the back of another staff member, as the girls decided to stop at one of the tents for refreshments. It seemed to have been pre-planned as she recognised the faces all around her. She'd barely had time to think before something was pressed into her hands. 'I made an executive decision on your behalf,' said Jonas.

She looked down and inhaled. The scent of sweet, warm chocolate filled the air. He handed her a spoon and she tackled the cream on the top first.

'What if I'd decided to opt for the mulled wine, or the lingonberry?' she queried as she savoured the sweet taste on her tongue.

'I figure you'll be back here enough to sample them all. And it was hot chocolate you mentioned first.'

'It was.' She nodded as she took a sip. 'Oh, that's nice. It's different from what I expected. What is it?'

'White hot chocolate. It's their bestseller.' He handed his cup to her. 'But if you want to taste the mulled wine you can try some of mine.'

She gave him a surprised glance. 'So, you *do* share. I'm surprised.'

'What do you mean I do share?' His voice was distinctly puzzled.

She took a step closer, her arm brushing against his. 'I got the general impression that you weren't particularly keen on sharing your NICU with me.'

'Why would I share what's mine?' he shot back, a smile in his eyes.

He knew she was teasing him, and it seemed he would give as good as he got.

'I thought you might make an exception for someone that you'd invited here.'

'Elias did the inviting—without consultation, I might add.'

'But you watched me today. Don't think I didn't notice. I'm an asset to the unit. Particularly when your staff numbers have been hit.'

He gave a slow, thoughtful nod. 'A senior pair of eyes is useful right now. But…' he raised his eyebrows '…you seem like the type that—what's the expression?—if I give you an inch, you'll take a mile.'

'Ouch!' She feigned a wound to her chest as she smiled. Then her expression turned serious. 'I don't want to run out of time to teach your staff what Elias asked me here to teach.'

She watched the tiny twitch at the corner of his blue eyes as she said the name. She got that Jonas was trying to do two jobs right now—be Head of Midwifery and run the NICU in Elias's absence. Maybe holding onto rules and regular practice was his way of ensuring a steadying hand in a time of uncertainty for staff while their regular head was off sick.

She decided to press on. 'I'm here to do a job. Why don't you let me do it? There's a full rota of staff tomorrow. I could start with explaining the science behind hypothermic neural rescue. It's one of my most important pieces of research. I understand that, at first, it can be confusing for staff. One of our natural instincts the second a pre-term baby is born is to get them into a warming cot. If I can get a chance to explain the science, then I can teach and explain the techniques.'

She could swear that right now she could hear him tutting internally.

She gave him her best smile. Boy, Jonas Nilsson was hard work to win around. Part of her was curious enough to want to know why, and the other part of her knew it was absolutely none of her business.

But Cora had always been curious about people and what made them tick. She was open with her close friends. They all knew why she'd become a neonatologist, which was because she'd assisted at her mum's unexpected early labour, and helped to deliver her little sister, Isla. They also all knew she'd then had to intervene when her mum had suffered a postpartum haemorrhage. It had been a scary, terrifying and exhilarating time all at once, and had cemented Cora's career path in her brain. When her parents had died, she'd tried to persuade Isla to come and live with her in London. But Isla had no intention of leaving the Scottish Highlands where she'd grown up, and had insisted on moving to stay with their aunt while finishing school. Now she was attending Edinburgh University, just as Cora had, but was studying physics instead of medicine. The two were still close and spoke every other day. Cora's close friends knew the moments that had impacted on her life, but it wasn't something she'd share with a casual acquaintance. Yet something was plucking at all the curious senses in her brain and making her wonder about Jonas.

She'd only known him a few days. He could be grumpy. He could be funny. He could be cheeky, and he could be deadly serious. She might only be here until just before Christmas, but she had to work well with this guy in order to meet the rigorous demands of the Kensington Project. She had to recognise which buttons she shouldn't push. At times, Jonas appeared like a closed book. At other times, she felt as if there were so many more layers beneath the surface.

As if he were reading her thoughts, he gave a conciliatory nod. 'A teaching session on research and knowledge seems reasonable. As long as there aren't any emergencies in the unit tomorrow.'

'Of course,' she agreed quickly with a nod. She held out her hand towards him.

He looked at her as if she were crazy.

'Shake on it,' she insisted.

'Why? I just told you that you can schedule it.'

She gave a shrug. 'Call me old-fashioned, but I like to shake on things.'

He put his gloved hand in hers and she gripped firmly, looking him straight in the eye. 'See, that's better. I always find it's harder for people to go back on their word, if they've had to look you in the eye and shake on it.'

'I don't go back on my word,' he said, shaking his head at her.

'But I don't know you that well,' she insisted as she finally let go of his hand.

As they dropped hands she raised one eyebrow, then winked. 'Yet,' she added.

CHAPTER FOUR

FOR SOME STRANGE REASON, Jonas had a spring in his step the next morning. He wasn't quite sure why. He was always happy at his work but today felt different.

His footsteps slowed as he realised when the last time was that he'd been this happy at work: the day he'd decided to propose to Kristina—the last time he'd told a woman that he loved her.

That day hadn't been so good. He'd been dating Kristina for a few months. It had been a kind of whirlwind romance. One in which Jonas had finally let his guard down. He'd been guarded with his emotions since the event at work. When he'd finally got up the courage to put his heart on his sleeve and tell Kristina that he loved her, it had seemed like the start of a new life for him.

But things had proved disastrous. He'd gone home early the next day, to collect the ring he'd had resized, and found a stack of bills in his post box. The bills were all for his credit cards, all of them run up to their maximum limits in the space of a month—the amount of time that Kristina had been staying with him.

He'd been short and swift with his actions. The ring had been hidden and he'd had a long conversation with Kristina when she'd arrived back at his apartment complete with numerous shopping bags. He'd wanted to give her the benefit of the doubt. Perhaps she had money troubles, medical bills, family debt, or some other reasonable issue that would have meant she'd had to use all of his credit cards, without permission, at short notice. But, no. Nothing that could excuse her behaviour. There had been tears, a bit of a tantrum, then she'd stuffed her belongings into a designer suitcase, grabbed the new shopping bags and left with a flurry of colourful language. Her last remark, a laugh, had been that Jonas was clearly a poor judge of women, and it had cut deep. A short conversation with the police had revealed Kristina was known to them for this kind of behaviour, but it hadn't made him feel any less of a fool.

Wearing his heart on his sleeve, sharing his history, his vulnerabilities, with a woman he'd thought he'd fallen in love with, had been a disaster. He'd learned the lesson hard. The last three women in his life hadn't stuck around for more than six months. The acute stumbling block of not actually being able to say the 'I love you' words again had proved a major hurdle for any relationship. He wasn't quite sure he ever would again.

Four years on, he tried not to waste any thoughts on Kristina. But something about his mood today had triggered the memories in his brain.

By the time he reached the NICU the spring in his step had disappeared. It was early, but, while everything in the unit seemed to be going smoothly, he was struck by the lack of visible staff. He moved instantly to Alice's side; the sister of the unit was calmly taking a reading from a pump and recording it in the baby's notes.

'What's going on?' he asked in a whispered voice.

'Nothing,' she answered.

'Exactly,' he replied. 'This place is usually a hive of activity. What on earth has happened?'

Alice nodded over her shoulder to the small teaching room in the unit. 'What's happened is, everyone heard about the hypothermic neural rescue research that Cora is presenting this morning. All the babies have had their care delivered, medicines given, recordings taken, and I—as the old girl on duty, am doing the observations while the staff listen in.'

Jonas couldn't hide his horror. 'They can't leave you out here alone while they listen to a presentation.' He could feel his fury building, but Alice could read him like a book.

'Dr Campbell is doing her sessions in twenty-minute bursts. Anyone would think this girl had worked in a NICU before. And you and I both know if I raise my voice above a whisper, I can have every member of staff next to me in less than twenty steps. Anyway—' she held out her hands '—look around. Even though it's seven-thirty a.m., it feels like four in the morning. This place is so peaceful. Isn't it a nice change?' She didn't give him a chance to answer. 'We also have three sets of parents with their babies, and now—' she changed her position so she could point at his chest '—I have you!' She said it as if he were some kind of Christmas gift. 'So, Jonas, you start on that side and I'll do this side. Record all observations and check all pumps. I think Baby Raff might be due for his tube feed.'

She moved off to her side quickly and Jonas spoke a little louder. 'I'm not sure I agreed to this.' He looked over at the training room and, seeing all the rapt faces, had to stop his feet from automatically moving in that direction. He really, really wanted to hear what Cora was saying that was enthralling his usually sceptical staff.

'You didn't,' Alice said over her shoulder with a laugh, 'but you're a good boy, you never let me down.'

He rolled his eyes. Alice was one of the most experienced and most senior of his staff. He sighed and picked up the nearest chart, having a quick check over the twenty-seven-week baby girl who was doing better every day.

It didn't take him long to remember how much he missed working hands-on every day. When he'd stepped in to assist in the labour suite the other day, there hadn't been time to think, let alone enjoy it. Here, things were quieter, and he took time to talk to each of the babies he was monitoring. Gently handling some, feeding another, changing two and saying a few quiet words to the sicker babies while gently stroking their hands.

A little boy, Samuel, was irritable and Jonas took him from his crib and placed him next to his chest and sat down on one of the rockers. He'd just managed to settle him when he caught scent of something light and floral behind him.

'Aw, look at you,' said Cora. 'Now I see the real Jonas.'

He shot her a frown of annoyance. 'I'm a midwife. Of course, I like babies. And when it comes to settling a disturbed preemie, I'm an expert.'

She walked around, gently touched the top of Samuel's head, then moved in front of Jonas, sitting in the seat opposite and scanning Samuel's chart.

When she looked back up, she tilted her head to one side. 'So, tell me, why did you become a midwife?'

He gave an exaggerated eye roll. It was a question he'd been asked time and time again—hardly surprising when only half a per cent of midwives in Sweden were male. He gave her his truthful standard answer.

'I love the idea of bringing new life into the world. Simple as that.'

She leaned forward and put her head on her hand. 'What, no family story of inspiration, or childhood experience of delivering a baby in a field or something?' She said it in a jokey tone but her eyes were staring straight at him.

'Is that what you expect from me?' His tone was a little harsher than he meant.

She sat back. 'It's just an unusual career choice for a young man. I guess I'm interested. Only half a per cent of midwives in the UK are male.'

'Same in Sweden,' he countered. Then he gave a small shrug, which Samuel didn't appreciate. 'Maybe I just wanted to rush up the ranks in the health service and decided midwifery was the easy route.'

She folded her arms across her chest. 'Not a chance,' she said as she looked at him in interest. 'I've heard the same tales. That in a profession mainly dominated by women, males in nursing, midwifery and mental health all seem to be promoted quicker than females. I don't think for one second that you came into this job to claw your way to the top.'

'Claw? Interesting expression.'

'It is, isn't it?' she agreed. Her gaze narrowed slightly. 'You didn't come and listen to my first session. You were here. I could see you.'

He held out one hand. 'Have you met Alice? Also known as Attila. As soon as she saw me, she put me to work, because apparently all my staff were listening to your research instead of taking care of their charges.'

She leaned back her head and laughed. 'Oh, no, you don't. There's no way you wouldn't have dragged out every single member of staff if you thought for one second that your charges were being neglected.'

'True.' He really was beginning to appreciate just how well Cora seemed to read him. 'Actually, I *was* quite interested. Can I read the notes?'

She grinned from ear to ear. 'Read the notes? Sacrilege. It's never the same as listening to the real-life presentation. You know, where you can look the researcher in the eye, see their passion for their project and ask the questions that dance through your brain as they inspire you.'

He tried to hold in the laugh that was building in his chest, desperately trying not to disturb the little sleeping form against him. He shook his head, and stood up, settling Samuel back in his crib.

He gave an enormous sigh and turned to Cora, who was right by his side. 'I'd hate anyone to think you're short of confidence.'

But Cora was glancing again at Samuel's chart. 'He would have been a good one to try my technique on. There's a note in his chart about birth asphyxia. Who knows how long it will be before his parents know if there is any permanent damage?' Her expression was sad, her voice melancholic.

'Samuel has done well since he's been in the NICU. He's starting to suck and he's managing without any additional oxygen now.'

Cora nodded, her eyes fixed on the little boy. She looked up. 'But you still won't know for sure until he's much older. Let's try my therapy on the next preterm baby. Let's not wait.'

Every muscle in Jonas's body tensed. But Cora had started talking again. 'You know that research has proved that hypothermia reduces neurological damage in infants who've suffered asphyxia during delivery. The next time you get a baby in the unit that meets the criteria, we'll both speak to the parents, get their consent and start the procedure.'

He didn't have a chance to answer before she'd put both hands on his bare arms. 'Just think, Jonas, we might actually save a baby from damage. Think of what a difference that could make to one tiny life? Isn't it worth a chance? If you've kept up with my research, you'll know we won't be doing any harm. But we could actually change the life course for a child.'

Boy, Cora was right. Watching her talk about the subject she loved with passion and commitment was mesmerising. Every cell in his body wanted to scream yes. He already knew that this had been Elias's intention.

He pressed his lips together for a second, trying to word things carefully. 'If I can, I'll come to your next few sessions. Once I've heard all your research, *then* I'll make a decision.'

She sucked in a deep breath. He could tell she wanted to argue with him, petition harder for her cause. But something made her take a step back and give a small nod. 'Okay.'

As his pager sounded and he went to move away, she put her hand back on his arm. '*But*, if you don't attend the sessions, if you get called away with work, you'll let me deliver the sessions to you later—after work. So we can still have this conversation later—no excuses.'

He paused for a moment and gave her a brief smile. 'You've clearly been taking lessons from Alice.'

Jonas could tell she was trying really hard not to smile. 'Maybe,' she admitted. 'Again.'

'Do you both just like to join forces against me?'

Cora gave him a soft look and leaned against the

nearest wall. 'That's what it is.' She said the words as if she'd just made some kind of amazing discovery.

'What are you talking about?'

'You,' said Cora. 'I'm talking about you. I couldn't quite put my finger on it, but that's it. You always seem to think that people are out to get you.'

'Don't be ridiculous.' He could feel every one of his defences closing like a steel trap.

But Cora wasn't matching his defensive posture—quite the opposite. She was still just smiling at him, staring with those green eyes and giving a little shake of her head. 'You get so defensive. So protective. I get it, I do. But sometimes I feel as if you're constantly looking over your shoulder, waiting for someone to grab you.'

His skin chilled. She had no idea what she was saying, but she was striking every chord in his body. Was he always this obvious? Had the rest of the staff just been more cautious around him?

But if Cora was generally good about reading people, it seemed that her enthusiasm had taken hold. 'Do you ever relax?'

'What do you mean?'

'You always seem on guard. As if you're waiting for something to happen. Don't you ever just kick back and go with the flow?'

Another baby started to make small sounds behind them and Jonas quickly moved next to the crib.

It only took him a few seconds to assess the situation. This little girl, Elsa, had respiratory issues. Most premature babies were vulnerable to infection and this little one had picked up a chest infection soon after delivery.

He moved as the oxygen saturation monitor started to sound. The little girl's colour was slightly dusky as her noises, which resembled mewing now, continued.

Cora turned to the wall and automatically handed him a suction catheter as Jonas lifted the protective shield around the crib and positioned himself at the top of Elsa's head.

Suctioning on premature babies had to be done gently, and with caution, but Jonas had years of expertise. Within a few seconds, he withdrew the catheter as Elsa coughed, pulling it back with a tiny lump of mucus that must have been blocking her airway.

He signalled to one of the NICU nurses. 'Roz, can you speak to one of our physios? See if they can make time to come and assess her again?'

Roz nodded and walked swiftly to the phone, as Jonas changed Elsa's position in the crib for a few minutes, keeping a light hand on her little rasping chest.

Cora thankfully didn't speak again, leaving their previous conversation forgotten. They hadn't even needed to speak about what to do for the baby. Both had read the situation and acted appropriately. There had been no panic, no raising of voices, just two experienced practitioners working together.

He tried to push down the momentary resentment that had flared at her words. She had no idea why he was a stickler for rules. Jonas didn't want any other person on his staff to go through the same experience. Rules and protocols supported staff to practise safely and he firmly believed that.

Just then Mary, one of the physios, walked through the door. She immediately came over to Cora and Jonas. 'You called?'

He nodded. 'Elsa just had an episode where her sats dropped and she had mucus blocking her airway. Can you assess her, please?'

'Of course.' Mary nodded. 'And if she needs it, I can

put her on our rounds for chest physio. Leave it with me.' Her eyes drifted to Cora. 'Heard the first session went well. I'll try and get to one of your others if I'm close by. I'm interested in getting involved.'

He could hear the intake of breath from Cora as she smiled and straightened up, immediately launching into her favourite topic of conversation. Jonas, satisfied that Elsa was in safe hands, moved away.

'Don't forget,' came the voice behind him. 'If you get called to other areas, I'll find you later so we can play catch up.'

Heads turned in the unit. There was a rapid exchange of glances and Jonas groaned inwardly. He knew exactly what Cora meant, but it seemed that others were interpreting a whole different meaning in those simple words.

That was the last thing he wanted. People getting ideas about him and the visiting doc.

As he pushed his way through the doors to the open corridor, his tense shoulders relaxed a little. If Elias were here right now, he'd be roaring with laughter.

As Jonas picked up the nearest phone and dialled the number on his pager, he made a mental note to call his friend later.

'It's Jonas,' he said when the phone was answered.

'How soon can you get here?' came the reply.

And all other thoughts were lost.

CHAPTER FIVE

CORA STARED DOWN at the pdf map she'd printed in a few hurried moments at work earlier. It still didn't make sense to her, but then, she'd never really been a map reader. When she'd first arrived in London, the underground had seemed to mock her.

But another week had slipped past, and this was the second staff event she'd been talked into. Maybe they wouldn't notice if she didn't turn up?

'Ready for the Christmas lights tour?' asked Jonas as he walked up alongside her wearing thick boots and a black fur-lined parka.

She glanced up and nodded. 'To be honest, I'm looking forward to getting my bearings in the streets around here. I never seem to know where I am.'

He looked at her, frowned and pointed. 'But you've got a map.'

She laughed and tapped the side of her head. 'I also don't appear to have the part of the brain that was designed for map reading. It's just a skill I've yet to accomplish.'

'Would it help if I give you a hint?'

She sighed. 'If your hint is pointing at the map and doing your best to explain to me in terms a five-year-old should understand how obvious the map is, please don't.'

'Anyone would think you take these things personally. No, I was just going to give you the tip of—' he held up his hand in the air '—following the lights. Believe it or not, that's what most people do.'

He gave her a nudge as she glared at him for stating the obvious, 'Then there's the other hint, that we're starting at the place we were at last week, Kungsträdgården Park.'

She wrinkled her nose. 'Does everything happen there?'

He gave a half-shrug. 'More or less. Gamla Stan really is the heart of the city. Tried the coffee shops and cakes there yet?'

Cora shook her head. 'Like I said, I'm lucky I can walk between the hotel and the hospital. My sense of direction has never been great.'

Once the rest of the hospital staff had gathered around them, there was a consensus that everyone should start by getting something to drink. This time Cora nudged Jonas out of the way. 'Ladies pick.' She smiled. 'And I'm paying.'

She returned moments later with some mulled wine. 'Hope this meets your approval,' she said as she handed it over.

The first sip took her by surprise as the hit of cinnamon, cloves, ginger and alcohol assaulted her senses all at once. 'Well, that certainly reaches places.'

Jonas let out a loud laugh and a few others turned to stare at them in surprise. Heat rushed into Cora's cheeks and she held up her steaming cup. 'First sample of *glögg*.'

She turned back to Jonas. 'I think my eyes actually just watered,' she whispered.

'Novice,' he joked, taking another sip of his.

'Show off,' she muttered as she leaned over her cup and inhaled. She pretended to sway. 'Wow, I think this could make me drunk by inhalation alone.'

He shook his head. 'That's why you're only allowed one. And why we recommend the Christmas Lights Tour. By the time you've walked four kilometres, you'll have forgotten all about the *glögg*.'

'Don't bet on it,' she murmured as the group started to move out into the streets.

They started walking down streets between rows of festooned shops. Above them were gold, green and red garlands. Every now and then they stopped to admire the displays in the shop windows, some intricate, some bold, but it seemed that nowhere in Stockholm hadn't been struck by the Christmas bug. And it was still only November!

There was a large department store, and every window had a different Christmas scene. By the time they'd worked their way along all of the scenes, the *glögg* had been finished.

When they reached a public square, Jonas turned towards her. 'This is the *svampen*—known as the mushroom. You can see it's a popular meeting place.' Cora tilted her head at the strange structure. A mushroom was exactly what it looked like, right in the middle of the square, with several groups of people gathered underneath and chatting together. Next to the mushroom was a huge lit tree. She stared at some of the designer shops surrounding the square, and the names of a few restaurants. 'I take it this is the posh bit?' she asked,

Jonas looked confused.

'The more expensive area—the place where the great and the good come to shop?'

He was smiling broadly as he shook his head. 'You

have some strange expressions. Sometimes I can hardly make out a word you are saying.' Now, he nodded. 'But, yes. I get it. If you want to eat or shop around here, bring your credit card. And make sure you've raised the limit on it.'

He glanced at some of the shops and for the briefest of pauses, Cora thought she saw something odd flit across his eyes. But a few seconds later, he was chatting to one of the nurses from Paediatrics.

They continued along the streets, which were all decorated in turn. Some had hearts in the centre of their strung garlands, others had stars. The lights tour wasn't for the faint-hearted. They had already covered half the route and Cora was very glad she had her comfortable walking boots on. She chatted to two of the staff from the NICU, and two surgical interns that had joined them.

At various points on the tour they stopped. The garlands changed to snowballs in the middle, and then to pinecones, and then frolicking angels. Near the palace were brightly lit royal deer. Cora stopped to admire the palace again. 'It's enormous,' she breathed.

Ana, one of the NICU nurses, nodded. 'I'm a history buff.' She smiled. 'And a bit of a data geek. Built in the thirteenth century, it has one thousand four hundred and thirty rooms. The national library is housed inside, and Parliament House is to the left.'

Cora laughed and put her hand on Ana's arm. 'I love that you know that.'

Ana tapped the side of her head. 'You have no idea the useless general knowledge I have in here.' She gave Cora a nudge and looked in the direction of one of the surgical interns. 'Think he'll like a bit of useless knowledge?'

Cora smiled. 'There's only one way to find out.'

Ana's eyes gleamed. 'True,' she agreed as she moved in that direction.

'What are you up to?' came the deep voice from behind her.

Cora jumped a little, then give him an appreciative smile as she continued to watch Ana. 'I'm playing matchmaker,' she said. 'And I'm just waiting to find out if I'm any good.'

Jonas followed her gaze and sighed. 'Oh, no. Not Rueben.'

Cora turned swiftly. 'What? Is he a chancer?'

'A what?' Jonas looked entirely baffled.

She threw up one hand. 'You know, a guy about town, someone who goes out with lots of women.'

Jonas was clearly holding back laughter again as he shook his head. 'No, he's an easily distracted intern, who needs to study a bit harder. Last thing I want is for him to fall in love and float off somewhere in the midst of his studies.'

'Oh.' Cora was almost disappointed.

Jonas took her by the shoulders and spun her around to where several members of staff had started walking again. 'And you seem to be easily distracted too. Come on, you don't want to get left behind.'

'No, I don't.' She cast another glance over her shoulder to where Rueben and Ana were clearly hitting it off and smiled again.

Jonas was right about one thing. This walk had certainly proved a distraction. The temptation had been high to snuggle up in her room with some chocolate and an old movie. But this was much better. The air might be stinging her cheeks, and she had to keep wiggling her toes, but just being in the company of all the other staff from the hospital, and with Jonas, was lifting her spirits in a way she truly appreciated.

These people didn't need to know about her past and her hang-ups with Christmas. She was just glad that they kept inviting her to all the activities.

'What are you smiling about now?' Jonas had fallen into step alongside her.

She gave him a sideways glance. 'What do you mean?'

'You always have that look about you—as if you're either keeping secrets or plotting something.'

Cora grinned. 'I quite like that description.' She pointed her finger at him. 'Okay, that's exactly the way I want you to think of me, at all times—as if I'm keeping secrets or plotting something. That way, I might get away with more and more.'

He rolled his eyes. 'I'm going to need eyes in the back of my head, aren't I?'

'I thought you already had them.' She pointed again. 'By the way, I tried to find you the other night to go over my research with you.' She blew on her gloved hand. 'But you'd vanished in a puff of smoke. There are three women in the antenatal ward who could go into labour imminently. All three of these babies would be pre-term—around the thirty-six-week mark. All three would fit the criteria for hypothermic neural rescue therapy.'

'You've read the mothers' notes?'

She nodded.

'Which one is your preferred candidate?'

Her eyes widened. 'Why, all three of them.' She kept talking. 'We have the chance to potentially improve the lives of three pre-term babies.'

'They're not born yet,' cut in Jonas.

But it didn't faze Cora in the slightest. 'Of course not, and I hope that all three stay safely inside their mothers for at least another three weeks. But, if they don't, I'd like us to be prepared.' She licked her lips, and caught his blue gaze. 'Most of your staff are prepared. It seems like you are the only sticking point.'

Was she being too direct? Probably. But Cora wasn't going to waste an opportunity. 'We can go over things tonight if you wish.'

For a second she thought he might agree. But, as his shoulders tensed and his back straightened, she knew she'd lost him.

'Let's talk tomorrow. Once we're both back at work.'

She knew it wasn't the time to push. But she really, really wanted to.

Someone handed her a piece of chocolate they'd just bought from one of the market stalls. 'Thanks,' she said, and popped it in her mouth to stop herself pushing him too far.

They moved back through the streets. The early evening crowds were starting to thin a little, but by the time they got back to Kungsträdgården Park and made their way past the skating rink, she noticed the large amount of people crowded around the herd of giant lit reindeer. Phones were flashing constantly as people posed next to the large structures, grinning and laughing.

'Go on, then,' urged Jonas.

Cora shook her head. 'No, not for me.'

He gave her a strange look and she shifted uncomfortably, hoping he wouldn't ask questions she didn't want to answer.

Several other of the staff members ran over and took their photos next to some of the reindeer. But Cora's stomach started to turn over. It was too much. She'd spent a whole night walking and admiring Christmas lights, and, while that had seemed fine, now, being here, back in the park, where everything was so concentrated, it all suddenly seemed claustrophobic.

Her breath was caught somewhere in her throat. Years of pent-up memories rushed up out of nowhere, and suddenly, the only place she wanted to be was back at the hotel and under her bedcovers.

'Cora, what's wrong?' Jonas was crouched down in front of her, his hands on both of her shoulders and staring her in the face. When she tried to breathe in, she caught a whiff of his pine aftershave. Concern was laced all over his face.

But the words just wouldn't come out. She wasn't ready to say them. She didn't know Jonas well enough to confide in him—not when she knew as soon as she started to tell her story, she'd get upset. She shook her head and pulled the hood up on her jacket in an attempt to try and hide part of her face. She didn't want him to see the unexplained tears brimming in her eyes.

Cora took a deep breath. 'Sorry, sudden headache. I'll go back to the hotel.' She was aware her voice was shaking. She tried to spin away, but he caught her.

'Let me help you,' he said.

She paused for a second as he moved his hand from her shoulder and for the briefest of moments his gloved finger touched her cheek.

She froze, not quite sure how to react. She wanted to grab his hand. She wanted to press his gloved hand next to her whole cheek just for a few fleeting seconds of momentary comfort. Although these warm, friendly people were new workmates, none of them really knew her.

She braced herself and blinked back her tears. 'I'm

fine,' she said quickly. 'Fine. Just need a few head-ache tablets.'

'Do you need a pharmacy? I can take you to one?'

She could see the concern in his eyes and for the odd-est reason it felt like a hand clasped around her heart. He was being nice to her. He was worried about her. And as much as she wanted comfort, she didn't want this.

She didn't want him to feel sorry for her—and that was exactly what would happen if she broke down right now and told him precisely how Christmas conjured memories she tried to forget and how painful she ac-tually found things.

Now it was her turn to straighten her shoulders. She ignored the way her stomach clenched and pasted a false smile on her face. 'Thanks, Jonas, but I have some back at the hotel. I'm sure a good night's sleep will do me the world of good. See you tomorrow.'

'You'll find your way?'

Boy, this guy was persistent.

'It's not too far. I'm sure I'll remember. I need to find my way at some point.'

It seemed he'd finally conceded. He gave her a nod. 'If you're sure, I'll see you tomorrow.'

He was staring at her with those blue eyes. And for some reason it seemed as if he could see further than he should.

So, Cora did the only thing she could do. She stuck her hands deep in her pockets, turned around and strode away as quickly as she could, ignoring the tears that started to stream down her cheeks.

CHAPTER SIX

HE'D SPENT MOST of last night worrying about her. There had been something in Cora Campbell's eyes. Something infinitely sad. It was almost as if he'd watched her retreating inside herself, even though he knew that was a completely melodramatic thought and he should probably just get over himself.

Over the last few years he'd lost a few members of staff who'd been burnt out by their emotional involvement in the sometimes heartbreaking cases they had to deal with. Hospitals were full of life and death, and the mental well-being of all his staff was a huge part of his responsibility.

Should he be concerned about Cora's mental well-being? She appeared capable and competent at work, but he had no idea what lay beneath.

His page sounded for the labour ward and he hurried down the stairs. Cora met him in the corridor outside Theatre, wearing a blue gown. 'Good. One of our ladies has delivered. Baby is born right on the thirty-six-week mark and meets all the criteria.' She counted off on her fingers, 'Less than six hours old, required prolonged resuscitation at delivery, and shows neonatal encephalopathy in a clinical exam.'

'I haven't had a chance to review the evidence.'

Cora looked him dead in the eye. 'No, but you did have the opportunity. And that's on you. What's on me is that I'm the doctor brought here to train your staff in these techniques. This baby has—' she pulled her watch from the pocket of her scrubs '—five hours and twenty minutes left to start treatment. Do you want us to sit in a corner and wait for you to catch up?'

His jaw clenched. They weren't alone. He wouldn't lose his cool. He kept his professional head firmly in place. ''Dr Campbell, these new procedures have to go to our ethics committee and governance forums for agreement.'

'Check your emails. Or, check Elias's emails. Because he did all that before I got here. Your paperwork is done, Jonas. The only person stopping this ground-breaking work starting is you.'

Every hair on his body bristled. He glanced at the clock on the wall next to him. 'Well, since I do have some time left, let me check. If I find the correct procedures have been followed, and my staff are safe to use these techniques, then I'll allow you to start.'

It was Cora's turn to look mad.

But he didn't wait for her response, he just turned around and headed into the nearest office.

He'd been given emergency access to Elias's emails, but had actually only put an out-of-office message on the account, notifying all people to send their emails on to him. He hadn't gone back through any existing emails on Elias's account—partly because it felt intrusive. But as he scanned backwards he found notifications from both the ethics and governance committees approving of Elias's proposals, along with safety protocols and guidelines for staff to follow. They'd arrived after Elias's collapse, which meant he'd put the applications in on the twenty-ninth of October—the day he'd found out Cora was coming, and just before he'd been taken unwell.

Part of Jonas wanted to be annoyed, but it looked as though Elias had just been laying the groundwork for Cora's visit—which was nothing less than he would expect from Elias. He just wished Elias had told him beforehand.

He printed out the documents, glanced over them to make sure he approved, then sent out emails to appropriate staff with the guidelines and protocols attached, asking them to read, sign and return, and to come back to him with any queries.

He tapped his fingers on the desk, moving to the coffee pot in the corner of the room and pouring himself a cup of the semi-warm liquid. It had only taken fifteen minutes. There were still five hours to start the new treatment with the baby—if the parents agreed.

He took one drink, then dumped the rest of the coffee down the sink before going back to find Cora.

The corridor was empty.

He grabbed the nearest midwife. 'Any idea where Cora, the new doctor, went?'

The midwife was carrying some equipment, obviously meant for one of the labour rooms. She looked momentarily confused, then smiled. 'Oh, the Scottish girl. Very pretty. She's away up to NICU with the new baby. I'm sure she said something about starting a new therapy.'

The papers in Jonas's hands started to crumple. He didn't look at the lifts. He ran straight for the stairs, taking them two at a time until he reached the fourth floor and the NICU.

By the time he was there, he could see Cora in one of the rooms, issuing instructions to the staff.

'What do you think you're doing?'

She looked up, completely unperturbed. All the other heads in the room turned towards him, and most of them *did* look perturbed.

'Outside. Now.'

'In a minute.'

'No, not in a minute. Now, Dr Campbell, or I'll order you out of my unit.'

Her cheeks turned pink and he could see her biting her tongue. She tugged at her scrub top to straighten it as she strode to the door. 'Carry on,' she said over her shoulder.

'*Don't* carry on,' said Jonas. 'Monitor the baby as you always would.'

He waited, letting Cora walk ahead of him. She thrust open both doors of the NICU and strode out into the corridor, turning on him in an instant.

'Don't you ever talk to me like that again.'

'Don't you ever attempt to put my staff in a vulnerable position again in my unit. I told you to wait. You moved, and attempted to start a procedure in *my* unit, without my permission.'

'We're running out of time. *She's* running out of time.' Her hands were on her hips, her words filled with passion.

'The research states the therapy should start in the first six hours after delivery. We are still well within that window.'

'Every minute matters.'

Jonas wasn't going to let this passionate woman beat him into submission. 'Dr Campbell, this is my unit. You don't go ahead without my consent. Have you even spoken to the parents—explained everything they need to know and gained their consent? Because I wasn't gone for long. Did you truly have time to have a conversation with them and explain what you wanted to do?'

He watched rage flicker across her face. 'Are you daring to suggest I haven't gained consent from the parents?'

'Can you show me it?'

'Of course, I can show you it! This isn't my first time at this.'

'Can you show me all the signed protocols and guidelines from every member of staff in the room with you in there? Can you show me your signed protocols and guidelines? I appreciate you've done this before, but not in this hospital. Not under the insurance of this hospital. And in order for you, and the hospital, to be covered, every *single* member of staff in that room involved in the therapy and the aftercare of that child needs to have read and signed the guidelines and protocols, *including you*.' He stepped right up to her. 'My job is to ensure the safety of both patients and staff. I will not allow you to bulldoze in here and put my staff at risk because you don't know how things work here.'

He saw her jaw tense. 'I gained consent a few days ago,' she said through clenched teeth.

'You spoke to the parents without clearing any of this with me?'

'I was giving myself a safety net. I always have this conversation with any woman who is in our antenatal unit if there is a chance they could deliver relatively early. It gives them a chance to ask any questions and take some time to think about it. I recognise that gaining consent after a difficult delivery, and with a very sick baby, can be fraught with difficulty. I only had to go back into Theatre and ask her if I could do what we'd previously discussed. And obviously she said yes.' Cora gave a giant sigh and ran her fingers through her messy hair, pulling it back again and redoing her pony-tail. 'I didn't realise you needed staff to sign individual paperwork here.'

'You would have if you'd paid a bit more attention to how the unit works,' he said in a low voice.

The glance she gave him was an indication she was clearly weighing him up, trying to know when to push, and when to retreat.

'My staff and your patient are left unprotected un-less all staff have read, understood and signed all the guidelines and procedures. That is what we do next.'

He didn't leave room for any argument, just moved past Cora and back into the unit. His instructions to his staff were clear. Two staff were to stay with the baby and monitor as normal, reporting any anomalies, while the rest spent the next half-hour reading all the new guidelines, asking Cora questions and then signing to say they knew what they were doing. Every additional staff member who was involved in looking after this baby while the new procedure was being trialled here would be required to do the same thing.

He knew she was agitated. She paced around the unit, planted a smile on her face to answer any staff questions, and wrung her fingers together while she waited for staff to read and sign what they should. When Jonas printed out a set of the papers and set them down in front of her, handing her a pen, she signed without even reading them. He raised his eyebrows.

'I sent the information to Elias. He won't have changed it—just completed it on your own templates.'

'Let's hope he did,' said Jonas with irony. 'Otherwise you have no idea what you just signed.'

He moved away to help a member of staff with another baby. The tension in the unit was palpable. Everyone had heard their spat. Everyone seemed determined not to get involved.

Once Jonas was satisfied everyone had read the protocols and guidelines, had signed, and it was recorded in their personnel files, he gave Cora a nod. 'Now everything is in place, you can get started.'

She almost flew across the unit in her haste to get started. Instructions flowed easily from her mouth. Jonas stood with his arms folded across his chest and watched the scene unfold.

She was direct. There was no ambiguity in any of her directions, and that made her a good teacher. 'Get the cooling blanket in place and monitor baby until the temperature reaches thirty-three degrees centigrade. Start the clock for a seventy-two-hour period. Continual monitoring of heart rate, breathing, blood pressure and temperature, with clinical observations of all extremities recorded every fifteen minutes. Any concerns at all, any readings that change, I'm right here. Talk to me. Use me. We want to do our best for this baby.'

Jonas watched as she put all instructions into the electronic records, and also set up visible charts around the crib. She'd just finished when both of their emergency pagers went off.

Jonas nodded to one of the other NICU doctors who'd signed all the protocols. 'Are you good here while we answer this?'

He nodded and they both ran down the corridor and back to the labour suite.

The sister met them as they burst through the stairwell entrance. 'You're not going to believe this. We have another.' She looked at Cora. 'You know, the sixteen-year-old girl you spoke to yesterday?'

Cora pulled back a little. 'The girl who presented with no antenatal care?'

The sister nodded. 'She's gone into early labour. Hard. The baby got in trouble with the cord around its neck. Assess for yourself, but I'm sure she'll meet the criteria.'

Jonas knew the sister of the unit well. 'Astrid, has there been a social-work referral?'

She nodded. 'The young mum is adamant she doesn't want to keep this baby. She's been hard to assess. She just turned up yesterday, with what turned out to be Braxton Hicks contractions. We kept her in when we realised her circumstances and that she'd had no ante-natal care. Emergency social worker saw her yesterday. Cora spoke to her yesterday, just as a precaution, in case she delivered early.'

Jonas put his hand on Cora's arm. 'This is a different set of circumstances. How was her state of mind? Did she understand what she was agreeing to?'

Cora nodded. 'She was a sad case yesterday. Very determined that she doesn't want to keep this baby, but close-lipped about everything else. I think she was dis-appointed she wasn't actually in labour yesterday. Told me she just wants to have this baby, sign the paperwork to give it up and leave.'

She took a deep breath and turned to Jonas. 'I know what you're asking me. Has someone pressured her into this? Is she actually a victim? Can she make rea-sonable and rational decisions?' She gave a nod of her head. 'She was very clear and articulate. Knew exactly what she wanted. When I asked her about the treatment she agreed immediately, but without any emotion. Just said, if it gives the baby a better chance of being adopted then fine.'

Jonas could hear a million thoughts crowding into his head about this case. 'Okay. She is the mum, and she's consented. We do want to give this baby the best possible start in life, no matter where it ends up. If she meets the criteria, then we'll take her up to NICU and start the therapy. But I want the duty social worker informed and I want someone to keep a special eye on mum.'

Jonas went to walk down the corridor, then stopped. He put his hand on his chest. 'Does she have issues with men?'

Astrid and Cora looked at each other, frowning. 'I'm not sure,' admitted Cora.

Astrid held up her hands. 'She's only met female staff so far. She hasn't told me she doesn't want to be treated by men.'

Jonas nodded. 'Okay, she knows both of you. Let's tread carefully here, because we don't know the background. Cora, you do the assessment of baby, Astrid, can you witness everything and record it, in case there are issues later?' He gave Cora a nod of his head. 'I'll wait here. If baby's suitable I'll help with the transfer back upstairs.'

He watched as they both made their way through to the delivery suite and picked up the phone to the unit. 'We may need a second team of staff for another baby. Can you start getting our other staff to read the guidelines and protocols? Call in extra if you need them. This could be a busy night.'

One minute she wanted to kill the man with her bare hands, the next he showed the maturity and professionalism of a manager who really understood a pregnant woman's journey.

She was struck by his thoughtfulness, even though she knew she shouldn't be. It only took her a few minutes to assess the newborn baby. She met all three criteria for treatment after her difficult delivery. Cora went to speak to the young mother, conscious that she couldn't let her own deep feelings affect her professional duty.

She'd been in the care system as a child and bounced from foster home to foster home. She'd finally been adopted by a couple who'd never had any children of their own and had a great life. When her adoptive mum had found herself unexpectedly pregnant, Cora had feared the couple wouldn't want her any more. But that hadn't happened at all. Instead, she'd managed to save her mother's life when she'd given birth unexpectedly and then suffered from a placental abruption. The emergency room operator had been cool and calm, giving the panicked fifteen-year-old Cora instructions every step of the way, and the whole event had set her career in process.

Cora couldn't remember her own mother, but had often wondered what set of circumstances had led to her being placed in the care of social services. She knew there could be a multitude of answers. She also knew what life in social care could mean for a child. After bouncing from place to place she'd got lucky with the Campbells, but she still had memories of feeling forgotten, left out and unloved in some of her foster homes. No one had ever been cruel or abusive towards her, but she'd lived her early days with the distinct impression that no one had really wanted her. And that stuck.

So, as she walked into the unit to speak to the young mum, she left all her feelings and memories at the door.

Five minutes later she blinked back tears and left the room. The young woman had been almost cold. Indifferent and uninterested in her new baby, she'd agreed again that her baby could have the therapy and was almost surprised she was being asked again. She was resolute in her decision, and also didn't want to go into her history or answer any other questions.

Cora respected the young woman's right to make a decision and knew she had to accept it.

As she came out of the delivery suite, Jonas was waiting near the crib, already monitoring the newborn little girl.

'She's really quite sick,' he said softly. 'Are we taking her for the treatment?'

Cora nodded as a tear slid down her cheek.

'You okay?' He touched her shoulder and she shook her head.

'Don't mind me, I'm getting old and emotional. Let's get this little one up to NICU where we can take good care of her.'

They readied the portable equipment to escort the little girl. 'What's her name?' asked Jonas.

Cora shook her head. 'She didn't want to give her daughter a name. Said whoever adopts her can choose the name.'

They both looked at each other. It was like a silent acknowledgement. They might have argued a short while ago, but things had to be put to one side right now. This baby was too important. There would be more than enough time to air their views about each other at a later date.

Jonas looked down and stroked the baby's hand. 'We'll pick you a name upstairs, lovely lady.'

Cora blinked back more tears. Today was just hitting her in all the wrong places.

By the time they got back upstairs, Astrid had solved their first problem. 'What a beautiful girl! You look like a Molly to me. What does everyone think of that name?'

There were a few nods, and moments later the temporary name was written on her chart. The next few hours flew past. Astrid had worked wonders and all staff currently in the unit had read and signed everything they needed to in order to be part of the team involved in the care of both babies. Molly's temperature was gradually lowered, and the clock was started.

Time ticked onwards and Cora watched both babies closely. Jonas had no interest in going home. This was a new procedure for his unit and he wanted to be there to support his staff. When the night shift filed in, none of them were surprised to see him near one of the babies. He often spent time in the unit if there were staff shortages, some really sick babies, or some parents who needed extra support.

Cora spent the first thirty minutes briefing all the new staff and getting them signed up. It was after midnight, when both babies were settled, that she finally sat down next to Jonas in one of the dimly lit rooms.

He pushed a box of doughnuts towards her. 'Perfect, I'm famished.' She sighed, then glanced around with her hand poised above the box.

He reached under the counter and pulled out a takeaway coffee.

'Where did you get that?'

He shrugged. 'There's a place nearby that does food

for nightshift workers. I gave one of our porters some money and asked if he could pick us up something.'

Cora looked around, clearly realising that most of the other staff were drinking from the same cups. 'You're really just an old softy, aren't you, Jonas Nilsson?'

He had an elbow on the desk and leaned his head in his hand. 'If you tell anyone that, I might have to stuff you in a cupboard somewhere,' he muttered in a low voice.

She gave a tired grin. 'It sounds like a half-hearted threat, but my brain is too tired to play verbal ping-pong.'

'And my brain is too tired to decipher what you just said to me.'

'Ping-pong. It's another name for table tennis?'

He shook his head and made a signal with his hands. 'You got me. My brain can't make the connection. No matter how much coffee and sugar I've had.'

She blinked. 'I think we've hit the night-shift slump. Let's get up and take a walk around. See if we can get some blood circulating again.'

He nodded and they slowly made their way around the unit, checking out monitoring stations and readings. Jonas nodded over his shoulder. 'Just as well those on the night shift haven't done a day shift too.'

Cora nodded thoughtfully. 'Your staff are good. I trust them.'

He smiled at her. 'So do I. Come on. There are a few on-call rooms just along here. You and I can grab a couple of hours' sleep. The staff will know where to find us if we're needed.'

She hesitated for a moment, looking unsure. 'Look,' he said as he pushed open the doors of NICU and took a few steps down the corridor. 'We're literally thirty steps away.' He pointed to the other door. 'And this one is forty steps away. It's better to lie down here than to have a parent see you sleeping in a chair in the office.'

She groaned. 'True.'

He ducked into the dimly lit kitchen in the corridor and grabbed two bottles of water from the staff fridge. 'Here, take one of these. There's a shower in the on-call room, and there should be fresh scrubs in there too.'

She leaned against the wall of the kitchen and closed her eyes. 'Are you trying to tell me something?'

He shrugged and leaned against the other wall. 'Some people like to shower before they sleep, some people like to shower after they sleep. I don't know your sleeping habits. Boy, you can be prickly sometimes.' The words came out in a jokey, sleepy droll.

She moved, coming shoulder to shoulder with him. 'Taught by the master,' she said ironically.

They stared at each for a few moments in the dim light. He could still see those green eyes staring at him. He wanted to know what she was thinking. What she was feeling right now.

The edges of her lips turned upwards. 'I can't work you out at all,' she whispered.

'Why would you want to?' came his throaty reply.

'Because you challenge me,' she said simply. 'And I think you might be the only friend I have in Sweden right now.' There was a wistfulness in her eyes that he'd only glimpsed before.

'Do you need a friend?' His hand moved automatically up to the side of her face, where he tucked a stray wispy strand of hair behind her ear. She instinctively took a step closer to him.

'Everybody needs a friend,' she murmured.

His own instincts took over, his mouth only inches

from hers. He could feel her warm breath on his skin and smell the light floral scent that danced around the edges of her aura. 'It's not nice feeling lonely all the time,' she said.

Her hand slid up to the side of his head, her fingers brushing through his short hair, pulling him forward so his lips were on hers.

Even though they were both tired, it was like a fire igniting some place beneath him. One of his hands wound around her waist, resting just above her bum, while the other moved to the back of her head.

Their kiss deepened. Not a mad, panicked kiss that he'd experienced at moments in his more youthful days, but something deeper, something more sincere.

None of this was normal for Jonas. He'd never dated a colleague before. He'd always just thought it wise not to. But Cora was different. From the moment he'd met her at the airport, she'd burrowed under his skin like some kind of persistent vice. Her confidence, demeanour and attitude both maddened and enthralled him. And the occasional flashes of vulnerability intrigued him. She'd already asked a few personal questions— ones he wasn't sure he would answer. One thing he knew for sure was that there was more to Cora Campbell than met the eye. Trouble was, did he want to push to find out more? She was only here for a matter of weeks. Could he really contemplate a fling with a visiting colleague?

Her hands moved and ran up the front of his scrub top, then she let out a little groan and rested her head against his, separating their lips.

He was surprised at how much that felt like a blow. So he stayed exactly where he was, feeling the rise and fall of her chest against his as they stood together.

As he watched, her lips turned upward again. 'I wondered,' she said with a hint of laughter in her tone.

'Wondered what?' he asked in amusement.

She leaned back. 'Just how good a kisser you would be.'

He was almost too scared to ask, but asked anyway.

She took a step back towards the corridor, her fingers curling around the edge of the doorway. She shivered before tossing a cheeky grin over her shoulder. 'A man of hidden talents. Definitely a ten,' she said as she moved out of his view and seconds later he heard the door of one of the on-call rooms close.

The temptation to follow her straight inside was strong. But she hadn't directly invited him. So he let out a long, slow breath, took a few moments to compose himself, then picked up his bottle of water and walked to the next on-call room, closing the door behind him and automatically flicking the tiny shower on.

What on earth had he just got himself into?

CHAPTER SEVEN

THEY DIDN'T DISCUSS the kiss.

For one whole, painstaking week, they didn't discuss that sweet, passionate, and extremely illuminating kiss—just danced around each other at work, exchanging small glances and smiles.

Jonas was a ten at kissing, of that there was no doubt. The ice Viking had ignited sparks that she'd kind of forgotten existed. Wow.

In fact, things at Stockholm City Hospital were turning out quite well. Both babies who'd had the hypothermia treatment seemed to have fared well. Of course, no one would know for a number of years if it had actually made a difference to their developmental outcomes. But Cora was positive as all the signs looked good.

A third baby had started treatment today and the staff, who had initially been a little nervous, were acting like experts now. They were a good team. Those who hadn't been present at either of the first sessions were all trained and on the rota for the third session to ensure everyone in the NICU got the experience and supervision they required.

Jonas had been around the last few days, helping with the supervision of staff. When he'd told her he was determined to make sure all staff had their questions answered, and would be confident and competent to practice, the man hadn't lied. He was diligent in his duty to his staff.

It was interesting to watch. She could tell that some staff loved his involvement, and a few thought it was a little interfering. But Jonas appeared to read his staff well, knowing who to back away from and who appreciated a glance over their shoulder.

So, if he could read all these staff well, why couldn't he read her?

She was beginning to replay the kiss over and over in her brain. The truth was, she wouldn't mind repeating it. But the even deeper truth was, she wouldn't mind getting to know Jonas a little better too. He intrigued her. It was almost as if he had a whole host of layers to break through before she finally got to the Jonas that lay beneath. Maybe things would have been better if they hadn't met in a workplace setting. He might be an entirely different person away from here.

All around the hospital, people were getting more and more in the festive mood. She was used to it. But Christmas sometimes made her feel as if the walls were closing in around her, especially as those particular dates loomed in the calendar. Even though they were still some weeks away, the twenty-third and the twenty-fourth of December were imprinted on her brain, a time when most people were entirely wrapped up in the chaos of panic buying and searching for that one last crucial element for dinner in the few days before Christmas.

What she badly needed right now was something to distract her from all this. Had she been at home, she'd have retreated to her flat, closed the door and the curtains and taken herself on some kind of sci-fi movie marathon. But being in the hotel was different. The Christmas decorations were beautiful. The maid had also put a small Christmas tree in her room and Cora felt like an old Scrooge when she tried to hide it every night by throwing her jacket or dressing gown over the top of it.

So, today when she was out walking through the older town, she was doing her best to scowl at all the beautifully decorated shop windows. Jonas and many of the other staff had encouraged her to explore Gamla Stan and they'd been entirely right.

The district felt like something from a children's story book. It was packed with cafés, museums, restaurants, tourist shops, galleries. Some of the building fronts were painted in vivid shades of red, yellow and green. Coupled with a dusting of snow and cobblestone streets, Cora half expected a witch on a broomstick to fly overhead, next to reindeer pulling a sleigh.

She lost several hours in the shops, buying some woodwork, jewellery, and then finding a sci-fi book shop with some very tempting board games. Wonderful smells continued to drift around her and it wasn't long before her stomach started to rumble.

She was peering in the window of one of the bakeries when she felt a tap on her shoulder. 'I'd recognise that green coat anywhere,' said the accented voice.

Her stomach leapt and she turned around to see Jonas holding a paper bag with a giant loaf inside. 'What are you doing here?' she asked.

He raised his eyebrows and lifted the loaf. 'I'm on a retrieval mission for the theatre team. I told them that when I came in at two p.m. today, I'd bring some bread for them.'

'You're working today?' He nodded. 'One of the

other managers needs a few hours off this afternoon. Her daughter is in a play at school.'

Those few words made Cora's heart swell. Jonas really was a good guy. 'What's the other bag?' she asked.

His face fell a little. 'It's Elias's favourite apricot pastries. I'll run them over to him later today.'

She nodded, then looked around and held up her hands, which were weighed down with bags. 'Okay, I've been shopping all morning and am looking for somewhere to go for a coffee and some cakes. Where do you recommend? They all look good around here.'

He nodded. 'Come along, I'll show you. Is it definitely cake you want, or something more substantial?'

'Oh, no, it's cake. Can you smell this place? I might just eat all the cakes. There's no way I can be here and resist eating cake.'

They walked along the street together, and when they were almost at the castle, Jonas nudged her, and pointed towards a cute-looking café. She spun around. 'Will you join me?' she asked. 'Or don't you have enough time?'

There was a large clock visible where they were standing and it was only eleven. But she had no idea what other plans he had for the day.

Jonas nodded solemnly and smiled. 'I think it's my duty to introduce you to all the cakes that Stockholm has to offer.'

He pushed open the door to the café and joined her at a table near the window. He glanced over at the glass-fronted cabinet. 'So, what's it to be? Scrumptious croissants, cinnamon buns, fruit and nut loaf, or blueberry and raspberry pie?'

'I swear I'm putting on ten pounds every time I inhale around here,' said Cora, watching as a waitress walked past with delicious-looking items on her tray.

'I want what they're having,' she said as the plates and mugs were slid onto the table.

'Well, that's easy, then.' Jonas said a few words to the smiling waitress as she passed by. She nodded and disappeared.

Cora gestured down at her bags. 'You didn't tell me how addictive this place is. Don't leave me unsupervised again. I'll likely buy everything and eat everything.'

She was smiling but Jonas's brow creased for a few moments. Didn't he know she was joking?

He looked down at the numerous bags she had sitting on the floor, the crease in his brow deepening as he stared.

Then he blinked and his pale blue eyes rested on her again.

'I'm sure that won't happen,' he said softly.

She unzipped her jacket, feeling instantly flustered. Cora had the distinct impression that she was missing something here.

The waitress appeared and put two delicious-smelling white hot chocolates on their table along with two portions of warm blueberry and raspberry pie complete with ice cream. 'Wow, ice cream in the middle of winter. I wouldn't have believed it if I hadn't seen it for myself.'

She wasn't quite sure what was on Jonas's mind, but she was determined to lift the mood. They'd kissed just over a week ago now, and neither of them had talked about it since.

As he took his first spoonful of pie, she decided to throw caution to the wind. 'So, tell me, do you kiss every visiting doctor that comes to Stockholm City Hospital?'

His eyes widened and he started to choke on his pie.

Several other customers turned to look and Cora had to jump up and give him a couple of claps on the back before he finally stopped. The waitress appeared with a glass of water and Cora sat back down in time to see Jonas wipe the tears that were streaming down his face.

'Are you okay?' asked the waitress.

He nodded. 'Fine. Sorry. It just went down the wrong way.'

She nodded, waiting a few moments before leaving.

Cora picked up her own spoon, now feeling badly instead of bold.

'Maybe a question for another time?'

Jonas shook his head and took a drink of the water. 'No. It's not. And no, I don't kiss every visiting doctor. You're the only one.'

She leaned her head on one hand. 'Ahh, so I'm special, then?' She wanted to joke, she wanted to flirt. She was still surrounded by all things Christmas and she wanted her mind to be someplace else.

He raised one eyebrow. 'Maybe.'

She grinned at him. 'You playing hard to get?'

His brow creased again and she waved her hand. 'Don't worry, it's an expression that probably doesn't translate well.'

He stirred his hot chocolate. It was clear he was thinking about something. 'Are you going to the Lucia procession?'

Now it was her turn to frown and shake her head. 'What's that?'

'It's next week. There are many processions of Lucia and they all take place in December. A young girl is asked to act as lady of light, or Lucia, as we call her. She wears a white costume and has candles on her head, and there is usually a singing procession following her.

There's always one in Stockholm and most of the hospital staff attend.' He paused for a second, then added, 'Or there's the night out beside the world's largest Christmas tree—you'll have seen it already at Gamla Stan. Or there's the living Christmas advent calendar. You might have seen it already. Every night, a window somewhere in Gamla Stan will open at six-fifteen p.m.—on Christmas Eve it opens at eleven-thirty a.m.—and one or more heads will pop out—an actor, a singer, a storyteller—and offer fifteen minutes of Christmas advent delight. If you look out for banners hung from windows that say *Här öppnar luckan*, you'll know where the surprise window will be that night.'

He was clearly waiting for a response, but, after flirting with him, Cora was finding it hard to say the word she wanted to: no.

She licked her lips and tried to find something appropriate to say. 'Is everything about Christmas? Isn't there anything that's just about Stockholm?'

She could sense his eyes on her for a few moments of consideration.

'Don't you like Christmas, Cora?' He asked the question in a gentle way that made her realise he already knew the answer. He was just giving her a chance to say what she wanted.

She bit her lip and met his gaze. 'I find it a bit tough. Family reasons. I want to be sociable with the rest of the staff—I do. But every single thing we do is about Christmas. I don't want to appear like a Scrooge because I don't love it quite as much as others.'

He reached over and squeezed her hand. 'You're right. Most of the trips this time of year are about Christmas. We can find something different to do. A visit to the Vasa Museum perhaps? Or we could do a boat trip—this city stretches across fourteen islands. You've only seen a few.'

She nodded gratefully as he kept talking.

'Maybe, though, if you don't have good memories of Christmas, it might be nice to create some new ones? And Stockholm is new to you—perhaps you could create some new memories here?'

Her skin prickled. He was being sincere, and it made her feel stripped back and bare. As if all her past experiences and fears were exposed. Her involuntary action was the same as always—to brush things off.

'Can I take that under advisement?'

Jonas looked puzzled again and she waved her hand. 'Just another turn of phrase. Ignore me.'

There was silence for a few moments as they both ate. The door to the café opened again, letting in a fierce gust of cold air, and another couple walked in hand in hand. Something twisted inside Cora.

She couldn't ever remember looking like that. So in love, so caught up in the moment that nothing else mattered. She tried not to stare as they stood at the counter together selecting cakes, then sloping off to one of the booths near the back of the café.

When she looked up she realised Jonas was watching them too. He shrugged. 'Oh, to be young.'

There was something melancholy about his throwaway words. And she was suddenly struck by the fact that for the last few minutes she'd been immersed in herself and not thinking about Jonas. She knew there was a story hidden deep down somewhere. It was in everything he said, everything he did, and the way he reacted to things. His need for process drove her crazy. But she'd seen how well he connected with patients. Part of her wondered if being in management was the right thing for Jonas. Management came with its own challenges—one of which was that it often took an excellent hands-on member of staff further away from the patients.

She glanced back at the younger couple. 'They're not so young,' she said, squinting a little to get a better look. 'Mid-twenties?'

Jonas nodded in agreement. 'Maybe.' There was still something wistful in his tone. She wanted to prod. She wanted to ask questions but wasn't quite sure how he might respond. Did kissing someone give her the right to dig deeper?

'You haven't mentioned family much—do you have family in Stockholm?'

He shook his head. 'My family stay in Sundsvall. It's about a four-hour drive. I moved to Stockholm to train to be a nurse and midwife and found that I liked it here. I've been here since I was eighteen.'

'Do you ever go back home?'

'Sometimes I visit my parents and my sister in holidays.'

'Are you going home for Christmas?'

He shook his head. 'I usually volunteer to work so other managers who have families can have the time off. I hope that when my time comes, someone will do the same for me.'

She was pretty sure her stomach was fluttering right now, and it wasn't the raspberry pie. 'You plan to settle down sometime?'

He leaned back in his chair. 'Some day. Doesn't everyone?' His eyes fixed on hers.

Cora hesitated. 'I sometimes wonder if I'm the settling-down type.'

His gaze was steady. 'Well, only you can decide that.

I guess it just depends what priorities you have in your life. And timing, of course.'

'You haven't met anyone you wanted to settle down with?' As she asked the question she noticed him shift uncomfortably and she cringed. Please don't let there be some dead wife in the background and she'd just monumentally put her foot in it.

His gaze was now fixed on the window to the street outside. Surely if there had been something, or some-one, significant in his past, one of the other staff might have mentioned it? But then, the staff were loyal to Jonas. Would they really tell a temporary newcomer something private or personal about their boss? Prob-ably not. Maybe she should tread a little more carefully.

'Not yet,' he said finally. She could almost see some-thing turn on in his eyes—as if he'd never really given it much thought before, but now…now it was something he might consider. 'I guess I've just not been lucky.' He took a sip of his hot chocolate. 'Not met the right woman yet.'

She could swear there was something glittering in the air between them. So much unsaid. Her brain was screaming *How about me?* And, maybe she was crazy, but as he looked at her the corners of his mouth edged upwards, as if he were having the same thoughts as she was. When he spoke again, his voice was low. 'What about you? No Mr Right tucked away somewhere?'

She shook her head and laughed. 'Plenty of Mr Wrongs, Mr Never-Could-Be-Rights, and Mr Abso-lute Disasters, though. I tend to get too caught up in work to pay much attention to whoever I'm dating. I think I'm probably the worst girlfriend in the world.'

He held up his hot chocolate. 'I'll drink to that.'

She laughed and held up hers. 'What—are you the worst boyfriend too?'

'Oh, no, but I'm happy to drink to you being the worst girlfriend.'

'Cheeky!' She clunked her mug against his and ate some more of her pie. 'You said you're going to meet Elias. Do you think I might get to meet him in person at some point, before I leave?'

He wrinkled his nose. 'What—you have another, nearly three weeks? I'll see how he is today. Elias is a proud man. He wouldn't want to meet you unless he was at a stage where he could converse properly with you.'

'He's not there yet?'

'Maybe. He's improving all the time. I saw him again last week, and he was able to walk with a stick. He was still stumbling with some words, and his thought processes were a little delayed. Let me ask him when I visit later today. I'll let you know what he says.'

'Will you tell him about the babies?'

There was the briefest hesitation. 'Of course, I will. He'll want to know all about it.'

'And you'll tell him it's been a success?' she pushed.

'I'll tell him the procedures went well, and our staff training and monitoring systems are in place. I can't tell him it was a success as we don't know yet that it is a success. We won't know the outcomes for these babies for a few years.' This time it was him who was pushing.

'But the immediate outcomes were evident.'

He nodded slowly. 'Yes, but we have to view these things in context.'

Cora sat back with a sigh and shook her head. 'You don't want this to succeed, do you? You're so against change that no matter how well this works, you just won't let it continue.' Frustration was building inside her. She'd thought they'd made strides towards this being an implementable procedure at Stockholm City Hospital. A step forward for babies affected by hypoxic ischaemic encephalopathy. But every time she thought they'd made some headway, they seemed to jump backwards instead.

Jonas looked at her with an incredulous expression. 'Where on earth did you get that from? I'm just asking you to have a bit of context around the work so far and not to jump too far ahead. We've used the treatment on three babies, Cora. *Three.* Since when did that become a number that makes this treatment the one to use? You've been involved in research studies. You know that's not how this works. And we won't know the true outcomes for these babies for years.'

She leaned forward, pressing both her hands on the table. 'But this is *not* a research study. This is fact. The studies have been done. I'm here to teach, not to tiptoe around every person and constantly ask permission to breathe!'

Her heart was racing in her chest and her voice had become a bit louder, causing people to turn around and look at them, with a few raised eyebrows.

But Jonas wasn't ready to back down. He leaned back across the table to her. His voice was low, and hissing. 'But your research was done in the UK. A different population. A different demographic. A different healthcare and social care system. Things aren't automatically translatable. I shouldn't have to tell you that.'

Cora stood up sharply, her chair tilting back dangerously. 'You're impossible.'

Jonas leaned back in his chair. While she was boiling mad, he looked completely unperturbed. It was as if he was baiting her.

'And you're irrational.'

It was like someone jabbing a red-hot poker into her side. How dared he call her irrational? She was so mad she couldn't speak—not that he deserved a response.

She slid her arms into her jacket, bent down and snatched up her shopping bags, fumbling to fit them all in her hands before turning and storming out of the door.

The freezing-cold air did nothing to cool her temper. She stomped down the street without a backwards glance, determined to get as far away as possible from Mr Ice Viking.

She had a job to do. And he wouldn't get in her way. She wouldn't let him.

CHAPTER EIGHT

TWO DAYS LATER and she hadn't set eyes on him.

Cora was the ultimate professional. In the NICU she was all smiles. She'd written a few more protocols for the procedure and asked Alice for advice on how to put them through all the relevant committees.

Alice had waved her hand. 'Jonas will do all that for you,' she'd said casually.

'I like to see things through myself,' she'd insisted. 'Plus, I like to find out all the procedures anywhere that I'm working. Each hospital works differently, and it's good for me to get a handle on different operating procedures.'

If Alice had been suspicious, she hadn't said so, just scribbled down some names and numbers of people for Cora to get in touch with.

Forty minutes later when there had been a page from the antenatal ward that another of their patients had gone into early labour, she'd decided to go on down.

Her phone buzzed as she ran down the stairs. It was Chloe. They'd been ping-ponging messages to each other after Cora had raged about Jonas a few days ago.

Just thinking. Can't remember the last time you ranted about someone quite so much. If you ask me, there's more to this than a disagreement about work. Exactly how attractive is Jonas Nilsson?

Cora's mouth bounced open. Chloe was too smart for her own good.

Viking-like. But far too arrogant for me to care how attractive he is.

Dots appeared. Chloe was immediately typing a response.

You've kissed him, haven't you?

Cora actually stopped mid-step.

Why on earth would you say that??????????

She was shaking her head as Chloe typed back.

Knew it.

She let out a sigh and put her phone back in her pocket. Chloe could always read her like a book.

As she reached the labour suite, there was that eerie kind of calm. There was no sign of any staff, and the corridor was silent—never a good sign in a labour ward.

She made her way along the corridor, towards the emergency theatre at the end. Just as she reached the swing doors, a midwife burst through them, wearing a blood-stained plastic apron. She gave Cora a quick glance up and down before a flicker of recognition crossed her face and she pointed a gloved hand. 'NICU doctor?'

Cora nodded without speaking.

'Good, with me. Emergency.' The midwife gave a sharp nod of her head and pushed open the doors.

Cora could tell immediately that this was where the majority of the staff were. Someone was lying on the floor, and it took her a few moments to realise it was a fellow doctor, who was pregnant. She went immediately to assist, but a voice from the theatre table stopped her.

'No, leave her. We need you here.'

Cora's head flicked from one place to the other. Every instinct in her wanted to help her fellow colleague on the theatre floor, but there were three members of staff already around her. One of them caught her eye. 'She's diabetic. Had a hypoglycaemic attack. We can deal with this.'

Cora didn't recognise the obstetrician in the cap and mask at the theatre table, but there were twelve at Stockholm City Hospital and she hadn't met them all.

His voice was deep. 'I need a neonatologist. This baby will need resuscitated.' He was already cutting through the woman's abdomen.

Cora stepped to the sinks and gave her hands a quick wash. Turning around, she found a theatre nurse with a gown ready for her to step into, and another with a pair of waiting gloves, and a third placed a cap on her head.

She recognised one of the NICU nurses waiting next to the neonatal crib. She thrust her hands into the gloves, just as the obstetrician lifted out the silent baby.

As Cora took the baby, her motions became automatic. She'd unfortunately done this on many occasions. A voice she recognised was at her side and she looked up to see Jonas appear and tie a mask around her face. Some babies needed encouragement to breathe after delivery, but Cora knew nothing about the circumstances of this case, and this little one looked a little too flat for her liking.

She spoke clearly to the NICU nurse, who was just as well versed in this as she was, assessing airway, breathing and circulation. Jonas handed her a suction tube, as she tried to stimulate the baby to breathe.

Nothing. There was a noise behind them and she turned her head in time to see her colleague on the floor thrash out with her arms and legs. It was clear she was confused. Hypoglycaemic attacks frequently did that, and it could be a few minutes before things calmed down. In an ideal situation they would have taken her somewhere else, but for the next few minutes, the floor was probably the safest place for her.

Cora continued her assessment of the baby as Jonas systematically connected her to all the monitoring equipment. It was a little girl and her colour was extremely poor. Her pulse was weak but rapid and thready, and there was no respiratory effort at all, even with a bag and mask. After another few moments she nodded to Jonas. 'I'm going to intubate.'

She moved to the head of the crib and Jonas automatically put everything she needed into her hands. Airways could be tricky, particularly in small pre-term babies, but Cora slid the tube in with no problem and started the procedures to connect the little girl to the machinery.

Now it was Cora's turn to hold her breath, until the little girl's skin finally started to lose the dusky tone and pink up.

She spent the next few moments inserting a line. Premedication was usually given prior to intubation in the neonatal unit, but wasn't appropriate for intubations in the delivery suite. Cora wanted to ensure that now an airway was established she could do her utmost to ensure this little girl was given the medications that would assist her.

Cora finally lifted her head to look at the obstetrician while another nurse put an ID bracelet on the baby. 'I'm going to take this little one up to NICU.'

As another alarm sounded, this time for the mother, the obstetrician nodded. 'Thanks for your assistance. Jonas said you would step in.'

She exchanged glances for the briefest of seconds with Jonas, and then the two of them started to push the crib and ventilator out to the lift. Their doctor colleague was now in a sitting position on the floor and drinking some orange juice.

Once they were clear of the theatre, Cora pressed the button for the lift and looked at Jonas. 'What on earth happened in there?'

He frowned tightly. 'Everything. Eve passed out. One minute she was there and talking, the next she was on the floor. I had already paged you about the delivery and knew you were likely on your way down. Just as well, as at that point they lost the baby's heartbeat.'

Cora shuddered. Her eyes on her little patient. 'As soon as I walked into the labour suite I knew something was wrong.'

'Chaos?'

'The opposite. Not a single person and complete silence.'

Jonas closed his eyes for a second. 'Never a good sign.'

'Nope.' She touched the cheek of the little girl. 'Do we know a name?'

He nodded. 'Her mother told me before we got to Theatre that she intended to call her Rose.'

'You were already down there?'

He nodded again. 'Yes. There had been some issues on the antenatal ward, and the labour suite today.'

'What?' The question came out automatically, and as soon as she noticed the dark expression on his face, she wished she hadn't asked.

'Two staff were involved in a car accident this morning. One worked in each area. Both are serious, and are in general theatres, right now.'

'Oh, no.'

He inhaled deeply. 'I had to send some staff home, and I had to phone the families.'

She reached her hand over and touched his. 'That must have been hard.'

'That's the job. I've called extra staff in, and another manager.'

'And what about that doctor? I've never met her before.'

'The neonatologist? Eve has been off during her pregnancy. She's a Type One diabetic and had been having frequent hypos. She literally came back to work two hours ago.'

'Poor soul. She'll need to go off again. Will someone check her over?'

'I'll make sure of it.' He glanced at Cora. 'It's a shame. You would have liked working with her. She's a great doctor.'

As the lift doors pinged open, two of the NICU staff were waiting for them and grabbed one end of the crib and the portable ventilator.

They rolled smoothly into the NICU and spent the next half-hour getting baby Rose set up in the unit. Jonas disappeared while Cora spent some time with the frazzled dad who appeared upstairs, explaining exactly what was happening with his newly born daughter.

By the time Jonas reappeared with two ham bagels in his hand, Cora didn't even realise that four hours had passed since she'd first received the page.

As he sat down next to her in the office, and wordlessly handed her a bagel, Cora took a deep breath. 'Wow.'

He took a bite of his bagel and a few moments later gave an agreed, 'Wow.'

'Is Eve okay?'

He smiled. 'Angry, embarrassed, annoyed, and frustrated, but definitely okay.'

'That's what matters.'

He gave her a sideways glance. 'She wanted to meet you. Wanted to hear about your work.'

'Ah, that's nice.' She took a bite of her bagel. 'Maybe some other time. I'd be happy to go over the principles with her. Take it she's having a tough time with this pregnancy?'

He nodded. 'She's one of our most reliable doctors and she's been diabetic since childhood. But since she became pregnant, she's been plagued by unexpected hypoglycaemic attacks. It's a shame. She sat with me at lunch one day, ate everything, then stood up and literally passed out cold.'

'She wasn't showing any signs?'

'About two minutes before she passed out, she got a strange look in her eye—but she was still taking part in the conversation. She's been so well controlled for years that her blood sugar goes really low before she gets any warning signs.'

'Is there nothing they can do?'

Jonas actually looked furtive for a moment and paused.

'What have you done?'

He pulled a face. 'I phoned a company rep that I knew. There's a new thing that's been trialled. It's a patch that fits to the skin and sends a constant cellulose sugar reading to a phone. The phone can alarm for either high or low levels.'

'Did you get one?'

He glanced at his watch. 'Eve—much to her annoyance—is being monitored for a few hours in the antenatal ward. The rep will be here within the hour.'

Cora gave him an interested look. 'You have a good heart, Jonas Nilsson.'

He held out his hands. 'What? She'd do the same for me if I was in that position, and I know it. We're a team. We've got to help each other.'

She gave him a knowing smile. 'That's right. We're a team. We should help each other. I totally agree.'

The change in her tone of voice got his attention. He set the bagel down. 'Why do I feel like I've just been played?'

Cora shook her head and pointed at the half-eaten bagels. 'Tell me you got us something other than this?'

He sighed and reached into his pocket, pulling out two chocolate bars. Cora took hers, opened it right away and broke off a square of chocolate, putting it in her mouth without pausing for breath.

'You didn't finish your main,' he teased, pointing at the bagel.

She shrugged. 'I like to mix and match. I'll finish them both.' She narrowed her eyes and said warningly, 'Don't try and police my food. Quickest way to make me your enemy.'

'I thought I'd already done that,' he said casually, teasing her.

She ate another piece of chocolate. 'You definitely try my patience. This chocolate might be the only thing that saves you.'

He stopped for a minute, pushing his food away. 'Do we want to talk about what happened between us?'

'The kiss or the fight?'

'Touché. How about both?'

He had her there. Cora wasn't quite sure what to say. Talk about being put on the spot. 'Are you brave enough to go there?' She kind of preferred this casual flirting. Jonas had already learned more about her than most people she'd consider acquaintances. She wasn't entirely sure she wanted to reveal any more.

But on the other hand, finding out a bit more about her mysterious Viking wasn't entirely unappealing.

She licked her lips. 'Okay, then. I'll start with the kiss. I liked it. It was…interesting.'

He sat forward. 'Interesting?' He said the word as if she'd just insulted him.

She smiled at his reaction. 'Yes, it was.'

He frowned. 'Not enticing? Or amazing? I'd even settle for hot.'

Now, she was definitely laughing. 'Well, how would you describe it?'

He folded his arms. 'Unsure.' He was watching her with those pale blue eyes.

'And what does that mean?'

He gave her a half-smile. 'It means I think I need to try again, to be sure.'

'You do?' She couldn't help but smile as he leaned closer.

'I do.' His lips were inches from hers. As she inhaled, she could smell his aftershave. The soap powder on his uniform. The balm on his skin.

She put her hand on his chest. 'But we haven't got to the fight yet,' she said quietly.

'I thought we could just miss that bit,' he whispered.

'We could,' she agreed, highly tempted. But gave his chest a little push back. 'Or, we could get to the crux of the matter.'

He gave a resigned sigh and sat back on his chair, cracking open his own bar of chocolate. 'Which is?'

'Why you don't like my research or my work.'

He shook his head. 'Your research I don't mind. I've read it all. It's your methods I find…questionable.'

'Questionable?' Her voice rose an octave as he gave her a lazy smile, knowing he'd tempted another reaction out of her.

He waved a hand. 'I think we've established you're a great hands-on doctor. Fearless. Practical. Able to teach. Able to assist in an emergency.'

She gave an approving nod. 'Carry on. I like these thoughts.'

'I thought you might.'

She sighed and waited for him to continue.

'But you don't always see the bigger picture.' He put his hand on his chest. 'And you don't need to, because that's my job as the manager of this unit and all the staff to make sure that I cross every t and dot every i.'

'Is that a Swedish expression?'

He shook his head. 'No, I looked it up online last night to be able to explain what I meant to you.'

'You planned this conversation last night?' she said with disbelief.

'I planned we'd have it at some point.'

She broke off another piece of chocolate. 'What made you think I'd talk to you again?'

He reached his hand over and touched her skin. 'This.'

There was silence as the little buzz shot up her arm and tickled every sense in her body.

Her eyes were fixed on the spot he'd just touched. 'So, I haven't imagined it,' she said in a low voice.

'No,' he said huskily. 'You haven't imagined it.'

'So what does that mean…for us?'

'It means we have a little less than three weeks left to get to know each other a bit better.' He'd moved closer again, his voice low, his warm breath teasing the skin at her neck.

He smiled at her. 'So, what's it to be? The boat trip, or a visit to the Vasa Museum?'

Something warm stirred inside her heart. He'd remembered. He'd remembered that she didn't love Christmas so much, and wanted to try something different.

That mattered. A lot.

Her green eyes met his gaze. 'You decide,' she said quickly, before sliding her arms around his neck, and sealing the deal with a kiss.

CHAPTER NINE

IT SEEMED THAT he was losing his mind. And Jonas was sure that the gorgeous woman, currently on his arm, was the cause.

This should be harmless. This should be fun. Cora was only here for another few weeks. He already knew that she was due to fly back to London on Christmas Eve.

It had struck him as kind of a sad time of year to travel. But from the casual chats he'd had with Cora, he could tell she wasn't really thinking about it. Others might be fretting about late flights, and delays, and hurrying home to their family, but he already knew Cora didn't like Christmas much, even though he didn't know the finer details.

Today, they were huddled at the entrance to the Vasa Museum—in amongst a long line of tourists. Cora looked up at him with a smile. 'You bring me to all the best places,' she said, her breath turning to steam in the freezing air as she shivered.

He put his arm around her. 'It's warmer once we get inside. Think of this as your cultural experience.'

She laughed. 'It's a chocolate museum, isn't it?'

'You wish. But I know a nice chocolate shop we can visit later.'

'Promises, promises,' she muttered as the line slowly moved forward.

They made their way inside, and it took Cora a few moments to unzip her jacket and realise what was the main exhibit.

She let out a gasp. 'A ship? The Vasa Museum is a ship?'

He smiled and nodded. 'A bit of history. Pay attention. It's the world's only conserved seventeenth-century ship.'

The ship was mounted just above them, so everyone viewing could walk around and underneath and get a feel for the size and quality of the ancient ship.

Cora shook her head. 'How on earth did it get here?'

'It sank,' he said simply. 'A few minutes after being launched in 1628.'

She looked at him in confusion. 'But I still don't get it—this was at the bottom of the sea?'

He nodded. 'After over three hundred years on the sea bed, the *Vasa* was retrieved and preserved for the museum.'

'No way!' she said as she continued to walk underneath. 'No way was this under the sea for three hundred years.' She turned and wagged her finger at him. 'I've watched all those *Titanic* documentaries. Everything just disintegrates. This must be a replica. Isn't it?'

'I'll have you know we Swedes are a talented bunch. Ninety-eight per cent of this ship is original.'

She reached out to try and touch it, even though it was way above her head. 'But…that's impossible.'

He smiled again. He wasn't sure what she'd think of the museum and deliberately hadn't told her what it housed. But it was clear she was impressed. 'Did Vikings sail on it?'

Now, he laughed. 'We'd have to go back a whole lot longer for that. No, it was a warship, and the upper hull was much too heavy. That's why she sank. It's in such good condition because Stockholm has uniquely brackish waters, which basically fossilised the ship and kept her in great condition until her recovery.'

'I can't believe it survived,' said Cora in wonder. She slipped her hand into Jonas's as they continued around the structure.

'Well, a bit like the Titanic, the metal parts suffered. All the iron bolts disintegrated; only things like cannon balls and the anchor survived.' He gave a laugh. 'And the guns and cannons. They were looted years ago.'

Cora slid her jacket off. 'It's quite warm in here.'

'It's kept at a steady temperature to stop the ship deteriorating. If you came in here in the summer, you'd find it chilly and want a jumper.'

'Well, it's so cold outside it feels positively pleasant in here today,' said Cora. They'd walked around the boat twice now.

'Want to visit the restaurant upstairs? The food is quite good here.'

She nodded and passed by an exhibit of the timeline of the ship's preservation as they moved to the stairs. The restaurant was busy already, even though it wasn't quite midday, and they were seated at a table quickly.

'Okay, there's a rule,' said Jonas as the waiter took their drinks order.

'What's the rule?' asked Cora cautiously.

'They have a daily dish here—and it's always Swedish meatballs in a cream sauce with lingonberries. You have to try it.'

Cora smiled. 'I haven't tried any meatballs since I got here.' She picked up the fork at her place setting.

'But I have, of course, tried the meatballs at a very famous store in the UK.'

Jonas groaned and shook his head. 'No, they are an imitation. Now you're in Sweden, you'll try the real thing.'

Jonas ordered for them both as Cora sipped her white wine, and he his beer.

Her mood was good today. He hadn't seen those hidden shadows that occasionally flitted across her eyes. And it was clear she was enjoying herself. She asked questions at an alarming rate, and eventually he had to admit he didn't know all the answers, and bought her a guidebook for the museum.

They joked back and forward as their meal was brought to them and Jonas watched in pleasure as her eyes lit up at the first taste of the genuine Swedish meatballs. She gave a nervous smile. 'I hated to admit that I loved the ones back home, but these are really spectacular.' She leaned back in her chair with a contented glow. 'I swear, if I could come here every day to eat these, I might just move to Stockholm.'

Her words made him curious. 'You've always stayed in London—you wouldn't consider moving elsewhere?'

She shook her head. 'Well, obviously I'm from Scotland, and I trained at Edinburgh University and worked in the hospitals around there during my training. But, as soon as I qualified, because it's a more specialist field, there just seemed to be more opportunities in London. I had an offer last year of a job in Washington, and then the year before in Germany, but...' she paused as if she were contemplating whether to be honest or not '... I wanted to be in the same part of the world as my sister, Isla, when she was at university. And it's only just over an hour's flight from London. She has her aunt and uncle, of course, but we're close—guess that happens when you're there at the delivery—and I just wanted to be nearby in case she needed me.' She smiled sadly. 'But the truth is, she's all grown up now. She's the most independent girl on the planet. I wouldn't be surprised if she announced she was going to Australia to do her final year of university or something similar.'

Jonas shook his head. 'Wait a minute. Rewind. You were there when Isla was delivered?'

Heat flooded into her cheeks. But she'd said it out loud now. There was no point in lying about it. 'I delivered her. My mum went into labour early, fast, and very unexpectedly. We stayed quite far out in the country. My dad was miles away trading sheep, and it was just me and her.'

Jonas sat back a bit further in his seat. He wanted to know all about this. 'That must have been terrifying. How old were you?'

'Fifteen. Let's just say it was a baptism of fire. The emergency operator was great, calm as you like, and gave me really clear instructions. Isla was born within a few minutes. She was early and needed a bit of assistance with her breathing. The scariest thing was when my mum had a postpartum haemorrhage. I'll never forget seeing all that blood on the floor.'

'What did you do?'

'Exactly what the operator told me to do. They decided to send an air ambulance at that point.'

'How long did that take?'

She gave a distinctly uncomfortable smile. 'Nearly too long. Obviously, I had no oxytocin, and I spent a long time massaging my mum's uterus, trying to get it to contract and stop the bleeding. It was all I could do.'

'Wow, that's brave.'

She nodded slowly. 'In the end, both Isla and my mum were okay. Both stayed in hospital for a few weeks, and it lit a fire in my belly.'

He gave her a strange glance.

'Maybe it's another UK saying. It made me curious. Made me want to be a doctor. To help small babies like Isla and see if I could learn to do things to help them.' She licked her lips and took a sip of her wine. 'Honestly, it made me who I am today.'

He sat back and watched her for a while, loving the way the sunlight from the windows was catching the tones in her hair, and the glint of her green eyes. She was beautiful. Inside and out. Passionate about her work too. Yes, they might disagree about things, but Cora challenged him. She was the first woman who'd brought some light into his life in the last few years. She made him laugh. She made him furious. And he'd honestly never been so happy around someone.

But somehow he knew there was more—so much more to unravel about this intriguing woman. She still hadn't really told him why she didn't like Christmas, and if he asked now, it would feel like prying. She'd already told him a little of herself, but he was sure there were many more fascinating pieces to the puzzle that made up Cora Campbell. His stomach clenched a little. He'd been burned once before with Katrina. Was he going to let himself be burned again? Could all this blow up in his face?

He took a breath and made an instant decision. He would be patient. He knew Cora still had some secrets. But Jonas hadn't told her everything about himself either. He was rapidly losing his heart to this woman, and, at some point in his life, he had to take the chance. He had to take the chance to be happy.

'What?' she asked.

The word jolted him out of his reverie and he straightened in his chair. 'What?' he countered.

'You were looking at me funny.'

'I was not.'

Her expression was affectionate and her voice lowered. 'Yeah, you were.' Her hands circled the stem of her wine glass. 'So, I've told you what made me who I am. Now you need to reveal a bit of yourself to me.'

It was like being under an instant magnifying glass. He tried the casual wave of his hand. 'Nothing. What you see is what you get.'

She shook her head. 'No, it isn't. Why are you so pedantic at work? Why are you such a stickler for rules and regulations? I get that they're important. I know we have them for safety reasons. But, in my experience, on the odd occasion, it's okay to think outside the box.'

He visibly shuddered and she noticed straight away. 'See? You don't even like those words.' She paused for a few moments, clearly thinking. Her gaze drifted to the stem of the glass as she stroked her fingers up and down it. 'I've met a few people who act the same way that you do, and all of them had some kind of bad experience at some point in their career that made them a stickler for the rules.'

Her gaze lifted and met his. It was as if she'd just reached her hand into his brain and read everything he kept hidden there. He wanted to deny it. But, for the first time in a long time, someone was reading him like a book.

And it was Cora.

He took a long, slow breath, followed by a sip of his beer. 'Guilty as charged,' he finally said. If he was willing to take a chance with Cora, surely she would be willing to take a chance on him? He knew he was about to reveal the part of himself he didn't talk about much. There was always a deep-down fear that if he revealed this part of himself, a colleague might find him wanting. Might think he'd made the wrong decision and let his patient down. Would Cora?

She gave the slightest shake of her head. 'No. I need more than that.'

He sighed. 'It's just like you said. I had a bad experience. I learned from it. And I do my best to ensure that none of my colleagues end up in the position that I did.'

'And what position was that?'

He looked away from Cora. Her gaze was unnerving.

'I was newly trained as a midwife. Believe it or not, I used to be quite laid-back. I loved being a midwife. I loved working on birth plans and formed really good relationships with my expectant mums.'

'So, what happened?'

He was conscious that she kept gently pushing him to reveal more.

'I had a woman in the late stage of labour. She'd been really clear in her birth plan that she didn't want a Caesarean section unless there was no other choice. She'd had surgery as a child that had left her traumatised and was terrified of undergoing anything similar again. Her birth plan was meticulous. She had control issues, and having every part of her plan detailed in advance helped her feel more in control and helped alleviate her anxiety.'

Cora shook her head. 'Oh, no. I can guess what happened.'

He nodded. 'I made a mistake. I made a promise I eventually couldn't keep. I told her I'd do everything I could to make sure she didn't have a C-section.'

Cora winced. 'Ouch.'

Even now, he could feel a weight pressing down on his shoulders as he talked about the case. 'So, things went just like you'd expect. Baby's heart rate dipped dramatically, the baby was deteriorating and...'

'There was nothing else for it,' Cora finished for him. 'Your patient had to have an emergency C-section.'

He gave an enormous sigh. 'Exactly. And both mum and baby survived.'

'Both healthy?'

He nodded. 'Physically, yes. But mentally? Not so much. For mum, anyway. She complained about me— claimed I'd let her down. She suffered a really severe postnatal depression after the birth of a baby she'd very much wanted.'

'But that could have happened anyway,' said Cora.

'I know that. But I'm sure the whole delivery did affect her mental health.'

'So what happened about the complaint?'

He leaned back in his chair, his hands twisting the napkin on the table. 'I was exonerated. They said that my actions had saved the life of both mum and baby.'

'So why do you look so miserable about it?'

He leaned forward. 'Because I *did* let her down. I made her a promise that, in the end, I couldn't keep.'

Cora shook her head. 'So, you never had the "what if" conversation with her?'

He frowned. 'Of course, I did. That's how we had it documented that a C-section was only if there was no other choice.'

'And there was no other choice, was there?'

He ran his fingers through his hair. He hated talking about this. 'Of course, there wasn't. But the only thing that saved me in all this was the fact I had documented *everything*. And I'd followed every protocol to the letter. If I'd strayed in any way, they would have found against me.'

Cora held up her hands. 'You did what every good nurse, midwife or doctor does.'

He was still frowning at her. She was saying it as if it made perfect sense.

'Your practice was good, Jonas. You didn't do anything wrong. But that doesn't make you feel any less responsible. Or any less guilty. That's natural. I still remember every patient where there have been questions about care, or a complaint. It doesn't matter that they are few and far between, they stay here—' she pointed to her chest '—inside, grinding and grinding away. Making me ask the "what if" questions constantly. Making me go over every drug prescribed, every conversation I had. Wondering if I didn't read a situation correctly. That's normal. And neither of us would be good practitioners if we didn't reflect. If we didn't try and learn from situations that we wished had turned out differently.'

He gave a slight nod. 'But staff are sometimes slack. They don't understand how important it is to follow all protocols completely. Documentation and safe protocols can, at times, be the difference between a member of staff being charged with something, or not.'

'I know. I get it, I do.' She looked him in the eye. 'But don't you ever just want to park the bad experience, know that you've learned from it, and shake off the guilt? I can still see it sitting there, like a baby elephant in a cloud above your head.'

He let out a surprised laugh at that comment, then instantly became serious again. 'I'm the manager. It's my job to protect my staff.'

Cora agreed. 'It is. But it's also all staff members' professional responsibility to protect themselves. You can't be looking over every shoulder all the time. You can't work twenty-four hours a day.' She held up a cautious finger. 'And remember that we also learn from our mistakes—or our maybe mistakes. Reflecting on those can be even more important. And if you terrify staff with rules, they might be too scared to tell you about mistakes, or about near misses.'

Jonas leaned back, both hands flat on the table, thinking about what she'd just said.

'I can remember as a junior doctor drawing up morphine, double-checking the prescription and the dose with a nurse, then almost giving it to the wrong patient. Someone had swapped beds around while we'd been drawing up the medicine in the treatment room. When we went in to administer the dose, with the chart in our hands, the nurse went to read the name and date of birth from the patient's wristband. I have to admit to not really listening. And it took a few more seconds than normal to realise that something wasn't right.'

'But you didn't give it?'

'No, it didn't even get out of the tray. But for me, that was a near miss.'

He nodded silently and she held up her hand.

'Let me tell you about another. I was part of the arrest team. I got paged to a ward I was unfamiliar with. I reached the scene, and a senior nurse was standing next to a bed, looking stunned. I *assumed* that the nurse had already done the basic ABC checks before she pulled the arrest buzzer. You know…airway, breathing, circulation. So, as the most junior member of the team, I put my knee on the bed and leaned over to start compressions.'

'What happened?'

'I did one, and the elderly patient sat up and said, "Ouch!"'

Jonas put his hand over his mouth. 'She never.'

'Oh, she did. I got the fright of my life and I learned a valuable lesson. Never assume anything.'

'Who pulls an arrest buzzer without doing ABC?'

Cora raised her eyebrows. 'Who, indeed?'

Jonas was still contemplating what she'd said. Could his behaviour mean that staff were reluctant to report things to him? There was an electronic monitoring system in the hospital for any incidents or near misses. It was part of the induction training for any new staff. He'd always just assumed that staff would report the way they should. The thought that his dictate about rules and protocols might actually stop reporting issues was genuinely disturbing.

'Have you seen any incidents that should have been reported and weren't?'

She sighed sadly. 'And that is where the problem lies. Why did your mind go there first? Why didn't your mind say, *Hmm, maybe I should think about that*?'

'It went there too.'

'But that's not what you said.'

He sighed. Boy, she was tough. He put his elbows on the table and leaned forward. 'Okay, I don't want staff to be scared to tell me if something goes wrong.'

Cora nodded and smiled. 'Okay, now we're getting somewhere. I just think you have to strike a balance.'

'How do you feel about a balance?'

'What do you mean?'

'Most of the reasons we've fought is because I think you rush on into things. How about you stop and take a breath too. Try and strike a balance.'

She pulled a face at him for turning her words around on herself. She lifted her glass towards him. 'Maybe we should drink to that?'

The words were out of his mouth in a flash. 'I'd prefer to seal the deal with a kiss.'

She blinked and licked her lips. Once. And then twice.

And then she stood up and walked around the table towards him. He stood to greet her.

'Deal.' She smiled, as she stood on tiptoe to plant a kiss on his lips.

For a moment he thought it was going to be a fleeting kiss. But his body reacted immediately, bringing his hands to her waist and pulling her close. Cora's hands wound around his neck and their kiss deepened. They were in a public space so he couldn't do exactly what he wanted to do. But as he kissed her he breathed in her shampoo, her body lotion and her light perfume, a collision of floral scents that invaded his very pores.

She pulled her lips back, smiling, and murmured in a low voice, 'Sometimes, it's worth the wait.' Her warm breath caressed his skin. She rested her forehead against his cheek.

He laughed quietly. 'More than worth it,' he said as he stepped back with the sexiest smile on his face that she'd ever seen.

CHAPTER TEN

CORA STRETCHED OUT in her hotel bed and smiled. Last night they'd gone to see a movie in English and she'd eaten popcorn and drunk soda with her head on Jonas's shoulder.

The day before, flowers had been delivered to her hotel room. The beautiful pink and white blooms had started to open and the aroma was drifting across the air towards her.

Today, they were going to one of the Christmas markets. That would mean coffee and cake, and a chance to see all the items for sale. She jumped out of bed and quickly dressed in a warm green jumper she'd bought the other day that was threaded through with glitter. She pulled on her jeans and boots and wrapped a checked scarf around her neck. She was just sliding her arms into her green coat when there was a knock at her door.

'Ready to go shopping?' she asked Jonas, whose frame filled her doorway in a way that was far too inviting.

He leaned down and kissed her. 'New jumper?'

She nodded and pulled it out. 'Isn't it fabulous? I saw it in a shop window on the way home the other night and had to dash in and buy it. It's the perfect colour—even matches the coat you bought me.'

As she zipped her coat and grabbed her gloves, she ran a hand down the front of the jacket. 'You know, I've worn this every day since you bought me it.' She gave him a wink. 'It's brought me good luck.'

'Luck has nothing to do with it,' said Jonas as he pulled her forward for another kiss. 'I just have incredibly good taste.'

She kissed him in agreement and grabbed her bag. 'Should we go for breakfast first?'

'Oh, no!' He laughed. 'Wait until we get to the market. There will be food galore.'

It was only a short walk to the square where the Christmas market was held. There were a few across the city, but Jonas had suggested this was the best place to start.

There were around forty stalls, all red-painted wood, with a whole variety of items, and, true to his promise, the first thing Cora noticed was the delicious smell of food.

The place was already busy, both with tourists and locals. 'Where do we start?'

Jonas reached over and took her hand, threading their way through the crowd and stalls and finally stopping at one where the vendor was making pancakes. 'How about here?'

'Oh, wow.' They ordered coffee and pancakes, which were served on a wobbly paper plate. Cora tucked the coffee into her elbow and ate her pancakes as they drifted between all the other stalls.

'No way,' she whispered in horror to Jonas as she pointed at a sign. 'That can't be true.'

He grinned. 'Reindeer sausages? Oh, it's true. They're actually really popular.'

'You eat Rudolph?'

He didn't even blink. 'And Dasher, and Prancer, and Vixen, and whatever the rest of them are called.'

Cora shuddered and moved on. The next stall had Christmas cheese, crispbreads and handmade mustard. 'This is much more like it,' she said as she tried a few samples. The next had sugared almonds, honey, marzipan, *pepparkakor*—ginger snaps—saffron buns, home-made jams and marmalades and penny candy. Cora was highly tempted, but groaned. 'Those pancakes and that taste of cheese have ruined me. Take me away from all this food and show me things that can't do me any harm.'

He laughed and directed her to a range of other stalls all carrying different goods. Christmas music was playing as they wandered around the various stalls. She could even hear a few carols being sung. But Cora was completely distracted by the tall blond on her arm. Everything else seemed to dull around him.

Every now and then, people would come up and speak to him. More than one had a small child in their arms or trailing after them. It was clear from the faces of the mothers and fathers that these were children and parents who Jonas had met through work.

One woman threw her hands around his neck and kissed him on both cheeks, talking rapidly. Jonas took it all in his stride, happily meeting the twins she had in a double buggy and introducing Cora to the two little girls. She was impressed that he remembered the names of both the mother and the girls instantly and was completely at ease. When the woman finally left she turned to him. 'Another patient?'

He nodded. 'Long-standing patients. Twins were born very early. They are still under our monitoring programme.'

'The same one that the babies who've had therapeutic hypothermia will go on?'

He nodded. 'We nurse these patients for so long, I'm always interested in the long-term outcomes.' He wrapped an arm around her shoulder. 'No matter what you think of me, I get paged when any of our previous long-term patients come in for review, and I always do my best to go along and say hello, then talk to the paediatrician later.'

She gave him a curious glance. 'Is this official, or unofficial?'

He waggled his free hand in the air in front of them. 'Let's just say it's both personal and professional interest.'

'I knew you were a secret softy at heart,' she said as they moved over to the other range of stalls. They browsed easily. Cora bought some hand-knitted mittens that were the same colour as her jumper and parka, some white and red glassware, and a couple of Christmas-scented candles. She inhaled deeply as she chose them. 'I'll take these home,' she said. 'They'll remind me of being here.'

Something inside her stomach twisted painfully. Although she loved Stockholm, she'd found the time of year tough, as always. But now, the thought of going back to her empty flat in London didn't fill her with joy. Sure, it would be nice to sleep in her own bed again. But the bed at the hotel had been very comfortable. The staff at the hotel were lovely and hospitable, and she got that genuine vibe from the city too. By the time she flew home, it would be almost Christmas Day, and, unless she asked someone back home to help her out, she'd be arriving home to a relatively cold flat with no food. She'd already turned down the invite to go to her aunt and uncle's in the Highlands—mainly because the travel would be too complicated.

Jonas put a hand on her shoulder. 'You okay?' His gentle voice was like a warm hug around her heart.

'Of course.' She smiled. 'More shopping?'

There it was again. That odd expression on his face for the briefest of seconds. Then he gave her another smile and put his hand around her shoulder again. It was starting to become colder. Behind them the school choir started to sing more carols as they wandered past a market stall with traditional reusable Swedish advent calendars.

Cora was half tempted to stop and look. It had been a long time since she'd had an advent calendar, and these ones could be filled with tiny gifts.

'Want one?' Jonas asked.

She shook her head and watched as a woman walked past with a delicious-looking bag of chocolates.

'I'd like one of those, though.'

'Oh, I know exactly where that stall is. Let's go.'

He took her around to the back of the stalls, then across the road to a glass-fronted exclusive chocolatier. As soon as he pushed open the door and her senses were hit by the delicious scents, she couldn't help the wide smile that spread across her face.

'You said it was a market stall.'

'I might have been a stranger to the truth.'

'This place costs a fortune, doesn't it?' she whispered.

'Absolutely.' He nodded.

An aproned assistant appeared and happily guided Cora around the huge range of single chocolates on display. She couldn't help herself, and picked a whole range that were wrapped in a gold box with a flamboyant red bow. As they exited the store she turned to Jonas. 'I think I've just been very, very bad.'

'It's allowed,' he said.

She shook her head. 'No, what I mean is, I'm going to take them into the NICU. The staff might be distracted for the next day or so.'

'You bought them for the staff?'

'Of course, I did. Your staff are a great bunch. I love working with them.'

'Then why don't you stay?'

It was clear that the words had come from nowhere and seemed to shock Jonas just as much as they shocked Cora.

He seemed to take a breath and then added on a slightly more serious note, 'I suspect that Stockholm City will be advertising for a new clinical Head of Neonatology in the next few months.'

'You don't think Elias will be back?'

He sighed, and she could see the pain on his face. 'Truthfully? I'd love him to come back. But I'm not sure that he'll want to. I'm sure his son and daughter will try and persuade him to retire. He might want to return a few days a week. But I think the running of the unit will all be too much for him.' He locked gazes with her again. 'So, at some point soon, I suspect we'll be looking for a new clinical lead.'

She was watching him carefully: he'd been partly shocked by his first direct invitation, but now she could see the idea start to settle on him.

'I'm not sure I would be the best person for the job,' she said, her automatic defensive mechanisms kicking into place. She wasn't entirely sure if he was suggesting the job, or maybe something else.

'Think you're not smart enough?' he joked quickly.

She rolled her eyes as they started to walk again. 'I definitely don't have a good enough handle on the language.'

'Try some immersive therapy,' he nudged. 'People always say it's the best way to learn. Move to a place, spend all day there, and try and speak the language constantly.' He gave a wicked grin. 'Or, there are some other immersive therapies we could consider.'

'Cheeky,' she nudged him right back, then stopped walking and looked around. 'It's a beautiful city, but I don't know enough about it yet. I know I've stayed at a great hotel. But I'd need to find out about renting or buying, where the good areas are, where the not so good are. The driving arrangements if I wanted to get a car. The living costs. Everything, really.'

'Sounds like you're trying to talk yourself out of the possibility.'

She gave a rueful shrug. 'I'm just not sure. I'd need to think about Isla. I know it's a short flight, but it's still a whole other country. Anyhow, we don't even know if a job will come up. There could be other amazing candidates. People that your hospital might go out to with offers, rather than advertise the job.'

He nodded his head slowly. She froze. The way he was looking at her was...unnerving.

'Is that what you're doing?' Every tiny hair on her body was standing on end.

The expression on his face told her everything she needed to know. 'They mentioned it to me yesterday. Gave me a few names that the board might consider. Asked what I thought of them.'

Something clicked in Cora's brain. She raised her eyebrows. 'But I wasn't one of them, was I?'

The pause was excruciating. 'No,' he admitted. 'But I think you should be.'

She leaned forward and grabbed the lapels of his jacket, heaving him towards her in the busy street. 'Jonas Nilsson, you didn't even consider me until right now, did you?'

He sighed as his arms folded around her. 'The truth is, I didn't consider *anyone* apart from doctors who are the heads of surrounding NICUs in Sweden.'

Cora held her arms above her head. 'But there's a whole world out there.'

He bowed his head and closed his eyes. 'I know that. But I think when any job comes up, you immediately look at all those you've worked with, and those close by. Heads of units that we speak to frequently because of transfers, or crib shortages, or imminent arrivals.'

She tilted her head to one side as she smiled up at him. Cora was feeling a little easier. For a few moments, she'd felt really on the spot. As if Jonas were asking about a whole lot more than a job. 'Think of all the wonderful people you might miss, thinking like that,' she teased.

He dipped his head, his slight bristles brushing the side of her cheek. 'And think of all the opportunities you might miss if you only look at the UK for job opportunities.'

'Touché.' She smiled and now he laughed out loud, knowing that she was teasing him about his word choice a few weeks ago.

She stared up into those pale blue eyes and her heart gave a little leap. What about staying here, living here, and working here? Jonas was the first guy she'd met in for ever who made her catch her breath, who made her skin tingle with one glance, and who challenged her, day and night. The sparks flew when they were in a room together. She liked it that he didn't always agree with her, and wasn't afraid to say so. Of course, he was wrong, but that didn't matter.

A tiny sprig unfurled deep inside her. The one that had been there since childhood. The one that told her she wasn't good enough, wasn't loved enough, to take up a post like this. She hated that it always appeared at times like this. Jonas hadn't thought of her first. He'd been working with her side by side—if he really thought she was good enough he should have thought of her first.

She pushed the feelings aside. He'd thought of her *now*. That was what was important. And he was enthused about it. Even though she didn't know if she wanted the job. The sprig inside was turning into something else—a beautiful rose.

'What are you thinking about?'

She smiled. 'A world of opportunities,' she admitted. She took a breath. 'I'm kind of cold. Want to come back to the hotel with me?'

He bent down again and whispered in her ear, 'I thought you'd never ask,' and slipped his hand into hers.

They walked along the street together, and she was conscious that her footsteps seemed to be quickening. She kept a firm hold of his hand when they reached the hotel entrance and she nodded to the doorman and receptionist as they crossed the lobby to the lift.

As soon as the doors slid closed, Jonas was kissing her again.

Now they weren't in public. He pressed her up against the mirrored wall of the lift and she wrapped her arms tightly around him as he kissed her until she was breathless.

When the lift slowed to a halt and pinged she stepped back and looked at him again. Her mouth was dry. But she knew exactly what she wanted the next step to be.

She licked her lips and held out her hand. 'Stay over.'

He hesitated, and for a second she felt a wave of panic. Was she overreaching? Misreading things between them?

But Jonas let out a soft laugh as the doors opened to her floor.

'Like I said earlier, I thought you'd never ask,' he said again, as this time he grabbed her round the waist, lifted her up and she wrapped her legs around him.

Cora couldn't help but laugh as she struggled to find her card for the door. 'Maybe a little unconventional?' she teased.

Jonas took it from her hand as she found it and swiped the door, carrying her inside and kicking it shut behind them.

Her heart swelled. A perfect day, and things could only get better.

CHAPTER ELEVEN

THEY'D QUICKLY FALLEN into routine. One night they would spend a night at Cora's hotel, then the next they would wake up together in Jonas's apartment.

He was surprised how quickly she seemed to fit into his life—in lots of weird ways. It felt entirely normal to see her snuggled up at the end of his pale grey sofa, or under the white blankets in his large bed. Within a few days her toothbrush remained in his bathroom, and he'd bought an extra one to leave in her hotel room.

'So, how're things going in love's young dream?'

The words jerked him from his thoughts. Alice was standing next to him in the NICU with a set of older notes in her hands. She was giving him 'that' look. The one that told him she could read every thought in his head and knew exactly everything he'd been up to in the last few weeks.

'I have no idea what you're talking about, Alice,' he said, doing his best to keep his face straight.

'Of course, you don't.' She smiled, patting his hand as she moved over to the computer screen.

'That's why you watch every step she takes, turn your head every time she laughs, and notice every time she talks to another member of staff.' She raised her eyebrows just an inch. 'And she, it seems, does entirely that same with you. The vibe between you both has changed.' She stepped a little closer and lowered her voice. 'And in case you think it's a secret…' she shook her head '…just so you know, we've been taking bets for a while.'

Jonas tried not to look stunned, but clearly failed when Alice started to quietly laugh. After another minute, he folded his arms. 'Who won?'

There was no chance for an answer as one of the alarms started to ping dangerously. As if by magic, all the staff in the unit moved smoothly. Resuscitating a tiny baby was always a delicate operation. One staff member automatically went to mum and put her arm around her, while moving her back, away from the crib, so others could do what they needed to.

Jonas and Alice joined the team, doing tiny heart compressions, bagging the tiny little boy and administering emergency medications, until finally the heart monitor started to blip reassuringly. A few moments later, the little boy's chest started to rise and fall rapidly as breathing was re-established, and his blood pressure started to come back up.

It was another hour before Jonas and Alice were back near the nurses' station. The phone rang and he answered it. 'Jonas, we've another baby on the way up. Meets all the criteria. Can you be ready? I'll be up in five.'

He put the phone down and gave Alice a nod. 'Another baby for the hypothermia treatment. Cora is on her way up.'

'Oh, is she?' said Alice wickedly, all the while moving off to prepare one of the side rooms.

Jonas shook his head as he moved after her. 'Is this

what it's come to? Is this what I'm going to have to put up with at work every day?'

Alice grabbed a drip stand to pull into the room and threw him an interested look as she attached the machine to the stand. 'You have no idea how much pleasure it gives me. How much pleasure it gives us all.' Her hand reached over to his arm as he was preparing the crib. 'Jonas, you seem so happy around her. Mad at times. Then delighted at others. Honestly, if you let this one get away, I'll make your life a misery afterwards.'

The words stopped him cold. He looked at the older woman, who might have made a million mistakes in her life, but he'd never know it. Her gaze was honest, sincere and playful all at once. It yanked at every heartstring he'd ever had.

'You wouldn't have to, Alice. I'd be there already.' The honesty of the words was like a bucket of ice-cold water emptying over his head.

He was frozen. Thinking about how much Cora actually meant to him.

Alice was routinely going about her business. 'Have you told her?'

His eyes darted to Alice. She was so cool and casual about things—as if this were an everyday conversation that they were having.

But it wasn't. And they both knew it.

He loved the way she could be so matter-of-fact about things. It was one of her greatest traits, and why the entire hospital staff looked up to the experienced sister of the NICU. She was unflappable, to the point, entirely professional, and all with a little gleam in her eye.

The slightly scary thing was, he knew she would make his life a misery if he didn't up his game and speak to Cora.

So he was entirely honest with her. 'Of course, I haven't told her. She's due to go back—' He stopped as something came into his head. He'd been about to say 'back home', but realised that he got the general impression from Cora that, right now, nowhere really felt like home to her. 'She's due to go back to London in two weeks.'

'Sounds like you're running out of time, Jonas.'

He shook his head as he plugged in some of the other pieces of equipment. 'Yeah, don't rub it in, Alice.'

She bumped him with her hip on the way past. 'Don't say I didn't warn you.'

The NICU doors flew open and Jonas pushed everything out of his head. It didn't help that Cora's face was the first one he saw, and he instantly drank in everything about her. It was amazing how quickly she'd got under his skin, and he didn't mind one bit.

But as he worked methodically, helping the team get set up for the treatment, his mind kept going back to Cora. He'd already unexpectedly asked her if she'd considered staying, and it was abundantly clear it had never crossed her mind.

To be honest, until that point, it hadn't crossed his either. But as soon as it had landed there, it had just made perfect sense, and it had made his heart lurch in a way that had surprised him.

But inside his head, there were a few tiny doubts. His judgement had been wrong before. His ex had proved that. And every time he saw Cora loaded down with shopping bags, it just rang alarm bells in his head. She'd done and said absolutely nothing to make him think she could be anything like Kristina. But then again, Kristina had done nothing to raise alarm bells either. Maybe his whole judgement was just questionable?

And if he couldn't get past that, how could he have any other kind of conversation with Cora? He shook his head as he put some recordings on a chart. He'd told Cora the most significant event in his life. And she'd talked it through with him with empathy, understanding and reassurance. She hadn't doubted his practice for a single second. And that meant something to him. But could he actually say those three little words to her? Last time around it had spelled disaster for him. Could he be brave enough to try again?

As the team set to work, lowering the new baby's temperature, he moved out of the room to let them continue their work. The start-up procedures were the most labour intensive and, once they were over, the unit settled down to a steady hum of activity. There, in the waste basket near him, were the remnants of a box of chocolates with a familiar logo. The first box Cora had brought in had disappeared in one day. She'd bought a second, and this was clearly the remnants of the third. It struck a chord with him about how she felt about the staff here. They'd wanted to learn from her, and it was clear she relished the opportunity. How would he really feel if Cora was a permanent fixture around here?

Jonas grabbed his jacket and took a walk. He was already long over the hours he should have worked and wanted to clear his head.

Snow crunched under his feet as he walked towards the city centre. Lights glowed everywhere. Before he knew it, he was outside her hotel—the one he'd taken her to on that first day. Cora was still back in the unit. He knew that. He took a few moments to walk around the square. Another Christmas tree had appeared, decorated with pink lights. There seemed to be trees all over the city this year. He hadn't got around to putting his own up back at his apartment. He was usually a bit more festive. But he knew there were still more layers to Cora Campbell. She'd told him she didn't like Christmas much, and it had seemed wrong to push it on her by decorating his apartment. She'd remarked that she frequently just closed the curtains in her room at the hotel to block it out.

As Jonas watched other tourists and some local families walk past, his heart was sad. Christmas wasn't for everyone and he could accept that. But what he really wanted to do was to make some new memories for Cora. Give her something else to think about. He'd already suggested it, but he still wasn't sure if she wanted to take him up on that.

As much as he wanted to do something, he knew deep inside he had to let that be Cora's decision to make. He had no idea what her experience of Christmas had been, or if she was ready to try something new.

Something flooded over him like a wash of warm water in the icy cold. Even though he'd compared Cora and Kristina in his head, he knew in his heart that Cora was nothing like Kristina. They weren't even in the same ballpark. And even though he'd said those three words to Kristina in the past, the way he felt about Cora couldn't even compare. It was so much more. So much better. So much fuller. Any feelings he'd had for Kristina were a pale comparison to what he felt about Cora.

This was love, pure, unadulterated love.

As he walked past a nearby shop, something in the window caught his eye. Before he had time to think much longer, he ducked inside, coming out five minutes later with the gift tucked in his pocket. Would she like it?

He wasn't sure. He could only wait to find out. Because he knew what he needed to say to her. He just had to find a way to let those words out again. His heart knew exactly how he felt about Cora. But could he actually tell her?

Cora looked around the unit. The little boy, Sam, was steady now. She'd been seriously concerned about him earlier, and she could only hope that the treatment would help him. Now, she needed to find Jonas. Something had happened today, and she wanted to tell him, and get a sense of what he thought.

'Anyone know where Jonas has gone?' she asked one of the nearby staff nurses.

The girl turned to a colleague and held up her hand for a high five. He slapped it and they both laughed. 'What?' asked Cora.

The nurse shook her head. 'We've just been waiting for confirmation—but it doesn't really matter, we already knew.'

Cora smiled. 'So, does anyone know where Jonas has gone?'

She nodded. 'He headed out earlier. I think he said something about a walk. He'd been here for around twelve hours; he probably needed some head space.'

Cora wrinkled her nose. When she'd woken this morning, Jonas had been gone with a scribbled cute note next to her bed. She'd just imagined he'd had some things to do. She hadn't realised he'd come into work early.

She made a few final checks, then grabbed her jacket, zipping it up and pulling out her phone to text Jonas. He answered straight away, and as she pushed open the doors of the unit, something came into her head. She looked over her shoulder. 'Okay, then, who just won the bet?'

'Alice,' they both answered in unison.

'Of course.' She nodded. 'I should have known.'

She couldn't stop smiling as she left the hospital and headed to meet Jonas. It was dark, but the streets seemed even busier than normal.

Jonas appeared through the crowd and slung an arm around her shoulder. 'Do you remember that boat tour I promised you?'

She nodded. 'But it's dark, I won't see anything.'

'This is a special tour. Perfect for night time. We cross under twelve different bridges and see most of the city.' He bent down and whispered in her ear. 'There's even Swedish *fika* on board.'

'Coffee and cinnamon buns? You got me.'

They boarded the boat at Strömkajen. Cora stood at the railing on the boat and watched as the white craft pulled out into the black water. All around them, across the city, white lights were sparkling, outlining buildings, and giving the whole city a glow. Soft music played in the background as a guide gave them a little information about the history of the city, and the bridges they passed underneath. They even passed through the lock that connected the Baltic Sea to Lake Mälaren.

As it got colder, they ducked inside and grabbed some coffee and a cinnamon bun. 'Want to sit down?' Jonas asked.

She shook her head. 'Actually, I'm really enjoying this. Can we take these outside?'

He nodded and they went back to the railing. Cora watched the wonder of the passing sights. The inner city, the Old Town, Södermalm and Lilla glided past. Her heart was warm. The twinkling festive lights only added to the experience. She put her head on Jonas's shoulder. Between the steam from their breaths, and the steam from their coffee cups, it made the cold night air seem even more special.

She was starting to love this city, and the people in it. For the first time in for ever, the thought of Christmas didn't fill her with sadness and dread. Jonas had suggested—without asking tricky questions—that it might be time to make some new memories. And somehow, being in an entirely new place, with a wonderful man and a great bunch of staff, was making it a whole lot easier. Maybe it was timing too. But it was almost as if the dark cloud that seemed to descend around her shoulders at this time of year had forgotten where she was.

Snuggling up with Jonas, and looking out at this new place, was perfect.

'Hey.' His lips brushed her ear. 'What's up?'

She turned towards him and slid her hands around his waist. 'Nothing's up,' she said with a smile on her face. 'I'm just happy.'

'Happy?' He pulled her closer. 'Now, that sounds good.'

She nodded. 'One of the directors of the hospital came and found me today.'

He didn't look particularly surprised. 'They did?'

She gave his chest a gentle slap. 'They told me that— as well as another suite of candidates—they were considering me for the position of Head of Neonatology.' Her voice was shaking a little.

'And what did you say?'

She stood on her tiptoes and kissed one of his cheeks. 'I listened carefully...' she kissed the other cheek '... and said thank you very much...' she dropped a soft kiss on his lips '...and that I'd wait to hear from them.'

She slid her arms around his neck. 'Do you think someone put in a good word for me?'

He gave her a small smile. 'They might have.'

'But is there any chance that person might be a bit biased?'

He laughed. 'It doesn't matter if I'm biased. The board listens to lots of people. They'll have spoken to your colleagues back at the Royal Kensington, they'll have asked many of the other professionals you've worked with over the last few weeks. They want someone they know will fit well with the unit. Someone who can help us maintain our standards and reputation.'

She let her fingers run through his hair. 'You think someone like me—a woman who makes your blood boil at times—can do that?'

He slid one hand under her thick jacket. 'Sometimes blood boiling means a totally different thing,' he said with a soft laugh.

She pressed closer as she looked over his shoulder. 'This place has been surprising. I've never really considered a proper move before. Even when I was offered a job in Washington a few years ago, I never truly, really considered it properly.'

'And now you will?'

She nodded and pressed her lips together. 'If they ask me.'

'Will you talk to your sister first?'

She blinked back some tears and nodded. 'Absolutely. But I have a feeling that Isla will tell me to chase my dreams.'

'And what are your dreams?'

The question circled around her brain. She immediately wanted to say that she didn't know. But, deep down, parts of her did know. Jonas drove her crazy and

she loved that. She'd never wanted to be around someone so much. Waking up next to him every morning
had quickly given her the vibe that she was entirely in
the right place.

But could she trust him with her heart?

She wanted to. She really, really did.

CHAPTER TWELVE

'HEY, HOW ARE you doing?' Jonas leaned forward and put his hands on Elias's shoulders, kissing him on either cheek as he opened the door.

Elias looked distinctly shaky. He had a stick in one hand and had limped slowly to the door. 'How's my unit?'

'Interesting,' said Jonas as he followed Elias inside and closed the door behind him. His heart fell as he saw a few boxes piled up in one corner. It told him everything he needed to know. But for Elias's sake, he pretended he hadn't seen them as they walked slowly through to Elias's large kitchen and sat down at the table. Jonas noticed that the coffee was already made.

He sat a bag on the table and started emptying it. 'Favourite marmalade, bread, biscuits, and those peppermint creams that you hide in your top desk drawer.'

Elias smiled, and Jonas breathed another sigh of relief. Both sides of his face were moving in perfect symmetry.

His hand shook a little as he determinedly poured the coffee. Another sign. These hands that had inserted thousands of central lines over the years into tiny veins would not be doing that again.

He kept all emotion from his face. He knew that

Elias's heart must be breaking. Work had been such a huge part of his life after his wife had died. And now that had been taken from him too.

'What do you mean by interesting?' asked Elias. 'How's the new doctor working out?' There. He had a glint in his eye. The main part of Elias was completely intact.

Jonas couldn't help the smile spreading across his face. 'She's good. Feisty. Challenging. But definitely an excellent doctor.'

'Asked her out yet?'

Jonas choked on his coffee. 'What?'

'A bright, intelligent, good-looking woman? What's wrong with you? From the first second I spoke to her, I thought you would be an excellent match.'

Jonas was incredulous. 'You invited a doctor to our hospital because you thought she would be a good match for me?'

Elias shook his head. 'Of course not. I invited her purely because of her research—which is outstanding, and I hope you've got everything set up for us to continue when she leaves. The match part came later. That video conferencing is a fine thing. Her manner. The passion for her job. That accent. She isn't married, is she? Because I thought she would be perfect for you. I'm just annoyed I haven't got to play matchmaker and take full credit for it.'

He dipped one of the biscuits that Jonas had brought in his coffee.

'You're an old rogue.'

Elias's eyes shimmered with pride. 'I knew it. You do like her.'

He sat back in his chair and gave a self-satisfied sigh. Then, his expression changed. This time his face was full of sadness. 'I tendered my resignation last week. But you know that, don't you?'

Jonas nodded his head. 'I suspected. The board of directors approached me about possible candidates for Head of Neonatology.'

Elias looked interested. 'Who did you recommend?'

'Franz Kinnerman from Lindesberg, Ruth Keppell from Lund, Astra Peniker from Kalmar...' He paused for a second. 'And Cora Campbell from the Kensington.'

Elias tapped his fingers on the table and nodded. 'I also recommended two out of the three. But I asked them to pay particular attention to the performance of our visiting consultant.'

He smiled at Jonas. 'I take it my matchmaking is going well?'

Jonas took a breath. He wasn't quite sure how to answer.

'Come now, Jonas. Tell me you've put that whole episode with Kristina behind you. It's time to make new horizons for yourself. Take a chance on love again.'

Jonas shook his head. Elias was one of the only people he'd confided in about what had happened with Kristina. He reached over and grabbed a biscuit. 'I don't remember asking for love advice.'

Elias tapped his hand on Jonas's arm. 'But I won't be around much longer to give it to you.' His expression changed again. 'My son has persuaded me to sell up and move down next to him and his wife.' Elias looked around his home with the wide windows showing the land around about him. 'Forty years I've lived here. But all good things...' He met Jonas's gaze again. 'It's for the best. But who will be here to keep an eye on you and give you advice about life? I feel as if I should leave you in a safe, but sparky pair of hands. And I think they are distinctly Scottish.'

Jonas burst out laughing. 'Wait until I tell Cora you called her sparky.'

'You should have brought her with you today. I would have liked to have seen you two together. See if there really are sparks flying.'

Jonas was serious now. 'She asked. She wanted to come and meet you. I told her I had to wait until I'd seen how you are.'

'Well, bring her back when she wants to know more about running the unit. I'll give her all the tips she'll need. Or...' there was a wicked gleam in his eyes '...you could always just invite me to the wedding.'

'Elias!'

'What?' He held up his hands, his face the picture of innocence. 'Can't let a good one slip away. And Christmas is always such a lovely time of year for a proposal. It's when I proposed to Ann, you know. Under the giant Christmas tree at Skeppsbron.'

Jonas took a sip of his coffee. 'Christmas isn't her favourite time of year. I don't exactly know why. I didn't want to push. I just suggested that since she was in a new place, it might be nice to make some new memories.'

'With a new person?' Elias gave a nod. 'Wise man. But you should ask. Always ask the difficult questions, Jonas. Then she'll know you care. That you want the good, and the bad.' He gave a soft smile. 'But you know that, don't you? You only have a few days left—don't leave it too late.'

Jonas nodded slowly. 'Let's just say, I have a plan.'

He glanced at his watch. 'I'll have to run. I'm the duty manager at the hospital this afternoon.' He stood up and reached over and gave Elias a giant hug. 'Next time I come, I promise I'll bring Cora with me.'

'Be sure you do.'

Jonas pulled on his jacket and left, pausing outside for a moment to take a deep breath. So much of what Elias had said to him rang true.

But what was most important was that he was right. Time was running out.

And it was time to look to the future.

CHAPTER THIRTEEN

SOMEONE HAD PRESSED fast forward on her life. Last time she'd looked at the calendar there had still been nearly two weeks left in her time here.

But it felt as if she'd blinked—and that time had gone.

Every night had seemed shorter than the one before. Waking up next to Jonas had become excruciating because she'd realised that soon it wouldn't be happening any more.

She'd spoken to Isla the other day, who'd told her she was spending Christmas with their aunt and uncle and wouldn't be coming down to London.

Cora had made a half-hearted scramble to look at when her flight got into London, and any possible chance of reaching the Highlands safely, even though she'd known it was completely futile. Alternative flights to Inverness airport were full. It seemed that most of the Highlands wanted to get home on Christmas Eve.

But what she couldn't get out of her head was the dark cloud that continually settled around her shoulders at this time of year. It had arrived again—even though she'd hoped it wouldn't.

Being in Stockholm had been the perfect distraction at first. But maybe it was time to accept that, no matter what else was going on in her life, she would never get over these feelings associated with Christmas.

And this, doubled with the fact that she hadn't quite managed to figure out exactly how she felt about Jonas—or how he felt about her—was making her lose sleep at night. She should be over the moon with the time she was spending with him. But now it just felt like a double countdown looming over her head. The countdown to bad memories. And the countdown to leaving Jonas behind.

She hadn't heard anything about the job, which likely meant they had another preferred candidate. It would seem ridiculous to let her go back to London, and then offer the job to her. And even that was completely crazy. She hadn't come to Stockholm even thinking about the possibility of a job change. It hadn't been on her radar at all. But, after falling in love with Stockholm, and the staff at City hospital, and falling in love with Jonas, she had such mixed feelings about going back home.

Cora froze. She was tying her shoelaces and her hands just stuck in mid-air. She *loved* Jonas. She loved him. The thought had entered her brain so easily, and the realisation struck her like a blow to the chest.

She sat back up and let out some slow breaths. It was early evening, Jonas would be here in a while, but she'd planned to go for some fresh air. She grabbed her jacket, and looked out at the square, and blinked back a few tears.

Did she really want to go out there? In amongst the glistening white lights and people excited about Christmas?

She pulled her hat over her head and grabbed her gloves. As soon as she reached the foyer of the hotel, the receptionist shouted her over. All the staff knew her by name now. There was a large tray of cookies on the reception desk and Cora could smell them instantly.

'Help yourself, Cora. They've just come up from the kitchen. They're still warm.'

Cora smiled. 'They smell delicious. Thank you.'

'We'll really miss you when you head back to England. Will you come and visit again?'

It was like a little light going on in her head. She'd been so encompassed by the thoughts of going home, and everything that was ending for her, that she hadn't even thought of her holiday time. Wow. Her head must be really muddled.

'I'd love to come back again, and if I do, I promise I'll stay here.' Her footsteps felt a little lighter as she walked out to the square and started to meander her way around in the dimming evening light.

The shop window displays were all familiar to her now, and she couldn't pretend that she didn't have favourites. The traditional carved pale wooden trees behind a white chequered window were lovely. Another shop had a whole array of small glass ornaments with splashes of colour. The effects were mesmerising. She'd already bought a little sculpture with splashes of green, and a mini square with a pink drop in the middle. Now a wall hanging with a flash of red across the middle was catching her eye. It was the size of a large dinner plate—did she have enough space in her luggage? Who cared? She could buy another suitcase if needed.

She continued along the street, stopping to buy a soft grey jumper for Isla, and a decorative studded bangle.

The air was icy and there were several stalls set up in the middle of the square. She wandered over and decided to be brave and try another cup of warm *glögg*.

She sat down on a bench, ignoring the cold as she watched the world go by.

She wasn't even seeing the Christmas decorations now. She was just seeing the people. The families and couples, all walking along laughing and joking. Tears blinked in her eyes as she saw a man and a woman with a teenager and a baby in a buggy. It gave her instant flashbacks to what her family must have looked like to others.

And before she knew it, she was in floods of tears.

'Cora!' The joyful shout came from the other side of the square. Jonas looked really happy. He practically sprinted across the square to join her, and she quickly wiped her tears away.

'I wanted to talk to you,' he said, slightly breathless, a wide grin across the face that she loved.

'What is it?'

There was a weird kind of pause. He sat down on the bench next to her and looked as if he was trying to decide where to start. He bent down and kissed her. Cora responded instantly, because Jonas's touch to her was as natural as breathing air.

When they separated, his arm was still around her shoulders. 'Have you made a decision?'

Her stomach squeezed. 'About what?'

'About where we're going for dinner tonight?'

Every muscle in her body sagged. For some strange reason she'd hoped it would be an entirely different question. Have you made a decision about wanting to stay here? Have you made a decision about when you're coming back? Have you made a decision about what happens next for us?

But maybe she was just imagining the connection between them both. After all, she'd only just realised herself that she loved this man. They hadn't talked about love. They hadn't talked about anything to do with when her time with the Kensington Project was up. And that suddenly struck her as odd.

If Jonas felt the same way she did, surely he would have started a conversation with her by now?

For reasons she couldn't entirely explain, tears started rolling down her cheeks again. It was as if every emotion had just burst to the surface and was overwhelming her.

Maybe he thought she wasn't good enough for him. Maybe he didn't want her the way she hoped he did. Maybe, yet again, she would be the child left alone at Christmas. The feelings were overwhelming, coming out of nowhere. There was no rhyme or reason to them. She knew she could try and be rational and think herself out of them. But she couldn't stop the heave in her chest, or the overwhelming feelings of not being good enough. They were swamping her, making it almost difficult to breathe.

'Cora?' There was instant concern on Jonas's face.

She stood up and shook her head, trying to breathe and stammer the words out. 'I...don't feel up to dinner tonight. I can't do this. I think it's best if I just go back to the hotel.'

He looked at her as if those words had stung, and she knew instantly it was the delivery. She hadn't added the word 'alone' to her dialogue, but her tone had made certain the implication was there.

He reached for her hand. 'No. Don't go. I wanted tonight to be special. I wanted to talk to you. What's wrong?'

The words just erupted from her belly. 'Nothing. Everything. I don't know.' She held out her shaking arms, letting the paper cup of *glögg* fall at her feet. She looked around her at the people, families, and all the signs of Christmas in every part of the square. Even though she knew they were outside, it was as if the walls were pressing in all around her. She couldn't breathe. She couldn't be here. She couldn't do this.

She turned and ran, ignoring the fact her clumpy boots slowed her pace. If her head had been straight, she would have gone back to the hotel. But nothing was making sense to her right now. Every corner she turned seemed to take her to another festooned street. Christmas lights and decorations had never bothered her quite as much as they did now.

Flashes appeared in her head. Holding her mum's cold hand. One minute she'd been there, full of life and laughing, and the next minute she'd been gone. Nothing could save her. Then the flash of her father's withered face on the pillow, his pallor sicklier than any shade of white or grey. The laboured breaths and wheeze. And the memories of hating every second of seeing the bright, vibrant man that she loved in pain. The cancer had come quickly after her mum had died, and Cora always thought he'd had no strength to fight because his heart was already broken. It was agonising, but that was what was left in her memory. And over the years it had grown bigger, instead of fading. It had pushed all the best memories out of place. And with it was the overwhelming sensation that Cora had failed both of her parents.

The final breath had been a relief to them both, and, for that as well, the guilt was overwhelming.

Cora had reached the harbour now, panting, and, catching hold of the barrier in front of her, she clung on, knowing there was nowhere left to run.

She didn't even hear his footsteps, but knew instantly the arm around her was his. For a few moments he didn't speak, just stood with his chest against her back, his arms around her, and his own rapid breaths matching her own.

'I hate seeing you like this. Tell me what's wrong, Cora. I want to help.'

She couldn't find the words; exhaustion was sweeping over her.

He turned her around to face him. 'I wanted this night to be good between us. I wanted to talk about what comes next.' There were deep furrows across his brow, and he was clutching her array of shopping bags in his hand.

'What comes next is, I get on a plane and go home. Isn't it a bit late to have the "what about us?" talk?' It came out much more bitterly than she wanted it to. But her heart was aching. Every moment felt like another realisation. If he'd wanted to talk about them, shouldn't it have been mentioned long before now?

He hesitated, and it made her heart plummet inside her chest. 'I was waiting,' he said cautiously.

'Waiting for what?'

She saw him swallow awkwardly. 'I thought they were going to offer you the job today.'

Those feelings that she was trying hard to push away swamped her again. They hadn't wanted her. She wasn't good enough to be offered the job.

His pale eyes looked fraught with worry, and she wasn't quite sure how to read it. 'Well, they didn't. But, so what? Why would that make a difference to any talk about us?'

She stepped away from him. 'What? Can there only be an "us" if I'm right here? On your doorstep, where it's convenient? Is that why you waited to have this discussion? And now I've told you that they haven't offered me the job, I can see how awkward you feel. I take it that rules out any discussion for us at all?' She put her hand on her chest. 'How am I supposed to feel? Has this all just been a convenience for you? Because it hasn't been for me. And now I'm finding out just how important I am in your life. I won't be working here. I'll be back in London. I've been here for a while now, Jonas. We could have had the "what about us?" conversation at any point.'

The words were coming out so quickly, she almost couldn't breathe. 'And today? Tonight?' She let out a hollow laugh. 'It couldn't be more fitting. This is my worst time of year. You nearly had me fooled for that too—that I should try and create new Christmas memories. But how can I do that? No matter where I am in this world, I'm always going to feel like this—alone.' She closed her eyes, hating herself for spilling everything out to him. Her voice shook. 'You've no idea how much I hate this date. This is the date that my mum died from an aortic aneurysm after going into hospital with back pain. A year and a day later, my dad died from cancer on Christmas Eve. And things don't get better with time—no matter what well-meaning people say. They just amplify and haunt me. How can I create new memories when the bad ones take me over—no matter how hard I try?'

Her shoulders started to shake. Jonas had his arms around her instantly, propping her up, taking her weight as her legs started to crumple. 'Let me help you, Cora. Let me help you. We can get through this together. You should have told me. I had no idea how hard this was for you.' His eyes glanced towards the bags he gripped in his hands—her bags. And there it was again. That weird look.

And his earlier words didn't soothe her, they just injected her with a force of solid determination. He still hadn't said the words that mattered most. And now, she realised, she didn't want him to. She didn't want him to react to this situation by saying something he didn't actually feel. He'd never given her a true indication that he wanted a long-term relationship with her. Her heart twisted in her chest. She loved this man, but it was clear he didn't have the same strong feelings that she did. It was easier to end things here and now and walk away with a bit of her dignity intact. But something inside her flared as she saw his eyes still fixed on the bags.

'Why do you do that?' she snapped.

'What?' He looked confused.

'You.' She thrust her hand towards him. 'Every time you see one of my shopping bags you get a weird look on your face. I know you don't like shopping, Jonas, but you really need to get over yourself. People all around the world shop!' She'd thrown her arms upwards now and the expression on Jonas's face changed, filling with hurt and regret.

He took a deep breath. 'I'm sorry,' he said slowly. 'The bags just reminded me of a past experience. Every time I see them, it just takes me back.'

Her eyes narrowed. 'What past experience?'

He shook his head. 'An ex, with spending habits that left me in a world of debt. Every time I saw you clutching shopping bags, it brought back memories.'

Her brow wrinkled. 'That's ridiculous. Why on earth would I leave you in debt with my shopping? I have more than enough money of my own.'

Her brain was spinning. Was this the mysterious

ex she'd heard a few of his colleagues hint at? One had even mentioned they'd thought Jonas might have planned on asking her to marry him.

Every part of her body bristled. He'd never mentioned his ex to her before. He'd never confided in Cora, and that made her realise that he'd never taken their relationship that seriously.

As the thoughts churned in her brain he nodded and closed his eyes. 'And when you say it like that, I seem like a complete fool. But I couldn't stop the memories, and it became more about my bad judgement than anything else.'

She stepped back as a cold wave of realisation swept over her. Nothing about this had been as it seemed. Maybe the connection between them had all been in her head?

She straightened and looked at him. 'I'm going home, Jonas. I'm going home tomorrow. I'm sorry that they didn't offer me that job, but, in a way, I'm not. Because now I know. Now I know this would never have worked between us. And it's better this way. It has to be.'

She turned quickly, walking swiftly back towards the centre.

He was alongside her in an instant. 'Cora, stop, let me talk to you. Don't walk away. I don't want things to be like this between us.'

She stopped walking for a second and looked him in the eye. 'This is exactly how things are between us, Jonas, which is exactly why I should leave. Now, stop.' She held up one hand. 'Leave me alone. I can't be anywhere near you right now.' She took a deep breath. 'I'm going to keep walking, and you—' she pointed at his chest '—are going to leave me alone.'

And she started walking as quickly as she could—

even though her vision was blinded with tears and her heart ached.

All she could do was keep walking. Right on back to London. She'd wanted to trust him with her heart, but it was clear that she couldn't.

CHAPTER FOURTEEN

HE WAS AN IDIOT. He was an absolute prize idiot. The words had been on the tip of his tongue last night—even before he'd noticed she was crying—and he half wished he'd blurted out the *I love you* as soon as he'd seen her.

Instead, he'd been distracted by the pile of shopping bags around her feet. And in that moment of distraction, which had made him think about bad memories, he'd lost his momentum and opportunity.

The way Cora had looked at him last night had been like a knife to the heart. Had he totally misread everything? She'd seemed almost cold. He couldn't help but wonder if she'd always meant to break up with him—had never considered anything serious between them. If that were true, his *I love you* would have been sadly misplaced and awkward for them both.

Although he'd wanted to run after her last night, her story about why she was so sad at Christmas had floored him. He'd known it was something significant. But the look in her eyes when she'd told him about losing both her mum and dad so close to Christmas, one year after the next, would have broken the heart of the coldest ice man. And when she'd told him to let her walk away, even though every cell in his body had protested, he'd known he had to listen. And his head had filled with crazy doubts. Maybe Cora had only ever wanted a temporary fling. Even with the potential job offer, she might just have been placating him. Letting him think she would consider it, when she really just wanted to head back to London and get on with her life.

He still couldn't believe that she *hadn't* been offered it. And it almost felt as if she'd blamed him for that too last night. Or maybe his head was just too full of conflicting emotions to actually think straight.

So, he'd let her walk away. If she didn't love him, then this was for the best.

But it had been an achingly long night. He hadn't been able to sleep for a minute. He'd played things over and over in his head. What if he'd done something different? What if he'd chased after her when she'd walked away, and admitted that he loved her?

He'd been in work since six a.m.—after toying with the idea to walk to the hotel and deciding not to. He would wait for her here. It was her last day in Sweden. He wanted her to come into work, say goodbye to the friends she'd made, and then he would ask if he could have some of her time.

He wanted to wear his heart on his sleeve and tell her that he absolutely loved and adored her. That last night, he'd had a special gift for her in his pocket. He wanted to tell her that was what his plans had been. A nice restaurant. Some good food. Some wine. And a chance to tell the woman he loved that he wanted to spend the rest of his life with her.

He only prayed she would still let him.

The clock ticked past in slow motion. He paced near the unit. He paced near the labour suite. He paced near the paediatric ward. But Cora was nowhere. He asked and asked, but no one had seen her.

He wandered the management corridors, wondering if she'd been called to some kind of meeting. He still couldn't believe she hadn't been offered the job. But it had never even entered Jonas's head that Cora would consider that part of a reason to be together. He'd already decided last night that if Cora wanted to return to London, he'd ask if he could join her.

But he had to find her first.

A colleague had asked him to verify some documents for him, and Jonas scribbled his signature and passport details, before ramming his passport in his back pocket and pacing the corridors again.

Alice came and found him in the corridor. Her face was sad. 'She's not here.'

'I know she's not here. I've been looking everywhere.'

Alice sighed and put her hand on Jonas's arm. 'Did you message her?'

'Of course, I did.' It came out much more snappily than intended.

Alice pressed her lips together and gave an understanding slow nod. 'Well, she texted me.'

His head shot up. 'What? What did she say? Where is she?'

Alice's voice was soft. 'At the airport. Her flight leaves in the next two hours.'

'What?' Panic gripped straight across his chest like a vice.

He looked around madly.

'You'll need to be quick,' she whispered.

Jonas didn't hesitate. He grabbed his car keys, his jacket and started to run.

His car was in the car park at the hospital. It was the middle of the day, so traffic wasn't too heavy in Stockholm, and he did his best to stick to the speed limit on the way to Arlanda airport.

By the time he reached the airport, the slow entry to the car park and the excruciating line of people trying to file into a parking space made him want to explode. He dived out of the car, and raced to the airport entrance doors, his eyes immediately scanning the boards for her flight. Some part of him felt a wave of panic when he couldn't initially find a flight to London. Then he realised. LHR—Heathrow. The abbreviation had thrown him.

He ran towards the security entrance, scanning all people sitting in chairs, around the washrooms and in the stores along the way. There was no sign of Cora.

As he reached the security entrance, one of the guards eyed him suspiciously. 'Ticket?' he asked.

Of course. He didn't get past here without a ticket. 'Can I put a call out for someone?'

It was as if the man could read his mind. He raised an eyebrow. 'Will they come if we call them?'

His stomach clenched. He darted back through the crowds of people slowly milling about the airport as if they had all the time in the world, straight to one of the ticket desks. He slammed his credit card on the counter. 'I need a ticket.'

'Where to?' asked the girl behind the desk, pulling back a little.

'Anywhere,' was his instant response.

Her brow furrowed and she gave him a suspicious glance. Just what he needed—her to call security, and him to get ejected from the airport.

'The love of my life is in the departure lounge. I need to get in there—and to do that I need a ticket.'

'The love of your life?' The girl gave him a hard stare.

Jonas nodded then screwed up his face. 'I just haven't told her that yet.'

The girl's eyebrows raised. 'Are you asking her to stay, or do you want to go with her?'

'What?'

'You said you need a ticket. Wouldn't it be wise to buy a ticket to the same place, instead of just any ticket?' She didn't wait for him to respond—just continued with her hard stare as she folded her arms. 'After all—you can't just expect her to come back home with you. If you love her, you have to be prepared to go where she is.'

Even though he didn't have time for this, and his heart was currently racing, he leaned forward and smiled at the girl. 'You're that kind of quirky character in the movie, aren't you? The one that almost stops the guy reaching his girl?'

She nodded. 'What can I say?' She made a sign with her fingers, 'Hashtag, team girl. Have you any idea how many stories like this I hear from hapless guys who just haven't got their act together?'

'Okay, I'm a shameful, pathetic human being. Now let me buy a ticket to London Heathrow and send me on my way.'

She gave him an approving nod, took his credit card and passport and her fingers flew across the keyboard. A minute later she handed him a printed boarding card, and a receipt. She sighed and said, 'Okay then, go be a hero and don't screw this up.'

'Thank you.' The words had barely left his mouth when he started running back through the hall towards the security check area.

He thrust his boarding card towards security.

The queue seemed to deliberately crawl forward. Pat-

SCARLET WILSON 177

downs took for ever. Jonas was watching the clock on
the wall behind the check-in desk; it seemed to be on
fast forward. He could also see a board filled with flight
information. The boarding gate number was up for Cora's flight, along with the flashing words *Go to Gate*.

He was a few seconds away from pleading with the
people ahead to let him skip the queue when another
checkpoint was opened and a guard waved him over.
He'd never moved so fast. He stuck his belongings in
the tray to be security scanned, held his hands out to
be patted down, collected his tray, pushed his shoes
on his feet and rammed everything else in his pockets,
and then he started running all over again in the direction of the gate.

A few people shot him an amused glance as he
sprinted past. The message on the flight screen had
now changed. *Now Boarding.* There were already a few
people in the line.

He ran straight to the front, ignoring the glares and
craning his neck to see the few people who'd already
walked into the tunnel to board the plane. He didn't
recognise any jackets. He took long strides and looked
at every face in the waiting line. Nope. None of them
were Cora.

He turned back and ran to the front again. 'Can you
check a name for me to see if they've gone through to
the plane?'

The attendant, who was scanning someone's ticket,
didn't even look up. 'Go to the back of the line, please,
sir.'

He wanted to argue. But that wouldn't do any good.
He'd only get thrown out, and right now he needed to
be in this airport, in the departure lounge.

His brain kept whirring. Maybe he should go back and check the shops? She might still be shopping.

He darted back and scanned the nearest tourist souvenir shop, the duty free, a perfume shop and a bakery and coffee shop. No Cora. No sign anywhere.

There was a buzz.

'Last call for Flight G654 to London Heathrow. Would the last remaining passengers make their way to the boarding gate now?'

When he ran back along the corridor, he was suddenly very conscious that there was absolutely no one waiting to board. There was only one attendant, glancing at her watch and looking slightly annoyed.

His brain freaked for a moment. What if Cora had changed her mind and gone back to Stockholm? Could he really take that chance? He might end up on a flight for no reason.

But he couldn't take the chance. Not for a second. Not when Cora was at stake. Worst-case scenario, he would end up on a flight for no reason and have to take one back.

He handed his boarding card over and walked down the longest flight bridge in the world. He hadn't even looked at his seat number.

The air attendant smiled and gestured to him to walk down the entire length of the plane. He could hear the door being closed behind him, but all he could do was scan the faces in the seats. As he got nearer and nearer to the back of the plane, his heart sank. He couldn't see her dark hair anywhere.

He got to the last row, and someone lifted their head.

A head with dark hair. Cora. She had been rummaging in her bag that was shoved under her seat. Jonas couldn't believe it. He glanced at his ticket. Then slid into the seat next to her.

She sat up straight away. And he realised she must have recognised his aftershave.

Her face was shocked. 'What are you doing here?'

She looked around as if it were some kind of bad joke. But no, the doors to the plane were closed, and the plane had started to taxi to the runway.

'I came to find you.'

Her face grew tight. 'But why?'

'Because I didn't get a chance to say the things to you that I should have.'

She blinked and waited a few seconds. 'And what should you have said?'

'That I love you, I'm crazy about you and I want to be where you are. And I don't care if that's London, Stockholm or anywhere else.'

She drew in a shaky breath and shook her head a little. 'I'm on my way back to London, Jonas. Why tell me now?'

'Because I'm an idiot. Because I was scared. Because I let myself get tied up in past experiences, because the truth is, for me, you were just too good to be true.'

'You got on a plane to tell me this?' There was an edge to her voice, and the last thing he wanted to do was upset her. He had a purpose for being here and had to get to the point.

'I waited all morning for you at the hospital. I was stupid enough to think you might show up at work today. I wanted to come to the hotel this morning, but thought that was just too creepy.'

The corners of her lips edged up for a second.

But they went back again as she slowed her breathing. 'I've been here for seven weeks, we got closer and closer, and you never told me that you loved me, you never really talked about the future—just danced around the subject.'

He reached over and put his hand over hers as the plane lifted off from the runway. 'You're right. And I'm sorry. But don't leave like this. I don't want you to leave like this. If you go, I go. I can't imagine not waking up next to you in the morning. This morning was the worst ever. To turn over and find a big empty space was the worst feeling in the world. I kept telling myself that I'd see you at the hospital. I'd talk to you. I'd persuade you to give me a chance to explain. Tell you all the things I should have told you last night before you walked away. Then Alice told me about your text.'

'She was texting me literally every hour, on the hour.'

'She never told me that.'

Cora raised an eyebrow. 'She's a very persuasive, persistent woman.'

She shook her head again. 'But your whole life is in Stockholm, Jonas. What on earth will you do in London?'

He kept his face grave. 'My whole life will be wherever you are, Cora. If you'll let me.' He slipped his hand into his pocket. 'I didn't get it. Your whole Christmas feeling. When you told me last night, you broke my heart, because I just wanted to be there for you.'

She closed her eyes and spoke quietly. 'And I pushed you away. Because that's what I've learned to do. I don't talk about it with anyone. Most of my colleagues back home already know—so no one brings it up. I just volunteer for the Christmas shifts, and no one asks why.' She lowered her head. 'I got so used to not telling anyone, that I just couldn't cope last night. I was overwhelmed.' She kept her head down, but squeezed his hand. 'You told me to try and make new Christmas memories, and I did. I started to. I started to make them with you. Then I felt guilty. That I didn't deserve to make them, and I was betraying my mum and dad by even considering moving on.' She looked up in surprise when Jonas wiped away a tear that slid down her cheek.

'We don't ever have to do Christmas, Cora. If you don't want to, then that's fine with me. We can take holidays and go off to some remote cabin for a few days and just be ourselves, just chill. Take some time away from everything.'

She shook her head and breathed deeply. 'No, Jonas. I'm going to do what I should have done years ago. I'm going to go to a counsellor and talk my way through this. Maybe I'll never feel better, but I have to try.' She gave a soft smile. 'Maybe I should try to make new memories.'

He stroked her cheek with his finger. 'And I want to be by your side. Whatever your decision, it will be fine with me. What I have with you is too special that I can't even contemplate a life where we're not together. I've never loved someone the way I love you. Not even close.'

By now the plane had climbed high into the sky. Cora glanced out of the window. 'You're actually coming to London? You know today is Christmas Eve?' There was still a wave of sadness in her eyes.

'And this is a day you shouldn't be on your own. I'm happy to fade into the background and give you space, or, equally, just give you lots of hugs.'

Cora didn't cry. She just laid her head on his shoulder. He whispered into her hair. 'I'm hoping a really kind-hearted woman will let me bunk up with her tonight, and maybe for a whole lot longer.'

'You really don't want to go back to Stockholm?'

'I can be a midwife anywhere,' he answered promptly, and he truly meant it.

'And I can be a doctor anywhere too,' she said simply.

'Then the world is our oyster.'

She nodded as the air attendant approached with drinks for them both. As she set them down, Jonas reached for the item he'd taken from his pocket. 'My timing isn't great. But I had something for you.' He smiled. 'I bought it a few weeks ago, but wanted to give it to you the day before you left—without realising what I was doing.'

She took a sip of her wine and wrinkled her nose. 'What is it?'

'It's a message.' His voice was steady. 'Things are a bit different in Sweden. You might think we do things in reverse.' He swallowed and flipped open the small velvet box. 'In the older days in Sweden, this was an engagement ring.'

Cora leaned forward, her eyes wide at the simple gold band, with a thicker one next to it.

'We both wear them,' he said steadily.

She hadn't said anything yet, and his nerves were making him fill the gap. 'I promise I'll buy you a diamond later—but we usually save them for the actual wedding.'

Her eyes were wide as she turned to face him. 'What exactly are you asking me?'

Jonas didn't hesitate for a second. 'I'm asking you to marry me, Cora, and pick where we live together. I love you. I was a fool not to tell you sooner, but I promise I'll spend the rest of my life telling you every day.'

Her finger brushed the gold rings in the box. She smiled. 'Aren't I supposed to buy you a ring?'

'I decided to save us some time.'

She kept staring at him in wonder. 'When did you buy these?'

He groaned. 'Will you just answer the darn question?' He'd drunk some of the wine given to them by the air attendant, but if she didn't give him an answer soon, he couldn't swear it would stay down. No one ever spoke about how nerve-racking it was for a guy to ask the woman he loved the biggest question in the world and wait for an answer.

She slid one hand up the side of his face and through his hair, pulling him towards her. Just as their lips were about to touch she gave him his answer. 'Yes,' she whispered.

And they kissed, forgetting about the world outside and concentrating only on each other.

EPILOGUE

'READY?' CORA GRINNED at Jonas as he tugged at the kilt she'd made him wear.

'Is this supposed to be comfortable?' he asked, straightening up.

'Absolutely not.' She kept smiling. 'You're supposed to spend the whole night in terror that you'll turn too quickly and the whole world will see what they're not supposed to.'

He shook his head. 'I'm not sure about all this "true Scotsman" tale. Did you make it up? Because I can tell you right now that any Norseman with this on would wear boxers.'

She walked up and put her hands on the lapels of his Highland jacket. 'But tonight, husband, you are an honorary Scotsman.' She winked. 'And you did lose the bet.'

He sighed and grabbed his wallet, stuffing it into his sporran. 'I never thought you'd hold me to it.'

'You're quite handsome as a Scotsman. Maybe we should try this more often.'

Jonas let out a disgruntled noise as he grabbed her hand. 'Let's go before this Christmas party starts without you.'

Cora took a final glance in the mirror at her floor-length red satin gown, grabbed her purse and made her way down the hotel corridor with her new husband.

They'd married quietly, only a few days before, with her sister as bridesmaid, and Jonas's friend as best man. Their reception would be held back in Sweden after Christmas. All their friends and colleagues back at Stockholm City should have received their invites in the mail today.

They'd arrived in London nearly a year before and as soon as they'd landed Cora had received the call from Stockholm City asking her to be Head of Neonatal Intensive Care.

She'd accepted immediately, then spent the few days after celebrating with Jonas, before packing up her things, renting out her flat and moving to Stockholm permanently.

Tonight was a double celebration. Their wedding, and the Royal Kensington Christmas party to celebrate the achievements of all the staff who'd been part of the Kensington project over the last fifty years. Organising had been a logistical nightmare, but Cora had taken on the challenge with pride after Chris Taylor had asked her to. Her first calls had been to her fellow three Kensington Project recipients that year. It seemed that the project had had a big impact on all of their lives. Tonight, she would get to see some of them for the first time in nearly a year.

The large ballroom in the hotel was decorated with green boughs and red bows.

Pictures of all those chosen to be part of the Kensington Project over the years lined the walls. Chloe, Scott, and Stella all stared back at her with pride on their faces. Cora glanced quickly at the four people who'd had the honour this year, wondering if their lives would change as much as her and her colleagues' lives had.

A waiter was standing in the entranceway with a silver tray of glasses filled with champagne. Cora had only taken a few steps when Chloe ran over and threw her arms around her. Chloe's green dress was gorgeous and her curly hair was piled up on her head.

'What took you? Aren't you staying here, same as us?'

Cora nodded and gestured to Jonas. 'My husband needed a hand with his kilt. It seems he's not used to wearing a skirt.' She kept hugging Chloe tightly. 'You look fabulous. Are we still on for tomorrow so I get to see this gorgeous baby?'

Chloe grinned, her eyes sparkling at the mention of the baby she'd had back in July. 'Can't wait. We'll meet you at St James's Park.'

A deep laugh sounded behind them as Chloe's husband stepped out from behind her to put a kiss on Cora's cheek. Sam, the general surgeon from Kingston Memorial who'd captured Chloe's heart, automatically started teasing Jonas. 'Don't bend over too quickly.' He laughed good-naturedly.

'Hey, don't start this party without me.' Stella, their colleague from Orthopaedics, glowed in a silver fringed dress as she wrapped an arm around both of them. With her dark bob, she looked as if she'd stepped straight out of a nineteen-twenties movie.

'You look fantastic,' said Cora, kissing her cheek. 'I wasn't sure if you'd want to make the journey from Toronto.' Like herself, Stella had decided to relocate after meeting Aiden and his small son when she'd travelled to Toronto as part of the Kensington Project.

She reached out to shake Aiden's hand.

'Where's Scott?' asked Chloe.

'Right behind me,' said Stella as she nodded over her shoulder.

They watched as Scott, their handsome American cardiology colleague, danced his way across the floor to them, his arm around his wife, Fliss. He clinked glasses with them all as soon as he arrived.

The girls all wrapped arms around each other and started to laugh and joke, ordering a bottle of champagne from a passing waiter and sitting down at a table to exchange stories.

As the music started a little while later, all four men appeared on cue to take their partners onto the dance floor.

Cora slid into her new husband's arms and wrapped her arms around his neck as the slow Christmas song started.

'Happy?' he asked.

'Delighted,' she whispered. 'And this year, I get to have my first Christmas Day in Stockholm. I can't wait to make a whole host of new memories to keep for ever.'

Cora had been seeing a counsellor back in Stockholm and was slowly unpicking her feelings of guilt and grief. Jonas was with her every step of the way, and she'd never been happier.

'So, what are our plans for tomorrow?' he asked. They only had another few days in London before flying home again.

'We're meeting a gorgeous baby, and then...' she gave him a special smile '... I have a few ideas about what we could get up to.'

He looked at her with amused suspicion. 'And what might that be?'

She spun around under his arm before pressing up against him. 'What do you think of this dress?'

Jonas's eyes ran appreciatively down the figure-hugging floor-length red dress. 'I adore it. Is this a trick?'

'Could be. My plans include doing my best to ensure I don't fit into this dress next year. But I might need some help with that.'

He spun her around the dance floor. 'Oh, I think I can help with that. I think we should practise.' He dipped her low, then pulled her back up. 'Let's do our best to expand this family.'

And Cora stood on her tiptoes and planted a kiss on her husband's lips. 'That, darling, is music to my ears.'

And they danced their way around the floor again.

* * * * *

COMING SOON!

We really hope you enjoyed reading this book.
If you're looking for more romance, be sure to
head to the shops when new books are
available on

Thursday 23rd December

To see which titles are coming soon, please visit

millsandboon.co.uk/nextmonth

MILLS & BOON

MILLS & BOON

THE HEART OF ROMANCE

A ROMANCE FOR EVERY READER

MODERN

Prepare to be swept off your feet by sophisticated, sexy and seductive heroes, in some of the world's most glamourous and romantic locations, where power and passion collide.

HISTORICAL

Escape with historical heroes from time gone by. Whether your passion is for wicked Regency Rakes, muscled Vikings or rugged Highlanders, awake the romance of the past.

MEDICAL

Set your pulse racing with dedicated, delectable doctors in the high-pressure world of medicine, where emotions run high and passion, comfort and love are the best medicine.

True Love

Celebrate true love with tender stories of heartfelt romance, from the rush of falling in love to the joy a new baby can bring, and a focus on the emotional heart of a relationship.

Desire

Indulge in secrets and scandal, intense drama and plenty of sizzling hot action with powerful and passionate heroes who have it all: wealth, status, good looks…everything but the right woman.

HEROES

Experience all the excitement of a gripping thriller, with an intense romance at its heart. Resourceful, true-to-life women and strong, fearless men face danger and desire - a killer combination!

To see which titles are coming soon, please visit

millsandboon.co.uk/nextmonth

MILLS & BOON

Coming next month

SECRET FROM THEIR LA NIGHT
Julie Danvers

Last night was just a fluke. It doesn't have to mean anything. It doesn't have to be a slippery slope back into old patterns. She'd simply had a moment of weakness, brought on by loneliness and old memories, and she'd given in to temptation. With time, she could forgive herself for that. But first, she needed to find her shoes.

Ah. She spied the pointed toe of one ballet flat poking out from beneath the bed. She gathered up her shoes, not bothering to put them on. Her own room was only a few floors away, and it was early enough that the halls were still empty. She turned the doorknob; the door creaked as she opened it, and she slowed so it would open quietly. At least she hadn't lost her silent creeping skills.

As she stepped out, Daniel turned over in his sleep, and her heart rose in her throat. His snores paused, and for a moment she was certain he'd woken up. But then she relaxed as his breathing returned to a slow, even pace. He really was very attractive, with his dark, tousled hair and his barely shaven stubble. But great hair or not, she needed to put last night behind her. Daniel, fun as he had been, represented a past she had tried her best to forget, and the past was where he needed to stay.

One brisk shower later, Emily was back in professional mode. She took a cab to the convention center and found the right conference room a few moments before orientation was scheduled to begin. She was the last one into the meeting, but only just; a few other stragglers were still hanging their jackets when she arrived. She took the last seat available, next to a dark-haired physician who turned to greet her.

Her stomach dropped.

His brown eyes widened.

Emily was completely tongue-tied, but somehow, he was able to speak.

"Dr. Daniel Labarr," he said, holding out one hand. "I do believe we've met."

Continue reading
SECRET FROM THEIR LA NIGHT
Julie Danvers

Available next month
www.millsandboon.co.uk